NAGUIB MAHFOUZ
KHAN AL-KHALILI

Naguib Mahfouz was one of the most prominent writers of Arabic fiction in the twentieth century. He was born in 1911 in Cairo and began writing at the age of seventeen. His first novel was published in 1939. Throughout his career, he wrote nearly forty novel-length works and hundreds of short stories. In 1988 Mahfouz was awarded the Nobel Prize in Literature. He died in 2006.

KHAN AL-KHALILI

A Novel

_____

NAGUIB MAHFOUZ

Translated from the Arabic by
Roger Allen

ANCHOR BOOKS
A DIVISION OF RANDOM HOUSE, INC.
NEW YORK

FIRST ANCHOR BOOKS EDITION, SEPTEMBER 2011

English translation copyright © 2008 by Roger Allen

All rights reserved. Published in the United States by Anchor Books,
a division of Random House, Inc., New York, and in Canada by
Random House of Canada Limited, Toronto. Originally published
in Arabic as *Khan al-Khalili* in 1946. Copyright © 1946 by Naguib
Mahfouz. This translation first published in English in hardcover
in Egypt and the United States by The American University
in Cairo Press, Cairo and New York, in 2008.

Anchor Books and colophon are registered trademarks
of Random House, Inc.

The Cataloging-in-Publication Data is on file
at the Library of Congress.

Anchor ISBN: 978-0-307-74257-5

www.anchorbooks.com

146119709

KHAN AL-KHALILI

1

It was half past two in the afternoon on a September day in 1941, the exact time when civil servants left their government offices. Streams of them came pouring out of the ministry's doors like a raging torrent. Their minds had long since become preoccupied with a combination of hunger and sheer boredom, and now they all scattered in different directions under the burning glare of the sun.

Ahmad Akif, whose job was at the Ministry of Works, was among them. At this time of day he usually made his way back to al-Sakakini, but today was different: for the first time he was heading toward al-Azhar. He had been living in al-Sakakini for a long time, stretching back many years, whole decades in fact. Those many years constituted a veritable storehouse of memories—memories of childhood, youth, adulthood, and then middle age. The incredible thing was that it had only taken the family just a few days to make up their minds to pack up and leave. They had all felt completely secure in their old house; they had never imagined leaving. But then during the short interval between one evening and noon the next day everyone had started yelling, "A pox on this awful quarter!" Fear and panic had taken over; there was no longer any point in trying to persuade scared folk to change their minds. The old house had soon become a memory of the past, and the new house in Khan al-Khalili was a reality from today and onward into the future. Well might Ahmad Akif quote the phrase, "Praise be to the One who changes things but who never changes Himself!"

The suddenness of the decision to move had left him in a quandary. His heart kept drawing him back to the beloved old quarter; he bitterly regretted the feeling of being tossed out and thrust into one of the ancient popular quarters of Cairo. But at the same time he could not forget the relief he had felt when he realized that he would now be far away from a kind of hell that threatened imminent destruction. Maybe tonight would turn out to be the first time he managed to get any sleep since that terrible night, the one that had given the people of Cairo such a terrible shock.

It was therefore with mixed emotions—sadness and forbearance—that he paced the sidewalk waiting for the trolley that would take him to Queen Farida Square. Sweat was pouring off his brow, and yet he could still feel a certain frisson of pleasure at the thought of new discoveries and the prospect of change: a new place to live, new environment, new atmosphere, and new neighbors. Maybe luck would turn out differently and good times would return once again; perhaps the ever-so-subtle intimations he was now feeling would manage to shake off the layers of dust left behind by so much lethargy and inject some new sense of life and energy.

This then was the sheer delight of exploration, taking risks, and pursuing dreams; not only that, but also a hidden sense of superiority that grew out of his moving from one quarter to another that was of lower status in both prestige and educational level. He had not even set eyes on the new house as yet because he had been at work in the ministry when he was notified that the furniture had been moved first thing in the morning. Now here he was, on his way to the new house following the directions he had been given.

"It's only temporary," he told himself. "They'll have to put up with it as long as the war lasts. Then things will get better."

Could it have turned out any better? Would it have made more sense to stay in the old quarter, even though it would involve watching and listening to the fearsome noises of death?

He could not stand spending ages doing nothing, so he kept pacing the sidewalk. By now his nerves seemed to have calmed down a bit, but the way he was smoking a cigarette so quickly was evidence enough of how preoccupied he was. His nervous gestures, anxious expression, and generally disheveled appearance made him look like an exhausted old man with heart problems; the look in his eyes was distracted, as though he were out of touch with his surroundings. Actually he was approaching his forties. The fact that he was so tall and thin might attract people's attention, not to mention the regrettably scruffy state of his clothes. To tell the truth, his torn trousers, the too-short sleeves of his jacket, the sweat and dust that accumulated at the rim of his tarboosh, the tightness of his shirt, the shabby necktie, his balding pate, and the creeping grayness that showed at his temples and the back of his head—all these features suggested that he was getting on in years. Beyond all that, there was his skinny, elongated face with its pale complexion, part of a small-sized cranium that sloped gently toward his fairly narrow forehead framed by eyebrows that were straight and widely separated. His eyes were widely spaced too and narrow, almost filling the entire contours of his face; whenever he squinted so as to concentrate on something or shield them from the sun's glare, they looked as though they were shut; their deep honey-colored irises simply vanished. His eyelids drooped, and their corners had by now acquired a reddish hue. He had a narrow nose, thin lips, and a small, tapered beard. Incredible as it may seem, there had been a time when people regarded him as someone who was fussy about his appearance, a trait that had made him appear quite acceptable. However, a combination of despair and thriftiness, followed by a peculiar aspiration to look like an intellectual, had robbed him of any concern about either his person or his manner of dress.

As he boarded trolley no. 15 he mustered a smile that revealed a set of teeth yellowed by smoking. From Queen Farida Square he caught another trolley, no. 19. Out of force of habit he had actually made a mistake by throwing away the ticket that he had bought on the first trolley. He needed to go to al-Azhar, and so he had to buy another ticket, all the while laughing at himself in exasperation.

His secret craving for sex gnawed at him; truth to tell, for some time he had inured himself to ever being head of a household, and to staying single, at least up until now. He never spent even a penny without thinking about it, so his cravings were not so strong as to prevent him from spending money, but even so he still found it painful when forced to do so. Finally he reached al-Azhar and headed toward Khan al-Khalili, his new destination. He made his way through a narrow alleyway in the direction of the quarter in question. To his left and right were new apartment blocks with countless alleyways and walks interspersed between them; they looked like row upon row of imposing barracks where you could easily lose your way. All around him he spotted cafés teeming with customers and the occasional store, some selling taamiya, others jewelry and trinkets. And there were hordes of people, a never-ending flow, some wearing turbans, others fezzes, and still others skullcaps. The air was filled with shouts, yells, and screams, all of them guaranteed to shatter the nerves of someone like himself. He felt ill at ease and jumpy. He had no idea where he was going, so he went over to a Nubian doorman sitting beside the entrance to a building and said hello.

"Where's the street to building number seven, please?" he asked.

The man stood up courteously. "You must be looking for apartment twelve, where people moved into today," he replied, pointing in the right direction. "See that passageway? Take it to the second alleyway on the right, then go as far as Ibrahim Pasha Street, then the third door on the left will be building number seven."

He thanked the doorman and proceeded down the passageway. "Second alleyway on the right," he kept mumbling to himself. "Okay, so here it is. Now, third building on the left." He paused for a moment and looked at his surroundings. The street was long and narrow, with four square apartment buildings on either side, all of them connected by side-passages that intersected with the main street. The sidewalks of these passageways and the main street itself were crowded with various stalls: watch repairer, calligrapher, tea maker, rug maker, clothes mender, trinket seller, and so on. Here and there cafés were scattered around, but they were no larger than the stalls. Doormen stayed close to the building entrances, their faces as black as pitch, their turbans as white as milk, with expressions languid enough to give the impression that the perfumed scents and wafts of incense that floated through the air had sent them into a stupor. The atmosphere of the place was enveloped in a brownish haze, as though the entire quarter never saw the sun's rays. The reason was that in many places the sky was blocked by overhanging balconies. The various craftsmen sat in front of their stalls, patiently and skillfully plying their trade and producing little masterpieces; the ancient quarter still preserved its long-standing reputation as a place where the human hand could make exquisite crafts. It had managed to withstand the influx of modern civilization and to confront the insane pace with its own calming wisdom; its simple skills stood counter to complex technologies, its reverie of imagination to an uncouth realism, and its drowsy ocher hue to the gleaming brilliance of modernity. As he took in the scene with confusion, he wondered to himself whether he would be able to get to know this new quarter the way he had the old one. Would the day ever come when he could make his way through this maze without even thinking about it, following the path wherever his feet took him because his mind was so distracted by other matters?

"In the name of God the Compassionate, the Merciful," he intoned as he approached the door.

He walked up the spiral staircase to the second floor and found apartment 12. When he spotted the number he smiled, almost as though he had known it for some time and was pleased to see it again after a long absence. He rang the bell, and the door opened. His mother was standing at the threshold, smiling in welcome.

"Do you see this wonderful new world of ours?" she said with a laugh as she let him in.

He entered the apartment. "Congratulations on the new home!" he replied with a smile.

Her laugh revealed yellowing teeth because she too, like her son, smoked a lot. "I'm sorry," she went on apologetically, "we haven't been able to put the furniture in your room or ours today. It's been a really exhausting day. In spite of our best efforts, a chair leg was broken, and the headboard of your bed was scratched in some places."

Ahmad found himself in a small room stuffed full of utensils, chairs, and pieces of furniture. In the middle stood the table with crockery and rolled-up rugs on it. The room had two doors, one to the right of the entrance, the other straight ahead. He took it all in without saying a word.

"God knows," his mother commented, "I've not had a moment's peace today. Pity the poor mother who's never given birth to a daughter so she can lend a helping hand when needed. You ran away to your ministry and your father's huddled in his room as usual. Even so he still found the energy—God forgive him—to ask a short while ago what I was preparing for dinner, as though I'm some kind of magician who can conjure up anything she wants! Fortunately this new quarter we're living in is full of food stalls. I've sent the servant to buy us some taamiya, salad, and zucchini.

At the word taamiya Ahmad's tastebuds began to salivate, and his anticipation was reflected in the gleam in his eye.

"So is my father feeling relaxed and at ease?" he asked his mother.

His mother smiled sweetly, showing that, even though she was now fifty-five years old, she had lost none of her feminine charm. "Yes, thank God!" she replied. "He's feeling relaxed and happy. Maybe he even trusts his own instincts. But the apartment's small and the rooms are narrow. We've managed to squeeze all the furniture inside, and, as the saying goes, 'whatever's imprinted on the forehead must be visible to the eye.'"

As he listened to his mother talking, he was looking around. A hallway stretched away to the left, and the kitchen and bathroom were in the opposite direction. His mother pointed to the room facing the outside door. "That's your room," she said. Of the two rooms off the hallway, the first was his parents' bedroom, while the second, to quote his mother, was to be put aside for his brother and kept empty for him. Ahmad went over to his parents' room and found the old man lying down on the bed, his expression one of calm resignation. Like his son, Akif Effendi Ahmad was tall and thin. He had a full white beard and wore thick spectacles that gave his feeble eyes a deceptive brilliance. He looked up at Ahmad with a cautious unease, ready to spring to the attack if he made the slightest hint of a sarcastic remark about moving to this new home.

"Congratulations, Papa!" Ahmad said by way of greeting.

"God reward you likewise," his father replied calmly. "Everything happens according to His will."

"True enough," replied Ahmad with a shake of his head, "but fear has now brought us to such a pitch that we've lost all sense of reason. Don't you realize, Papa, that the airmen flying over Cairo aren't going to distinguish between al-Sakakini and Khan al-Khalili?"

"But this quarter is close to the Mosque of al-Husayn," his father responded firmly. "He has found favor with God. This is a quarter of religious faith and mosques. The Germans are too intelligent to bomb the heart of Islam when they're trying to win us over."

"But what happens if they bomb this area by mistake," Ahmad asked with a smile, "the way they did al-Sakakini?"

"Don't quibble!" his father replied, now out of patience. "I'm optimistic about this place, and your mother's happy, even though she keeps chattering on without expressing any sense of gratitude. You're feeling more secure too, but you keep playing the phony philosopher and putting on a false display of courage. Come on, change your clothes and let's have dinner."

Ahmad smiled. "Father's right," he told himself as he went to his own room. He took a closer look at it and discovered that with the addition of his furniture it had lost all sense of proportion. To the left was his bed and to the right his wardrobe; close by was the desk with a pile of books beside it. The room had two windows, so he decided to take a quick look out of both of them. He went over to one and opened it. It looked out on the street he had come along to get to the house. From this height he could make out the main features of the quarter: the apartment buildings had been constructed as sides of a big square; in the middle courtyard smaller quadrangles had been built consisting of small shops with narrow alleyways leading off from them. The apartment windows and front balconies overhung the roofs of the shops and blocked out a fair amount of air and sunlight. Nothing blocked the view of the other apartments; looking out from the front windows of one of the four sides of this large square he could see a large quadrangle of apartments; down below there were many other square patterns made up of shop roofs, the scene being broken up by a complex web of alleys and streets. Beyond it all he could make out the minaret of the al-Husayn Mosque whose soaring height bestowed blessings on all those who lived around it.

When Ahmad saw that he could see open sky from his window, he relaxed; the thing he had feared most was that he'd only be able to see blank walls. He now made his way over to the other window opposite the door to his room and opened it too. This time the view was completely different. Down below was a narrow street leading to the old part of Khan al-Khalili; its shops were closed, and it looked deserted. On the other side of the street was the side of another apartment building whose windows and balconies were very close to those of the building he was in. He now realized that the roofs of the two buildings were actually connected at several points and that their different floors were also linked by balconies, all of which made him think that it was in fact a single apartment building with two wings to it. On the left side of the street you could see the old Khan al-Khalili; from where he was standing it looked like a series of dilapidated roofs, collapsing windows, and wood and cloth canopies to give shade to the network of streets below. The space beyond that was filled with minarets, domes, and the tops and walls of many mosques, all of which gave the viewer an impression of the Cairo of al-Muʿizz's time. This was the first time he had ever seen that view, and it only served to intensify his dislike for this new quarter. He started gazing at the strange, sprawling scene, a truly amazing sight for eyes accustomed only to paper and unversed in the real wonders of nature and historical monuments. But he had no time to indulge in such sensations, because he heard a knock on the door.

"The taamiya's ready, esteemed sir!" his mother called.

He shut the two windows, changed out of his business clothes, and put on a gallabiya and skullcap. "God bless this house!" he intoned to himself. At that very same moment and before he had had a chance to leave his room, he heard a gruff voice coming up from the street below.

"God destroy your house and damn your eyes, you son of a...!"

Another voice retorted with an even viler curse, all of which proved that the two men were merely following the custom of the quarter in swearing at each other in such a disgusting fashion.

Ahmad felt furious and cursed them under his breath. "I seek refuge with God from bad luck and pessimism!" he said, and then left the room.

2

The taamiya was the best he had ever tasted; he praised it to the heavens. His father liked it too, and turned his praises into an encomium on the new quarter where they were now living.

"You know absolutely nothing about the al-Husayn quarter," he said, warming to his subject. "It's not only the tastiest taamiya and ful mudammis, but kebab, goat meat, trotters, and sheep's head as well. You won't find tea or coffee like it anywhere else. Here it's always daytime, and life goes on day and night. Al-Husayn, the son of the Prophet's own daughter, is here; he makes for a good neighbor and protector!"

After dinner, Ahmad went back to his room and threw himself down on the bed, hoping to get a bit of rest. By this time he had decided that the move to the new quarter had as many plusses to it as minuses. He looked round the room again, and his eyes fell on the piles of books beside the desk that still needed to be organized. He stared at them, his thoughts a mixture of pleasure and contempt. There they were, his beloved books, all of them in Arabic. He had had so much trouble learning English—and not very well—that he had been forced to neglect his Arabic books; by now he had almost forgotten about them. More than a third of them were school textbooks on geography, history, math, and science. Quite a few were reference books on law, and an equal number consisted of works by al-Manfaluti, al-Muwaylihi, Shawqi, Hafiz, and Mutran. There were also some yellowing tomes from al-Azhar on religion and logic, all of which still confounded him; he had come to regard them as symbols of that most difficult of subjects whose truths very few people manage to penetrate. There were also a few works by contemporary writers, the acquisition of which he regarded as an act of courtesy. So all these were his beloved books; truth to tell, they were his entire life. He was a voracious reader. For the past twenty years, from 1921, when he graduated from high school, until now in 1941, he had devoted himself to reading books. It consumed his life inside and out and served as the focus for all his feelings, whims, and aspirations. However, from the outset, his reading activities had had their own particular characteristics, and they had stayed with him for all twenty years. All his readings were general; there was no specialization or depth involved. While there may have been a certain inclination toward classical learning, it was both cursory and disorganized. The reason for this lack of focus may well have been that he had been compelled to abandon his studies after his high-school graduation, so he had never had any kind of planned opportunity to specialize.

This decision had had profound ramifications for Ahmad's life, both socially and psychologically, and they had clung to him ever since. The major reason for the decision was that his father had been pensioned off before he had even reached the age of forty. As a result of sheer negligence he had failed to perform his administrative obligations adequately; what made it worse was that he had then adopted a supercilious attitude toward the civil service investigators who were examining his case. Because of his father's behavior, Ahmad had been forced to terminate his studies and take a minor administrative post in order to provide for his shattered family and support his two younger brothers. One brother had died, and the other had taken a job as a minor employee in Bank Misr. Ahmad himself had been an excellent and ambitious student with broad aspirations. At first he had wanted to study law, by following his great idol, Saad Zaghlul, by completing a legal degree, but his father's dismissal had swept all that away. The decision to abandon his studies had been a severe blow to his hopes. At first it sent him reeling, and he was overwhelmed by a violent, almost insane fury that completely destroyed his personality and filled him with a sense of bitter remorse. To him it was obvious that he was a martyr to injustice, a genius consigned early to the grave, a victim of malicious fate. Thereafter, he was forever ruing his martyred genius and invoking its memories, whether or not the occasion demanded it. He kept on complaining about what fate had wrought and enumerating its crimes against him to such an extent that the routine turned into a sickly obsession. His colleagues inured themselves to listening to him repeating the same things over and over again.

"If only I'd been able to complete my studies," he'd say in his shaky voice, "needless to say, I would have done well. And then just think where I'd be now. I'd be a real somebody!"

"I'm in my forties now," he'd complain in a resentful tone. "If things had gone the way they were supposed to and cruel fate had not stood in my way, just imagine what I'd be doing. I'd be a middle-aged lawyer, someone whose services to the legal profession would have been widely acknowledged for almost twenty years. What else could have been expected over a period of twenty years for someone as serious and dedicated as me?"

"We've been robbed of the most fruitful era in Egypt's history," he would go on regretfully, "one where considerations of age and inherited wealth have been thrust aside and the younger generation has leapt forward to occupy ministerial positions."

He kept a relentlessly close watch on the careers of some of his more distinguished school contemporaries who had managed to continue their studies. Quite frequently he would look up from reading the newspaper and say something like, "Do you know this person they keep writing about?" he would ask incredulously. "He was at school with me, grade after grade. He was a very poor student; he never managed to beat me at anything."

"Good heavens!" he would scoff. "The man's an undersecretary of state! That scruffy boy who could never remember anything he was told? What's happening to the world?"

He would then go on and talk about what an exceptional student he himself had been at school and what a promising career his teachers had predicted for him. All these sentiments only managed to have negative effects on his temperament; he became obstreperous, bad tempered, and arrogant, always ready to wax hyperbolic about his talents. His life was thus turned into a continuing succession of lies and sheer misery. This alleged genius thereafter found himself stuck in the eighth administrative level in the archives department at the Ministry of Works, but he adamantly refused to settle down and accept things. Never giving up, he kept searching for ways to rid himself of his chains and beat a path to freedom, glory, and authority. Many avenues were tried, and one attempt followed another. His first idea was to undertake home study for a law degree, that being the field he had aspired to from the start. He had to get a degree because practicing law was no longer the kind of endeavor it had been in the old days of Saad Zaghlul and al-Balbawi, so he started collecting books on law and borrowing reports, then spent an entire year studying before presenting himself for the examinations. He failed in two subjects. This was a savage blow to his pride, and he felt acutely embarrassed when dealing with all those people who had been assiduously following the tales of his exceptional talents. He started using his job in the ministry as an excuse for his failure and pretended he had an illness that made it impossible for him to continue his studies. In fact, he kept up this pretense of an illness even afterward as a precautionary measure against further embarrassment. He was scared to try the exam again and decided to avoid subjecting his talent to more obvious public experiments, where people could easily gauge the results.

He now decided to try free thinking instead and immediately made his colleagues aware of the contempt he felt for exams and degrees. He managed to convince himself that the reason for his failure in the exam had nothing to do with any failings or inadequacy on his part, but was simply due to the fact that he had not had enough time to prepare for it.

With that in mind he abandoned his studies so he could discover the most natural outlet for his unquestioned (and martyred) genius. Thus he had managed to waste a year and acquire a sizeable quantity of law books for his library. Now he decided to concentrate on science, but could not make up his mind between more theoretical research areas and practical discoveries; which of the two should he choose? It was the latter area that he turned his back on, the pretext being that the country was completely devoid of factories and laboratories, which is where experiments were conducted and creative inspiration flourished. Instead he pinned his hopes on theoretical science. His dearest wish was one day to discover a theory that would transform the horizons of modern science; as a result he would find himself elevated to the eternal heights of fame and glory alongside Newton and Einstein. Once again ambition caught hold, and he started buying as many texts on physics and chemistry as he could lay his hands on. He read them all avidly, but after a solid year of study he found himself exactly where he had started, not having advanced a single step toward his ultimate goal. He now convinced himself that real involvement in scientific research demanded preparatory studies of the kind that he had never had.

At this point he panicked again, as was often the case. He gave up theoretical science as a field of study; such was his desperation, he managed to convince himself that theoretical research was no different from more applied investigations in its need for laboratories and research institutes. The intellectual atmosphere in Egypt in general was not yet ready for science. This time he felt no need to justify his failure to anyone. By now he had learned to keep his goals hidden from everyone, but even so that did not stop him telling his colleagues and friends that he was devoting all his spare time to knowledge and learning. The untrammelled domain of knowledge, something that far outclassed school-based learning and government-issued diplomas, and in-depth reading that would turn its practitioner into a scholar of enormous profundity.

Another year was squandered while his library acquired yet another category of scientific works. After a while he paused in his endeavors. "Precisely what is it," he wondered in an exhausted quandary, "that my particular talents are cut out for?" It was obvious enough that he himself did not know the answer as yet; if he had, he could have saved himself some time—it would have been much better if he had—rather than wasting his energies to no effect.

What really interested him? By now he was finished with both law and science, but they were the be-all and end-all of everything. Even so, there was something else that was just as worthwhile and wonderful. How he adored the works of the poet Shawqi and the essayist al-Manfaluti; what bewitching eloquence in their writing! Could his real calling be literature? What a great mode of art it was, one that did not require a degree to practice it nor school learning either. Reading, that was all that was involved; reading poets like Shawqi, Hafiz Ibrahim, and Mutran, just as he had done before. His library soon welcomed some new additions in the form of poetry and prose anthologies that he devoured with such enthusiasm that it aggravated him. During his literary excursions he came across Ibn Khaldun's quote: "We have heard from our revered shaykhs in literary salons that there are four major sourceworks when it comes to literature studies. They are: *The Complete Work* by al-Mubarrad, *The Scribe's Manual* by Ibn Qutayba, *The Book of Eloquence and Clear Expression* by al-Jahiz, and *The Book of Anecdotes* by al-Qali from Baghdad. All other sources apart from these four are derivative." He let out a sigh of satisfaction; it was as if he had stumbled on a treasure and had acquired the four pillars of literature. With that he read them all with his characteristic zeal and speed. When he had finished, he asked himself—with a good deal of relish—whether he had now become a literature scholar. Grabbing a pen he decided to test his resolve by writing something. The piece he wrote was called "On the Banks of the Nile," and into it he poured his artistry and inspiration. When it was finished, he sent it by mail to a journal and started picturing the admiration and amazement with which readers would greet it once it had been published. This would be the first stage on the path of glory and fame. For him that would be enough, since the only reward he was looking for was literary recognition. The journal was duly published, and he thumbed through it looking for his article, but it was not there. He began to lose heart, and his high hopes took an awkward tumble. But he did not give up hope and told himself he had to wait another week. Weeks went by, and still the article did not appear. Here he was, someone who had read the four principal pillars of Arabic literature from which all other sources are considered to be derived. According to Ibn Khaldun that made him a literature scholar—Ibn Khaldun, no less! So how could it be that his article had not been published? Was it because the author was unknown, or he had not gone through an intermediary? Was it possible they couldn't understand his argument? For a short while he thought he might go to the journal in person and find out what had happened, but he soon decided he could not; his innate diffidence was always there as a roadblock.

He now decided to put the shock of the first rejection behind him and wrote a second article about justice. He had no more luck with it than he did with the first one. He wrote a third piece entitled "Poverty's Crime Against Talent," but it fared no better than its two predecessors. When that happened, he set about writing with all the dogged stubbornness of someone who sees it as his final hope, all his previous efforts having been destroyed on the frozen rocks of cruel neglect. He rewrote most of them and sent them out to a number of different journals. However, none of them showed any mercy toward his tortured aspirations or seemed ready to rescue him from the pit of despondency. The last article he wrote was on "The Triviality of Literature," and it too sank without a trace. Shattered in spirit and deeply hurt, he abandoned any further attempts. Bad luck—his enemy of old—had conspired against him yet again, and malicious intent had done the rest. Not for a second did he doubt the value of what he had written about literature. Indeed, he believed it was better than anything al-Manfaluti himself had written, not to mention the effusions of any number of contemporary writers. It was all a question of malice and evil intent. All his dreams had come to nothing. How utterly constricting and unfair life was! Discarding his pen, he now allowed his anger, sorrow, and recalcitrance free rein and finally gave up all aspirations for prestige and authority. His heart was full of anger and resentment, against the world in general and people, especially men with social renown and power. How could you define prestige, he asked himself, particularly its Egyptian form? He answered his own question with a single phrase: favorable circumstances. He was devoted to the memory of Saad Zaghlul, but even so he noted that it was Saad's father-in-law who had paved the way for his successful career; but for that, he would never have become the figure we know.

"Behind every high-level position in Egypt," he would often say, "there's always a tale to be told. If you want to get ahead in this society of ours, then make sure you use deceit, hypocrisy, and impertinence; and don't forget a fair dose of stupidity and ignorance to go with it!"

Either that sort of thing, or else, "Who are these literary types, the ones who write for newspapers and journals? How can it be real literature if the only way to succeed is to meddle in politics and party feuds? Is it only a person of honor who is incapable of achieving the phony prestige they have earned?"

"By God," he would say angrily, "I couldn't be a person of prestige in Egypt now, even if I wanted to...but may God Himself launch a campaign against the very idea of dignity!"

This anger kept burning away inside him until all that was left was an unholy flicker of flame and a pile of ashes. However, life cannot endure anger on a continuing basis; there have to be some intervals of calm, even if the calm involved is actually more akin to resignation. Thus, whenever his anger got the better of him, he would resort to despair.

"What's the point of stubborn persistence in this world of ours?" he would tell himself. "If we're all going to die like animals and rot in the grave, what's the point of thinking like angels? Just suppose I'd filled the world with writings and inventions. Would the worms in the grave respect me? Would they instead devour me like some common murderer? No! The whole world consists of lies and vanities; in such a context the quest for glory is the acme of lies and vanities."

Therefore, he surrendered himself to a bitter isolation of mind and heart. He despaired of life in general and fled from it. But, even as he was turning his back on it in impotent despair, he was still arrogant enough to imagine that he was in fact the one who was depriving life of the benefits of his own personality. For that reason he did not give up reading, the idea being that books were the things that provided man with the kind of life he wanted. He used the world of books as a way of looking down on the ordinary world and adopted them as a kind of salve to treat his wounded pride. From them he derived a kind of strength, one that he kidded himself was personal. It felt as though the ideas they contained were actually his own; their authority and eternal validity were his too.

After his succession of failures, he stopped reading things in an organized and goal-oriented way, and started reading whatever fell into his hands. He had a particular fondness for old volumes with yellowing paper because they were valuable and hard to find. He now began to read voraciously and quickly. He felt on edge and no longer enjoyed reading anything useful or serious; it gave him a kind of mental indigestion. He may have learned all sorts of different things but he was master of none of them. His brain was not used to indulging ideas in and of themselves, and he relied on books to do the thinking for him. Ideas and reflection on them did not interest him at all; his only real concern was that he be able to address the morrow on the basis of what he had read the day before and to harangue his friends and colleagues (all in a learned philosophical tone) with the inspired fruits of his memory. For that very reason the employees working in the archives section of the Ministry of Works nicknamed him "the philosopher." That delighted him, even though the gesture was as much one of derision as of respect.

This "philosopher" had no fixed views on anything because, while he may have been reading things, he never reflected on them; he might well forget what he had said the day before and even totally contradict everything he had said earlier. He would always rush to adopt an opinion that served to boost his own arrogance, delusion, and total concern with superficialities. He relished confrontation and argument. If an interlocutor said "right," he would say "left"; if the former said "white," he would reply "black." He would then plunge headlong into an argument, becoming more and more angry and worked up until he would almost be grabbing his opponent's lapels. None of this implied that he was stupid; in fact, he was of average intelligence. His mind was one that never sank to the level of stupidity, but neither did it rise to any kind of excellence, let alone the notion of genius. The thing that totally deceived him about his own person was his crushing ambition to achieve prestige and his delusions of genius, all of which led him far from the path of reason. What made his sense of misery even more acute was that he was extremely sensitive and easily roused. Patience, perseverance, reflection, and contemplation—these traits were in short supply where he was concerned. As a result, his brain was full of an intellectual mixture of facts rather than being the focused mind of a penseur. There can be little doubt too that the insomnia that had afflicted him for fully six months of his life had had a negative effect on his mental make-up. It had brought him to the very brink of madness and death; he had spent countless nights wide-awake and raving. But then God's mercy had descended on him, and despair had been replaced by cure. He attributed the reason for his illness directly to a risky venture that he had embarked on without considering the possible consequences.

He had long believed in magic and never doubted the veracity of the tales he had heard about it. One day he happened to meet an old civil servant who was a fervent believer in magic and demons, so he began to devote himself assiduously to getting to know him better. Once their friendship was firmly established, the old man lent him some ancient tomes dealing with magic and the invocation of demons, such as *Solomon's Ring*, *The Magic Bottle*, and *O Mighty Lords*. He had been utterly thrilled and treated the entire subject as the loftiest kind of knowledge and truth that he had yet laid hands on. With the enthusiasm of conviction he embarked upon a process of solving its mysteries and penetrating its secrets; with all his heart he longed for the arrival of a time when he would gain control over the forces of the universe and acquire exclusive possession of the keys to knowledge, power, and authority. The idea almost drove him crazy, and the desire took complete hold of him: when would he be given infinite power to take and leave whatever he wanted, to toy with whomever he wished, to raise and lower, to make rich or poor, to give life and death? But his nerves could not stand the prolonged efforts involved, and he was incapable of spending long nights in seclusion with demon spirits. His confidence let him down and his nerves collapsed; he found himself hounded by fears and delusions. His health deteriorated rapidly and he felt the approach of insanity and death. At this point he realized that he had to stop these activities and give up his plans. He returned the books to their owner and for the last time gave up on the idea of achieving glorious heights now that he had tried every single avenue in an attempt to get there.

"What's my problem?" he asked himself sorrowfully. "Is there any solution for a corrupted soul? Why is it that I am forever struggling when only an arm's length separates me from my goals?"

He now collapsed beneath the rubble of his failed initiatives, dashed hopes, and lost illusions. As day followed day, he grew older without ever losing that profound sense of injustice; quite the contrary in fact, he even began to feel some obscure sense of pleasure in the pain it still gave him. He would now imagine injustice to be occurring, with or without due cause, and would proceed to counter it with this same peculiar blend of pain and cryptic pleasure.

"Isn't it just great," he would tell himself with a defiantly sarcastic tone, "that the entire world rises up in order to fight the individual?"

Didn't his disillusioned self find great comfort in the thought that the abundance of bad luck he had suffered was an indication of other people's envy and fear? Indeed he managed to surrender to the ancient notion that genuine misery is the lot of all rare geniuses in this world.

This decision of his to relish his own misery had an effect on his fluctuating political leanings. He always sided with the losing party, whatever its political principles may have been, and regularly placed himself in the role of the party leader who has to take all the inimical and malicious blows aimed in his direction and bear the brunt of all kinds of responsibilities and pressures. In all of it he discovered almost limitless pain and at the same time unparalleled pleasure.

Truth be told, this trait of his did not happen merely by chance or as a consequence of his failures; instead it traced its origins back to his early years when he was his parents' firstborn child. He had become used to being cared for, loved, and even spoiled, but he was also the child whom fortune had kept in reserve so that he could take on all the responsibilities of his shattered family when he was not yet twenty years old. The world may have pandered to him just a bit, but not for a single hour had it treated him kindly!

He lay there stretched out on the bed, but didn't close his eyes. He started looking round at the ceiling, walls, and floor of his room. Could he ever find contentment living in this strange quarter, he wondered. He felt a wave of nostalgia for Qamar Street, the Sakakini quarter, and the old house, but at the same time he still had that emerging sensation of hope alive with aspiration. Once again the apartment began to be filled with the sound of movement, and he listened to the noise as his mother and the servant started moving the furniture around and arranging the various rooms. From the street below came the sound of an annoying din. Listening more carefully with a disapproving ear, he made out that it was a group of children playing and singing. Shaken out of his slumber he went over to the window looking out on to the apartment buildings and opened it. Looking down on the street below, he could make out groups of boys and girls yelling and laughing. They had divided themselves up into teams, and each team was playing a particular sport. It was as if the entire street had been turned into a primitive sporting club; one group was playing with new stuff, and another amused itself with old rags. Some were skipping, others fighting. The young ones stayed on the sidewalk, dancing, singing, and clapping. Dust flew up in the air and noise was everywhere. He realized that from now on an afternoon snooze was out of the question. He heard some amazing tunes too: "Dear friend, what a beauty!" "Children of our alley, mulberries ahoy!" "That's a high mountain, my friend!" and so on and so on. He did not know whether to feel amazed, angry, or happy. Just then he heard a nasty, gruff voice let out a yell like a clap of thunder: "God damn the world!" and then intoned the same phrase to a clapping rhythm. The voice was almost certainly coming from the store immediately below the window, but from inside. He could not see who this person was singing curses against the world in general, but he could not stop himself laughing, something that put a bloom on his pale face. He stretched as far as he could out of the window and was able to make out the sign over the store: "Nunu the Calligrapher," it said in elegant script. So, he wondered, did this craftsman make signs that cursed the world and then sell them to grumblers and malcontents? He needed to buy some himself in order to slake his own thirst for such things!

3

He watched as the sun's rays, reflected in the glass of the upper windows of the apartment blocks opposite his own window, started to disappear, a sign that the sun was setting behind the domes of al-Mu'izz's Cairo. He looked up at the lofty minaret of the al-Husayn Mosque soaring in splendor over the fine mesh of sunset shadows. Leaning on the windowsill, he looked out on the roofs of the stores in between the apartment blocks and the windows and balconies that overhung the fronts of the buildings and the various alleyways that branched off. He could see fully locked windows and others that were half open. On the balconies housewives were busy collecting the washing or filling pots. By now the street was almost empty of children, as though the approach of nighttime had managed to scare them away. He secretly longed to venture outside, see the sights of the quarter up close, and explore the streets and alleyways, but he had spent so much energy organizing his room that he gave up on the idea. In fact, he usually stayed at home these days; once he arrived back from the ministry, he would only go out once in a while. He decided to postpone his little expedition for a later time. That decided, he left the window and sat cross-legged on his mattress, that being his favorite position for reading. Taking a book from his library shelves he proceeded to read until it was time to go to sleep.

His father, meanwhile, was sitting cross-legged on his prayer mat with the Qur'an open in front of him. He was reciting portions of the text in an audible voice, not paying any attention to the numerous mistakes he kept making in the reading of the text. Akif Effendi Ahmad was in his sixties now; he had a long white beard, and his face had a haggard and august look to it. After he had been pensioned off in the very midst of his working life and with great aspirations for the future, he had imposed a severe isolation upon himself. He seemed to be spending his entire life on devotions and Qur'an recitation. He only left the house on rare occasions, and then it was for a solitary stroll or to visit a particular shrine. The fact that he was financially hard up (his pension amounted to no more than six pounds) was probably primarily responsible for the regulated life he led, but eventually he reconciled himself to his new way of life and fell into its routines; indeed, he even felt grateful and grew to like it. The time that had been most painful for him had been the period after he had been dismissed and pensioned off. He had lost his entire source of income, or almost so, and a life of poverty loomed over his wretched family. He had been forced to leave his work and the activities it involved and to abandon the prestige that came with his position. With that he sprang to his own defense like a madman and started looking for intermediaries who might intercede on his behalf.

However, all that went up in smoke, so he started submitting petition after petition and application after application, but all to no avail. Eventually he came to realize the sad truth, namely that the doors of government employment were now firmly and forever closed. In fact, he had not actually done anything wrong, but his general lassitude and his insolence toward the people who had investigated his conduct only made things that much worse. Once it was all over, all he could talk about was how he had been wronged and who had done it to him, calling down curses on all of them. Anger, hatred, and despair took hold of him, and he started scoffing at government work and civil servants in general. He claimed he had been pensioned off because he refused to do anything corrupt; government jobs were simply too constricting for someone like himself who insisted on keeping his self-respect. At first he had denied that he had been insolent when questioned by the government investigators, but then he turned that round and took pride in it to the point of exaggerating about the way he had behaved. It became his only topic of conversation, to the extent that he became the butt of jokes and started to drive his friends and relatives away.

Initially he maintained his relationships with people he knew; he used to frequent the Gita Café in Ghamra and play backgammon with his friends. But then his misfortunes had a bad effect on his demeanor, and he started becoming more and more intolerant and irascible. One day he lost his temper with someone who was playing backgammon with him. "You can't talk!" roared the man.

"You've been fired by the government!" From that day he never went back to the café and retreated from the world and its people. His refuge was the world of religious devotion; there was no longer any trace of the past. What speeded his recovery was the fact that his son Ahmad was able to take on responsibilities for the family, inheriting thereby his father's obligations and ailments.

At the same time, we should not overlook another key factor in the father's recovery, namely the role of the mother. When it came to keeping the family content, she possessed a number of estimable qualities. She was a beautiful woman; when she was young, she had attracted the attention of Cairo's menfolk who clearly admired her looks.

By now she was fifty-five years old, and yet she was still comely and elegant, well made-up and colorful in her choice of dresses. Full-figured and well padded, there was just a touch of flabbiness about her. She knew all there was to know about cosmetics. Above all, she was known everywhere for her sense of humor, her funny stories, and jokes; no other woman came close to her when it came to making friends and telling stories. She had lots of friends, and would spend a lot of time welcoming visitors and visiting people. She would be gladly welcomed into homes by women, married and unmarried alike. That was how it came about that, when her husband's tragedy struck the house, she was not really affected. When her husband was no longer able to provide her with the things she needed, other hands, those of her female friends, were glad to step in and offer her presents; all of which meant that she was able to keep herself well presented and made-up. She was able to stay one step ahead of her husband too; her gentleness, sense of humor, and optimism all combined to sweep away any residual feelings of sorrow.

"You're done with the government, Akif Effendi," she would chuckle, "so now you can concentrate on me!" "If it's roses you're after," she would say as she toyed with his beard, "then you have to water the weeds as well!"

But in spite of it all, she still felt sad when she watched her husband bent over the Qur'an and her eldest boy at his desk.

"Why don't you both teach me how to read?" she would yell at them, "so I can sit by you."

The way Ahmad neglected his appearance made her furious. She used to rub her cheeks as though she were about to slap them. "You've made your mother feel old," she yelled in exasperation, "and ruined her reputation! Get your scruffy clothes properly ironed and your beard nicely trimmed. There are all kinds of celebrations going on in the world, and all you do is sit there pouring over those yellowing books of yours. How come you've let yourself go bald and your temples turn gray? You've made me feel so old, so old!"

Ahmad would smile sarcastically at her. "You can slap your cheeks all you like," he would reply to aggravate her. "But you're in your forties, aren't you?"

The brutal frankness with which he told her the truth horrified her. "Shut your mouth," she yelled at him, "and watch that insolent tongue of yours! Has any son ever before dared to mention his mother's actual age?"

For all that, her life was not without its sorrows. She was ill, or at least she thought she was, and yet no one around her showed any sympathy. As the years went by she became convinced that secret powers were at work and the only way she could be cured was through the zar ritual. Many times she had asked her husband for permission to hold such a ceremony, but Ahmad disliked the idea, even though he had no doubts about the existence of such spirits. At the time he could vividly recall his own experiences with the occult, something that had almost driven him mad. The mother had eventually despaired of ever convincing the two men and made do with attending zar rituals at the homes of friends.

One day Ahmad broached the topic. "Truth to tell," he said in amazement, "our family is a genuine victim of the devil. Didn't he tempt my father to be so insolent to that dog of an investigator, with the result that he lost his job? Then didn't he tempt me to learn about magic until I almost went mad? And now here he is harassing my mother, and that'll end up destroying us all!"

But—God be blessed!—Sitt Dawlat, Ahmad's mother, managed to show her cheery side more often than the sorrowful one, and judicious use of henna managed to keep strands of gray duly hidden.

Ahmad found he could not concentrate on reading because the change in location made him edgy and nervous. For an hour or so he tried to read in a desultory fashion. The daytime din outside had died down by now, but in its place came an even louder, sharper kind of noise that soon turned the entire quarter into a kind of stage for popular drama like the ones in Rud al-Farag. The source of this din was all the cafés scattered around the quarter, where the radios would be broadcasting songs and stories at full volume; the noise was so loud that it felt as though the radios were in his room. The waiters kept yelling out the orders like tuneful chants: "Black coffee," "Mint tea," "More coals," "Shisha!" Then there was the clicking of the backgammon and domino pieces and the voices of the players.

"I feel as if I'm right in the middle of a street full of passersby," he told himself, "not in an apartment!" He asked himself in amazement how people in the quarter could possibly stand so much noise or how they ever managed to get any sleep.

He sat there on the mattress until nine o'clock, then stood up to get ready for bed. Turning out the light, he decided to close the windows before getting into bed. Even so, the noise still filled the room and battered his ears. He recalled how quiet the suburb of al-Sakakini had been at this time of night, and that made him regret the move his family had made. He cursed the air raids that had forced them to abandon their nice, quiet neighborhood. At the same time, it all brought to mind that hellish night when the whole of Cairo had been shaken awake; the very memory of it frazzled his nerves, and the whole thing was only made worse by the ongoing din from the street below.

On that terrible night the whole world had been sound asleep; the time was close to dawn. As usually happened in Cairo at such an hour, the sirens had started their dire, intermittent wailing. The entire family had got up; Ahmad turned off the light in the outside hall before going back to bed and his habitual snoring. Before this particular night Cairo had only ever experienced air reconnaissance missions; there had never been any anti-aircraft fire. This time, however, he could not get back to sleep; lifting his head off the pillow he listened with increasing concern. He could clearly hear the whining noise made by the planes; that was obvious enough. But this time it went on and on. There was no let-up; in fact, the noise intensified and came even closer, and that alarmed him. But there was one thought that managed to calm him down: the gap in time between the sirens going off and the noise from the planes was only a minute or so; needless to say, that was not enough for fighter planes to arrive since the usual interval in such cases was at least fifteen minutes. On that basis he assumed the planes were British; they were circling overhead to launch an attack. He waited for the noise to stop, but it went on and on, getting louder all the time; it almost felt as if the planes had selected their house as a focal point for their circling. The din was totally nerve-wracking.

He got up again, left his room and felt his way slowly in the dark toward his parents' room.

"Are you both awake?" he asked when he reached the doorway.

"We haven't managed to get any sleep yet," his mother replied. "Did you hear something?"

"Yes, planes buzzing overhead. I heard them as soon as the sirens went off."

"They're probably British," said his father.

"Could be," Ahmad replied.

After sharing this opinion with his father he decided to go back to his own room. But before he had even made it back to his bed, his entire room was lit up by an incredibly bright light in the sky. It was followed by a horrible screeching sound and loud explosion that reverberated across the city of Cairo. In a panic he leapt out of bed again and, heedless of everything else, rushed toward the door like a madman. What made him panic even more were the bright bomb flares that were still lighting up his room; they managed to penetrate through the windows all the way into the interior of the room as though to direct the bombs right toward their intended targets. There now followed a whole string of powerful bomb blasts, each one preceded by that dreadful screeching noise. The ground shook, and the whole house kept rattling. The bombs kept falling one after the other, as though a fit of overweaning obstinacy was causing the sky to maintain this fiendish barrage.

He found his parents in the lounge, his father's arm wrapped around his mother; he looked as though he was about to collapse from sheer panic. Ahmad rushed over to them and grabbed his father by the arm.

"Come on," he yelled, "let's go down to the bomb shelter."

They hurried downstairs, preceded by the servant.

"What's that bright light?" his father asked in a quaking voice. "Is there a fire outside?"

Ahmad was busy trying to control his own breathing and make out the staircase steps in the dark. "They're magnesium flares," he said, "the ones we've been reading about in the newspapers."

"God protect us!" his father replied.

The stairwell was crowded with people making their way downstairs, praying to God with fearful hearts as they did so. With each explosion the walls shook. That would be followed by deafening screams from the women and crying from the children. All of a sudden the flares went out and the bombing stopped; the deadly rain of bombs came to an end, and everywhere was dark. All sorts of chaos ensued as people kept slipping and bumping into each other. Everyone started to panic. Eventually after a good deal of effort they reached the shelter in the basement; it was lit by a dim lamp, and the windows were all covered with a thick, black cloth. The ceiling rested on horizontal beams and vertical steel pillars. There were piles of sand all around. In the faint glow of the lamp you could glimpse people's faces, their expressions as pale as death itself; eyes agog, limbs aquiver, and tongues raving. The three of them stood there huddled close together, craving for a single moment of release so that they could catch their breath. But the pounding had gone on and on; in fact, it had intensified and seemed to be coming even closer to where they were.

At this point Ahmad's distress at the memory of what had happened that night was so strong that he had to move his legs around in the bed. "What a lousy night that was!" he muttered to himself. With a deep sigh he opened his eyes. The din in the street below once again impinged upon his consciousness. He recalled that, going to bed, his intent had been to sleep, not to relive the worst night in his life. But now that was exactly what was happening, and the way the memories kept flooding back was irresistible. Yes, indeed, the bombing had come even closer; in fact, one bomb had landed so close that everyone imagined that it had actually exploded inside their very hearts and minds. They all raised their hands as though to protect themselves in case the ceiling fell in on them. There was more screaming and praying; the word "God" was on everyone's lips.

Everyone started to imagine that the next bomb would fall directly on top of them. The next bomb did indeed fall. Good God, how can anyone possibly forget that awful screeching sound—the screech of death itself—as it made its inexorable way in their direction; how the entire building had shaken and the windows had rattled before it actually landed. There had been a huge explosion, at which everything had been shattered—hearing, nerves, breathing; backs bowed in anticipation of the inevitable, total despair; everyone preferred to die instantly rather than endure the long wait for its arrival. Yes indeed, at this point all that separated them from death was a single bomb that might be leaving its slot inside the airplane at that very moment. But the bomb had never come—at this point he allowed himself a sorrowful smile; either that or else it fell somewhere else far away. The sound of explosions receded just as quickly as it had come. This time death did not come the way they had imagined it would; it had showed them its face but did not give them a taste of its impact, at least not until some other night. The explosions moved off and the noise diminished, then became intermittent, then stopped. All that was left was the sound of gunfire, then everything fell silent.

At this point everyone recovered their breath and stared at each other in a mixture of doubt and hope. Suddenly people recovered the power of speech and started raving like madmen. A hellish quarter of an hour went by before the all-clear siren sounded. For God's mercy! Had death really passed them by? Would they really see the light of a new day? People started moving, lights were put on, and everyone headed for the outside where they found other people coming from neighboring quarters. Stories started doing the rounds: Abbasiya was in ruins, you could kiss Misr al-Gadida good-bye, and Qasr al-Nil was a pile of rubble. The trolley depot had been hit, and there were piles of workers' bodies all around.

As Ahmad and his parents made their way back upstairs to the apartment, they all felt a tense exultation, the kind of feeling people have when they have just managed to escape death and yet their hearts remain in the clutches of fear's sharp claws. They spent the rest of the night awake and talking to each other. Next morning the entire quarter looked as though everyone had made up their minds to leave; trucks were carrying all essential property to other quarters which people considered safer or else to villages close to the capital city. Whole buildings emptied of their occupants, and the sight of this mass emigration made the family feel even more worried, particularly Ahmad's father whose weak heart had already been badly affected by the air raid. The notion of leaving the quarter along with everyone else took root inside him. Already influenced by Islamic propaganda, he was firmly convinced that air raids would never target a religious quarter like al-Husayn. He had conducted a thorough investigation that resulted in finding this particular apartment. Even if he managed to forget the move itself, there was no way he would ever forget the day after the air raid. The whole of Cairo could talk about nothing else; everyone engaged in nervous chatter and their laughter was a blend of happy release and fearful tension.

As far as Ahmad was concerned, this time death seemed to have been so close that he could feel its breath on his face. And there were fates even worse than death: being abandoned in the middle of the road limbless and with a severed head, for example; or perhaps become permanently disabled; or to survive death but have the house and all its contents destroyed. He and the family would have nowhere to live, no furniture and no clothes either. He started praying to his Lord and begging his Prophet to intercede. His life may have been miserable and frustrating, but it was still one that he wanted to live. Even more remarkable was the fact that he now started coddling himself a bit and making his way of life as enjoyable as he could. Suppressing his natural instincts, he bought a box of chocolate biscuits on his way home, something that he had long craved but had deprived himself of, instead putting the sum into a savings account regularly each month. But with the arrival of evening the entire family was feeling anxious and unhappy; everyone was still jumpy, and no one slept a wink. Memories of that horrendous night came back to haunt them, and everyone's senses were on edge. Every single siren that went off, every door slam became a bomb blast; every rustle the screech of an airplane.

Now they had moved. Even so, did they feel any safer in their new location? The apartment blocks were newly constructed and sturdy; they all had bomb shelters that were models of their kind, and it was in the al-Husayn neighborhood. But then, castles could fall and mosques be destroyed! Oh my, how often we find ourselves being tortured by our love of life, and done to death by fear! But, when all is said and done, death knows no mercy. Merely thinking about it turns anything noble into mere trivia.

How often had Ahmad endured feelings of sorrow and anger that were almost intolerable? And why? With that thought he heard the radio announcing the royal good-night and realized that he had lain there awake and fearful for a good two hours. That worried him, and he started putting such thoughts aside in a quest for some sleep. But he failed, and instead the thoughts took over. He found himself inundated with this flood of memories. He recalled how he had suggested to his parents that they move to Asyut where his younger brother worked and they could be really far away from danger.

"No," his mother had told him, "we're going to stay near you. Either we stay together, or else...." And with that she had chuckled and asked for God's protection.

He wondered what he would be doing now if his parents had moved south. The best solution would have been to live in a pension. Truth to tell, he would have welcomed the idea, because, although he wasn't aware of it himself, he relished change. How could it be otherwise when he was still a bachelor, someone who had spent forty years living in a single house and enduring a routine that never changed from one day or year to the next and left him with a devastating sense of isolation? However inured he was to such an existence, something deep inside him was bound to push him toward change, even if he himself was not aware of it; it would need to be a complete change at that.

On this occasion, however, he did not completely surrender to his thoughts because a strange smell managed to bring his dreams to a grinding halt; it penetrated his nostrils as though carried by some previously dormant breeze. What made him aware of it was that he had never smelled anything like it before. He could not describe it: neither sweet-smelling nor foul, yet pleasant. There was a serenity and depth about it, allowing it to penetrate to the very core of his senses. For a while it would disappear, only to come back again. Were people really burning incense at this hour of the night? Or was it that this strange new quarter possessed its own particular scents that hovered over the depths of the night's silence?

All this made him forget his previous thoughts. Without even being aware of it he started to doze off and, before very long, slumber invaded his eyelids and closed them tight.

4

Next morning at seven o'clock he was seated at the table eating his breakfast. It normally consisted of a cup of coffee, a cigarette, and some bread along with a few pieces of cheese and some olives. Leaving the apartment, he went out into the hall. Before he reached the stairs, he heard the soft sound of feet behind him. Looking round he saw a young girl wearing a blue school-jumper with a satchel of books under her arm. For a fleeting second their eyes met, then he looked away feeling all confused, something that always happened whenever he looked at a female. He could not decide whether it was more polite to go ahead of her or to let her pass. That made him even more confused than before, and he blushed. So here was the philosopher of the Archives Department in the Ministry of Works acting just like an immature teenager falling over himself out of sheer embarrassment. The girl looked surprised and stopped where she was, while the extent of his confusion conveyed itself to her. The only thing he could do was to stand to one side.

"After you, Miss," he whispered in a barely audible voice.

The girl went on down the stairs, while he was left to follow her, wondering whether he had done the right thing or not. What impression did she get from his hesitation and confusion? When he reached the building's main door, his thoughts were rudely interrupted by a loud voice shouting, "Damn the world!" Looking to his left he saw Nunu opening his store, just as he had suspected. He relaxed a bit and gave a smile, before muttering, "O God, Opener, All-Knowing!" With that he went on his way, with the girl just a short distance ahead of him. When she reached the New Road, she branched off to the left toward al-Darrasa, while he made his way to the trolley stop.

All he had seen of her was her eyes. Once he had realized she was there, he had been looking straight at them. They were large and limpid, with honey-colored irises; her lashes were so long that they looked as though she had used kohl. They managed to suggest both softness and attraction and made their way straight into his affections. The girl was obviously only just approaching the age of maturity; she could not be more than sixteen. He, on the other hand, was forty; over twenty years between them! If he had married at the age of twenty-four—that being the sensible age at which to marry—he might well be father to a young girl of her age and youthful vigor. As he got on the trolley he was still thinking about that fatherhood that had never come to pass.

The powerful impact of those two eyes soon faded, as did his nostalgic enthusiasm for fatherhood. In their place came a vicious and black feeling that beset him every time he was near a female. And all because his love for women was the forbidden love of a middle-aged man that made him as afraid of them as a shy novice. He hated them all as a desperate old man. Every time he saw a pretty girl, he felt a strong emotional pull, a blend of love, fear, and loathing. His early childhood had had a profound effect on his peculiar instincts in this matter: he had been exposed to a father who dealt with him strictly and a mother who doted on him. The father's strictness had regarded oppression as a sign of affection, while his mother spoiled him to such a degree that, if she had had her way, he would never have learned to walk in case he fell down. As a result he had grown up with a peculiar mélange of fear and coddling, afraid of his father, people, and the world in general, and escaping from all his fears in the affection of his mother. She had done everything for him, even the things he should have done for himself. As a result he was still a child at the age of forty, afraid of the world, going into despair at the slightest failure, and recoiling immediately from any kind of confrontation. In such cases his only weapons were the ones he had had from the start, tears or self-torture. But by now they were useless. The world did not consist of his loving mother; it didn't care if he stopped eating, nor would it soften when he started weeping. Quite the opposite, it would turn away in disinterest and leave him to his own devices, sinking still deeper into his isolation and mulling over his own agony. Would his parents have ever imagined, one wonders, that this balding failure of a man was actually a victim of the way they had brought him up?

But in spite of all that he had left a historical record when it came to matters of the heart.

The first instance occurred during his first year in secondary school, which only need bother us for what it shows about his particular temperament. At the time he was a well turned-out and attractive young man, traits he may well have inherited from his parents. He managed to attract the attention of a pretty young Jewish girl who was the daughter of his neighbors. There was a time—it would appear—that Ahmad Akif was actually attractive! She used to play on the same street and would watch from her window for him to come home from school. Her pert femininity was abundantly evident to him and distracted him with the fires of love, and yet it was not enough to arouse in him the necessary courage and daring. His heart may have been aflame, but the only thing his timid nerve would allow him to do was to stare at her in silent longing and then retreat exhausted as soon as she stared back at him. Even though he was so bashful, he did manage to share some passionate moments with her, but it was at her instigation. She was a daring coquette; nothing could hold her back. Her brazen behavior managed to overcome his bashfulness. One afternoon she chased after him and caught up. She called out his name, and he turned round, his face pomegranate-red. She gave him a gentle smile, and he responded with an abashed one of his own.

"Let's walk down Abbas Street!" she said.

Without uttering a single word he went with her. They walked side by side as the sun headed toward the horizon. She made a point of sidling up and gently rubbing against him. That made him move away; it was as though he were afraid she might think he was the one taking the initiative, whereas in fact he longed to brush against the person alongside him. She now put his right arm through hers, laughing diffidently as she did so. He looked all around him.

"Are you scared?" she asked playfully.

"I'm scared that someone from your household might see us," was his gentle reply.

"Who cares?" she retorted with a shrug of her shoulders. Seeing how shocked he looked, she went on, "Are you still scared?"

"Yes," he replied after a little hesitation, "I'm scared someone from my own family might spot us."

She burst into laughter. With that she took him to a garden. "Now," she whispered, "we're out of range of all those spies!"

They walked around in silence as the sun continued its descent and sunset shadows grew longer, erecting a pavilion to welcome the onset of night.

"I had an amazing dream," this brazen girl now said, trying to work her way round his shyness.

"A nice one, I hope," he said, beginning to warm to her conversation.

"I dreamed that I met you somewhere. You told me that you wanted.... Then you said a word that I'm not going to tell you. You have to say it. Can you guess?"

That made him feel even more flustered. "I d-d-d-don't know," he stuttered.

"Yes, you do," she replied sweetly, "you're just pretending! Go on, say it...."

He swore to her that he really didn't know.

"There's no point in lying to me," she said. "You'd better remember. It's a word whose first letter is K...."

He remained silent, heart pounding.

"The second letter is I...."

He still said nothing and turned away.

"The third letter is S," she went on. "So what's the last one?"

He gave her an embarrassed smile, but still had no idea of what to say.

"If you don't say something," she said, squeezing his arm, "I'm never going to talk to you again!"

That threat had the desired effect, since he drew another S in the air.

"So now at last you've told me what it is you want," she laughed in delight, "and I'm not going to stop you." She leaned toward him, totally frustrated by his incredible bashfulness.

He stole a quick kiss that seemed to last for whole decades. How he longed for more of the same! But that is the way he was: intense passions but along with them desperate shyness. This pretty Jewish girl liked to poke fun at his face. He took her seriously and started hating his own face to an unnecessary degree. Now he had yet another excuse for his innate shyness, which only intensified. Had it been possible for a man to wear a veil over his face, he would have been the one to do so. It was one of the key factors in the excessive attention he paid to his personal appearance, something that transformed itself into utter neglect when despair got the better of him.

The pretty Jewess suddenly disappeared from his life. No sooner did a young man from her own community become engaged to her than she abandoned her playful ways and adopted a more serious lifestyle, entirely oblivious to the bloody wound she was leaving behind in a tender heart. But then tender hearts can salve their wounds very quickly. So it happened that in the final phase of his time at secondary school the proximity of neighbors brought him into contact with the pretty and youngest daughter of a widow who was one of his mother's friends. An affection developed between the two young people, duly encouraged by their two mothers who were soon referring to them as the "bride and groom." This second relationship was not like the earlier one that had served as a wake-up call to a heart that was now ready for sentimental education. However, this girl by contrast possessed strength of character and determination. As a result, when she fell through his fingers, he regretted it bitterly. Afterward he would often tell himself that if he had followed his and her mother's advice and married that girl, he would have enjoyed a married life of unparalleled happiness. However, no sooner had he obtained his high school diploma than his family was struck by disaster. His father was pensioned off, and it was now up to him—Ahmad—to face the dire consequences. Cruelly snatched from the gentle havens of hope, he found himself instead cast into the sheer hell of despair. If this girl was willing to stay with him, she would have to wait for at least ten years until his younger brother had completed his education. It became obvious that her mother was not going to encourage such a sacrifice since it would involve a long wait. In fact, it was the girl herself who made the decision to ignore her feelings; she cut off the relationship, and all their dreams came to nought. From then on Ahmad lost all faith in love and women, just as he had already done with the world as a whole. The love that in the presence of the Jewish girl had filled his heart was nothing but a false illusion, a teenage disease just like teething in babies. Harsh reality had imposed its own severe sentence on someone who had decided to rely on a woman's word; it didn't matter whether she was like his fiancée when it came to both intelligence and virtue, or whether she was like the Jewish girl who had flirted with him to her heart's content and then left him, like a guest at a hotel on Station Square leaving his room.

Now twenty years had gone by and his heart was still a void. He continued to endure a life of poverty filled with a variety of concerns that augured little hope for the future. If only he had managed to control his rage, he might have been able to be successful at something. In fact he still nourished a hope—after all, life cannot be without any hope at all, can it?—that one day he might find some happiness. Even though he had eventually despaired of ever gaining any prestige or authority, he could still aspire to be happy.

He tried getting engaged to the daughter of a merchant who lived in Ghamra, but her father rejected his offer in the nicest possible way. The middle-aged Ahmad learned that the girl's mother had noted that he was of a certain age and yet his salary was small. This blow to his pride left him reeling, and he went into a towering rage. It was more than he could tolerate to be rejected by some woman or other, when he was the genius against whom the entire world was conspiring. What's more, she had rejected him because he was insignificant! How could anyone say he was insignificant? So who exactly was supposed to be significant? With sparks flashing from his eyes he clenched his fist and vowed dire vengeance on the world. Only yesterday his beloved had rejected him because he was still young and had few prospects, where today another girl was rejecting him because he was too old and still had no prospects! So when exactly was he supposed to have prospects? Had his life been wasted? All glory was past, happiness was lost, everything was finished; was that it?

Thereafter he developed a habit of criticizing women and accusing them of every kind of shortcoming. They were cunning creatures, using ambition, lies, and sheer stupidity to work their wiles. Soulless bodies, sources of pain for man, and grief for humanity in general. Their superficial interest in science and art was merely a sham they could hide behind whenever victims fell into their clutches. But for the wicked lust implanted in our instincts they would win neither hope nor love. They...they....

"I've made myself a solemn vow, thank God," he would often tell his friends, "that I'm never going to get married however many chances I may have to do so. I totally refuse to be taken over by some dirty creature with neither mind nor soul!"

If his complete failure to achieve anything turned him into an enemy of the entire world, then his failure with women made him their enemy too. Even so, deep inside him there still lurked rapacious illicit desires and emotions.

The way that a passing girl affected him, as had happened today, stirred up some of those latent feelings and immediately brought to mind his previous experiences with women. It annoyed him, and provoked that profound and familiar sensation that combined love, fear, and hate. In the sheer relish he felt for his self-sacrifice and doing what was necessary he found a certain consolation for all his failed hopes, but this time his anger stubbornly refused to soften. He still felt angry, peevish, and full of hate. After all, anyone who has become used to having sacrificial offerings come to him to be slaughtered is never going to be willing to be the sacrificial lamb himself. He decided to wallow in his own misery and the life of a recluse; as though, after allowing his heartstrings to play sweet melodies, he was now throwing it all down a fetid well where it would languish. He now lived his life without hope, without anyone to love, without a heart, refusing to stay in touch with life or enjoy the pleasures it could offer.

By now he had despaired of ever achieving anything worthwhile. That pushed him into a life of seclusion, while his despair in matters of love drove him to consort with prostitutes. It was as though the negative feelings he had about women in general now threw him into the hands of those wretched and defiled women who would only accentuate the unhealthy sentiments he already had. His malicious attitude now served to convince him that the only genuine women were prostitutes. The veils of deceit regularly used by other women had been ripped away; they no longer felt any need to pretend that they were in love and could remain loyal and pure. However, consorting with prostitutes robbed him of more than his respect for women; it also killed off any vestigial sense he had of his own worthiness as a man. He was convinced that, if a prostitute loved a man, it was only for his natural masculine attributes and had absolutely nothing to do with either social values or relationships through family or neighbors. The Jewish girl may have fallen in love with him because there was no one else around. With his would-be fiancée it had been the fact that they were neighbors and their mothers had encouraged it. But with a prostitute none of those factors were involved when she chose a lover from among the dozens of men who regularly consorted with her. So, if he had not managed to attract a prostitute for such a long time, it must be because he was not sexually attractive. Having reached that conclusion, he could now add sexual incompetence to the ugliness he had been using as an excuse before.

Once his brother Rushdi had finished his college degree in commerce and obtained a job with Bank Misr two years earlier (his other brother had died a while ago), Ahmad genuinely felt that his major task was not merely complete but duly celebrated.

5

After lunch he made his way back to the new quarter. "Second alleyway on the right, then the third door on the left," he mumbled to himself as he drew closer. As he made his way up the winding staircase, he remembered the young girl he had seen that morning, the one with the lovely olive complexion and honey-colored eyes. Would he see her again, he wondered? What apartment did she live in and on which floor?

By now his mother had organized things in the apartment. He stayed there until sunset, but then decided to wander around the streets of the quarter in order to explore and find out as much as he could. He put his clothes back on and headed outside. He paused for a moment by the apartment entrance and looked around him as he tried to decide in which direction he should start his exploration. But before he had a chance to make up his mind, he was aware of someone coming toward him. Turning round, he spotted the person whom he had identified that morning as

Boss Nunu. The man approached him with a heavy tread, beaming with pleasure.

"A hearty welcome to our new neighbor!" the man said, extending a hand as rough as a camel hoof. "What a wonderful day for all of us!"

Ahmad greeted his new neighbor, hardly expecting such a warm welcome from the source of "God damn the world!" "And greetings to you too, Boss!"

The man gestured to a chair in front of his store. "Please join us for a minute," he went on, the broad smile still on his thick lips. "This is a happy day indeed!"

Ahmad hesitated for a moment. It was not so much that sitting down with the boss would mean negating the purpose of his expedition, but rather that his shyness would never allow him to accept such an invitation without due hesitation.

"I swear by al-Husayn himself," the boss went on in his usual loud voice, "that, unless you have some really urgent business to attend to, you be my honored guest. Gaber, bring us some tea and a shisha too!"

In spite of his hesitation Ahmad was delighted to accept the boss's invitation. He went over to a chair, while the boss came back with another. They sat facing each other. The calligraphy store was exactly like all the others in terms of its size and neat appearance. It was covered with beautiful signs, with a table in the middle on which bottles of colored inks, pens, and rulers were arranged. Leaning against one of the pillars was a large sign at the top of which was written in gaudy colors "The Khan Gaafar Grocery Store," with the name of the owner etched out in pencil but not colored in yet. The boss was wearing a gallabiya, white coat, and skullcap. He was about fifty years old, stocky, and well built. He had a large head with pronounced features, an equally large mouth, and thick lips. His complexion was wheat-colored, with a red tint to it.

"Nunu the Calligrapher, your humble servant," he said once he had sat down.

"I'm delighted to meet you," Ahmad replied, raising his hand to his head. "This humble servant is Ahmad Akif, civil servant in the Ministry of Works."

He had never liked mentioning where he worked as a way of salving his own sense of pride. Every time he had to introduce himself, it was a moment of sheer torture. But this time he did not feel the same way because he was well aware that people like Boss Nunu had great respect for civil servants. The man raised his hand to his head as a token of respect, then gave a gentle smile.

"It would be an honor to welcome you at any time," the man said with his characteristic bluntness, "but was it really fear of the air raids that brought you here?"

Ahmad was utterly amazed that people already knew why they had left the old quarter when they had only been in the new one for a single night.

"Who told you that?" Ahmad asked, staring disconsolately at the man.

"The driver who brought your furniture," he replied in all simplicity. "These days everyone's moving somewhere else."

That was a cue for Ahmad to launch into a defense of his family's courage. "Actually," he said, "all the quarters that have been subjected to the danger of air raids have emptied out. What drove us to leave our old quarter was the fact that my father has a weak heart, and we were worried about it. We really didn't want to leave."

At this point the waiter came with the tea and shisha. He put the shisha pipe down in front of the boss, then brought a chair from the store, placed it in front of Ahmad, and put the teapot down on it. The boss urged his guest to take some tea, while he himself grabbed the shisha pipe with relish and took a long puff from it, filling his nostrils.

"It's always okay for people to go looking for security, even though in fact everyone's life is in God's hands and fate decides what's going to happen. Ahmad Effendi, I'm one of those people who places complete reliance on God. I have no idea how to get to the bomb shelter. Which bomb shelter are you talking about, for heaven's sake? Have you ever listened to the words of Salih Abd al-Hayy's song? 'Whatever your share of life may be, that is the way it is!' Even so I pray to God that He will be a sufficient protection against calamity. At the same time I also pray that our luck may be good. After all, if it weren't for decisions made by some people, we wouldn't have the good fortune to be new neighbors, would we?"

Ahmad was aware that what the boss had said at first was intended to poke a bit of fun at him, even though it may not have been malicious. The rest of it obliged him to show some gratitude.

"Thank you, Boss," he replied with a smile. "Prudent people have often told us that there is security to be found in the al-Husayn quarter."

The other man took another huge puff and let out a cloud of thick smoke. "That's true enough," he said. "It's a blessed and much loved quarter, much honored because of the person it's named for. In days to come you'll realize that from now on you won't be able either to forget it or do without it. A deep-seated emotion will continually call you back. Here, take a puff from the shisha."

Ahmad thanked him but declined. As he listened to his companion, he kept enjoying the sips of tea. Wanting to join his companion in a smoke, but of his own kind, he took out a cigarette and lit it with a smile. He felt very relaxed as he sat there talking to his new neighbor, probably because there was a strange quality about him, something he had never encountered in anyone before. His simplicity, frankness, and forceful presence, they all surprised him, but what was more important than any of those things was that Ahmad felt a sense of superiority that stroked his own tortured vanity. That impression made Ahmad want to get to know him better.

"Why don't you like the shisha?" Boss Nunu asked. "It's just like a cigarette except with water. The smoke's filtered and purified. Beyond that, it conveys an aura of authority, and the gurgling sound it makes has a music of its own. And its very shape has sex appeal."

Ahmad could not help laughing, but his laugh was drowned out by the ringing guffaws from the boss himself; they sounded like a continuous loud mooing and culminated in a burst of coughing that went on and on until he ran out of breath.

"Do you think we locals are stupid?" he asked Ahmad, his face still smiling. "Do you realize that English tourists come to visit this quarter in droves; many, many more than Arabs. But, in any case, by al-Husayn's faith and God's, may you find untold happiness in his quarter and may our relationship and your time here be a happy one too, in spite of whatever Hitler and Mussolini decide to do."

"God willing, that will be so."

"A number of distinguished government personnel like yourself live in the area," the boss went on by way of encouragement.

"Oh Boss, please! I'm not that important." Ahmad hurriedly replied.

"No, I swear by al-Husayn and his beloved grandfather, the Prophet himself. Most of my friends in the neighborhood are officials. The new apartments have attracted a lot of good families here. You'll find everything you need: coffee, radios, kindness, and shishas. In fact, there's enough available here to make God happy and angry in equal measure."

"Heaven forbid we should make God angry!" Ahmad said with a laugh.

The boss stared hard at him, then carried on with his usual bluntness. It was as if he had known Ahmad for many years, not just a few minutes. "Pleasing God and angering Him are like night and day, inseparable from one other. Beyond them both lies God's mercy and forgiveness. You're not a Hanbali, are you?"

"Certainly not!"

"You surprise me!"

"But how can this quarter be big enough to cater to things that anger God?"

"Ah well, disaster always lurks, so they say, wherever people don't pay attention. Just wait and make sure for yourself. But I have to say that whatever faults there may be are not the fault of our quarter but of others. The corruption has spread so far that they can't keep it within their own walls. They keep sending their excess over to us; and that's exactly what the radio keeps telling us about world trade. Here we export primary goods and other quarters import them ready made. In some parts of our quarter they export servant girls; the other quarters convert them into barroom singers. Because of this the world's been turned upside down. Just imagine, my dear sir, yesterday I heard the radish-seller's daughter using English with her sister. 'Come here, darling,' she said."

Ahmad laughed. By this time he was feeling much more relaxed and at home. "In spite of all that, Boss," he said, his strategy being to get the other man to do the talking, "your quarter is pure enough. The level of corruption in other quarters is beyond conception."

"God protect us! It's obviously a good idea not to let our anxieties get the better of us. So forget about such things, laugh, and worship God. The world belongs to Him, whatever happens is His doing. His command is certain, and the ending belongs to Him as well, so what's the point of spending time bashing your brains and feeling miserable? God damn the world!"

"Well, Boss, that seems to be your favorite expression. I've heard it many times from my room upstairs."

"Yes, God damn the world! It's a phrase of derision, not a curse. But can you really curse the world in actuality as you do when you use those words? Can you despise the world and laugh at it when it makes you poor, leaves you naked, and brings hunger and disaster down on you? Believe me, the world's just like a woman: kneel in front of her and she'll turn her back on you; beat her or curse her and she'll come running. With the world and women therefore I have just one policy. Before and afterward I rely totally on the Lord God Almighty. There's been many a day when we have no idea where the next penny is coming from; the family has nothing to eat and I can't even buy myself a shisha, but I still keep on singing, cursing, and joking. The family might as well belong to my neighbors, and poverty be a mere passing cold. Then things change; I'm asked to do some work and grab the money I get. Then it's, 'Be happy, Nunu!' 'Thank God, Nunu!' 'Zaynab, go and buy us some meat!' 'Hasan, get some radishes!' 'Aisha, run out and buy us a melon!' 'Fill your stomach, Nunu!' 'Eat up, children!' 'Be grateful, you wives of Nunu!'"

That phrase "wives of Nunu" attracted Ahmad's attention. He wondered exactly how many wives Nunu had in his harem. Would he be prepared to share his domestic secrets with the same frankness as he had used to detail his personal philosophy? The only way he could see to find out was to ask a trick question: "God is always there to help us. You obviously have a large family."

"Eleven stars," the man replied simply, "and four suns. Oh, and a single moon!" he went on, pointing to himself.

"You have four wives?" Ahmad asked after a pause.

"As God wills."

"Aren't you afraid of not being fair to them all?"

"And who's to say that I'm unfair?"

"Do you rent four separate houses for them?"

"No, like you, sir, I've just one apartment. It has four rooms, and there's a mother and her children in each one."

Ahmad's expression showed his astonishment as he stared at his companion in disbelief.

Boss Nunu's laugh was filled with a certain pride. "Why are you so astonished, Ahmad Effendi?" he asked.

At this point Ahmad discovered a sense of daring that was unusual for him. "Why haven't you been satisfied with just one?" he asked.

"One?" came the reply. "I'm a calligrapher. Women are just like calligraphy; no single one can make up for the others. One's naskh, another ruq'a, another thuluth, and a fourth farsi. The only thing I have one of is God Almighty."

"But aren't four more than you need?"

"If only they were enough. God be praised, I can satisfy an entire city of women. I'm Boss Nunu, and my recompense is with God!"

"But how can you keep them all in one apartment? Don't you know what people say about women's jealousy?"

Boss Nunu gave a contemptuous shrug of his broad shoulders, then spat on the ground. "Are you going to believe everything people have to say about women, their jealousies and cunning? It's all a smokescreen created by puny men. At base woman is a moist, malleable dough; it's up to you to shape it as you wish. She is a creature deficient in both mind and religion, and you have to use two things to make her function properly: shrewd tactics and the stick. Each one of my wives is totally convinced that she's my favorite; none of them has ever needed more than one sound thrashing. You search in vain for a home that is as happy and serene as mine; my wives are unrivaled for their modesty and competitive desire to keep me happy. That's why none of them ever dared to get me angry when they found out that I have a girlfriend!"

"A girlfriend?" Ahmad shouted.

"Good heavens!" Boss Nunu said, "You get shocked by the smallest trifles! Here's what I say: the taamiya at home is delicious, but then what about the stuff you can buy in the market?"

"So are your wives happy about you having a girlfriend?"

"If you're used to being content, then you're content. With your own sense of manliness you can craft a woman just the way you want; she'll do whatever you want and believe whatever you want. A strong man has no need to resort to divorce unless his own passions dictate that he should."

"May God forgive you, Boss," said Ahmad with a smile.

The man took some more puffs from his shisha. "And are you married, Ahmad Effendi?" he asked his guest.

"No," he replied resentfully.

"Not even one?"

"Not even half of one."

Boss Nunu laughed. "I get it," he said with his habitual frankness, "you like to play the field."

Ahmad gave a cryptic smile, neither confirming nor denying this statement.

"May you be forgiven too!" Nunu commented with a chuckle.

Boss Nunu had managed to get further with Ahmad than anyone else before him; he had delivered a violent jolt to his psyche. He represented Ahmad's diametrical opposite in terms of forcefulness, health, and good humor, not to mention his verve for life, his success, and his happiness. Ahmad admired the man, something he derived from his awareness of his own inability to match the man's accomplishments. At the same time he resented him for the things he did so well and for his contentment. But the resentment he felt was trivial and certainly did not compare with the sense of superiority that he felt toward the man. Thus the attraction he felt for him overcame his resentment and rekindled his desire to get to know him and his remarkable quarter a lot better.

"You should try the Zahra Café," Boss Nunu said as Ahmad stood up to leave. "It's small, but all the most respected government workers in the neighborhood congregate there. You'll find the very elite among your neighbors. How about going there this evening?"

"If not this evening," Ahmad said as he made to leave, "then tomorrow, God willing."

Saying a grateful farewell, Ahmad now proceeded on his journey of exploration into the different parts of his new quarter.

6

Next evening Ahmad left the apartment building, heading for the Zahra Café. He found it at the start of Muhammad Ali Street, just before it turned into Ibrahim Pasha Street. It was as large as any store, with two entrances, one of which was on Muhammad Ali Street itself, while the other was on a long passageway leading to the New Road. There were dozens of cafés like this one in the quarter; he estimated that there must be a café per every ten inhabitants. He approached the café with a certain hesitation because he was not a habitué of such places and was not used to their atmosphere. But no sooner had he entered the place than he spotted Boss Nunu sitting in the middle of a group of government officials including some locals as well. Nunu noticed him and stood up with a smile.

"Welcome, Ahmad Effendi!" he shouted in his usual loud voice.

Ahmad moved over in his direction, with a bashful smile on his face. He held out his hand in greeting, and Nunu grabbed it with his own rough palm.

"This is our new neighbor, Ahmad Effendi Akif," he said turning to the assembled group. "He's a civil servant in the Ministry of Works."

Everyone stood up in unison out of kindness and respect, something that made Ahmad even more nervous and shy. He went round shaking hands with everyone and being introduced by Boss Nunu: "Sulayman Bey Ata, primary school inspector; Sayyid Effendi Arif from the Survey Department; Kamal Khalil Effendi, also from the Survey Department; Ahmad Rashid, a lawyer; and Abbas Shifa, an eminence from the provinces."

They cleared a space for him and made him feel very welcome. He started to feel more at home and forgot about his shyness and discomfort at coming to the café. Before long he was feeling happily superior to them all, although he managed to keep it well hidden by smiling sweetly and exchanging amiable looks.

There was not the slightest doubt in his mind that he was superior to these people in every conceivable way. After all, he was from al-Sakakini, and families who lived there were the children of quarters like al-Darrasa and al-Gamaliya. He was an intellectual, with a fully fashioned mind, while these folk had none of that. Indeed, he pictured his presence in their midst as a nice gesture of sympathy, an engaging display of humility on his part. What continued to baffle him was the question as to how he would make these people aware of his importance and introduce them to his sterling intellectual and cultural qualities. How on earth was he going to convince them that he was a person of real significance and earn their respect? Needless to say, as long as this new friendship developed and they continued to get together, such respect would inevitably follow; so there was no harm in delaying things for a couple of sessions.

He looked round at the people sitting there and studied them carefully. There was Sulayman Ata the inspector, fifty years old or more—ugly to the point of contempt, small, and with a stoop. His face reminded you of a monkey: sloping forehead, bulging cheeks, round, tiny eyes, wide jaw, and stub nose. Even so, he had none of the deftness and energy of monkeys. He wore a fixed glowering frown as though to reflect his own outrageous ugliness. The best thing about him was his amber rosary; his fingers were incessantly playing with the beads. The amazing thing is that, even though he looked so ugly, it did not provoke any hateful feelings, but rather sheer mockery and sarcasm.

The person called Sayyid Arif was about the same age, small and thin, with a soft complexion and an innocent look about him. By contrast, Kamal Khalil's expression exuded an aura of respectability; he was obviously meticulous about his appearance, of average height and somewhat portly. He was the one who gave their new guest the warmest welcome. Ahmad then concentrated his attention on Ahmad Rashid. He discovered him to be a young man in the prime of his youth, with a round face and large head, although the heavily tinted dark glasses he wore almost completely obscured his facial features. Ahmad was particularly interested in this young man because he was a lawyer and thus an educated person. The legal profession had been one of his aspirations when he still had hopes in life but had yet to inure himself to failure. He still hated lawyers just as much as literature scholars and learned people; his feelings were like those of a man toward one who has married a girl he himself was in love with. For that reason he immediately regarded him as an enemy and made ready to pounce on him at the earliest available opportunity. The other member of the group was Boss Abbas Shifa, a youngish man with a dark complexion whose coarse, ugly features suggested a humble obsequiousness. He was wearing a loose-fitting gallabiya and slippers and had left his head bare so that his peppery-colored hair stuck up all over the place. All of which made him look even more ugly; sufficiently vile, in fact, that all he needed was a prisoner's uniform. Even though the group was fairly small, it took up a good third of the café. The café owner sat by the cash register nearby as though he too was a member of the assembled company and one of the participants in their conversation.

Boss Nunu and Kamal Khalil extended the warmest of welcomes to Ahmad Akif, but Sulayman Ata maintained his frowning posture as though he had completely forgotten about the new arrival. Ahmad Rashid started listening to a broadcast on the radio.

"We've heard that you've just come here from al-Sakakini," said Kamal Khalil to open the conversation.

"Yes, sir," replied Ahmad lowering his head, "that's correct."

"Is it true," the man asked anxiously, "that very few people made it out of their houses?"

"The truth of the matter is," replied Ahmad with a laugh, "that only one house was destroyed."

"So much for rumors! What was it then that made such

a terrible noise, the one that sounded as though it was inside our very homes?"

"That was in the sky!"

At this point Ahmad Rashid turned away from the radio; he obviously had not been paying much attention to it. "Is it true that a bomb landed but didn't explode?" he asked.

Ahmad was delighted that the young man was now talking to him. He replied, "People say that two bombs did fall, but they were cordoned off and experts defused them."

"What we need," Ahmad Rashid went on, "is that Canadian specialist whom we've read about in reports on war news. Apparently he's saved whole quarters in London."

Sayyid Arif was an admirer of the Germans. "Are there any whole quarters of London left?" he asked with a scoff.

Ahmad Rashid smiled. "As you can tell, our friend supports the Germans!" he said.

"For medical reasons!" laughed Boss Nunu, completing Ahmad Rashid's comment.

That made Sayyid Arif blush, but Boss Nunu refused to spare him. "Our friend, Sayyid Arif believes," he went on with one of his enormous laughs, "that German medicine can restore one's youth."

Sayyid Arif frowned angrily. Obviously it was utterly inappropriate to make such a statement in the company of someone who had only just made their acquaintance. Ahmad Akif was well aware of what Boss Nunu's motivations were in saying it, and yet he made sure that his facial expression showed no sign of having heard anything. Boss Nunu was anxious to repair any damage his remark may have caused, so he started telling their new guest about the new quarter he was living in, praising its virtues to the skies.

"This quarter is the real old Cairo," said Ahmad Rashid, commenting on Boss Nunu's description. "Crumbling remnants of former glories, a place that stirs the imagination, arouses a real sense of nostalgia, and provokes feelings of regret. If you look at it from an intellectual perspective, all you see is filth, a filth that we're required to preserve by sacrificing human beings. It would be much better to knock the whole thing down so we could give people the opportunity to enjoy happy and healthy lives!"

Ahmad immediately realized that his new conversation partner had a seriousness about him that suggested that he might well be a smooth talker, and indeed someone of genuine intelligence; especially as his law degree gave him the kind of prestige that ignorant and naive people respected enormously. He was afraid that this man might outshine him, so he immediately assumed the offensive, ready to counterattack at any cost: "But old quarters do not necessarily imply filth; there are the memories of the past that are far more worthy than present-day realities, memories that can serve as the impetus for any number of qualities. The Cairo you're anxious to wipe off the map is the city of al-Mu'izz, reflecting the glories of eras past. Compared with that city, where does today's Cairo, all modern and indentured to others, belong?"

This ringing statement by Ahmad had a positive effect on the group, as was obvious from their expressions. That made him happy. Feeling pleased with himself, he was eager to use the moment to display his knowledge. "Forgive me,

Ahmad Sir, but I've read many, many volumes about our history. I can tell you that what I've just said is established fact."

"It's clear," Sayyid Arif commented, "that our friend Ahmad Effendi is fond of history."

Ahmad was thrilled because this comment allowed him to show off his learning even more. "Actually," he went on, "I am no fonder of history than any other branch of learning. Truth to tell, I've spent over twenty years in a quest for knowledge of all kinds."

Everyone in the group looked in his direction with considerable interest. That made him feel even happier; it was the kind of admiration that made his heart leap for joy. He would have liked to read Ahmad Rashid's expression behind his dark glasses.

"But why are you studying all these things, 'Professor'?" Kamal Khalil asked Ahmad Akif. "Are you studying for a degree or something?"

Ahmad was thrilled to be called professor, but he didn't like the rest of the question. "What degree is there," he asked arrogantly, "that could possibly justify the long and comprehensive study that I have made of things? Degrees are just a kind of game young people compete over. My studies have only one quest, genuine learning. Maybe one day I'll have done enough to think about publishing something."

"But what do you mean when you say that degrees are merely a game?" Ahmad Rashid asked him with the kind of smile on his face that made the other Ahmad furious.

"A degree is no indication of learning," Ahmad replied, doing his best to control his anger.

"Does it indicate ignorance then?"

His temper kept rising, so much so that he had to consciously suppress it. "What I mean," he went on, "is that a degree merely demonstrates that a young person has spent a few years memorizing certain topics. Genuine learning is nothing like that!"

Ahmad Rashid gave a cryptic smile but then let the subject drop. In fact, he felt some sympathy for the sentiments that Ahmad Akif was expressing about university degrees. Beyond that, he was well aware of the passion with which the opinion was being expressed. All of which led him to surmise that there had to be other reasons for adopting the posture beyond the ones that had already been discussed. Ahmad Akif in turn was delighted by Ahmad Rashid's withdrawal from the argument because he assumed it meant he had won in front of the group of plebeians he was sitting with in the café.

For a moment no one said anything. Boss Nunu started pouring more tea into the cups. Ahmad Akif looked around. For the first time he noticed a young boy sitting on a chair alongside Kamal Khalil Effendi; he could not decide whether the boy had been there when he arrived or whether he had come in while Ahmad was preoccupied with his argument about degrees. However, it took no more than a moment to confirm that the boy was Kamal's son; even a passing glance made the family resemblance clear. Ahmad looked around some more, but soon focused on the boy again. There was something about his face, but he could not put his finger on it. He obviously could not stare at him for a long time, so he started sneaking perplexed glances in the boy's direction from behind his teacup, from which he kept taking sips. What was it that so attracted his attention to that face and made him almost forget about the fierce argument he had just been having? He had a vague feeling that he had seen him before, particularly those wide eyes with their sweet, simple expression. Such feelings will nag their owner till some recollection will shed light on memories shrouded by the past. As a result he fell back on asking himself where and when he had seen that face before. Was it in al-Sakakini? On the trolley? At the ministry? In response to his stubborn inquiries, his memory treated him with a cruel mockery: an image would float up into his consciousness with glimpses back into times and places past, and he would tell himself he almost had it, but then everything would vanish into a profound darkness. The image would disappear, leaving behind yet more obscurity, ambiguity, and despair.

Eventually he reached the point of not wanting to recall anything that was not relevant to his chief concern, but the truth of the matter was that at this point his memory was not the only thing impinging upon his consciousness and confusing him. In fact, deep down he could feel something pulling his heart back in the direction of those honey-colored eyes and their sweet, simple expression. Every time he sneaked a look in that direction, a wave of longing and attraction swept over him. He was totally confused and felt abashed by the whole thing. The watchful eyes of the assembled company were warning enough. Clutching the handle of his teacup he stared at the floor, his heart pounding. Yet his imagination totally refused to forget about the boy, something that showed in both his facial expression and the look in his eyes, while his heart overflowed with affection and longing. His eyes were on the point of giving him away, but a combination of fear and anger managed to keep them under control. What on earth had come over him, he wondered.

It was Boss Nunu who dragged him out of these personal reveries. "Do you play any recreational games?" he asked.

Ahmad looked at him, his expression that of someone who has just been jolted awake. "I don't know anything about games," he said.

Kamal Khalil laughed. "Our professor, Ahmad Rashid, is exactly the same," he said. "You can chat to each other while we play a game for an hour or so...."

"Come on, Muhammad," he said turning to his son, "It's time to go home."

Ahmad's heart gave a flutter. He looked at the boy once again and followed their progress as they made their way toward the door and then vanished from sight. Once again he asked himself in frustration how it was he could not remember where he had seen that boy before. By now the company had split up into separate groupings: Boss Nunu and Kamal Khalil were playing dominoes; Sulayman Ata and Sayyid Arif were playing backgammon; and Abbas Shifa had moved his chair so he could sit with the group around the café owner. Ahmad Rashid moved his chair to make room for the game players and came over to sit beside Ahmad Akif. The latter realized that he had come over, and that made the feelings he had just been having disappear, to be replaced once again by argument and conflict. Out went all notions of love, and in came anger and hatred.

"How are you, sir?" Ahmad Rashid asked, turning in

his direction. "By the way, I don't want you to think that I've known Khan al-Khalili for a long time. I came here just two months before you."

Ahmad was delighted that the other man wanted to befriend him. "Was it the air raids that made you move as well?" he asked.

"Pretty much. The fact is that our old house in Helwan was vacated for military reasons. I thought that a move into Cairo would mean I was much closer to work. I found it difficult to locate a vacant apartment until a friend happened to point me to this district."

Ahmad Akif lowered his voice. "What an unsettling neighborhood it is!"

"You're right. Even so, it has its consolations. It's weird, but it's also full of art and amazing examples of humanity. Just take a look at the café owner to whom Abbas Shifa is talking. Notice the drowsy look in his eyes. He takes a dose of opium every four hours. He goes about his work without ever really waking up; or, to put it another way, without ever wanting to wake up."

"And does this improve life?"

"I don't know. The only thing that's certain is that he and others like him totally abhor the state of wakefulness that we enjoy and try to maintain by drinking tea and coffee. Were he to be compelled for some reason or other to remain in a wakeful state, you would find him yawning all the time, bleary-eyed, bad-tempered, and completely incapable of staying on an even keel until he found a way of canceling the world and floating in the universe of delusion. So is it some kind of nervous pleasure habitually obtained, or a purely illusory sense of happiness to which the human soul resorts as a way of escaping the hardships of reality? Only the café owner can provide the answers to that."

Ahmad told himself that he too was scared of the hardships of reality, just like one of these drug addicts. He too ran away from it regularly in order to seek refuge in his isolation and his books. Was he any happier than they were? He felt an urge to explore the subject further.

"How can I concentrate on my studies," he asked with a changed tone of voice, "with all this hubbub going on?"

"Why not? The noise is very loud, it's true, but habit is that much stronger. You'll get used to the noise, and eventually you'll be disturbed if it's not there. At first, I found it annoying and despaired of ever getting anything done, but now I can write my briefs and review legal materials in a completely calm and relaxed fashion amid this incessant din. Don't you think that habit is a weapon with which we can face anything except fate itself?"

Ahmad nodded his head in agreement. Not wanting the other to outdo him, even with such a trite phrase, he said: "Here's what the poet Ibn al-Mu'tazz has to say on the subject: 'Adversity brings a sting of distress; should a man suffer it for a while, it lessens.'"

Ahmad Rashid gave another of his cryptic smiles. He never memorized poetry and hated hearing it cited. "So, Professor Akif," he asked agreeably, "are you one of those people who are always citing poetry?"

"What's your opinion about that?" Ahmad asked dubiously.

"Nothing at all. It's just that I notice that people never cite modern poetry, only the old stuff. What that means is that, if they cite poetry a lot, it is always ancient poetry. I hate looking back into the past."

"I don't think I understand you."

"What I'm trying to say is that I hate to hear poetry cited because I hate any resort to the past. I want to live in the present and for the future. When it comes to the provision of guidance and direction, I'm quite content to rely on the sages of this era."

Unlike his colleague, Ahmad Akif was someone who believed that genuine greatness resided in the past. Or rather, the only examples of greatness that he was familiar with were in the past; he had no knowledge of greatness in the contemporary era. As a result, the other Ahmad's statement made him angry again.

"Why would anyone wish to deny the greatness of times past," he asked, "with their prophets and messengers?"

"Our era has messengers of its own!"

Ahmad was about to express his sense of outrage, but he didn't want to express it in words unless it was his companion's ignorance that was involved rather than his learning. "So," he asked calmly, "who are the messengers of this era?"

"Let's take those two geniuses: Sigmund Freud and Karl Marx."

He felt as though a hand had grasped his neck and was throttling him. Indeed, he felt as if his honor had just suffered a deep wound, because he had never heard either of those two names before. He was now insanely angry with his companion, but was obviously unwilling to display his own ignorance. He shook his head as though he was well acquainted with the views of the two men.

"Do you really see them as being the equals of geniuses of the past?"

The young lawyer was thrilled to come across another educated person and was eager to argue points of principle. He pulled his chair up so close that they were almost touching.

"Freud's philosophy concerning the individual," he said in a low voice so no one else could hear, "has shown us the way out of the ills of our sexual existence that play such an essential role in our lives. Marx for his part has provided us with ways to liberate ourselves from the miseries of society. Isn't that so?"

Ahmad Akif's heart was pounding and his fury was barely suppressed. This time he did not know how to object, let alone to come out on top. All of which led him to dodge the whole issue.

"Take it easy, Professor," he said gently, although his chest was bursting, "take it easy! In the old days we were all as enthusiastic as you are, but the passage of time and further thought on the matter both demand that we maintain a certain balance."

"But I do think a great deal about the things I read!" protested Ahmad Rashid.

"I'm sure you do," he replied, "but you're still young. As you get older, you'll acquire genuine wisdom. Haven't you heard people say, 'Someone one day older than you is a whole year wiser'?"

"Some ancient proverb, no doubt."

"A sage one too!"

"There's no wisdom in the past."

"Oh yes, there is!"

"If there were any genuine wisdom in the past, it wouldn't have become just our past."

"What about our religion then?"

The young man raised his eyebrows in amazement. If Ahmad Akif had been able to look behind the dark glasses, he would have spotted a look of sheer contempt.

"Utter naiveté!" the young man muttered.

Ahmad Akif had read the religious philosophy of the Brethren of Purity. There were two reasons why he was anxious to summarize it for his obnoxious companion: firstly to defend himself against the charge of merely following the popular view of religion; and secondly as a means of baffling his companion just as much as the latter had done to him.

"Religion constitutes a sensory phenomenon for people in general and a rational essence for intellectuals. It involves truths that intellectuals should have no problems believing in, such as God, divine law, and the active intellect."

His companion gave a contemptuous shrug of his shoulders. "Come now," he said, "our contemporary scholars know about the elements contained in the atom and the millions of stars that lie beyond our own galaxy. Where is God in all that? A load of religious myths! What's the point of thinking about issues that cannot be solved, when we face any number of problems that can and must be solved?"

The young man gave Ahmad a furtive smile. "Needless to say," he went on, altering his tone of voice, "we mustn't include anyone else in this particular conversation."

"Of course, of course! But never forget that disbelief is always the point at which knowledge begins."

Their conversation was interrupted by an angry outburst from Sulayman Ata. Apparently Sayyid Arif, his opponent at backgammon, had finally provoked him with all his blather.

"What a wise and just God who's deprived you of your powers!"

Ahmad Akif recalled what had been said about Sayyid Arif just an hour earlier and smiled at Ahmad Rashid, who smiled back meaningfully.

"Our friend keeps taking those pills," he said, "with sincere hope and belief in their effectiveness!"

At this point both of them noticed a group of men in gallabiyas gathered around the café entrance, each of them clutching a huge wad of bank notes. The entire scene was astonishing for the contradictions it implied.

"Maybe they're war profiteers," Ahmad Akif suggested.

"You're right," his companion responded. "They're leaving one class in order to join another."

"The war's managed to lift a number of people out of the lower classes."

"Lower classes, you say! True enough, but there's no real gap between lower and upper classes any more. Today's aristocrats are yesterday's poor. Surely you realize that in the past marauding mobs could grab our land by right of conquest. The same is true now with the upper classes. They all wallow in their prestige, power, and privileges without limit."

For the first time he was inclined to concur with his companion without any argument.

"I agree with that," he said.

"It's Marx's view," the young man went on, "that the

working classes will eventually win, and the world will turn into a single class where everyone can enjoy the necessities of life and human fulfillment. That's what socialism is."

Neither of them said any more, as though they were both exhausted. Ahmad Akif started pondering: What ideas! Freud and Marx, atoms and millions of planets, socialism! His facial expression showed signs of a burning hatred and disgust. It had never occurred to him that in Khan al-Khalili he would come across someone who could challenge his own cultural identity and force him to acknowledge that there was always going to be more to be learned. Would he never be able to find any peace in this world?

With that the young man took off his glasses to wipe his eyes with his handkerchief, only to reveal that his left eye was actually made of glass. For just a moment he was astonished, but then a wave of malicious satisfaction poured over him as he realized that the other man's eye condition gave him at least one way of exerting his sense of superiority.

He stayed there for a short while longer, but then left to go home, his mind churning and his dignity outraged. Fortunately for him, at that very moment he remembered the young boy, and that completely changed his mood. A cool moist breeze wafted across his burning senses and blew away the anger and hatred. Those honey-colored eyes appeared once again, with the coy expression. He gave a deep sigh. "I'm bound to see him again," he told his heart.

7

When he woke up the next morning, he was full of energy. Opening his window, he leaned out and found his amazing new quarter gradually rousing itself. Storefronts were being raised and window shutters opened; milk and newspaper sellers were wending their way through the patchwork of streets yelling their wares in non-stop chorus. He noticed a group of religious school students heading for their school in groups, wearing black jubbas and white turbans. They reminded him of popcorn in a pan. He listened with pleasure as they intoned a verse from the Qur'an: "*Has there ever come on man a period of time when he was a thing unrecorded?*" He let his gaze follow them as they proceeded on their way; eventually they reached the end of the sura: "*He allows whomever He wishes to enter into His mercy; for evildoers he has reserved a painful punishment.*" That last phrase immediately put him in mind of Ahmad Rashid, the lawyer: there was someone for whom God had reserved a painful punishment, and he thoroughly deserved it!

That afternoon, he sat with his mother in the lounge drinking coffee.

"Today I had a visit from the neighborhood women," she told him, obviously very happy. "They came over to welcome me and make my acquaintance as is the custom."

Ahmad was well aware of his mother's ability to get to know people and her fondness for visiting other families. "That's very nice for you," he replied with a smile.

With a laugh she took a cigarette from him and lit it. "There were some really nice women," she went on. "They'll be able to fill the void in our strange new surroundings with their warmth and contentment."

"It could be," said Ahmad, "that you'll soon be forgetting your old friends in al-Sakakini, al-Zahir, and Abbasiya."

That was too much for her.

"How can a decent person ever forget her true friends?" she exclaimed. "They're my heart and soul. However far apart we may be, distance will never be able to separate us."

"What are the women in this quarter like?"

"They're not lower-class folk," she replied carefully, fully prepared to leap to their defense if needed, "nor are they uncivilized as you may have imagined. Remember that it's not fair to judge people without really getting to know them. One of them is married to an official in the Survey Department named Kamal Khalil, and another one is the wife of yet another official from the same department named Sayyid Arif. I also had visits from the wife of the owner of the Zahra Café and his sister. The wife's a nice lady, but the owner's sister needs to be watched; the mean streak in her was obvious enough from her expression, even though she made a big effort to keep it hidden."

"Flatter her and people like her. She'll only show her true colors when she can dig up some dirt about you."

"Heaven forbid, son! Something even more odd happened today. I met Sitt Tawhida, the wife of Kamal Khalil Effendi—who is as broad as your own mother when she was younger—she's an old friend of mine! I used to know her well from Bahla the perfumer's shop in al-Tarbi'a."

"You'd both try to outdo each other with diet pills!"

"That's right. We said hello many times, but never really got to know each other."

"So now's the opportunity."

It was then that he remembered that the lady in question was the mother of the young boy Muhammad whom he'd seen at the café. It was only the mention of his mother's name that had brought him to mind. He wondered to himself in amazement how he could have managed to forget all about him, whereas a mere twenty hours ago that had been all he could think about. However, his mother gave him no time to reflect.

"We had a long chat about women's deceitful ways," she said with a loud laugh. "One of the women has a father who's a major expert on law; people feel blessed if they can kiss his hand. Another is the daughter of a very wealthy merchant. Still another is related to the director of accounting in the Ministry of the Interior. And a fourth has been ill and has spent dozens of pounds on a cure."

They both laughed.

"And what lies did you have to tell?" he asked her with a laugh.

"Oh, nothing to cause me grief on Judgment Day. I told them that your father had only recently been pensioned off; he'd been an inspector in the Ministry of Religious Endowments. Your grandfather was a merchant, I told them. As for you, my dear sweet son, you're a department head in the Ministry of Works. You're thirty-two years old, and no more. Don't forget!"

"What on earth?"

"There's no point in complaining about it! Make sure you don't say anything to call these little white lies into question. I'm thirteen years older than you. I'm forty-five."

"You mean, you had me while you were still a child?"

"Girls can give birth at twelve!"

"That makes you more of a sister than a mother."

"You're right. The eldest child is always a brother to his own parents. Your brother's a bank manager in Asyut."

He shook his head in amazement. "How can you possibly make up such stories when they can't possibly stay a secret for very long?" he asked. "One day, people are bound to find out."

"Starting tomorrow, we'll all get to know each other much better, and then we can all find out the truth bit by bit. Don't worry, it won't involve any blame-giving or mockery. If I hadn't embellished the truth somewhat, they wouldn't have believed me; in fact, they don't believe me even now. But we'd have lost the principal as well as the interest."

"What a load of unmitigated liars you all are!"

"What's your problem? No one can object to a few white lies when a bit of social one-upmanship is involved. Women's lies are a soothing balm for bloody wounds. May God grant you a wife who'll treat you to the very best lies there are!"

Even though her mention of the word "wife" made him angry, he still managed to laugh. "What a load of unmitigated liars you are!" he repeated.

"And you men," she said, giving him a wink, "you never lie, of course!"

For a moment he said nothing, not because he did not have a response ready, but rather because he was thinking about the various kinds of lies in his own life. "Oh yes," he replied, "we lie as well, but about more significant things."

"Maybe the things we find trivial are important to you men. But do you really regard life, prestige, and respect as trivialities?"

"Men's lies are as noble as manhood itself. Where do all you women fit in the context of lies told by merchants, politicians, and men of religion? Men's lies are the very pivot of the noble life whose effects you can all see on the battlefields of government, parliament, factories, and academic institutes. Indeed, they are the pivot for this dreadful war that has brought us to this strange quarter!"

He realized that she only understood part of what he was saying, and that made him even happier. Just then he remembered something.

"Did you have a visit from the wife of Boss Nunu?" he asked.

" 'God damn this world' you mean? They all told me a lot about him, but he won't allow his wives to go outside the house or look out of the windows. They may well have to spend year after year cooped up inside the house, happy and content!"

"It's fair enough for someone who curses the world not to trust it."

"By God, my son, women are just as wronged as the world is. But never mind. Have you heard of someone called Sulayman Ata?"

"The inspector?"

"Tawhida Hanem calls him 'the monkey.' "

"That may well be the first true statement you've heard!"

"She told us with a great chuckle that he's thinking of getting married."

"Which girl would ever consider taking that monkey as a husband?"

"Untold numbers of women. Money makes up at least half the value of beauty. The girl in question will be the one who manages to track him down and go after him in earnest so she can marry him before he's fifty-five."

"So is it true," he asked her with a laugh, "that men are finished at that age?"

"Good heavens, no! But she has no rights to his pension if she marries him after that."

"So when she marries him, she's gambling on the fact that he's going to die! And who pray is this judicious woman?"

"Tawhida Hanem told me that it's the daughter of Yusuf Bahla, the perfumer. Apparently, she's a genuine beauty, and in two specific ways, natural and artificial!"

As Ahmad pictured the aged monkey he felt sick. He was shocked that such a man could manage to attract beautiful women whereas he was a total failure at it. After all, hadn't a woman—who wasn't even beautiful—rejected his hand with the words, "He's too old!"? He wanted to picture the beautiful daughter of the perfumer, but instead what came to his mind right out of the blue was that beautiful brunette girl with the honey-colored eyes whom he'd met in the hallway.

"Does the perfumer live in our building?" he asked, his heart in his throat.

"No," she replied. "He lives in Bayt al-Qadi."

He gave an inner sigh of relief, then wondered to himself which family the lovely girl belonged to. He only just managed to stifle a groan. At that very moment he remembered the eyes of the young boy, Muhammad, and realized that the place where he had seen them before was in those honey-colored eyes in the hallway! That's what he had been trying so hard to remember. So, the young boy was the girl's little brother; there could be no doubt about it! His heart gave a flutter, but, now that he had found a release from all his doubt, confusion, and shyness, he also felt a profound sensation of pleasure and relief. So powerful was his joy at this discovery that he was no longer paying any attention to what his mother was saying. She kept on talking, but he was lost in his own dreams.

8

In the evening he made his way to the Zahra Café again. He did not do so without a certain hesitation; frequenting cafés was not something he was used to doing, it was entirely new. His long-standing desire for cultural seclusion now found itself matched by his favorable impression of the café and its denizens. But for his desire to joust with Ahmad Rashid and lord it over the others, he certainly would not have found it so easy to abandon his normal reclusive habits. When he reached the café, he did not find Ahmad Rashid; when he asked after him, he was told that the pressures of work often prevented him from coming. Even so, the assembled company was by no means dull; both Boss Nunu and Boss Zifta, the café owner, managed to enliven it in their own unique way.

Ahmad Akif talked a lot and laughed a lot. He started enjoying spending time with people, and especially the more refined types; for him at least, consorting with such folk was just like someone who is dead tired surrendering to sleep. He returned home at ten, and spent a couple of hours reading; all the while the images from his new life were dancing in front of his eyes as he perused every line on the page (something he had never done in any detail before). Then he went to bed and fell asleep. He had no idea how long he slept, but he woke up with a start to hear a hateful sound. At first he did not realize what it actually was, then he did, and his heart gave a terrified leap. He jumped out of bed like a madman, felt his way into his slippers, and rushed over to the door. There he bumped into his parents, with a young servant leading the way.

"How do we get to the shelter?" his father asked in a quavering voice.

"I know the way, sir," the servant replied for him.

The family rushed to the front door in total darkness and went out into the hallway, feeling their way down the spiral staircase. By this time everyone was awake, and the silence was broken by the sound of doors slamming and footsteps rushing down the stairs. There were anxious voices and nervous laughter. The caravan clung to the banisters and stumbled its way downstairs through the darkness, gripped by fear and panic. Ahmad's family did not need their servant to guide them; the shadowy figures and sound of voices showed people where to go. Outside, the covered streets were just as dark as inside the houses, but the dim starlight made the other streets slightly less gloomy. They all felt the same as they had on that other hellish night—scared out of their wits; they kept lifting their eyes to the heavens whenever they loomed into view. They reached the entrance to the shelter amid a flood of people and went downstairs into the bowels of the earth.

They found themselves in a wide space; the powerful electric light blinded eyes that by now had become accustomed to the pitch darkness. The firm and well grounded walls and ceiling were enough to give observers a profound sense of relief. Long wooden benches were attached to the side walls while in the middle were piles of sand. Ahmad's family made for one of the corners and sat themselves down, while other people distributed themselves on benches and in corners. There were not enough seats for everyone, so many people had to stand in the middle. At first everyone was scared. Neither the fact that they were together, nor the light, nor the solid walls were of any help in easing their intense anxiety. There followed a tense period of waiting, during which the looks in people's eyes gave eloquent expression to what they were feeling inside.

"It's 2 a.m.," muttered his father, looking at his watch. "Same time as on that dreadful night!"

Ahmad was as scared as his father, or even more so. But he made an effort to appear calm. "That raid was a mistake. God willing, it won't be repeated!"

Minutes passed in total silence. As time went by, a sense of security began to insinuate its way into the assembly. People started whispering and talking to each other. There was a lot of laughter, and people kept trying to reassure each other. Ahmad looked at the faces of the people next to them, but they were all strangers. Now everyone rushed to say something.

"They'll never harm the place where al-Husayn's head is buried!" said one man.

"Say, 'God willing,' " responded another.

"Everything's according to God's will," said a third.

"Hitler claims to have a profound respect for the Islamic countries."

"Not only that. People say he's actually a closet Muslim!"

"That's not so surprising. Didn't Shaykh Labib al-Taqi say that he saw in a dream Ali ibn Abi Talib—may God bless him—giving Hitler the sword of Islam?"

"Then why was Cairo bombed in the middle of the month?"

"That was al-Sakakini, the quarter where the majority of the inhabitants are Jews."

"What do you suppose the Muslim peoples can expect from him?"

"Once the war is over, he's going to restore Islam to its former glory. He will unite the Muslim peoples, and then alliances and treaties of friendship will be signed with Germany."

"For that reason we pray that God will support him in his war efforts."

"And he would not be victorious if his motives were not pure—our reward is ultimately a measure of our intentions."

Ahmad listened to this conversation with a mixture of pleasure and disapproval. True enough, most of them were local folk, but even so it had never occurred to him that their sheer naiveté could reach such a level of illusion or that propaganda—if there were such a thing—had managed to achieve such a comic effect. In spite of that he was unwilling to deny himself the pleasure of this unconscious humor and would not have done so had he not spotted at that very moment his great rival, Ahmad Rashid, walking slowly past him. He jumped up, and they shook hands.

"I didn't see you today," Ahmad Akif said.

"No," replied Ahmad Rashid in his dark spectacles, "I was busy studying a legal case."

The very mention of the subject aroused his jealousy, and he made no comment.

"I see all our colleagues are here," the lawyer went on, casting an eye over the assembled company, "but of course I don't see Boss Nunu."

"I'm surprised by his strange behavior," said Ahmad with a smile.

"All summarized in the single phrase 'God damn the world!' "

"For him it's a slogan; you could almost call it his theme song."

"He would have paid more heed to death if he were younger."

"For him it's a matter of faith."

"He has a profound sense of God's presence. Wherever he is, he keeps Him in mind and puts his trust in Him with all his heart. He has not the slightest doubt in his mind that God will never abandon him. That's why you can see him indulging in every conceivable kind of outrage, firm in the belief that he's going to receive God's forgiveness and mercy."

"I suppose he's a happy man," commented Ahmad Akif with a sigh.

"Fool's paradise is more like it," the young man retorted with a scoff. "That's the happiness of ignorant fools and blind faith, the kind of happiness that tyrants enjoy by virtue of controlling the lives of simpletons. It's really funny that I've despaired of ever discovering happiness among people of wisdom, and yet you seem to find it in such a stupid form. You need to search for genuine happiness within the framework of science and knowledge. If that makes you feel anxious, angry, or miserable, then look on that as a sign of a genuinely virtuous human existence, one that will rid society of its faults and the human soul of its illusions. When it comes to real happiness, Boss Nunu's version of it only credits our suffering—those of us that support science and reform, that is—to the extent that he can privilege death with its would-be repose over the boons of life with all its struggles and tensions."

The atmosphere in the bomb shelter had already made Ahmad Akif feel tense, so he did not feel up to arguing with him. "Don't you think," he responded with a smile, "that the very unthinking happiness that you've just talked about is letting him sleep soundly while we're all down here sweating it out through the night?"

The young man had more self-control than Ahmad Akif and simply laughed. "He's undoubtedly sleeping soundly at this very moment, undisturbed by anyone except for the quarter's 'husband lover.'"

The look on Ahmad Akif's face made it obvious that he did not understand what his companion was talking about.

"Haven't you heard about her?" the young lawyer asked with a smile. "She's a terrific woman. Her official role is to be Abbas Shifa's wife. Do you remember him? Every evening her house provides a warm welcome to a whole crowd of heads-of-household from this quarter. Boss Zifta, the café owner, calls her the quarter's 'husband lover.'"

This information startled Ahmad Akif. "You mean...."

"Yes!"

"What about Abbas Shifa?"

"He's her official husband, one who's found both a trade and a profit in playing that role."

"Is that why everyone makes such a fuss over him even though he's so ugly and coarse?"

"He is a much esteemed personage!"

At that moment the image of the despicable man with his disheveled hair popped into his mind. Simultaneously, however, the young man moved away, and Ahmad went with him. Very slowly they passed by all the people standing and sitting until they spotted Sayyid Arif sitting beside a pretty young girl with a baby on her lap.

"That's Sayyid Arif and his wife," the young man whispered.

"His wife?" Ahmad asked abashed. "How did he get married to her?"

"The way people do," Ahmad Rashid replied. "He's a perfectly normal man, apart from a critical condition about which he remains hopeful, especially given those German pills, and he won't...."

Ahmad Rashid had no time to finish the sentence because at that moment he was interrupted by a loud bang followed by a whole string of others. Ahmad Akif's heart skipped a beat. He felt as if his whole body gave a jolt, and that bothered him in case his great rival noticed. Total silence followed, and everyone looked panicked and scared.

"Those are the anti-aircraft guns," people said as a way of reassuring themselves and everyone else, but all it managed to do—whether intentionally or not—was to make people even more nervous and angry.

A man came rushing in from the outside. "The sky's full of searchlights," he said.

That made people even more anxious. There were other

explosions farther away which lasted for a while and then stopped. Once again there was complete silence, which went on for quite a while. People started to relax a bit. First there were a few whispers, then everyone burst into conversation.

"The disaster of random air raids won't happen again!"

"Radio Berlin has apologized for the raid in mid-September."

"It was an Italian raid. The Germans don't make mistakes!"

Ahmad Rashid allowed himself a smile. "Do you see how fanatical these people are in supporting the Germans?" he said. "What about you? Are you the same way?"

As usual, Ahmad Akif relished the chance to empathize with the underdog. Since the majority were supporting the Germans, he was glad to express an opposing viewpoint. "No," he replied, "I'm for the Allies, heart and soul. What about you?"

"I've just one hope," said Ahmad Rashid, adjusting his spectacles. "I want the Russians to win, and then they can liberate the world from chains and illusions!"

They both moved away from the people who were chatting. At the very end of the other side of the shelter, to the right of the entryway, they spotted their friend Kamal Khalil with his family. Ahmad Akif looked at them carefully and saw a very fat woman, the young boy, Muhammad, still in his pajamas, and the beautiful girl with the honey-colored eyes. Now he could see for himself the game that love had played with him; he was thrilled to discover that the connection he had made a few hours earlier was correct. He could not keep on staring at her, so he turned away feeling delighted and fulfilled.

"Kamal Khalil and his family," he heard Ahmad Rashid say.

"Is the girl his daughter?" he asked.

"Yes, he has Muhammad, Nawal, and an elder daughter who's married."

He sneaked another glance at her in order to fill himself with that lovely, simple expression so full of charm. She had wrapped herself in a winter coat, and her long black hair was done up in a thick plait. She was looking drowsy and let out a big yawn. At that point Kamal Khalil spotted them both and came over with a smile. They stood there chatting. Ahmad Akif realized that the fact that Kamal had come over to talk to them meant that the family must be paying attention to them; it was not out of the question that those two honey-colored eyes were looking him over—if they had not done so already—with his flowing gallabiya and white skullcap. He suddenly felt shy and blushed. Did she remember him, he wondered. But they did not stay talking for long, because the all-clear siren went off and the shelter resumed its normal busy routine. Ahmad Akif said farewell to his two companions and went back to his parents.

"So you leave us alone while the raid's on," said his father angrily, "and you come back when the all-clear is given!"

"God is always with us, whatever the circumstances!" said his mother with a laugh.

Moving very slowly they made their way amid the mass of people toward the shelter's exit and climbed the stairs to the street. The light from windows illuminated the way as they climbed up to their apartment. As they went upstairs with everyone else, Ahmad could recognize Kamal Khalil's voice. Ahmad hurried to his bedroom in the hope of getting to sleep again, but for a long time all he could see were those two honey-colored eyes and the lovely image they presented.

9

The fasting month of Ramadan now approached; there were just a few days left before it started. But Ramadan never arrived unexpectedly, and its advent was always preceded by preparations to accord with its sacred status. Ahmad's mother was never going to be one to shirk her duties in that regard, she being the person in the household primarily responsible for making sure that the month was properly observed and respected. One day she made it the topic of family conversation.

"It's a month that brings its own rules as well as obligations," she said, obviously directing her remarks at Ahmad.

He was well aware of the point she was making. "For sure Ramadan has its rules," he replied defensively, "but war is a bitter necessity for all of us. It overrides all other obligations."

His mother was very unhappy at that remark. "God forbid that we should ever break our customs," she said.

That managed to arouse his miserly streak. "Ramadan

can pass just like any other month," he said in an exasperated tone. "We can make up for the things we missed doing sometime in the future when there's peace."

"But what about Ramadan treats: candied almonds, honey cakes, and mini-stuffed pancakes?"

Even though he was feeling annoyed, the very mention of those treats had a magical effect on him, not merely because he loved them so much but also because they invoked happy memories of the beloved month and especially his childhood. Even so, such memories, wonderful though they might be, were not enough to counteract the bitter reality of inflation or to soften his frugality.

So, even though in his heart of hearts he longed to go along with the idea, he delivered a firm refusal. "Let's forget about such luxuries as long as we're living through these difficult times. Let's beg God Almighty to help us with the bare necessities of life."

His father gave the impression of not paying much attention, but in fact he was listening carefully to what his son was saying. He was inclined to agree with his wife's position, but did not have the necessary courage to say this in so many words. However, he intervened at the crucial moment.

"There's no need for us to either stint or be extravagant," he said.

His son realized full well that his father was taking his mother's side, and he certainly could not talk to him as bluntly as he had to his mother. From a very early age he had learned to respect his father. As was always the case, the last thing he wanted to do was to ignore the hand extended to him for help now that he had become his father's primary source of support. With that in mind, he made no comment although he felt awkward and unsure of what to say.

It was his father who eventually spoke. "We can make do," he said, "with some pine-nuts and raisins for stuffing and a packet of apricot drink mix to whet the whistle. We need only have honey-cake just once, and the stuffed pancakes twice; they don't need to be cooked in fat. All that won't cost a lot."

The whole thing appalled him. He was sure that during Ramadan they would spend what little he usually saved every month. He might even have to withdraw an additional amount from his savings account. That idea really stuck in his craw. Just then he remembered something else that was even more significant than the honey cake and candied almonds.

"What about meat?" he asked.

"The government has allowed the purchase of meat throughout the holy month," said his mother, mustering all her resources. "That's because a piece of meat is something that the heart of an exhausted faster really comes to rely on."

"But our budget's too small," protested Ahmad. "We can't afford to buy a pound of meat every day along with all our other necessities!"

"You're right," said his father, but then used a certain amount of cunning as he went on to say, "so it'll be better for us to eat no meat once every three days."

In the few days left before Ramadan actually started, the mother busied herself getting the kitchen ready, cleaning pots and pans, and storing away almonds, sugar, onions, and spices. Even though she had only been observing the Ramadan fast for a few years, the advent of the fasting month was still a source of pleasure and delight for her since it was always a month devoted to the kitchen as much as to fasting itself—even though the latter was its primary purpose. What was best about the month were the long nights and enjoyable visits where conversation would be accompanied by the cracking of nuts and melon seeds. This particular year they were lucky because Ramadan was falling in the month of October when the weather was usually mild and the temperature would be reasonable. That would make it feasible to stay up until the initial crack of light announced the arrival of dawn.

The night of the moon-sighting arrived; after sunset everyone was waiting and wondering if today would be the day. At dinnertime the lights on the minaret of the al-Husayn Mosque were turned on to announce that the moon had indeed been sighted. Because of the war emergency, they had decided not to fire off cannons but to make the announcement by illuminating the minaret. The entire column had been decorated with lightbulbs that emitted a pearly light over the entire neighborhood. Groups of people with drums now toured the quarter, calling out "Time to fast! To the fast let us aspire, just as Islam's judge requires!" Young men greeted the group with shouts, while the girls ululated. A feeling of joy spread throughout the quarter as though borne on a night breeze.

"I wonder how Ramadan is being celebrated this year in our old quarter?" Ahmad could not help asking.

"How much of our city have you even seen, my boy?" his father asked with a smile. "Did you ever see the beginning of Ramadan in this new quarter of ours before the war started? Everything filled with light and happiness; nights spent awake, nights replete with conversation, recitations, and innocent games. In the good old days when we were all young and healthy, a group of friends and I would walk for an hour before the dawn fast-breaking all the way from al-Sakakini to this quarter. Once here we would eat a breakfast of trotters and sheep's head meat in the al-Husayn Café and smoke a shisha. We used to listen to Shaykh Ali Mahmud recite the call to prayer and then return home in the early morning."

"When was that?" Ahmad asked.

"When you were ten," his father replied without even having to think.

Ah, what a wonderful time those childhood days were, days of merriment, happiness and being spoiled! That was an era that both father and son could cry over.

That evening Ahmad indulged in his new habit, making his way to the Zahra Café. By so doing he was cutting his reading time in half, but he found that the company gave him quite as much pleasure as did reading and seclusion. There he met the group of friends whom he was getting to know much better, as they were him. The conversation revolved around Ramadan nights and how they were going to spend them.

"Don't wear yourselves out thinking about it," was the raucous advice offered by Abbas Shifa (the husband of the so-called "husband lover"). "We have our own past Ramadan nights to use as a model. After we've broken the fast, we come to the café and stay here until midnight. Then we make our way to 'you-know-where' and spend the rest of the night there until the dawn fast-breaking."

Ahmad pricked up his ears when he heard the phrase "you-know-where" and wondered to himself if the group indulged themselves in sinful practices during the month of repentance. But he decided that his own plan was clear enough: he would stay with them in the café for as long as they did and then return home. Once there, he could read until dawn and keep doing that until the month came to an end.

10

On the first day of the fast Ahmad Akif felt really tired; he found it difficult not to drink his cup of coffee and have a cigarette whenever he felt like it. As he made his way to work, his head was throbbing and he kept yawning. He was feeling so completely exhausted that his eyes started tearing from all the yawning and his eyelids were drooping. At that point he remembered that Ahmad Rashid and his like would not be suffering the way he was, and the contempt and superiority that he felt gave him a small dose of pleasure.

When he returned home at noontime, he was totally wiped out. He threw himself on his bed and immediately fell fast asleep. An hour before the end of the fasting period he woke up again; heading for the bathroom he splashed some water on his face. On his way back to his room he noticed his father sitting cross-legged on his prayer rug reading the Qur'an and walked by in silence. He poked his head into the kitchen and saw his mother working there with her sleeves rolled up. The very thought of the kitchen led him to pause by the door for a moment. Looking round, he could sniff a big tray full of salad ingredients—parsley, watercress, carrots, onions, and tomatoes, and bright green and red peppers; all of which made him unconsciously lick his lips in anticipation. When he turned his attention to the tureen full of beans, he could not stand it any longer.

Abandoning his spot by the doorway he walked past the table in the big room and noticed that it was already laid: bread in one corner, cups of water placed in front of each chair, and a plateful of radishes in the center. He hurried back to his own room and shut the door. The last hour before people broke their fast was known to be by far the toughest to live through, so he had made it a hard and fast rule to divert himself during that period by doing some concentrated reading. When he had finished the task, he took a look at the clock and saw that he still had another half-hour to wait. That brought a frown to his brow, but he decided that the best thing to do as a way of killing time was to open the window and look outside.

There was Boss Nunu closing his store. His children, who were standing there waiting for him, almost blocked the entire street. Once he had finished, he went on his way, surrounded by young bodies, with the young ones grabbing on to his legs and the whole assemblage causing enough din to make a radio station envious. Apart from a few yogurt sellers, the street was now virtually empty. Ahmad watched as the last rays of the sun gradually faded from the walls on the buildings opposite his window behind the large square of stores. Open windows served to advertise tables heavily loaded with food inside. Pitchers had been put outside on balconies to cool, and plates of fruit compote garlanded with egg had been laid out. The evening breezes carried with them the smell of food being fried and the crackle of roasts. Ahmad allowed himself to wander off into a reverie inspired by the magic realm of food.

He left the window, went over to the other one that looked out on the old part of Khan al-Khalili, opened it, and leaned on the sill. That part of the quarter seemed quiet and still; the domes of the al-Mu'izz period loomed in the sky, almost as though doing obeisance to the setting sun. Immediately opposite this window was the left-hand side of the apartment building with its closed windows. Just at that moment he heard a slight movement from above. Looking up he could see his neighbor's balcony, opposite his window but higher up. A young girl was sitting there embroidering a shawl, the end of which twirled into her lap. She was sitting there on a chair, legs crossed. He recognized her at once—almost before he looked up— and his heart jumped. He hadn't realized that Kamal Khalil's apartment was on the side of the building facing his room or that his daughter was this close. He was overjoyed. The girl looked up, gave him a quick glance, and then went rapidly back to her needles. He looked at those honey-colored eyes for a third time. At that fleeting moment when their eyes met, his emotions overcame him and he blushed deep red in sheer embarrassment. He did not know how to behave or what was the best way to get out of this predicament. He lowered his balding head, dearly wanting to move away from the window while he caught his breath.

He wondered whether she was looking at him again. Could she see his bald patch? He could actually feel the part of his head where her gaze would be falling getting hot, just as leaves will burn up under the concentrated rays of the sun.

He had no idea how much time went by, but he came to himself when he heard the scraping sound of her chair. Looking up again, he saw her get up and go back inside. As she did so, he thought he caught the tiniest glimpse of a smile. As he made his way over to the other window, he wondered what exactly that smile might imply. Why had she smiled? Was it to scoff at his baldness? Was she laughing because he had looked so confused and bashful? Or perhaps she was pleased to have the amorous attentions of a man who was her father's age. Good heavens, that was right—her father's age! Needless to say, if he'd married at the appropriate point in his life, he might have had a daughter who by now would be of her age. Then it would have been impossible for a fleeting glance to embarrass him and send him into such a dither. But fate had decreed that he would lose his mind over this particular girl. The most innocent of glances had managed to make him feel both hungry and bashful.

He allowed himself a sheepish smile of despair, one that revealed his yellowing teeth. Just then, the cannon went off, and all the children started shouting. He was amazed that the last half-hour had passed without him even thinking about how hungry and thirsty he was. The muezzin chanted, "God is great, God is great," in a beautiful voice, to which Ahmad audibly responded, "There is no god but God!" Moving away from the window, he headed for the main room. All three of them gathered around the table. To quench their thirst they all downed some apricot juice, then the mother brought in a plateful of beans. They all devoured it with relish and left the plate completely clean.

"It would have been a good idea, I think," said the father as he sipped some water, "if we'd kept the beans back for a while until we'd eaten some of the other dishes. We'll fill ourselves up on beans alone!"

"You say that every year," the mother replied, "but you never remember until the beans have been eaten!"

In fact there was still plenty of room inside their stomachs. Lima beans were brought in, followed by stuffed peppers and roasted meat. Hands, eyes, and teeth all cooperated in silent resolution. It was not just the food that Ahmad was enjoying so much. His small balding head was teeming with happy thoughts, triggered, no doubt, by his enjoyment of the food. That lovely girl was his neighbor; her apartment overlooked his own. They would inevitably encounter each other; their gazes might well meet again, sentiments would certainly fly, and emotions were sure to be roused. Who knows what might happen after that? He planned to toss his heart into a bottomless ocean topped by hope and with disillusion as its seabed; hope in one direction, despair in the other. The darkness on the horizon worried him, but at the same time a safe haven on the far shore gave him some reassurance. How could he possibly know where security lay and when the final goal would be reached? It was surely enough that happiness had managed to waken a moribund heart; the very process brought its own particular delights, even though they might well cost a man his own blood and peace of mind. How could he possibly deny the fact that his heart was frozen stiff from the cold? It had long since tired of sleep and peace of mind. But now, here it was, alert and awake again; the scene on the balcony suggested that it would continue that way. Who knows what the outcome might be? For the time being he was so happy that he didn't care what the morrow might bring. Let the horizon have its sunrise or its sunset! Fate might either smile or frown on him. For him it was enough that his heart was alert. For days now he had been quivering with nervous energy, happily unsettled, joyfully perplexed, hopefully confused, fearfully hoping, and joyously scared. Yes indeed, this was life, and life was better than death, even though the living might endure hardships and the dead find peace.

11

After dinner he went to the Zahra Café to join his friends. They started chatting and sipping tea. Conversation revolved around fasting and the way that many people, particularly in Cairo, were not keeping the obligatory fast and for the feeblest of excuses.

Sayyid Arif decided to poke fun at both Boss Zifta and Abbas Shifa.

"Both of them can stop eating and drinking," he said with a chuckle, "but when it comes to hashish…that's entirely different, and religion isn't in the picture!"

"Wouldn't you rather be a real man, like us?" Abbas Shifa replied with a scoff, "even if it meant embracing some illicit activities?"

"There's a readily available medicine for my illness," Sayyid Arif commented, "but there's no known cure for what you have, my dear 'Thou Lord of all husbands'!"

Without blushing or batting an eyelid, Abbas Shifa simply shrugged his shoulders. "Don't blame me, and I won't blame you."

"No, no!" retorted Sayyid Arif, "we'll ask Boss Nunu to adjudicate. So, who would you rather be: Abbas Shifa or Sayyid Arif?"

"May I never have to make such a choice!" Boss Nunu replied with one of his enormous guffaws.

"Praise be to God who can revive decaying bones. Tomorrow those pills will prove all those scheming enviers wrong," said Sayyid Arif fervently.

Abbas Shifa gave a salacious laugh. "When that happens we can all congratulate ourselves," he said.

Sulayman Ata told them to stop this obscene kind of talk during the holy month of Ramadan. It was not that he was either sincere in his beliefs or annoyed with them for soiling the holy month with this kind of chatter, but rather that the refrain of "those pills" had long since become tedious; no one had any illusions about coming up with any new witticisms on the topic.

Kamal Khalil started reminiscing about Ramadan nights less than a quarter century ago before the current wave of irresponsible conduct had arrived to overwhelm all the established religious traditions. He talked about the way that the mansions of the patriarchs of the quarter would remain open throughout the night to welcome all kinds of visitors. Famous Qur'an reciters would be asked to perform until the break of dawn. He told them all that his own home—his father's house in other words—had always been one of those mansions crammed with visitors. Ahmad Akif wondered whether the man was actually telling the truth or merely emulating his corpulent wife?

They chatted for a full hour, and then, having exhausted the conversation, started playing games. Once again,

Ahmad Akif found himself alone with the young lawyer. This time, he realized, there would be argument and confrontation; however, as he eyed his adversary, he gave no sign of the pent-up anger inside him. But before either of them had a chance to utter a single word, a group of boys and girls came walking past the café waving lanterns, chanting Ramadan songs, and asking for coins. The young lawyer watched them as they disappeared into the distance and their loud voices diminished.

"We're a nation of beggars," he commented, turning to his companion.

Ahmad looked at him and smiled. He had started having deep doubts about the wisdom of engaging the other Ahmad in conversation, despite an apparent disregard. He embarked on a furious confrontation.

"Yes, a nation of beggars," Ahmad Rashid repeated in exactly the same tone of voice, "and a handful of millionaires. Cheap labor and begging, those are the only jobs available to Egyptians. And cheap labor is no better than begging."

Ahmad Akif shook his head and gave his companion a blank look. He remained silent, silence in such circumstances being by far the safest strategy since he could avoid getting involved in topics he knew nothing about and at the same time prepare a secure groundwork for grabbing opportunities when they arose.

"There's nothing worse," his companion continued, "than a system that requires people to lower themselves to the level of dumb animals. How can life afford intelligent people any pleasure when they are well aware that the majority of the country's citizens are starving and never have enough to eat? They're so ignorant that their minds never make it any higher than the brains of riding animals; they're so sick that bacteria of every conceivable kind infest their emaciated bodies. Has it never even occurred to them to demand equal rights for peasants and animals? No one can question the fact that in the countryside animals have the right to demand that their owners feed them, give them shelter, and keep them healthy. Peasants don't have the same guarantees!"

At this point Ahmad Akif could no longer resist the urge to protest; it was simply too much for him to allow the young lawyer to continue with this harangue and for him to have to listen to it like some student.

"If peasants have rights, as you say," he commented, "then why don't they demand them?"

"Peasants are kept in a state of total oppression and at the very lowest levels of humanity," the lawyer responded angrily. "They can't demand anything. But anyone who reckons that they deserve the privilege of belonging to humankind should feel honor-bound to remove that oppression from the overburdened shoulders of the peasantry. In the old days it was free men who battled slavery, not slaves!"

Ahmad found himself struggling with conflicting emotions. There was a part of him that was pleased to hear what the young man was saying. After all, if the scales of equality in his country had been genuinely balanced, nothing would have prevented him from completing his own education and he would have obtained the level of respect that he longed for. But the other side of him detested the young man's committed focus on social problems. For him such things did not deserve the attention of a genuine intellectual, someone who needed to focus on more cerebral things such as logic, mysticism, and literature. At that moment he remembered how strongly the young man expressed his opinions and how certain he was of his own rectitude. That riled his sense of superiority, and he felt compelled to react.

"If peasants really deserved more than they're allotted," he replied testily, "they would have obtained it by now. Rights pertain to those people to whom they are allotted. Anything beyond that is nonsense!"

The young lawyer adjusted his spectacles in a nervous gesture. "Are you a follower of Nietzsche, Professor?" he asked.

Heavens above, who on earth was Nietzsche? Wasn't it possible for a school of thought to exist—even if it was inspired by anger and hatred—without needing a spokesman from among all these philosophers of whom he was in complete ignorance? How was he supposed to respond to the nasty little devil? He allowed his mind to direct him toward the single way of getting out of the trap that his foe had set for him.

"My dear Professor Rashid," he replied in a much less angry tone, "you're trying to push me to talk about things I don't even care about."

"You mean, you don't care about your own life?"

"Just forget about peasants. Let people who need to be concerned about them deal with all that. Haven't you read Aristotle or the Brethren of Purity? Haven't you had any kind of spiritual education?"

The young man looked uneasy. "We're just like the

captain of a ship," he said, "one that's ploughing its way through a turbulent channel stirred up by ferocious winds. The waves keep pounding, and the wind howls. The ship heaves up and down and to the left and right, shaken to its core and buffeted hither and yon. In such circumstances can the captain simply turn his back on the steering wheel and stare at the horizon in fond hope?

"At this stage in our history we are passing through the straits of death, enveloped by misery on every side. So let's make use of those miseries as ammunition for our thoughts about the future. Ivory towers certainly have their particular delights, but for the time being we must resist our own egotistic tendencies."

"So, while you're busy rescuing the downtrodden from the pits of animal status, you're sacrificing the humanity of intellectuals and destroying their spirits!"

"I specifically said, 'for the time being.' Just think of the wartime situation we're now in, and the way that religious scholars—the most moral of people—have turned into outright criminals."

"But you have your own store of outrageous ideas—the universe and the atom!"

For the first time Ahmad Rashid let out a loud laugh. The game players all looked up.

"You laughed!" said Boss Nunu. "So tell us what it's about."

The two of them said nothing, and eventually the game players went back to their games.

"Knowledge is indispensable for the true revolutionary," the young lawyer went on, "not to bury ourselves in its contemplations but rather to liberate ourselves from the bonds of illusion and humbug. There was a period when religion was able to liberate us from idolatry, but now it's the turn of science to liberate us from the bonds of religion."

At this point, Sulayman Bey Ata lost his temper, a normal occurrence when he managed to lose a twenty in a game. Sayyid Arif decided to tangle with him. The whole thing soon degenerated into a vicious slanging match in which all the resident debauchees were eager to participate. Thus ended Ramadan's first evening of conversation.

With the arrival of midnight Ahmad Akif stood up to go home.

"I'm going home too," said Boss Nunu as he stood up. "I want to get my coat. The weather's very wet and chilly close to dawn."

They walked together.

"Why don't you stay awake until dawn?" he asked Ahmad as they were walking.

"Between midnight and dawn I normally read," Ahmad replied wearily.

"You read books?"

"Yes. That's all I read."

"What's the point?"

"It's my hobby, Boss Nunu!" Ahmad replied with a smile.

"But any hobby is supposed to have some point to it. Do books make you live longer? Stop you getting sick? Stave off the inevitable? Avoid hardship? Fill your pockets?"

By this point Ahmad was feeling so superior, he was

thrilled. "I fully intend to write a book as well!" he went on with a smile.

"That's even worse! Are you a journalist, or what?"

"Suppose I said yes?"

"Impossible!"

"Why?"

"Your parents are decent folk!"

That made Ahmad laugh so loud that it released all the evening's dark tensions. "But I really am going to write a book," he said.

"There are more books in the world than people. Just take a look at the Halabi Bookstore just below the Egyptian Club. It has so many books—good heavens!—if you stacked them all side by side, you'd have more than all the students at al-Azhar! Why go to all the bother of adding yet another title to the pile?"

"Okay, okay. But every book has its own qualities."

"You should develop some other hobby that won't cost you so much effort."

"Such as what?"

"You don't know? Have a guess."

"I've no idea, Boss."

"People call it Ramadan's best entertainment and life's greatest joy."

"So what's it called?"

"It comes out of the ground, but its true pasture is above the clouds."

"Amazing!"

"You'll find it either in a prison cell or by the Sultan's throne."

"There's nothing in the world like that."

"Craved by pauper and minister alike."

"That much?"

"Consolation for the desolate, quaff for the merry."

"How eager I am to make its acquaintance!"

"Just a tiny bit, and for every tight spot it's fit."

"That's magic!"

"They've brought it from the land of the elephant for the delectation of the people of the Nile."

"Are you serious?"

"Haven't you ever heard of hashish?"

At the very mention of the word Ahmad started. For his part, the boss laughed.

"Oh, come on," he said, "play along with me! Life's full of things that give much more pleasure than books!"

Ahmad's curiosity got the better of him. "Where?" he asked.

"If you agree and do me the honor," the Boss continued, "I can take you there."

"Aren't you afraid of the police?"

"Let's just say that I know how to keep them at bay. What about it?"

"That magical pastime doesn't interest me at all. But thanks anyway, Boss."

Back in his room he did his best to forget about his conversation with Nunu and his questionable pastimes. Instead he pictured Ahmad Rashid, the young lawyer, with all his complaints, enthusiasms, and violent gestures, and that made him feel angry, jealous, and vicious. He asked himself sadly how he could possibly have failed to absorb the world of modern knowledge, and how he would be able to fill in what he had missed. When would he be able to hold forth on Freud and Marx the way he could on the Brethren of Purity and Ibn Maymun? He spent some time pondering these issues and found it impossible to clear his mind for reading or even focus on it. Even so he stayed there, bent over his book without ever looking up. Such a posture— even when he felt distracted—was enough to convince him that his day would not have gone to waste by not acquiring some piece of culture, that being the thing he worried about the most. As a result an hour slipped by with his sense of superiority going through its own agonies.

Just then he had an idea, one that wafted its way into his heart like a gentle, moist breeze. It managed to douse the flames in his angry heart and leave it clean and fresh. He beamed. How lovely and joyful life would be, he thought to himself, if only chance and fate, coincidences and agreements, people and characters, all of the things he encountered could be like those two honey-colored eyes that exuded such sweet simplicity. Just then he recalled— somewhat to his own surprise—that Ramadan had long had a place of affection in his own heart. It had been in that month that his heart had first fluttered with love. Just like seeing the light of the world for the first time, it was a strange sensation, one that never again hits one with the same impact. It was then that he had seen the girl with whom he had wanted to share the rest of his life, but he had failed. Now here was Ramadan again, and once more his heart was brushing away the cold, dank fog from its surface in order to open up to rays of sunshine with their invigorating warmth. His mind was one of those that can find a piece of worldly wisdom in every little coincidence. Whereas other people might regard such things as mere coincidences with no real significance, for him they all contain hidden wisdom. That is why he now stared dreamily in front of him, his face a blank. Eyebrows raised, he opened his mouth. "So, Ramadan," he whispered excitedly to himself, "what will you bring this time?"

12

Next afternoon he jumped up and stood in front of the mirror to shave, something he usually did only twice a week. Normally he was not bothered if people saw him unshaven, but now he had decided to change his ways; from now on, he was going to shave every day.

Once he had finished, he put on a clean gallabiya and a gleaming white skullcap (needed to hide his balding head), then sat on the edge of his bed staring hesitantly at the window. It was not merely a matter of shaving or wearing a white skullcap. He had to ask himself what lay behind this burst of enthusiasm and this abrupt change in behavior. Was he careening ahead without any pause for thought or reflection? What exactly was it he wanted? Today it might well seem like a game, but tomorrow things could become serious. Above all he had to keep in mind his own bad luck and miserable history. Would it not be better, he wondered, to leave the window shut and forget about the implications involved in opening it? However, life never listens to logic of such a kind; neither prudence nor caution has a role to play. He was burning with thirst and consumed by desire.

He stood up again, his expression a study in determination, went over to the window, and opened it. Leaning on the windowsill he looked down, then slowly raised his gaze until it reached the floor of the balcony above. He could see the chair legs and the edge of the shawl—the one she had been embroidering the evening before—dangling between them. Just then, shyness got the better of him, and he looked down again, like some bashful child. He kept looking down, fully aware all the while that her eyes were boring a hole in his head. He was afraid the opportunity would be lost and he would miss the chance to look at her. Overcoming his shyness, he looked up again, only to find the chair empty and the shawl draped over the chair. Had she been there when he had opened the window and then had to go back inside? Or had she not been there at all? Whatever the case may have been, he felt frustrated and his enthusiasm flagged. Even more than before, he was now afraid he might not see her at all that day. The possibility of seeing her tomorrow was not enough to let him forget missing her today. He had gone to great pains to insure that today she would see him looking his very best, but now that entire hope had gone and the effort had been totally wasted. He looked down again in despair, but then, just a few moments before the cannon was fired, he heard a rustling sound from the balcony. Looking up, he spotted the girl coming out and bending over the chair to pick up the shawl. For a fleeting second their eyes met, but then she stood up straight, turned around, and went back inside again. That was all he needed. Had she looked at him any longer, he would have been all flustered and bashful. In fact, she had looked away as quickly as had been needed for her to grab hold of his very soul; a beautiful offering, without travail or pain. Thereafter, that particular sunset hour turned into the conjunction of all his hopes, the beaming smile of his dearest wishes; it gave the entire day its essence, its goal, its very meaning. As far as he was concerned, it was enough that he had had his fill of those elements of perfect simplicity and delight that flowed from her honey-colored eyes; for the rest of the day he could sate himself on the pleasure and dreams that they held in store. Two afternoons in a row she had come outside to sit on the balcony, and their eyes had met.

By now he was growing accustomed to seeing her lovely person, and perhaps she too was getting used to seeing him. Even so, he still felt flustered and shy. Every time the wonderful moment arrived, he looked at her with the staid, serious, and timid expression of someone who was on the point of running away. In his imagination he could now see her clearly. Her honey-colored eyes exuded a blend of purity, simplicity, and loveliness, eyes whose expressions suggested both inquisitiveness and acceptance, while their sprightly quality lent them a veil of wisdom and warmth.

Then came the evening when he was on the point of leaving his room to go to the café. The doorbell rang just as he was getting to the door. When he opened it, he found himself facing Sitt Tawhida and her daughter Nawal! For a moment, he simply stared at them both, taken aback by the joy that had hit him so suddenly. But then he recovered his senses and stood aside. "Please come in," he stammered.

He called out to his mother to come and greet the two guests, then went on his own way. Nawal's mother noticed how flustered he seemed and could not understand why a man of his age could be so awkward and act so bashfully simply because he had met two women. As Ahmad went down the staircase, he was ecstatic. He could recall very well—something he kept reminding himself to allay his doubts—that the young girl had given him a dazzling smile when he had greeted them at the door. It could have been the kind of smile a guest gives to her host at the door or even a shy, hesitant smile. On the other hand, it could also have been the kind of smile a woman bestows on a man as a way of rewarding him for his eagerness and persistence in looking at her every single day at sunset for a week or more. Whatever the case might have been, it was certainly a very sweet smile, the kind his heart had craved for twenty long years. He was loath to go to the café immediately; he wanted to give himself time to think.

He was one of those people who like to take a walk if they have something to ponder. With that in mind he headed for the New Road and walked along it for a while, feeling exultantly happy and relishing the joy of it for as long as he could. Needless to say, he was not as young as he once had been and life had not brought him much good luck—how could it be otherwise, bearing in mind the misfortunes and missteps in his earlier life? All he wanted at this point was to enjoy the happy feeling for an hour, even if it meant fooling himself and getting the entirely wrong idea. He had also decided to use this opportunity to reexamine his fortunes: where was he precisely with regards to his long suppressed hopes for the future; was it even possible for him to try all over again? For his part, he considered himself to be free, having now fulfilled all his obligations to the letter. Hadn't he taken on all of his father's burdens once his life had collapsed? Wasn't he the one who had given his family support when at one point it had seemed threatened with imminent disaster? Hadn't he looked after his brother until he had grown into a man? With all that in mind, he felt perfectly entitled to consider his own happiness and leave the family burdens to his younger brother. None of them could begrudge him that. But was there still enough time?

The rush of joy and triumph he was currently feeling forced him to think hard and use his imagination. His postal savings account had a fair amount of money in it, although it was paltry compared with the amount of time he had been working. As for the way he looked, there was no shame in being unattractive; and, in any case, he could really try, as he had done today, to make himself presentable, in spite of his gaunt appearance and baldness. He could even have a new suit made and buy a fez that was not as faded and crumpled as the one he now had. Now there was an idea! But he was middle-aged. He was over forty, and the girl was still in her teens. Only some kind of miracle could overcome such an age gap, but where would he ever find such a miracle? For the first time since he had opened the door to the two visitors, his heart sank. His doubts about his sexual attractiveness now came back to haunt him.

With a frown he finally woke up from his joyous dream. Walking along the street in the dark, he could picture the girl smiling at him. "She's just a silly, inexperienced girl!"

he muttered to himself. Even so, there was one thing that had not occurred to him: he could volunteer to proffer his hand to the life that was pulsing inside his own heart, albeit to throttle it in the serenity of death. Let it pulse and bloom then, and he would wait for that shelter that lies beyond the veil of the unknown. One thing was certain, he would never find himself in a situation any worse than the ones that fate had already thrown at him.

On his way back it occurred to him to ask himself whether this painful sensation he was feeling was actually love, the hidden passion that grows within the folds of the heart, the longing that coats one's very breath with the soul's essence, that heavenly ecstasy that brings delight to soul and world alike, the agony that fears any failure or return to loneliness and desolation. Wasn't it love when that lovely, simple vision settled inside his heart and became the stuff of his dreams and the source of all his hopes and agonies? Yes indeed, this was love, and he knew it perfectly well.

He went back to the Zahra Café where he found his companions chatting and sipping tea. He noticed the young boy, Muhammad, sitting beside his father and looking around the assembled company with those same honey-colored eyes. Ahmad was delighted to see him again—the boy being the envoy of his hopes—and his heart went out to him. He took his usual spot alongside Ahmad Rashid and started listening to what Sayyid Arif was saying.

"The Germans will take advantage of the thick spring fog," he said enthusiastically, "and attack the shores of England. Then the war will be over!"

"You mean, the same way Hesse fell?" Kamal Khalil asked jokingly, so as not to be too provocative.

Sayyid Arif chose to ignore his colleague's sarcasm. "England with all its arrogance will be flattened before it even has a chance to recover from the attack."

"But how can Germany invade England," Ahmad Rashid asked, "when its troops are bogged down in the terrible fighting in Russia?"

"The Fuhrer has special forces ready for the invasion of England. It's likely England will fall even before Russia, or at least they'll both collapse at the same time."

"It's obvious you know nothing about Russia," Ahmad Rashid replied. "Socialist Russia is not the same as Czarist Russia. People in the Soviet Union are now a solid front, united by common conviction and determination. They may have retreated a bit to recover their breath, but they'll never lay down their arms or even contemplate surrender."

"And what about Bunker 13?" asked Sayyid Arif.

Rubbing his hands together Boss Nunu chimed in, "That must be the place to get the pills you need...."

"If what people say about Hitler is true," Ahmad Akif asked, "then why wouldn't he use the contents of Bunker 13?"

"As an act of mercy on humanity in general. The Fuhrer will never resort to using that dreadful warehouse unless he finally gives up all hope of winning by normal strategic methods—God forbid!"

At this point Boss Nunu clapped his hands, called the waiter over, and asked him to bring the domino board. "Curse the whole lot of them!" he yelled in exasperation. "The Germans aren't our mother, and the English aren't our father either. The devil take them all to hell!"

Boss Nunu's intervention divided them into two groups—one to play games, the other to talk. Once again Ahmad Akif found himself sitting alone with the young lawyer. He did not feel like talking and told himself he should go home again, especially since Nawal and her mother were there. But what could he do once he arrived? He would have to stay in his room. He was still pondering these ideas when he heard the lawyer talking to the young boy, Muhammad.

"It's time you went home, Muhammad, and did your homework."

The boy stood up with a smile that suggested he was a bit embarrassed and immediately left. Ahmad Akif was surprised at the imperious way the lawyer had spoken to the boy and equally that the boy had responded. The tone he had used was neither one of gentle counseling nor of affection for the boy's father.

The lawyer sensed Ahmad's surprise. "It's amazing how much better girls are than boys." he said. "The boy's sister is hardworking and obedient, but Muhammad treats his lessons like nasty medicine and finds every conceivable excuse for not studying."

How could this creep be talking about the daughter so freely? Just then an idea occurred to him, one that made his heart leap.

"Do you tutor them privately?" he asked.

Ahmad Rashid responded that indeed he did. That aroused so much resentment in Ahmad Akif that he was forced to fabricate a smile so as not to reveal what he was really feeling. Did this creep really sit down next to his girl as a tutor? Did he teach her things, tell her to learn them, and then perhaps pretend to be serious and scold her? Didn't he have to be alone with her sometimes? Did he ever look at her with something other than a teacher's eyes? What did she think of him? An educated young man with a bright future. His serious mien and glass eye would not stand in the way. In fact, truth to tell, he—meaning Ahmad Akif—was no better than Ahmad Rashid, although at the same time he wasn't any lower in status either—at least as far as the plebeians and illiterates were concerned. So should he simply give up before the battle had even started?

In situations like this he wasn't the kind of person who could muster a great deal of fighting spirit and courage; quite the contrary in fact, he would usually shrivel up and take to his heels out of a combination of embarrassment, cowardice, and arrogance. Whenever the going was tough, he would still crave the coddling atmosphere in which he had grown up. Whenever it let him down—as it inevitably did on occasion—he would withdraw into himself with a wounded heart, licking his wounds and laying all the blame on the bad luck that dogged him. If only it were men's role to be chased after and not to do the chasing, to be the object of desire and not the initiator of it, then things would have been that much easier and the matter of love would have worked itself out. But things were not that way, indeed they were the exact opposite. What was needed was a certain manliness, suavity, and élan. How on earth did he ever expect to be successful in love? If innate traits of character could be made subject to the will of mankind, then he would have been willing to abandon his culture and his intellectual talents—his purported talents, that is— if in return he could become a skillful lover and attractive man. But there was little chance of that, so all that remained was for him to despise love, loathe women, and learn to enjoy the pleasures of lonely seclusion.

He now avoided any further conversation with the young lawyer and pretended instead to be paying attention to the radio. Time passed, and neither of them said a word. The prevailing silence was only broken when Sulayman Bey Ata was provoked by Sayyid Arif and let out an angry yell. The frenzied thoughts preoccupying Ahmad's silence drove him to some poisonous wells from which his traumatized imagination drank deep. He surrendered to some truly demonic and terrible desires: that some insane air raid on Cairo would drop lava that would level all its buildings and pummel its inhabitants until nothing was left standing and the entire area was reduced to rubble. Only two people would be left alive, him and the girl. She would be completely his and his alone, without fear, despair, jealousy, or effort! Before his darkened eyes he could picture the city of Cairo smashed and destroyed, with two lonely people, one of them running to the other to seek shelter and protection in his arms. The other would be content to have his companion seeking shelter with him alone, forgetting all about the dust and rubble that covered him. This strange longing on his part was provoked by an overwhelming sense of oppression and suffering.

13

It was after midnight when he returned home. He shut himself in his room, feeling annoyed. Would it not be better, he wondered, to stop opening the window and instead to lock his own heart in the face of this new emotion that was rapidly turning into agony? Surely dying in peace was better than living a life of agony and torture? But in spite of everything, by the following morning he had forgotten all about his concerns. From then on he kept his daily appointment by the windowsill every afternoon. He no longer doubted for a single moment that the girl was well aware that her new neighbor was deliberately appearing at the window every afternoon and directing that bashful, timid glance at her. What, one wonders, was her heart telling her? Was she laughing at his appearance, scoffing at his middle age? Or did his shyness and apathy merely aggravate her? The amazing thing was that, as days passed, he still kept the same appointment, adhering rigidly to the time, and feeling incapable of doing anything else until he had taken a timid glance upward to the balcony. But no sooner did their eyes meet than he would immediately look away, eyelids twitching.

He was beset too by the image of Ahmad Rashid. His jealous heart wondered whether he too was the recipient of such lovely looks from the girl, or was he, Ahmad Rashid, the beneficiary of something even lovelier and more charming? Even so, those happy afternoon moments managed to take his mind off such lingering doubts. He now started to calm his own fears. He convinced himself that if she were in love with the young lawyer she would hardly be bestowing such charming glances on him one afternoon after another; and that gave him back his hope. He realized, however, that it was not normal to settle for such exchanged glances and that he had to adopt a new approach. But could he do it? Was he actually capable of launching himself into life again just as he had managed to run away from it for all of twenty years? Why didn't he stare at her until she was the one to look bashfully away, if only just once? Why didn't he greet her with a smile? The very idea of staring at her and then smiling made him blush and sent him into such a dither that he was utterly incapable of doing anything. Good grief, could a middle-aged man really be that fearful of a youngster? Does a forty-year-old run away from some girl aged sixteen? How often had he told himself in the past that shyness was a disease that would disappear as one got older? But in his case it had lingered and turned into a brand new middle-aged disease.

Why did God create people like him who could not handle life? In this moment of despair he came up with a new tactic: people who were scared of staring and smiling, he told himself, could always write. Why didn't he try writing to her? The idea appealed to him, and he gave the matter serious thought. All he would have to do was to write a few words on a piece of paper, fold it up carefully, and toss it up to the balcony. That was fine. But how was he to begin? Should he say, "My beloved Nawal"? No, that would be too familiar. How about "Dear Nawal"? No, mentioning the name was still forward of him. So just "My dear"? That was more in line with his sense of decorum. But then what? Letters usually began with greetings, so he could do that, but then what? Should he declare his love to her? No, that was something to keep under wraps for the time being. He should begin by expressions of admiration, but how was he supposed to compose the right expressions, the apposite phrases? What kind of style would impress her? What choice of words would have the right impact on her? And, even supposing he managed to solve all those issues, what was he going to ask her? To send him a reply? To meet him? In fact, there was something else that was far more important than any of these questions. What led him to believe that she would welcome the receipt of such a letter? How was he to know that she would not tear it up and throw it right in his face? Either that, or she might even get angry, in which case she would reveal his secret and expose his behavior. His ever-diffident mind had been on the point of grabbing a pen, but now it retreated to seek a safer solution.

The problem was that the window still maintained its loyal connection to the balcony above; both of them seemed to be adhering to a pledge that neither of them had actually undertaken. Eyes had met; acquaintance and even familiarity had followed. Spirits had felt a mutual attraction unimpeded by either silence or shyness. By now he had started to believe that—taking his beloved's sweet and unsullied glances into consideration—he had misjudged her teacher, Ahmad Rashid, allowing his emotions and thoughts to get the better of him. That young man was much too involved in socialist ideas and the eradication of outworn beliefs to be bothered about matters of love and flirtation. That thought allowed him a brief taste of the purest nectar of hope, and soon afterward fate dealt his hope and self-confidence a boost.

One afternoon late in Ramadan his father kept him busy and he wasn't able to make his expected appearance by the window. Next day he waited patiently at the normal time, but discovered that the balcony was shut! He waited and waited in the hope that the balcony would open and the girl come outside, but it was in vain. He would have thought that the same kind of thing was keeping her inside as had been the case with him the day before, but he caught a glimpse of her shadow behind the balcony door. It was now clear that she had shut the balcony door on purpose just as he had done with the window the day before. All of which meant, if he was interpreting things correctly, that she had noticed his absence yesterday; in fact, she may have been annoyed and decided to get her revenge. And now, here she was, doing just that. He was inclined to believe this interpretation of events, and yet the revenge did not cause him any anguish; quite the contrary in fact, he was utterly delighted. He was so happy that he started snapping his fingers and pacing his room totally oblivious to everything around him.

The next day he approached the window with an entirely

new outlook, full of confidence and hope. He could feel that she was there even before he lifted his eyes. He had decided to give her a quizzical look, as though to ask her, "Why did you disappear yesterday?" Now was the time to implement the plan. He lifted his small head, and their eyes locked on to each other. He summoned every ounce of courage in his body to raise his eyebrows and move his head in a questioning gesture. He gathered his determination, as one does just before plunging for a dive in a swimming pool for the first time. But he waited just a moment too long, and his mind snatched the opportunity to inject a sense of doubt and fear into his thinking. He was afraid of making a mess of things once again. With that his determination flagged, and he abandoned his plan.

That night he blamed himself for what had happened and banged his bald pate. "Where's your masculinity?" he asked himself angrily. Here he was in love with her, with her honey-colored eyes, her sweet naive looks, her sense of fun. He loved her because his dreams—they being the sole art in this world that he had truly mastered—refused to be apart from her for a single hour. He loved her because he was hungry—at the age of forty—and hunger was a primary instigator of dreams.

14

Then came the Night of Power during the blessed month of Ramadan. The family celebrated it in style: the breakfast table was graced with roasted chicken and a tray of kunafa. At suppertime Sitt Dawlat started by wishing her husband good health and her children long life and happiness. Akif Effendi, the father of the household, went to the al-Husayn Mosque to witness the celebration put on by a group of Qur'an readers on this most favored of nights.

The night was a happy one, but just before dawn, as the family was going to bed, the air-raid sirens went off. They put on their clothes and rushed down to the shelter along with all the other inhabitants of the apartment building. By now they were all so thoroughly familiar with the route that they did not need any help from servants. Ahmad felt both alarmed and secretly happy, the latter because the shelter would bring him that much closer to Nawal; he could feast his eyes on her beloved countenance. Once in the shelter, he noticed Ahmad Rashid and Sayyid Arif chatting, so he went over and joined them. They were standing close to the most visible corner of the room.

"Have you heard what Sayyid Effendi has just told me?" Ahmad Rashid asked as soon as he saw Ahmad Akif. "He says that Sulayman Ata was engaged to the daughter of the perfumer today!"

"That's right," said Sayyid Arif with a smile, "a truly blessed event!"

"Just see how money can have its way with beauty," Ahmad Rashid commented angrily. "The very worst aspect of this world of ours is the way lofty virtues and values can be subjected to animal necessities. How could that lovely girl have allowed herself to give her hand to such a foul ape? Their union is not a real marriage, it's a double crime: robbery on the one hand and rape on the other. Her beauty will continue to reflect his ugliness, while his ugliness will reflect her crass greed."

He gave a cryptic smile, then went on, "Such a crime could never be committed in a socialist system!"

Someone else chimed in at this point. "Didn't they tell us," he asked angrily, "that the Germans wouldn't be conducting air raids during Ramadan?"

Sayyid Arif looked in his direction. "The English are bombing Tripoli," he said, "and they're Muslims too." He then turned to his two companions. "There's no military reason for the English to bomb Tripoli," he said with complete confidence. "They just want to force the Germans to bomb Cairo!"

Ahmad Akif did not pay any attention to the discussion; but stared silently through the indifferent throng. However, he did not have much time to enjoy it, because a gruff voice suddenly yelled, "Shut up, everyone! Aircraft noise!" With that, the entire place fell silent, with everyone listening.

"No, it's not," another voice chimed in. "That's the police car!"

"Yes it is," the first voice insisted. "It's aircraft noise. Listen!"

Everyone listened, and sure enough, there was the sound of a plane diving from high in the sky. Ahmad's heart gave a leap. He looked over at his parents; his mother had her eyes aimed at the ceiling, while his father had his closed. Then they heard the sound of an anti-aircraft gun being fired in the distance, followed by intermittent gunfire. For a moment the noise stopped, but then it resumed even louder than before. Now the gunfire was non-stop and completely random. Everyone began to panic and started blathering hysterically.

Someone who was feeling scared tried desperately to sound calm. "That explosion was Almaza for sure," he said.

Everyone took comfort from what he said, albeit unconsciously.

Ahmad went over to his parents. "How are you, Papa?" he asked, even though he was feeling as scared and edgy as everyone else.

"God our Creator is here!" was his father's quavering response.

The sound of gunfire continued, and its sources became even more numerous. Sayyid Arif started identifying the source of every single round of fire, as though he was some kind of expert on the subject. "Abbasiya that one," "Almaza," "Bulaq," "that one's from the Citadel," and so on.

This was followed by a round of fire that was the

loudest yet. "That's a German gun," said Sayyid Arif. "The government purchased it from Germany before the war."

People started getting aggravated at this kind of talk and told them to stop. The noise intensified, and there were yet more moments of extremely violent gunfire which went on for quite a while. Everyone's nerves were on edge. In actuality, it was not a very long time, but the tense period involved needed to be measured more in terms of rapid breathing and pounding hearts. It felt as though everyone was carrying the burdens of fate on their shoulders.

Gradually, the gunfire began to slow down, and then it could only be heard from one direction. Finally the last gun fell silent, and silence ensued. No one knew, needless to say, whether the firing would resume or the night's punishment was at an end. Even so, people who had been feeling as if their very souls had come close to being seared, now began to relax a bit. There was a short period of silence, then the all-clear sirens went off. Everyone stood up, intoning the shahada as they did so.

Ahmad glanced over at his beloved goal. She was looking in his direction, and their eyes met. That made him so happy that it swept away all the traces of fear and panic he had just been feeling. He watched as she went ahead of her family toward the shelter door; when she reached it, she turned and gave him a very meaningful look. With that she went quickly up the stairs. Ahmad was so overjoyed by the situation that he assumed that she wanted him to follow her; after all, eyes are like instincts—they have their own secret and silent language. His innate shyness held him back, and yet the way she had rushed outside gave him a temporary courage that managed to overcome his shyness and hesitancy.

He headed toward the door ahead of his parents and their servant and made his way up the stairs, wondering all the while if he would run into her in front of the door. What was he supposed to say or do? However, he saw that her shadow had moved several yards away in the direction of the apartment. They were the only two who had left the shelter thus far; if he quickened his pace, he could catch up with her.

In less than a second, he would be able to walk with her along Ibrahim Pasha Street and go up the staircase together, alone. These ideas occurred to him immediately, but he didn't make a move; actually he did move, but just a few steps. The distance between them actually increased until she was almost at the entrance to the building. Once again his bashfulness got the better of him. He started looking behind him as though asking his parents to catch up and get him out of this fix. With that, all fear, hesitation, desire, and hope came to an end.

In the company of his parents he made his way silently back to the apartment building, feeling a heartfelt sense of regret. As they started climbing the stairs, he looked up sadly, fully aware that if he had only been able to overcome his fears he could have had her to himself. Even so, he was still asking himself what he would have said to her. Just suppose he had plucked up the necessary courage and greeted her, and she in turn had greeted him with a smile, a word, or a gesture—notwithstanding the entire issue of how he should greet her, which posed a problem of its own. What was he supposed to say? "Good morning,"

"Hello!" "Peace be upon you!" or what? Suppose he had done that, and she had replied, then what? Would they have said nothing else until they parted company by the door of his apartment? What are lovers supposed to say in situations like this? How many of them there are! In streets and on boats they whisper and confide in each other, so how was it he had lost the knack of speaking in their favorite tongue?

As he went back to his room, he was full of remorse, but still delighted. In fact, he was veritably drunk with the kind of happiness that is the heart's most pleasant sensation of all. Whatever the case might be, he could not forget the way her look had issued a call to him—that in itself being one of the wonders of delight in the canons of emotion. In and of itself, that was enough to justify the particular joy he was feeling despite his bashfulness and regret. He glanced over at the window—which by now he was calling "Nawal's window"—and his besotted heart urged him to look up to the balcony. Opening the window he looked up and, to his astonishment, saw that the door was open, the light in the room was lit, and the girl was standing right by the door. What on earth could have led her to stand by the door at this early hour? He could see her shadow, but the features of her face were obscured because the light was behind her. It was the same with his room, meaning that she could only see his shadow too. That was enough to encourage him to stay and stare at her. He had not been standing there for very long when he had the most wonderful surprise in his whole life: she greeted him with a gesture of her head! He was stunned, but this time it was not enough to stop him; he too nodded his head in greeting. The girl was obviously shy; as he watched, she went back inside and closed the balcony door. Then the light was turned off. Ahmad just stood there for a while, unaware of either the passage of time or of his own self. Shutting the window, he sank to his knees, placed his palms on his chest, and prayed in a low voice, "O God, praise and thanks be to Thee!"

15

The next morning he woke up exhausted. After all, joy is just like grief—an ancient foe of slumber. He was feeling so happy and full of joy that he simply brushed his tiredness aside. When in the past twenty years had he ever experienced such a joyous morning? He left the house happy and smiling, his heart beating like someone in the prime of youth. Now at last he had become a member of the particular group he had always regarded with envy and hatred: lover and loved. That morning his emotions were pure, completely unclogged by feelings of hatred and rancor. Even if it were just for a short while, he could have some respite from the specters of failure that swooped like bats over his dark memories. He felt no need to argue, confront, or get angry with any of the other employees at work. Instead, a dancing wave of contentment washed away the putrid, stagnant slime that lurked deep inside him.

When he went home at lunchtime he found a letter

waiting for him. As soon as he took a look at the envelope, he recognized the handwriting—small, neat letters very similar to his own. He opened the letter with a smile and read its contents to the end.

"Rushdi is coming home on the morning of the day before Eid al-Fitr."

Even though his parents had known ahead of time that his younger brother would be spending the Eid in Cairo, they were still thrilled by the news. However, the letter went on to convey some even happier news for the two parents.

"Rushdi goes on to say that an order's been issued transferring him from Asyut to the headquarters in Cairo. He's to get his new post there immediately after the Eid holiday."

The parents were utterly delighted.

"We'll have two festivals to celebrate," Sitt Dawlat proclaimed. "I've missed him so much. I wonder how he's managed to spend the entire year on his own in Asyut."

"You'd better hope and pray," Ahmad replied with a smile, "that he's adopted a different lifestyle from the one he was following in Cairo before he left!"

Ahmad went to his room, took off his clothes, and lay down on the bed as usual to take a nap before evening—or rather, until his "love appointment" (as he now had to term it after such a notable day). The letter he had received from his brother temporarily distracted him from thoughts of sleep and the joyous feelings he was enjoying. Instead his mind was filled with memories of his younger brother.

It was rare for anyone to provoke such contradictory feelings as did Rushdi Akif in his elder brother's mind, ranging from anger to love. Ahmad had felt a sense of real grievance when the need to stand surety for his younger brother had meant that he, Ahmad, would have to sacrifice his own future and the application of his genius! Then again, he had been annoyed when his brother had squandered his young adulthood by indulging in all kinds of diversions and pleasures and had refused to listen to reason. On the other hand, he loved his brother more than anything on earth, because the young man had shown his love for him in ways that far surpassed the love and respect he showed to his parents. He always remembered the way Ahmad had taken care of him and served as his benefactor. Rushdi adored his elder brother because the latter had crafted him with his own two hands, nourished him with his spirit, and spent his own money on his younger brother's upbringing. Ahmad was both elder brother and loving parent. He had enjoyed his younger brother's childhood, carrying him in his arms, teaching him to talk, and training him to walk. He had watched over him as a boy and directed his education. Later on, the younger brother's success—after so much toil and trouble—had come as a reward for all the struggles his elder brother had undertaken and a proud achievement for his efforts. He was forever recalling his elder brother's sacrifices on his behalf. Beyond all that, Rushdi was a lovable person: kind and cheerful, he had inherited from his mother the ability to open other people's hearts without the slightest effort on his part; both of them—he and his mother—were generously endowed with beauty, sincerity, loyalty, and a fondness for company and conviviality. Unfortunately, those qualities were not accompanied by a similar level of moderation, poise, and commonsense. For him life was to be lived on the edge, at full throttle; everything had to be done to the maximum, and his natural bent pushed him forward without the slightest hint of restraint.

From the outset he had been brash and forward in his approach to life in general; and all this while the person who was supposed to be looking after him—namely his elder brother—was the exact opposite, trammeled by the fact that he was both spoiled and scared. As a result, Ahmad had tended to rely on the younger brother he was helping to bring up—who was reliable along with other people—when it came to doing things for him, buying whatever he needed, and borrowing books for him. The younger brother had thereby gained world experience, along with self-reliance, initiative, and masculinity. His elder brother needed him just as much as he needed his elder mentor. However, while he may have learned about the world and operated within it, he still had no fixed set of principles to protect him from its pitfalls. Ever since Akif Effendi had been pensioned off, he had kept to himself and left the running of family affairs to his elder son and his wife. As far as Rushdi was concerned, neither of those two dear people had the necessary resolution to provide him with guidance and restraint. He preferred to make his own way and to do everything on impulse. In fact, had he not been even-tempered and considerate, he might well have crossed the line from youthful indiscretion to criminality.

His early educational career in primary and secondary schools had often heralded great success; to such an extent that even Ahmad declared that Rushdi seemed to have inherited some of his own intellectual abilities. But once he had enrolled in the School of Commerce things changed. Corruption bent his will. He found himself drawn toward a group of young men who indulged in heavy drinking, betting on card games, and in general living a dissolute life. His behavior became more and more crazy; he went into debt several times and neglected his studies, to such an extent that it almost caused a rift between himself and his brother. Things reached a climax when he started thinking seriously of abandoning his university studies and becoming a singer, and all because he had heard a lot about the bohemian lifestyle of singers and their success in attracting women, quite apart from the fact that he was well aware of what a sweet, harmonious voice he had. With that, Ahmad's patience snapped; he warned his brother that he would cut off his allowance if he didn't immediately stop behaving in such a debauched and reckless fashion. Sometimes he became so angry that he really felt as though he hated his brother. So strong was his feeling of resentment that he found himself doing some things that he himself was actually incapable of undertaking on his own, one or two of which caused him no small amount of heartache.

And yet, in spite of everything, the two brothers still remained very fond of each other, due in no small part to the talents of the younger one. Whenever the elder brother applied pressure, the younger one slowed his pace a little; whenever the former frowned, the latter smiled; if Ahmad cursed and swore, Rushdi used to laugh and then either kiss his brother's hand or nudge his shoulder; if Ahmad clenched his fist, Rushdi would tease him ever so gently.

This phase came to an end with a miracle. Yes indeed, a miracle in the form of a BA degree. All of which drove Ahmad to observe that here was a student being awarded a degree that gave its holder precedence over himself! But then he gave a deep sigh and realized that now his own responsibilities were over. He would not have to concern himself—to an excessive degree—with his younger brother's raucous behavior any longer; Rushdi was in charge of his own life. All that meant that the atmosphere between the two brothers calmed down a lot; their mutual affection returned to the way it used to be when Rushdi was a boy, with nothing to mar the picture. In fact, they were so comfortable with each other that Rushdi would often share with his brother stories about his love affairs, drawing from his wide experience involving both chaste and distinctly unchaste episodes. He was just as likely to look for adventure in low dives as he was to chase pretty girls across roads and squares. He managed to collect a number of photographs of pretty girls with this odd expression scribbled in pleasant handwriting: "To my beloved fiancé, Rushdi." It was not that he meant any harm to these young women or that he found it in any way easy to plot dirty tricks against them. The truth of the matter was that it was all too easy for him to fall victim to his own intense passions. For him nothing was easier than to become a lover, a genuine and sincere one at that. But, once he was involved, he would never actually swear a lie, all too often he would break his word.

When his emotions became really intense, it often happened that he would take it further and make a genuine, truthful promise; then there would be an engagement. But not long afterward, his emotions would calm down or something else would happen. In his life there was no such thing as peace and quiet; it provided fertile ground for pleasures and passions, so much so that he actually wore himself out. He grew thinner and downright skinny, so much so that, according to his parents, he looked like a beanpole. Ahmad, who loved him and felt sorry for him, kept looking at him anxiously. "Have pity on yourself," he told his brother, to which Rushdi replied with his usual merriment, "God have mercy on us and you!" When the bank had sent him to work in the Asyut branch, his family had been secretly delighted—even though they were sorry to see him go so far away. They clung to the single hope that in his new posting—his exile to the South—their younger son might adjust his lifestyle and regain some of the health he had lost. They also hoped that he would be able to save some of his salary as well. For that very reason they were delighted when they heard he had been moved back to Cairo, all the while keeping their worries to themselves.

16

There were just three days left in the month of Ramadan. Ahmad was actually sad that the blessed month was coming to an end. After all, how could he possibly forget all the benefits and mercies it provided? How could he commune with the sunset hour about his rotten luck and lonely heart? What would tomorrow bring, he wondered to himself, and what of the future? His mother, Sitt Dawlat, and the servant girl were both busy getting the room ready for his brother who was coming home from Asyut. It was the room next to his parents' bedroom and looked out onto the street that led to the old part of Khan al-Khalili, as did one of the windows in Ahmad's own room. They swept and cleaned the room, then put some furniture in it so that it was completely ready for the young man's arrival. Their mother then embarked on one of her seasonal campaigns—as usual, one that involved her son, Ahmad—all connected with the arrival of the first day of the Eid, or "the Cookie Feast," as she liked to call it. After they had all broken the fast, she took advantage of the fact that she was alone with him and started bidding a fond farewell to the Ramadan days with their particular rituals.

"Just a couple more days," she said, "and we'll all be enjoying the smell of cookies!"

He was expecting something of the sort and realized that there was no avoiding an argument about it; he was bound to lose no matter what he said or however much he objected. Even so, he was not in the habit of surrendering even a single solitary penny without putting up a fight as a way of salving his conscience.

"In times like these," he said by way of justification, "people won't be smelling cookies! They'll be asking God to keep them safe and provide them with life's bare necessities. You're always keen to get us trivial luxuries, Mother. You don't think about how much money I have. Have mercy on those who dwell on earth, and He who dwells in heaven will have mercy on you!"

The look she gave him was a blend of reproach and entreaty, but then she smiled. "Oh, you're impossible!" she responded with a blink of her bespectacled eyelids. "How many times have you started an argument with your own mother for no reason at all, as though she isn't the one who has loved you and spoiled you to death? Are you pretending to be so poor, when you're obviously well-off? Are you pretending to forget that it's your turn now to spoil your mother a bit? I've no intention of ever causing you, the best of sons, any hardship. We always manage to make do with just a little, in honor of you!"

He was well aware that she would never give up until she had her way.

"Uh-huh," he sighed in despair.

"Uh-huh to the idea of a feast day with no cookies. Are we supposed to celebrate the feast day without cookies, when you're the man of the house?"

"Cookies are for kids!"

"And men and women as well. The feast's for everyone. Haven't you noticed that your father's bought himself a new cloak for the feast-day prayers? You've bought yourself a new suit, fez, and shoes—good for you in the name of the All-Merciful! As far as I'm concerned, celebrating the feast involves kneading, sculpting, sprinkling sugar, and stuffing with honey-sesame paste!"

The next morning, the day before the Eid, he made his way to the Cairo train station to await his younger brother's arrival. It was damp but not too cold, so he sat down on a bench on the platform for trains coming from the South. There were only a few minutes left before the train was supposed to arrive. As usual, he felt a bit panicky around steam trains puffing smoke and blowing shrill whistles. He had never had to meet a train before; in fact, he had never left the boundaries of Cairo itself. He had absolutely no desire to travel or take trips. As far as he was concerned, a prison term would be more tolerable than living in a distant country. No doubt it was his fear of any encounter with the outside world that fueled this hatred of travel, but the way he himself explained it—following his usual pattern of justifying his behavior and temperament—was that it was the natural path for an intellectual who much preferred the world of ideas and avoided material things as much as possible. After all, hadn't the great poet Abu al-Ala' al-Ma'arri lived his entire life in devotion to religious obligations? The thing that managed to lessen his sense of panic was the joy he was feeling because his brother, Rushdi, was coming back to Cairo—his own brother, almost his son. Not to mention his assumption that Rushdi would be able to help him shoulder the family burdens that up until now had fallen on his shoulders alone. He was hoping as well that his brother would manage to bring some fun and pleasure into his life.

Before long everyone's necks were craning toward the southern direction, and the place was full of all kinds of movement and activity. He too looked in the same direction and watched as the train slowly made its way into the station. Almost immediately the din of the engine could be heard and the ground started shaking; as it gradually approached the platform, the train filled one's entire field of vision. Heads were poking out of every open window as it drew to a halt alongside the long platform. Everyone rushed forward. With people rushing all around him, Ahmad scanned the windows until he caught sight of his brother at the front of one of the second-class carriages. Rushdi was handing his suitcase down to one of the porters. Ahmad yelled out his name and gave his brother a wave as he ran toward the carriage. The young man turned toward him, then leapt down from the carriage, and stood in front of his brother. The two brothers greeted each other warmly.

"I'm glad you've arrived home safe and sound!" said Ahmad, clasping his brother's arm. "How are you?"

"I'm very well, brother," Rushdi replied happily, his face somewhat flushed as a result of the journey's exertions.

Amid a horde of other people the two brothers walked side by side toward the exit. They were of roughly the same height and had the same thin build. Even though Ahmad looked somewhat crumpled and his younger brother much fresher, there was no mistaking the fact that they were brothers. Their facial features were similar too, except that in Rushdi's case they were more handsome while Ahmad's face sagged a bit and more often than not he was frowning and looking tired. Rushdi had the same long, thin face, but his cheeks were not as pale as Ahmad's, and, while his olive skin may have turned a bit sallow recently, he still looked in the full flush of youth. His eyes were elongated and widely spaced, but their irises were larger. That made his looks seem more piercing; his eyes had a glow to them that suggested a sharp mind, a propensity for fun, and a willingness to take risks.

As they walked shoulder to shoulder, they soon felt the irresistible urge to chat, as is only to be expected with people who have been apart for a long time. They had no idea where to start, what to talk about and what not. It was the younger brother who started things.

"Before anything else," he asked his brother, "how's Mother?"

"As well as you could wish her to be. She's still pursuing those childish fancies of hers without caring in the slightest about the way it affects me. So go ahead and grab your portion of it!"

"All the time I've been in Asyut, I've never forgotten my portion of it! I've bought her some ivory ornaments, nice plates, and subtle scents that will suit her lady friends, I hope." (He gave a loud laugh at that.) "And how's Father?"

"Just as you remember him: prayers at home and visits to the mosque. Now we're living close to the al-Husayn Mosque, so may he find blessings there."

Smiling, Rushdi said, "I must say, I was amazed when I heard you had all moved to the al-Husayn district."

By now they had reached the Station Square, where they took a taxi. Rushdi paid the porter a tip, and then the taxi took off and crossed the broad square. Rushdi's lovely light brown eyes scanned the scene, taking in all the cars, carts, trolleys, and pedestrians.

"My head's almost spinning," he said, banging his forehead with a finger. "It's as though I'm seeing trolleys and the metro for the first time ever. Do you remember the joke about the country yokel who comes to Cairo for the first time? No sooner does he look at this teeming square than he panics. He goes straight back to the train. 'I've arrived too late,' he tells himself sorrowfully, 'everyone's leaving!' "

Ahmad laughed out loud. He had always loved his brother's sense of humor and his basic simplicity. Luckily Rushdi was no university type in the literal sense of the term; not for him academic topics or any concern with memorizing their technical terms. But for that, he would have been a clone of Ahmad Rashid. What's more, he was one of the people actually taken in by Ahmad's pseudo-erudition; he regarded his brother as a genuine intellectual and was as convinced as his brother that the other possessed a fine mind. For his part, Ahmad was delighted by the way his brother believed in him and regarded him as a symbol of the Egyptian University's certification of his superior genius.

"Cairo's one of God's gifts to mankind!" enthused

Rushdi. "It's this world and the next all rolled into one. Day and night, heaven and hell, East and West. The entire process is a miracle!"

"You must have been very bored in Asyut."

"Any place other than Cairo would be equally boring!"

Ahmad stared at him. "For people like you, prison's the best place. In any case your expression doesn't look very relaxed."

The younger brother smiled, revealing a set of near-white teeth. "Whenever two bureaucrats get together anywhere," he remarked with a leer, "the gambling table will always be their companion."

Ahmad sighed. "I hereby rule," he said, "that you be deprived of the blessing of sleep forever!"

"The blessing of sleep?" his brother replied. "Sleep's actually a curse. It involves purloining a huge and priceless chunk of our short lives."

"You've no idea what you're talking about!"

"My dear brother, you're a very sage man, and I'm a crazy youth. That's the way young people like me think."

"So you're going back to...."

"God willing, yes. In Asyut I met a man who's a devotee of comedy. He used to say that the best nourishment for good health is drama. If that's so, then rowdy behavior must be a very precious vitamin!"

"And what if it's not so?"

"Let's pray to God that it is. But tell me, when did you start getting so fat?"

"You know I'm continually studying and contemplating."

"True enough. Maybe it's natural for our family to be skinny."

"And what about your mother?"

Rushdi gave a hearty laugh at that. He took off his fez and revealed a gleaming head of hair with a nice clean parting in the middle. "But then," he said with great affection, "she's always relied on the drug store to work wonders! How I've longed to see her all this time. Tell me, does she still talk about exorcism ceremonies?"

"No longer quite so blatantly," Ahmad responded with obvious disgust. "But once in a while she still complains about how cruel people are to prevent her from participating in them."

"Our mother is as gentle as an angel. She never loses her temper. I can hardly ever remember her being anything but happy and full of laughter."

Ahmad smiled.

"Devils are certainly something to believe in," Rushdi continued. "I have to admit though that I've never actually seen any despite a lengthy relationship with deserted streets late at night."

"Mankind is the worst devil of them all. Just think of this war."

Rushdi laughed again. The mention of the war reminded him of the family's move from al-Sakakini. "Indeed it's this devilish mankind that's forced us to leave our old quarter. Amazing! Don't you realize, Ahmad, that up until now I've never even set eyes on the Khan al-Khalili quarter?"

The mention of the quarter's name aroused a profound sense of joy in the elder brother's heart. "You're going to be seeing it morning and night," he said with great affection.

"Did things get so bad that you had to all leave al-Sakakini?"

"Certainly. Many people were convinced that the air raids were going to destroy Cairo the way they had London, Rotterdam, and Warsaw. But God decided otherwise. Father was in very bad shape, so we decided to get out."

The younger brother shook his head sadly. He looked at the street outside and noticed that they were crossing Queen Farida Square on the way up al-Azhar Street. The scene called to mind memories of unforgettable love affairs that now wafted across his heart the way a breeze does over gently glowing embers.

"So how do you find the new place?" he asked, perking up considerably.

If he had been asked that same question earlier on, he would have been almost totally negative. But now...! "Just wait until you can see it for yourself, Rushdi. It may take a while, but you'll get used to it."

"What are the neighbors like?"

"Mostly lower-class types, but some of the people living in the new apartment buildings belong to our class."

"Have you found somewhere suitable to think and do your studies?"

The question delighted him, as anything would that reminded him he was an intellectual. "As the proverb says," he replied, "'Wear the appropriate clothing for every occasion.' That's why every evening I go to the local café and sit there with some friends. Once the radio stops or the general din dies down, I return home to study."

"So at long last you've learned how to visit cafés!" Rushdi commented with a laugh.

"One of the requirements of our new quarter," Ahmad replied with a smile.

The taxi came to a halt by the entrance to Khan al-Khalili. The two men got out, and the driver followed behind with the suitcase.

"Take good note of the things around you," Ahmad warned as they plunged into the labyrinth of streets. "Learn the streets by heart, or else you'll get completely lost."

As they approached the apartment building, Ahmad noticed his mother looking out of the window in his room. Grabbing his brother by the arm, he pointed up to her. Looking up, Rushdi saw his mother with a brown scarf tied around her head; she was fully made up just like a bride waiting for her groom. No sooner did their eyes meet than she was opening her arms to embrace him. It only took a few moments longer until she was actually giving him a warm embrace.

17

They all gathered around the table. By this time Rushdi's father had appeared and the younger son had kissed his hand. They embarked upon their conversation with relish. Rushdi told them about Asyut and its people, about his feelings of loneliness, and longing for his family and home. The father spoke about air raids and the incendiary bombs dropped by planes. Rushdi's mother talked about her neighbor, and about Boss Nunu and his four wives. Just then she noticed that Rushdi had not gained a single pound while he was away. Transferring her attention to the cookies, she let him know that he was about to taste cookies the like of which no one in Egypt had ever before savored.

With that, she took him to his room. Once Rushdi was on his own, he could no longer control his temper; it was written all over his face. Ever since he had taken in the scene at the entrance to Khan al-Khalili, he had felt his heart sinking. When he entered the apartment, he was astonished at how tiny it was, and he knew for sure that he could never feel at home in this new place. What made him even angrier was that all his friends were still in al-Sakakini and neighboring suburbs. From now on, he would be spending the evening with them; then he would have to trek all the way back to this quarter, meandering his way in a drunken stupor along its narrow alleyways. Seething with anger, he told himself he would have to make his way back to their old house or another one nearby, however much it cost.

He opened his suitcase and took everything out. Humming one of Abd al-Wahhab's songs as was his habit, he started arranging his clothes in the wardrobe. After changing his clothes, he made his way to the bathroom at the opposite end of the long, narrow hallway from his own room. He took a cold bath to get rid of the dust and fatigue of the journey, then went back to his room looking and feeling a lot better. He closed the door behind him so that he could sing as loudly as he wanted, and opened the window. He applied Vaseline to his hair and combed it very carefully, then put on some of his favorite cologne, all of which made him feel much better. He was drawn to the window and looked outside so he could see what kind of view he had. He could see the alley below leading to the old part of Khan al-Khalili, but his view in the other direction was blocked by the next building. That aggravated him and made him feel as though he had come to some kind of prison. Where now was that window he used to have on Qamar Street in al-Sakakini looking out on the square where the observant eye could always manage to spot clusters of lovely Jewish girls?

With a sad sigh he looked around. His gaze was attracted

by a window opposite his own but slightly higher, on the side of the building facing his own. Both shutters were open, and he could see the face of a young girl, an exceptionally beautiful face adorned with a pair of eyes that sparkled with simplicity and grace. Their eyes met. Her look was one of disapproval, but his was that of a hunter who'd just spotted his prey. At this point, the way he was staring at her made her feel awkward, so she lowered her eyes and moved away. He gave a gentle smile, and his whole expression brightened at the thought of her pretty face and her flustered looks. He stayed where he was and kept his eyes riveted on the window. He expected her to come back; as far as he was concerned, it was only natural for her to want to take a second glance at the new neighbor who had stared at her so fixedly and shamelessly. He stood where he was, watching and waiting, his feelings a blend of desire, patience, and sheer stubbornness. Eventually the girl did poke her head out again, albeit cautiously. Their eyes met a second time, and the girl retreated yet again in apparent annoyance. He chuckled quietly to himself and left the window with a smirk of satisfaction. Sitting at his small desk chair, he muttered to himself that for the first time something nice had happened since he had entered this miserable quarter. Drumming his fingers on the desk, he thought for a moment. "She's our neighbor, that's clear enough," he told himself. "Her room's right opposite mine."

He pictured her face and had to admit that she was pretty and graceful. He was feeling all the inward happiness of someone who has acquired something precious. Where love was concerned, he had limitless self-confidence, based on one success after another. It was all founded on tremendous patience, an iron will that never gave up, and an innate suavity much assisted by artifice. He was patient for sure, and yet he never stopped insisting, urging, chasing, day after day, month after month, year after year—if need be—until he had achieved his goal. Among his well-known maxims on the topic of love was, "Anyone responding to love's call cannot afford to shackle his quest by being shy, worried, or scared. If you're chasing a woman, forget about honor. If she rejects you, don't get angry; if she swears at you, don't be sad. Rejection and curses are merely fuel for love's fire. If a woman slaps you on the right cheek, offer here the left one as well. You'll be the master in the end!"

There had once been an occasion when he took upon himself to chase after a determined young girl who was both well brought up and had a mind of her own. Things went on for quite a while with no sign of softening or change on her part. With that he simply spoke to her one day in a totally unaggressive way: "Listen," he said, "I'm a disgusting, heartless, annoying rogue. Don't even dream that you can send me away by throwing reproachful looks or rude words at me. That won't help, nor will punching me or calling the police either. I'm going to force you to talk to me one way or another, whether it's today, tomorrow, the day after, in a year's time, or a century's time. I really don't care. But, since the ending is a foregone conclusion, then for heaven's sake, make the process shorter!"

That's the way he was. Now once again he was wondering to himself what kind of young beauty this particular girl might be. Was she bold and adventurous, in need of taming by her lover? Or was she experienced and sophisticated, making it impossible to fool around with her? Or could she be naive and yet lively, something that would require a degree of patience in her lover? At this point he realized that Khan al-Khalili was becoming that much more tolerable thanks to this young girl and others like her. He raised his hands to the side of his head, "In the name of God, the Compassionate, the Merciful," he said. "If love is the intention, then God Himself is the helper!"

He was actually planning to fall in love. But he had no way of knowing the kind of blow he was about to aim at the happiness of his elder brother whom he both loved and revered.

18

Rushdi had not slept very much the previous night on the train, so he now simply surrendered himself to his bed and slept soundly. He did not wake up until four the next afternoon. As he sat on his bed yawning and gradually opening his eyes, he was aware that, for the first time in a year, he was actually waking up to the laughing light of Cairo. He remembered the order to relocate from Asyut, and that made him feel happy and relaxed. His room was shrouded in darkness, so he went over and opened the window. Instantly, he thought of the pretty girl and looked up at her window, but it was closed. He left his room and went out into the hall. His father was asleep, and his mother was preparing a fish for frying. For a while he stood by the kitchen door chatting to her, then he went to his brother's room. He found Ahmad standing by the window. When he was aware that Rushdi had come in, he quickly looked away—although Rushdi had no idea quite how much that had cost him. He gave his younger brother a gentle smile, and they both sat down, Ahmad on the mattress and Rushdi on the chair.

They started chatting, just the way you would expect with two affectionate brothers who had been separated for a while. Rushdi remembered the way his brother had always been fond of writing.

"Haven't you started writing things yet?" he asked.

The question stung Ahmad a bit, but he didn't dwell on it. "I've a head stuffed full of knowledge," he replied, "but what should I select and what should I leave out? Truth to tell, if I really wanted to write, I could fill up an entire library! But what's the point? Do the Egyptian people really deserve writing in the true sense of the word? Can they really digest such material? Or is it a question of one set of rabble reading another?"

Rushdi was always prepared to accept whatever his brother said. "It's a shame that your valuable ideas should go to waste."

Ahmad, too, believed in what he was saying, forgetting the arguments he had been having with Ahmad Rashid. "I'm ahead of my time," he said, "so there's no hope at all of my reaching some form of mutual understanding with these people. Everything in life has its faults, even absorbing oneself in research and knowledge."

"But, my dear brother, how can you be happy if all the effort you've made comes to nothing and has no impact on people?"

That comment pleased Ahmad a lot; in fact, it made him happy enough to compensate for having had to look away from the window a short while ago. "Who knows, Rushdi? Maybe one day I'll be able to change my mind about people and respect them more."

They kept on talking until the cannon was fired to announce the breaking of the fast. With that, the family

sat down to its final Ramadan meal. The traditional plat-
ters of fish were served, and they all ate and drank their
fill. As soon as coffee had been served, Rushdi put on his
coat and left the house without any further ado. He wanted
to get to the Ghamra casino at the right time; in other
words, he needed to get there before all his friends—who
regularly gathered at the casino every evening to drink and
play cards—took over the gaming table. For anyone who
knew as much about such things as he did, there was wisdom in getting there early. It was not just a matter of getting a place at the gaming table, but the fact that once the
players involved were engrossed in the game they would
not bother to greet any late arrivals, even if they had been
away for a full year! The best one could hope for was a
terse greeting, while eyes would remain glued to the cards.
If out of some reluctant sense of politeness they were forced
to actually stop the game, it was no boon for the new
arrival. Everyone would invoke all manner of mute curses
under their breath. Furthermore, latecomers who interrupted the players in the middle of the game would be considered good luck for the winners and the opposite for the
losers; as a result, one group of players would always be
staring daggers at the new arrival.

Some of his companions had suffered a string of really
bad luck and had acquired bad reputations. One of them was
a young lawyer whose friends believed him to be a jinx—as
long as he was anywhere close to the people playing, they
were bound to lose; none of them had any hope of winning.
Gamblers are very superstitious and prone to rumor monger-
ing, believing in omens and worshiping the notion of chance.

As he got on the trolley to al-Azhar, his memory took

him back to the days when he had first started indulging in gambling. It had been during his first year at the School of Commerce. He had been invited to join a game on the pretext that it was an innocent way to kill time. At the time they had bet milliemes—but with no thought of making a profit. After all, the millieme was such a small unit of currency, and the idea had been simply to lend a bit of excitement to the game and give the activity a serious aspect. Fairly soon, however, the amounts had gone up, until the entire contents of their pockets were involved. Gradually, their passion for the game became so overwhelming that it completely obliterated all thought of time, duty, and the future. After all, gambling is a fairly risky pastime; it's a masochistic form of pleasure, a manic compulsion. You are playing with the unseen and jockeying with chance; pounding on the door of the unknown and crunching together the clashing instincts of fear, aggression, curiosity, recklessness, and greed. Beyond all that, it's an echo of that feeling we all have, that aspect of our daily struggle, which derives from the energy and calculation we use in order to deal with life; the way we handle the powers of fate that control us, the requests we make of chance and the particular circumstances that envelop us, and the gains and losses we suffer as a consequence. How often had Rushdi devoutly wished that he would never have to leave the gaming table! What was remarkable about his behavior is that after an exhausting evening of playing he never once got up from the table without asking God's forgiveness for his folly. And yet, no sooner did the appointed time approach on the next day than he was rushing off to the casino without bothering about anything else.

Thus did this chronic disease grab hold of them all, turning people who were trying to kill time into victims. Rushdi became a hard-core gambler who worshipped chance and submitted to the dictates of omens. When he opened the window in the morning, he might say something like, "If I happen to meet two passersby, then I'll have good luck; if only one, then today I'll be a loser." Or on his way to breakfast he might mutter to himself, "If there's beans in ghee for breakfast, then today'll be a winner; but if they're in oil, then too bad!"

All these thoughts were interrupted when he got off the trolley, and took the number 10 that would take him back to the quarter where they had lived before. His nostalgia began to make itself felt now. As al-Sakakini drew close, he began to feel a deep sense of pain and powerful emotion. Getting off the trolley he made his way to the casino. He spotted his friends in their usual place in the garden outside, or rather he saw their silhouettes, because by now it was completely dark. All of which made him realize that he had arrived at just the right time, before everyone went into the gaming hall. He made his way over with a broad smile on his face and placed himself in the middle of the group. They all recognized him and yelled in unison, "Rushdi Akif! Welcome back, Lionheart!"

He was delighted to hear his nickname, one that they had given him because of the reckless way he used to gamble. They all embraced each other warmly. Like him, they were all in their mid-thirties. Some of them had gone to school with him, while others had grown up with him in al-Sakakini. But, where crazy and anti-social behavior and flagrantly reckless decisions were concerned, they were all of one stripe.

"So that's the way things are, is it?" one of them said. "We were inseparable day and night, and now you only show up at feast time?"

Rushdi took his seat. "From now on," he replied with a laugh, "you're going to be seeing me every day, or, to be more precise, every night!"

"How can that be?" one of the others asked.

"I've been transferred back to Cairo," he replied.

"You're not going back to Asyut ever again?"

"No!"

"May God so will it!"

"How did you manage to survive a whole year without playing cards?" another friend asked. "We've certainly missed seeing your cash!"

"Oh, there are gaming tables in Asyut as well," Rushdi replied. "As for the rest, the feeling is reciprocal."

They started talking about Asyut, until Rushdi asked, "How do you plan to spend the time tonight?"

"The way we've spent all the others. We're going into the gaming hall pretty soon."

"That's fine. But what about two or three glasses of cognac?"

"How about four or five?"

"Or six or seven?"

At this point someone else made a different suggestion. "Look," he said, "tomorrow's the Eid. Let's postpone getting plastered until tomorrow."

"Never postpone today's work until tomorrow!"

"What's the sex life in Asyut like?" someone else asked him.

"Don't even ask. Involuntary celibacy!"

"Here it's almost as bad as in the provinces now. The

allied armies are devouring meat, fruit, and women as well."

"At long last," another friend commented, "Jewish girls have discovered the virtues of knowing English."

"You can easily spot them, all decked out in silk. If you block their path, they stare daggers at you and tell you in a genuine Scottish accent to please behave like a gentleman!"

"My dear Rushdi, all the servant women have broken their contracts and gone to work in the cabarets."

"This war's provided a wonderful occasion for them to discover their hidden artistic talents."

Rushdi seemed perplexed. "So what's to be done then?" he asked with a smile "Are we supposed to start thinking about getting married?"

"If this war goes on and things get worse and worse, you and I are going to be the only bachelors around!"

"Friends, you're not being entirely fair to either the Jewish girls or the servants. The truth of the situation is that they've been alarmed by the lack of any involvement in the war on our part. That's why they've decided to use their own honor as a way of participating in the Allies' cause."

"Women now have become more expensive than fertilizer!"

"Even harder to get than coal."

"What if the war were to come to an end tomorrow? What are all those women going to do?"

"They'll become even cheaper than a Japanese woman!"

"And love-making will take place in groups. Any young man will be able to find three women in a single night: one for kissing, one for chatting, and a third for fondling, and so on."

"Unless the government intervenes, of course, in order to maintain the normal prices!"

Rushdi's laugh was that of someone who had been deprived of their company for a whole year. They all continued drinking and chatting until nine o'clock, at which point they got up to go into their beloved gaming hall.

That night Rushdi made a lot of money, at least by their reckoning: his total winnings before midnight were three pounds, added to which was the sum of thirty piasters as midnight itself approached—that being the agreed time to close the session. They then all got up from the table. Rushdi had seemed absolutely delighted during the game itself, being someone whose emotions are clearly visible on their face. He had started singing quietly as though humming a serenade and only stopped when one of his companions who was losing badly yelled at him, "For heaven's sake, stop singing. You're getting on my nerves!"

When they were out on the street, one of them suggested that they continue the game at his house.

"So be it!" they all responded in unison.

"What about you?" he asked Rushdi.

"I agree," Rushdi replied with a laugh, "but only on condition that you let me sing!"

They all made their way to their host's house on Abu Khudha Street. Once they had prepared the gaming table, they started playing again with an insatiable relish. The windows in the room were closed, and the heat came from their own breath. Alcohol had inflamed their innards, and they were pouring sweat. At two o'clock in the morning, someone said, "Enough! If we don't stop now, we'll be spending the whole Eid day asleep!"

With that they stopped playing. By this time, Rushdi had lost everything he had earned and the thirty piasters as well.

One of them joked with him, "That license we gave you to sing didn't get you very far, did it?"

They all laughed. Rushdi managed to keep his anger under control and laughed along with them. With that he said goodnight and headed for Abbasiya, but all public transport had long since stopped. He set out for the al-Husayn quarter where the family now lived and found the road totally empty; there was total silence, and the darkness was all-encompassing. He felt hot all over and was plastered with sweat; his throat felt dry as well. He felt as though he were being swallowed by the thick humidity that fall always provides in profusion, especially in the very early morning. Before long a shiver of cold ran through his body, wracking his chest and clogging his nostrils. Being the last night of the lunar month, everything was pitch-black. What made him even angrier was that it was cloudy, and so the stars were hidden. On both sides of the road the old mansions looked like ghosts sitting cross-legged as they dozed. He started talking to himself. "It would have been a much better idea not to go to the house with them. But fat chance of that ever happening!" Unfortunately, his regret was just as weak as his will. Die-hard gamblers usually accept their losses fairly calmly; the principle being that you accept the losses of one day in the hope of gains on the next.

He noticed how long and filthy the road was, and sighed in anger and frustration. When he got to the entrance to Khan al-Khalili, he remembered what his brother had told him: second alley on the right, and third door on the left. He felt his way in the darkness until he reached the apartment building and managed to make his way up to his room quietly. He turned the light on. No sooner did he spot the closed window than he remembered the other window that overlooked it. His face broke into the first smile it had formed since midnight. In his mind's eye he surveyed that lovely face with its olive complexion. The troubles of the night made him feel sad. "The way things had gone badly tonight were painful, true enough. But there were good things about it as well." After changing his clothes, he went over to his desk and took out his diary. He sat there recording his thoughts before falling asleep.

19

The father of the family was the first one to wake up. After performing his ablutions, he left the house at dawn, heading for the mosque to perform the Eid prayers. The fresh breeze of the new day greeted him, and he was aware of the beautiful dawn hour teeming with people going in the same direction as himself, making their way through its dreamy purplish waves as they intoned their praises of God Almighty.

Ahmad woke up second. He got out of bed, full of a joyful energy, and shaved his beard carefully. He was putting on a brand new gallabiya and skullcap when his mother came to greet him in his room; she had already done her hair and make-up. He kissed her hand and cheek, and she kissed him back on the cheek, praying that the entire family would be granted long life, happiness, and comfort. They both went into the lounge and sat side by side chatting and waiting for the rest of the family to appear—the one who had gone out to perform his duties to God and the other one who was still sound asleep and snoring. The father arrived home soon after sunrise and came into the lounge, parading his flowing overcoat, still pronouncing praise to God. They both stood up. His wife kissed his hand, and Ahmad did likewise. He gave them his greetings on the Eid day, and they all sat down.

"Happy feast!" he said. "May the Lord make it a propitious one for us and all Muslims!"

Glancing across the room he looked at the closed door. "Has the boy woken up," he asked, "or hasn't he gone to sleep yet?"

His mother rallied to his defense as usual. "He got home late yesterday," she said, "because he met some of his friends after being away for a year. Needless to say, he came home on foot."

Even so, Rushdi did not keep them waiting for long. The door of his room opened, and he emerged to make his way to the bathroom down the hall. A quarter of an hour later, he came strolling toward them in his pajamas, after combing his hair and putting on some aftershave. His face looked a little pale, although it still retained the handsomeness of youth. He had a sweet smile on his face that only his ever-cheerful mother was able to match. He was, of course, unaware of the criticism that his father had been aiming at him, and went over to him. Bending over, he kissed him reverently, and then bent over to kiss his mother on her hand and cheek. He then kissed his brother on the forehead.

"What about my gift, gentlemen!" she said with a laugh as she spread her hands. "Happy feast!"

Each one of them usually gave her half a pound as a

special present on the feast, which made her as happy as a small child. In fact, she spent it like a small child as well, using it to buy chocolate and clothes to her heart's content. Then she brought in the meal for the Eid-day breakfast, pastries and milk, which they all attacked with relish. People who have been fasting feel an unusual reluctance when it comes to taking that first mouthful on the morning of the feast, but before long this feeling is replaced by a delightful sense of enjoyment. After all, what greater pleasure can anyone feel at such a happy moment, one that separates the performance of a religious obligation dutifully observed from the sheer enjoyment of the reward and clear conscience that it brings about? They all grabbed pieces of pastry and munched them with unmitigated pleasure until there were circles of powdered sugar around their mouths. They washed it all down with milk, only stopping when they had drunk their fill.

"How we long for good old days of peace!" their mother exclaimed. "Ghee was real ghee in those days, flour was flour, and pastries were real pastries!" their mother exclaimed.

Rushdi was well aware that his mother was trying to fish for compliments. "These pastries are just fine!" he said. "There's absolutely no reason to feel wistful about the way they were in other times."

They all went into different rooms. Ahmad's heart was all aflutter with the intoxicating spirit of youth; he had felt that way ever since the girl had given him such a friendly greeting on the Night of Power. He could not forget the picture of her delicate shadow as it bestowed a greeting on him. Since then the emotions aroused by that magical greeting had not calmed down at all. He still felt happy and enthused by a feeling of joy, which convinced him that he was on track to recover his youthful energy. The somewhat faded branch would now bloom once again and the essence of life would course through him. His temples would again sprout luxuriant curls to cover up his bald spot, and his eyelashes would reassume their tinge of kohl.

However, since that wonderful moment he had not set eyes on the girl again; she had not kept her usual appointment at the window. There was no doubt in his mind that it was shyness that was making her stay out of the way and not venture out into the daylight. That made him feel a tender affection toward her; after all, who could possibly know more about shyness than himself? He was absolutely delighted by the thought that he had discovered someone who needed to keep her shyness hidden from him, of all people! However, this was Eid morning, and his heart told him that she was not going to deprive him of a glance that would both delight his heart and revive all his hopes.

He looked upward and found the balcony open wide, bathed in sunshine, ready to scatter its pearls on the beautiful face that looked down from there. He waited for a while, looking out over the quarter as it happily celebrated the feast. The spirit of the occasion seemed to have permeated everything. You could see it in the colors, hear it in the air, and smell it in the atmosphere. The wilderness, bounded by the apartment buildings, was now dancing and singing for joy and proclaiming out loud the intensity of pleasure. Children were running all over the place, all decked in their festival finery with bright colors, plaits, and ribbons flying behind them. Horns were blown, and firecrackers popped. Everyone was chewing desserts and mint-flavored delights. Songs and ditties filled the air with noise. Cafés were thronged with city and country folk alike. Earth and sky alike were decked out for the feast.

He watched the entire scene, the faces and sights, with a distracted eye. Eventually his patience had the best possible reward; his lovely girl appeared by the balcony door wearing the most beautiful outfit. He looked up at her lovely olive-colored face and plucked up the courage to give her a smile without automatically looking down. All the while his heart was throbbing violently. He gave a slight nod; for her part she was watching him with her honey-colored eyes and gave him the sweetest smile in return. She kept on looking at him, and that made him feel shy and anxious, but, just as he was about to lose his courage, she gave him another smile, then moved away and disappeared from view. He sighed in sheer delight and stood there, hoping against hope that he might see her again and be rewarded with a third smile. However, a servant came hurrying out and closed the balcony door. With that he moved away from the window, feeling a bit sad and disappointed.

By now it was almost nine o'clock, and he remembered that he was supposed to meet his friends at the Zahra Café, having finally become one of those people who have rendezvous in cafés. He put on his fresh clothes—suit, fez, shoes, and shirt—and looked at himself in the mirror. He was impressed by his own elegance and seriousness. He recalled times past, the days of his youth—before time had frowned on him—when he had been famous for his neat appearance. He left the apartment full of happiness and walked slowly, relishing all the hopes and dreams filling his mind. "What comes after a smile?" he asked himself with all the perplexity of one distracted by joy. "What comes next, O Fortune?"

20

Rushdi went back to his room, lit a cigarette, and started to smoke by the window. His gaze was riveted to that particular window, all in the hope of catching a glimpse of his lovely neighbor once in a while. His hopes were rewarded when she did indeed appear at the window, wearing her new outfit and with a gray coat over her shoulders. However, she quickly withdrew, almost as though she needed to escape from his piercing stare. The young man had taken due note of the coat and surmised that she was on the point of going out. He quickly took out some clothes and started getting dressed. Within minutes he was out of the apartment.

He wondered where was the best place to wait. Just then he remembered the narrow passageway that connected the quarter to the New Road. He rushed over there, then stopped on the sidewalk at the spot where it joined the main road. The entire street was teeming with people. Carts had come down from the Darrasa district loaded with boys and girls singing, dancing, and banging drums. He stayed where he was, one eye happily watching the crowds in the street and the other glued hopefully to the passageway. He was an old hand at this type of situation, so he was not worried.

As it turned out, he did not have long to wait. The girl soon appeared at the entrance to the passageway accompanied by a young boy who closely resembled her. He avoided looking straight at her by lighting another cigarette. He had no doubt that she had spotted him, but he still wondered whether she had realized that he was actually waiting for her. As she made her way toward al-Azhar, he followed close behind and was able to get a good look at her for the first time. She was sixteen at the most, of medium height, and nicely turned out. However, it was her face that was the loveliest part of her, and her honey-colored eyes were its loveliest feature.

He did not manage to enjoy looking at her for very long, because she soon reached the trolley stop and got on the women's carriage along with her brother—that was his assumption about the young boy. He too got on the trolley, one carriage back so he could see where she got off. The trolley began to move, and he had no idea where this particular chase was going to take him. He now started an assessment: a young girl, seventy-five percent for face; sixty-five percent for figure; and it wouldn't take long to find out whether she was easy prey or would present more of a challenge. Would she get swept up in the romance, or was she dreaming of getting a wedding ring? We'll know soon enough, he told himself. If it's the wedding ring she's after, then things might rapidly become tricky; even

worse, annoying. At this stage, however, the most important thing was to cajole her into chatting and then see what
happened.

When the trolley reached Queen Farida Square, they all
got off—the girl and her brother first, and then him. Just
then she happened to look round and noticed him staring
directly at her. She immediately turned away and pretended to be deep in conversation with her brother. Now
he was sure that she realized he was deliberately following her.

The pair boarded the first trolley that came, the one
going to Giza. He immediately boarded it as well. "Are
they going to visit a relative," he wondered to himself, "so
they can celebrate the Eid with him?" At that moment he
decided, out of the sheer goodness of his heart, that he
would leave the day to her. But at just that moment they
both alighted at the Imad al-din stop. He now realized that
they were going to the cinema, a thought that delighted
him. They all crossed the road to Imad al-din Street, the
pair first, then him behind them, poised and ready to
respond to a smile or any kind of gesture she might make
if she looked behind her. But instead, she kept staring
straight to the front, grasping her brother's hand as he hurried to keep up with her. Rushdi kept his gaze firmly on her
back and legs, her gait, and the way she walked. He was
happy to discover that the view of her from the back was
just as nice as from the front. Her rear view earned her a
solid eighty percent. It all took him back to the old days.
"Well, well," he told himself, "these days there's beauty to
be had in Egypt."

When they got to the Ritz Cinema, she looked behind

her and noticed him still staring hard at her. Quickly looking away, she hurried off in the direction of Studio Egypt, leaving him flummoxed by the lack of any clear signal. He regretted the fact that their eyes had not had a real conversation, and yet her choice of cinema pleased him a lot. It was showing the film, *Dananir*. He realized that this little chase he had embarked upon would now offer him a double pleasure. He was eager to sit next to her, so he managed to work his way to a spot right behind her in the queue at the box office; that way he could select a seat right next to hers. The young boy was standing to one side, looking at the pictures. Rushdi moved up close behind her, so close that it felt as though his breaths were actually touching her ponytail; it gave him the same sensation as the purest of scents. He watched her fingers as they picked out two seats on the cinema chart for herself and her brother. He noticed that there would be a single vacant seat to the right and three to the left. Which side would the girl be sitting on? he asked himself. To find out, he used the old guessing game, "eeny meeny miny mo," and came up with the seat on the right. He chose it with a degree of confidence and then moved away. Looking around he could find no sign of either the girl or her brother, but that did not bother him. After all, he had the ticket in hand; that was enough to put him next to her, no matter where she had disappeared. He had no idea why, but it all reminded him—the power given him by the ticket, that is—of the sanctity and magic of marriage, all of which gave his heart a jolt.

He was still feeling the effects as he entered the cinema. As the usher escorted him to his seat, he was hoping that

his choice had been the right one, but he discovered that
the boy was sitting between himself and the girl. The girl
saw him coming and looked away in alarm; she refused to
even glance in his direction. He sat in his seat, delighted,
and kept stealing glances in her direction. On two occasions he noticed that she was staring straight in front of
her; the way she was blushing and looking thoroughly
awkward made him fully aware of how bashful and agitated she was feeling. That made him feel sorry for her,
and he decided then and there not to bother her any more.
Instead, he contented himself by looking around at the
boxes and rows of seats and fondly surveying the bosoms,
necks, mouths, and wrists on display. He did not have long
to wait. A bell sounded, lights were dimmed, and the
screen prepared itself to unwrap the world of dreams. He
was happy enough to be sitting close to the girl with whom
he had fallen in love, even though his heart was actually
not fully involved as yet. The heavenly voice started to sing
the spring song, "How sweet the gentle breeze!" and he
allowed himself to float off into another world. He had
always loved singing, so much so that one day it had even
occurred to him that he had been born to be a musician.
As the film continued, he felt himself swept up in a divine
melody.

When the film came to an end, the lights went up.
Rushdi looked over at the girl and saw that she was standing up with her eyes closed, shielding them from the bright
lights after spending so long in the dark. He stood there
waiting until she opened them and saw him staring at her.
Once outside the cinema, he made a point of looking carefully at her fingers and noticed that she was not engaged.

That made him smile. He then proceeded to trail her all the way back, just as he had on the way to the cinema. However, he decided not to follow her to al-Azhar since he did not want to reveal his little secret to anyone from his new quarter. Returning to the family apartment, he found his family waiting to eat. It was not long before his mother was happily summoning the family to the table with the words, "It's time for the Eid stew!"

21

Nawal was quite upset when she got home. "How can this boy be so brazen?" she asked herself. "He's been chasing me ever since he set eyes on me yesterday!"

At this point she was just over sixteen years old. She was certainly pretty. Her prettiness resided in two principal features: her naiveté and her charm. But, one might well ask, what did those things imply exactly? The naiveté was of the kind invoked by beauty in its most basic form, to be seen in a pure, bright-eyed expression and a straightforward look; certainly in no way linked to stupidity or simple-mindedness. The charm resulted from the neat way she dressed and the kindly disposition she showed toward people. Apart from that, she was not the slightest bit flirtatious or silly, nor did she seem particularly intelligent or clever. She had a lovely olive-colored complexion, something that her mother always maintained was the epitome of beauty and a source of charm. Actually, her mother preferred a whiter complexion. She was convinced that being a little plump gave the complexion a particular glow, and that is why she tried to counteract her daughter's slim figure by regularly plying her with fattening foods to make her gain weight.

The daughter's progress at secondary school suggested that she would do well. However, truth to tell, she may have been willing to go through the process but it was not what she really wanted; school was not the focus of her heart's desires. Her dreams remained firmly fixed on the home, and she continued to regard her mother as her primary teacher, the one who was teaching her household skills such as cooking, weaving, and embroidery. As far as she was concerned, education was merely an accessory to be added to her femininity, a precious piece of jewelry that would require a larger dowry. For her, life was entirely focused on a single goal: heart, home, and marriage. After all, wasn't that the very first prayer uttered by any prospective bride? What a wonderful prayer it was! That was precisely what she was aspiring to, and she was prepared to wait for her chance with patience and hope. That is why she had chosen to sanctify marriage long before she herself was ready for it. She was in love with "the man," although that remained for her both an unknown dream and an unclear feeling. She was therefore a ripe piece of fruit, ready for plucking and waiting for the right person to do so.

The young lawyer, Ahmad Rashid, had been the first man ever—apart from her own family members, that is— to have any close contact with her, and that was in order to give her some tutoring. From the outset she had greeted him shyly and had eyed him with both curiosity and hope.

As far as she was concerned, he was not so much a teacher as a real man. Her heart softened a little, and life began to quicken its pulse. However, the young lawyer was far more strict and serious than necessary, and she was totally incapable of gauging the real feelings that lurked behind his dark eyes. At first he merely patronized her, but, when he started actually scolding her as well, she came to regard him as being both gloomy and somewhat frightening. With that she changed her mind about him and lost hope.

He would often talk to her in ways that she could not understand or make nasty comments such as, "It seems to me you don't appreciate learning the way you should, even though you're not lacking in either initiative or basic intelligence. You should appreciate it as much as you do life; after all, the two are linked in the same way the mind is to the person: you must use learning to feed your mind in the same way as you use food to nourish your body. Where is that longing for the world's great secrets? Where is the passion for knowledge? When it comes to the realms of knowledge and the unknown, it is simply not right for a woman's heart to be in any way less advanced than that of a man."

"What are you planning to do after you get your high school diploma?" he asked her on another occasion. "Haven't you thought about what you want to study at university yet?"

"I don't know," she had replied at the time.

"Oh, I see!" the young man replied angrily. "You're still feeling negative about knowledge, is that it?"

She obviously did not realize that this young man was trying to mold her into the kind of woman that he wanted her to be; she thought instead that all he was doing was mocking her. And that made her dislike him even more.

Then along came Ahmad Akif, the new arrival in the neighborhood. Rumor had it that he was still a bachelor. She was overjoyed when she saw him sneaking glances in her direction; her heart was edging its way in his direction just as a pair of hands will move toward a brazier of hot coals on a freezing cold night. "He's not young any more," she told herself, "but he's still in the prime of middle-age. He must be a well-regarded government employee; by the time such a person is his age, they have to be respected." Whatever the case, she could not ignore the glances that he was directing at her with such amiable diffidence or fail to realize that love was the motivating factor. If that were not the case, she asked herself, why on earth would he spend hour after hour every afternoon waiting by the window? And why, she wondered, wasn't he taking the next step, but seemed content just to steal glances at her? Hadn't he smiled at her, and signaled a greeting to her? Did bashfulness affect men's minds the way it did women's? If so, why didn't he talk to her father? Or why didn't he ask his mother to act as intermediary? Nawal was a lively girl, and needed someone to be pursuing her. Now chance had sent her a middle-aged man who desperately needed someone to pursue him. By this time she had despaired of his plucking up enough courage to make the first move, so she took the initiative. She waved at him from her balcony and received a beautiful response. Now her heart told her that her aspirations might soon be fulfilled.

But at about noon on the day before the festival a new face had appeared in the very same apartment; in fact, in the room that directly faced her own bedroom. She realized at once that this new young man was the younger brother of her middle-aged acquaintance. But where had he been before, she wondered. What did he think he was doing staring at her in such a brazen fashion, something that sent the blood rushing to her cheeks from every extremity in her body and made her run away? What a nice-looking young man he was! And how he stared at her, enough to send the heart into palpitations. Did he behave this way with every pretty girl he spotted, or had he detected something unusual about her face? Would he be staying in that same room from now on, or would he disappear again just as suddenly as he had appeared? Her heart told her that this young man was inarguably better than his middle-aged brother, and yet the elder brother wasn't a stranger any more. They had exchanged greetings. If he asked for her hand, he would be the favorite. She needed to bear in mind that they had made a silent pact, one that, God willing, would soon turn into the noise of wedding instruments, glittering chandeliers, and bright confetti to delight onlookers.

On the morning of the feast she had put on her new clothes. Her heart told her she should make an appearance on the balcony so that her middle-aged friend could see her looking her very best. She had found him standing by the window looking as fine as he possibly could; his gallabiya and skullcap reminded her of her own father. They exchanged greetings, then she went back to her room. At that moment her feelings urged her to take a look at the other window as well. There she found the younger brother, apparently waiting for her. When he stared straight at her, she quickly withdrew.

She had convinced herself that his brazen behavior would never go beyond the window, so it was a total shock to find him waiting for her by the New Road. On the trolley she kept asking herself whether he was actually following her or she was simply imagining things. It did not take long for her to realize that he was quite deliberately following her and was not to be diverted from his purpose. Funnily enough, he had managed to forget about her while they were in the cinema because he was so entranced by Umm Kulthum's singing, but she spent the entire time fully aware of the fact that he was sitting very close to her.

When she went home, she was feeling happier than she had ever known. "If all young men were as persistent as he is," she chuckled to herself, "there wouldn't be a single unmarried girl!" Now her heart started scolding her for being so quick to exchange greetings with the elder brother. But then, how was she supposed to have any knowledge of the unseen? She was completely flustered, and did not enjoy the special Eid stew or the fish either.

That afternoon she left her family's apartment, intending to pay a visit to Sayyid Effendi Arif's wife. But before she paid the visit, she decided to go up to the roof and cast her eye over the minarets and domes of the old city. Now that she could no longer play with the younger girls in the street, the roof had become her favorite spot. She walked slowly alongside the parapet, taking in the view and looking out toward the horizon. Just then she felt a strong urge to look toward the entrance to the roof. She was amazed to find him standing there, his tall form completely filling up the doorway. He was staring straight at her, a gentle smile evident in his beautiful eyes. The very sight of him gave her a jolt and made her feel scared and a bit panic stricken. However, she soon recovered her composure. Realizing that the situation was serious and required something more than a simple display of bashfulness, she gave him a glare that registered both disapproval and dismay.

22

Looking away, she turned her back on him and gazed toward the distant horizon, although she actually saw nothing. Commonsense told her that she should leave, but she did not move. An inner voice screamed at her to pretend that he was not even there and not to rush away in a panic, so she stayed right where she was, feeling both nervous and shy.

For his part, Rushdi gave a happy sigh when he saw that she preferred to stay rather than leave. "Well," he told himself with a certain satisfaction, "we've hooked the fish, but now we're going to have to be very careful how we handle it." He had discovered that she had gone up to the roof quite by chance. He had been watching the closed window of her bedroom in disappointment, but then he had looked up at the roof parapet just at the moment when she had passed by. He had already dressed for the evening, so his innate brashness and initiative drove him to go up to the roof immediately.

Once he was sure she was not going to leave, he surveyed his surroundings carefully and found that there was no one else around. With that he walked slowly to a point close by her. His insane boldness was still working overtime, but with this girl he preferred to take things slowly because she was obviously very shy. In between the place where he was standing and the spot where she stood, he noticed a wooden pole by the wall with washing on it. A dove had alighted on it.

Looking up at the dove, he said, "Good evening, my little dove!" all the while glancing at the girl.

He smiled as he noticed her sneak a quick look at the dove. "What a lovely color you have!" he went on. "A brown that is so attractive and charming. Do you know the song 'O my tan beauty, my life in tawny hues'?"

The girl was listening closely to what he was saying, although she pretended not to be. She liked the sound of his voice and smiled secretly to herself without it showing on her lips. Just then her shyness got the better of her, and she moved away a couple of steps and turned her back on him.

"Why do you not return my greeting, little dove?" he asked, addressing the dove again. "Why do you avoid me? How can cruelty possibly be a part of such delicate beauty?"

Now she started wondering whether it was time for her to go. Shouldn't she worry in case the doorman of the apartment came up to the roof or some of the residents and started getting suspicious about finding them together? Why was it that she felt glued to the floor?

"Don't you realize, little dove," Rushdi went on, "that I

am your neighbor? From now on, the merciful heavens will not be able to keep you apart from me. I shall always be where you are."

Nawal now turned her head to look at the dove, but found that it had flown away. Meanwhile, there he was staring at her in his usual brazen fashion. There was no longer any point in addressing the dove.

"Hello!" he said quietly.

Once again she turned her head away and slowly moved toward the door. With that he moved toward her in alarm.

"Aren't you going to say anything to me?" he asked.

Still she said nothing, although she was blushing and her eyelids were blinking hard. He moved even closer.

"Won't you say just one word, one single word? If you like, you can tell me off or even rebuff me!"

Instead, she hurried toward the door. He moved to stand in her way.

"Get out of my way," she said faking her exasperation. "You should be ashamed of yourself, behaving this way to a neighbor!"

"Can a neighbor be blamed for falling in love with a beautiful girl?"

"Yes!"

"But what if her beauty compels him to fall in love with her. Who's to blame then?"

"Don't start dragging me into conversation. Now stop blocking my way."

But, in spite of her warning, he did block her way. She started to panic and rushed toward the door, slipping under his outstretched arm. He was not able to catch up with her. Her heart racing, she rushed downstairs and headed for Sayyid Arif's apartment. She was neither angry nor exasperated, quite the contrary in fact. She sat on the balcony waiting for her mother to arrive, with the image of the handsome face of the young man and the affectionate tone of his voice still in her memory. She started to recall the stories her school friends had told her about the wiles of young men, love letters, and famous tales of romance. From tomorrow, she wondered, should she enact her own love story? But what kind of young man was he?

After a while, Rushdi too came downstairs, his face wreathed in smiles. As of yet, his heart had not felt any genuine emotion; it was almost as though he were playing a much-loved role. Even so, he was one of those genuine actors who get so involved in playing their part that his heart catches fire and sparks fly, in laughter or in tears. Soon after, he took off for the casino with a renewed appetite to spend an evening drinking and amusing himself.

23

For Ahmad Akif, the Eid went by without him seeing her again. He assumed that she was busy with the feast itself and the various entertainments associated with it. With all his heart he wished her happiness. At this stage, all he wanted was for her to see him dressed in the new suit that he had had made especially in her honor.

"This suit will last me for a long time," he told himself, "and at some point she's bound to see me wearing it with pride."

He too was busy with the Eid, although he spent most of it with his friends in the Zahra Café. Sulayman Bey Ata was the only one not there, since he had gone to celebrate the festival in his village. What was amazing was that even though he had by now been spending a lot of time with this group, not a single one of them had become a real friend. That was because when it came to friendship he was always looking for a pair of traits that were never combined: firstly, an acknowledgment of his own superior intellect and education, and secondly, that the friend be cultured—albeit only to a certain extent—so that he could enjoy his company. What he normally found was that the person in question was somewhere in the middle: one friend might be a bit plebeian in outlook (or at least in popular opinion), someone whom he liked as a person and who was prepared to acknowledge Ahmad's intelligence, while another who was better educated would not be willing to submit to his will and would prefer to argue with him. It might well be that he could love the first and hate the second, but, truth to tell, neither of them could fulfill the role of a real friend. That was why he liked Boss Nunu, Kamal Khalil, and Sayyid Arif but hated Ahmad Rashid. And that was why he remained friendless, or rather his brother Rushdi was his only real friend in the world.

The Eid passed without his setting eyes on her again. Even so, he never stopped thinking about her, nor did he ignore the need to think about the more important things in his life and future. His emotions had become engaged, his heart was awakened, and hope was bestowing a smile. This was doubly true—two hearts were awakened, not one. After thirty years deprived of love, now here he was experiencing love, and that with a heart that was bidding adieu to his youth. He would have to cling to love as a last hope for real happiness in this world. This sensation had arrived quite by chance when he had almost abandoned all hope. An old song had now come back into his heart, fresh and sweet, almost as though risen from the dead. That meant that he had to look at his affairs carefully and organize his life.

As the Eid passed, he was much involved in thought and planning. Life was now erasing the frown from his brow and affording him a golden opportunity to try his luck once again. He had no intention of either flinching or hesitating. He was keen to be much more frank with himself and uttered the magic word "marriage" to himself. Yes indeed, but he was forty years old and she was under twenty. He was old enough to be her father, but what was wrong with that? Hadn't she shown that she was fond of him? His heart gave a flutter at the very thought. Wasn't he the one her heart had chosen? Thinking of his friend, Kamal Khalil, Ahmad assumed that he would welcome the idea of giving his daughter to him in marriage, even if it was a bit of a shock at first. Ahmad imagined that people would be making inquiries about him. They would find out that he was forty years old, a clerk in the record department at the Ministry of Works, eighth level, someone as inconspicuous within the government hierarchy as he was in the world in general; his salary was fifteen pounds. Wouldn't Kamal Khalil be a bit anxious about that? After all, he thought Ahmad was a department head. Wouldn't Sitt Tawhida—Nawal's mother—say that he was very substantial in years and yet very insubstantial in salary? That thought made him bite his lip, and the old feelings of despair and misery came flooding back. He was on the point of losing his temper and saying something that he had said once before when faced with this particular situation: "Whenever someone persuades themselves into belittling me, the weight of the entire world is not worth a pile of garbage!" However, his determination to try his luck denied him any indulgence in fits of temper. All thoughts of despair were wiped from his mind, bringing in their wake feelings of joy and fond hopes for a new life.

As the three days of the Eid came to an end, he was thinking about all the things he needed to do immediately before acting. The first Friday after the Eid arrived, he had yet to put any of his plans into effect. However, that morning he saw her again for the first time since the first day of the Eid, and his lovelorn heart was thrilled. It was early November, and from time to time the fresh air wafted a cool breeze in his direction. The sky was covered by a thin veil of white clouds that shielded the bright light of the sun. He opened the window—"Nawal's window"—and looked up. There was his beloved girl looking down at him like a radiant hope, a wonderful dream. He smiled at her and gave her a wave, and she smiled back. How he adored that smile of hers! He stayed there for a while, taking in the pure loveliness of her complexion. Just then it occurred to him that he should try to signal to her, to the extent possible, that he was about to talk to her father about marrying her. But she beat him to it, resting her head on her arm as a way of indicating that she wanted to take a nap. She pointed to her head, frowned, then twisted her lips to imply that she had a headache. With that she turned away and went inside. He was sorry to have lost the opportunity, but his determination now became even stronger. He needed to have a cigarette, so he went over to Rushdi's room to get one from him. The door was ajar, so he pushed it and went inside. He noticed that his brother was standing by the window looking upward. Rushdi was so involved in whatever he was doing that Ahmad was halfway across the room before his brother even realized he had come in. From where he was standing he could clearly see the other window that his brother was looking at. From the middle of the room he managed to spot Nawal's head—no one else's—which proceeded to withdraw at lightning speed! The way in which she disappeared—or, more appropriately, ran away—made Rushdi aware that his brother had arrived. He turned round and gave his brother a smile. For his part, Ahmad was totally shocked by what he had seen, a shock far worse than the one he had experienced on the night of the bombing raid. This hit him like a bolt out of the blue, stripping away his initial equanimity and pulling him apart like clouds during a sudden lightning strike.

He was well aware of the way his younger brother had turned to look at him, so, in an instinctual gesture, he closed his eyes and called up all his hidden reserves so as to seem calm. He even managed to fake a smile, then looked at his brother who was coming toward him with a sweet, innocent smile of his own.

"I'd like a cigarette, please," he said calmly.

Rushdi took the cigarette pack out of his pajama pocket, opened it, and offered it to his brother. Ahmad took one and thanked his brother by raising his hand to his forehead. With that he went back to his room.

24

Once back in his room, he was so distraught that he could barely see straight. He threw the cigarette on his bed, then went over to the window and looked up. He could see the balcony just as she had left it, open and empty. He lowered his gaze with a frown and closed the window so loudly that it made the glass rattle. Going back to his bed, he sat down on the edge.

"I didn't realize," he muttered to himself, "that there was another window in her apartment that looked out directly onto his just like this balcony. I honestly didn't realize."

By now his blood had turned into oil, sending tongues of flame to his heart. Hadn't he seen her moving backward in shock when he had appeared in his brother's room? Was it a feeling that she was doing something wrong that shocked her? If not, then what had made her go to the window when she had convinced him that she was going to take a nap? It could only mean one thing, and it was not pleasant: the girl had been deliberately deceitful, and that meant an end to all his futile hopes. The amazing thing was this younger brother had only come home ten days ago, and in that short time everything had changed—the very idea hit him like a slap on the face. From now on his heart would declare all his passions to be invalid; any smiles of welcome were simply examples of hypocrisy and outright deceit. How could these changes happen so fast, he wondered. Could it be this easy and noncommittal, almost a victimless process? Or was there bound to be an appropriate level of reluctance and pain? Was the girl toying with both of them? Behind that sweet smile could there really be a thoroughly nasty and cunning little vixen? Why had she exchanged greetings with him just a few minutes ago? Did she feel awkward and shy, or was it more a matter of sheer cunning?

His younger brother was blameless; he was totally unaware of the circumstances involved. Rushdi had set eyes on her and found her attractive, so he had started flirting with her (as he usually did with girls). He had managed to attract her attention, and she had fallen for him. With a single glance and gesture she had forgotten all about the elder brother. That was all there was to it! She had forgotten the older man, with his balding pate. He had only himself to blame. Did he not know enough by now about his own hard luck and his negative view of the world in general and women in particular to steer well clear of false hopes and glimpses of happiness?

As he stood up, his expression was one of profound sadness and utter despair. He started pacing back and forth in his room between bed and desk until he began to feel dizzy.

He went back to sit down on the bed. Was there any point, he asked himself, in engaging in a contest with his own brother? The very thought aroused his innate arrogance. No, it was out of the question for him to lower himself so far as to engage in any rivalry with another human being; genuine rivalry could only take place between equals. It was also out of the question to let his younger brother know about his secret love. Ahmad's sense of his own self-importance made it absolutely impossible for him to even contemplate begging for happiness or love. No, someone like him should rather stand aloof from such trivialities—love, the girl, and whoever wins her. He was far above all that. But what about the agony he was feeling? Why did this dreadful pain not appreciate his genuine worth and simply disappear? Jealousy kept stinging his heart like a scorpion bite. And what was the point of all this pain and grief? Truth to tell, he had stretched out his hand to unveil his bride, but, when the embroidered veil had been taken off, what was beneath it turned out to be a skull. In his imagination he could see a picture of the two of them together: Rushdi in the prime of his youth, and she with her lovely, honey-colored eyes. The very idea was painful and only managed to make him feel even more disdainful and supercilious.

How was it that Rushdi always managed to interfere with his happiness, he wondered; especially since Ahmad loved no one else to the same extent as he did his brother? It was his younger brother who had forced him—twenty years ago now—to sacrifice his own future in order to devote himself to his brother's education. Now here was Rushdi plucking the fruits of the happiness that should

have been his and trampling all over his hopes with hob-
nail boots.

At this point raw anger got the better of him, and he
surrendered totally to an erupting volcano of hatred. Even
so, he could not find it within himself, even for a single
instant, to hate his own brother, even though he was the
focus of his towering rage. The love he felt for his brother
certainly suffered a kind of spasm during which it was
unconscious; but while it may have fainted for a short
while, it didn't actually die. Not only that, but he did not
feel any hatred toward Nawal either, even though she was
guilty enough. It seemed as though his anger could go on
forever, but, as it turned out, his temper calmed down
remarkably quickly; indeed, it was a total surprise to see
how soon it disappeared. The anger, malice, and supercil-
iousness all disappeared, to be replaced by a profound sadness, despair, and sense of failure, all of which lingered
and refused to go away. He recalled the happiness he had
felt just the day before, but, instead of feeling any sense of
regret or sorrow, he was contemptuous and not a little
embarrassed.

"The time for deceit is long past," he told himself in a
muted, sad voice, as though addressing someone else.
"There's no escaping the bitter truth. You're an unlucky
man. In fact, that's by no means all that's involved. You're
actually someone set up by fate to be the target for arrows
of frustration and failure. You've been assigned to a foul
and devilish power, one that makes sure that every good
opportunity or happy chance that comes your way is
removed. You imagine that the only thing separating you
from hope is a single word that needs to be said or a hand

to be extended. But no sooner do you extend your apron to catch the fruit off the tree than some bird of ill omen comes down, grabs it in its claws, and flies away with it. No sooner do you reach the top of a pyramid in your endeavors than the entire thing collapses and you find yourself in a deep pit. Your horizons glow with the flares of false hopes; your position on the earth is dark and gloomy. Does there exist in this world any other man who is beset by such stubborn ill fortune?

"As people go about their daily lives with smiling faces, they all have the benefits of good health, a nice family life, a satisfactory station in life, and enough money. But what about you? You don't have a single one of them! Early on it was your father's fall from grace that first broke your back, then your genuine affection for your younger brother shattered all your aspirations, and finally the entire boorish environment in which you were living crippled your undoubted intellectual gifts. What dreams remain in this rotten world of yours? By now youth is long gone. All it managed to produce was a beautiful memory seeking shade from the midday heat of time's inexorable march. And now here comes middle age, poking you in the ribs as you relentlessly broach the ranks of the elderly. How on earth can you stand this foul existence? Any man can divorce his loyal wife if he finds out that she's barren. So how can you stand a world that is not merely barren but that only brings you pain and grief? Why do you exist at all? Is there no end to this ongoing torture and stultifying boredom? Beyond all that, what use has your mind ever been to you? All that knowledge you have?

"In the name of all these pains put together," he told

himself, "I hereby swear that I intend to close books forever and burn this pesky library. It's a much better idea to become addicted to some drug that will dull the brain enough for an even more powerful stupor to take over. Life is one extended tragedy, and this world is merely a tedious drama. The amazing part of it all is that the actual plot is really disturbing and yet the actors are all clowns. The entire purpose is to make people feel sad—not because it is intrinsically distressing—but because it is supposed to be very serious. What it produces is the ultimate in farce. Since we find ourselves unable most of the time to laugh at our own failures, we end up in tears, and our tears only succeed in deceiving us about the truth. We imagine that the plot involves tragedy, whereas in fact it's one gigantic farce."

He paused for a moment, frowning and disconsolate, then stood up abruptly. "Very well then," he muttered angrily, "to the dark cave it is, the cave of loneliness and desolation; the cold grave, the grave of despair and disillusion. The world, the low world that is, has kicked me enough, so now I in turn will kick it back from a loftier position. Eunuchs have no need of women. If I choose to deprive myself of all false hopes in that direction, then I can use despair to block out the world entirely. So then, to the cave of lonely desolation. From its darkness we can supply a curtain to shield our eyes against life's never-ending perfidy!"

With that he turned toward the window—Nawal's window—that was now firmly locked. "Closed forever," he said angrily, "closed forever!"

25

He decided to make his way to the Zahra Café. While he usually went there on Friday mornings, he realized that the distress he was feeling provided him with an extra-powerful incentive to go; he really needed to find a way to console himself. He started putting on his new suit, remembering all the while how he had had it tailored and how much it had cost. With a sigh of exasperation he left the apartment.

As he descended the staircase, he recalled the first morning he had spent in the apartment building; how he had looked behind him and spotted Nawal's eyes for the first time. How can anyone guard against predestined misery when it reveals itself in such bright hopes and vibrant colors? Even so, he was also aware that his current feelings of agony, persecution, and injustice were perversely pleasurable, albeit a somewhat obscure kind of pleasure whose features had not as yet made themselves clear.

As he plodded his way slowly toward the café, he could

not help thinking about the way an underage girl had managed to bring down so much sorrow and despair on an intelligent elder man like him. He found the entire thing too much to bear.

"Good grief!" he scoffed at himself, "how can it have happened? A little girl just out of nappies doing this to me? How could she possibly pull me up to the very heights of delight, only to dump me into the depths of hell? Why behave sensibly if infectious desires could toy with us in this despicable fashion? Shouldn't we expect—I ask Your forgiveness, O God!—to be created better than that? If the entire world has turned itself into a gloomy wasteland simply because some insanitary microbe or other has gone berserk or run out of hope, wouldn't it be better simply to piss on the world and everything in it?"

At this point he reached the café, which ended this conversation with himself. He found that his friends had already arrived, except, that is, for Sulayman Bey Ata who was still in his village. Boss Nunu was with them; on Fridays he always closed his store from ten in the morning until after prayer time. As usual, Abbas Shifa sat beside Boss Zifta, not far removed from the circle of friends. The men started chattering, while the radio broadcasted some recorded music. Kamal Khalil decided to include the new arrival in their conversation.

"So what's Professor Ahmad's opinion of singing?" he asked. "Which style does he prefer, the old or the new?"

Damn it! As the age-old proverb puts it: "Woe to the person with troubles from the one who is without!" But after all, hadn't he come to the café specifically to take his mind off things by listening to their normal drivel? Yes indeed, he had. Okay then, he should dive in and be grateful. In fact, he adored singing (would his mother have given birth to anyone who didn't love singing?), but he preferred the old style; he had never developed a liking for the more modern stuff, not only out of habit but because of his early upbringing. He had listened to the songs of female vocalists and records made by singers like Munira, Abd al-Hayy, and al-Manyalawi.

Just then he stole a glance at his old foe, Ahmad Rashid, who seemed to be concealing his thoughts on the matter behind his dark glasses.

"The old style of singing," Ahmad told them all, "is the only one that can arouse the emotion and effortlessly ensnare our hearts."

Boss Zifta shouted "God is most great!" enthusiastically while Boss Nunu clapped his hands three times.

"But what about Umm Kulthum and Abd al-Wahhab?" asked Sayyid Arif.

Ahmad Akif sneaked another quick glance at his foe. "To the extent that they repeat aspects of the old style, they're both terrific, but beyond that they're nothing."

"Umm Kulthum's wonderful," said Sayyid Arif, "even when she's singing 'The Tender Radish!'"

"There's no arguing about her beautiful voice," replied Ahmad Akif, "but we're talking about the artistic aspect of singing."

Kamal Khalil chimed in at this point. "Professor Ahmad Rashid loves the new style of singing. Not only that, but he likes Western music too!"

It was obvious that the young lawyer was not in the mood to argue. "My views on singing are not those of an expert," he responded lackadaisically. "I don't really bother with it that much."

Boss Nunu was determined to have his point of view heard. "Listen, folks," he said in his usual gruff tone, "the Prophet Muhammad's people are still in good shape. The English have been with us now for over half a century, but tell me, for heaven's sake, have you ever heard anyone English who could sing 'O Night, O Eyes'? The truth of the matter is that anyone who prefers Western music is just the same as someone who likes eating pork!"

As a rule Boss Zifta was preoccupied with his work and had little to say, but this time the subject interested him. "Okay," he chimed in, with a lisp that suggested that he had lost at least a couple of his teeth, "here's the scoop. The very best singing you'll ever hear is Si Abduh with 'O Night,' Ali Mahmud doing the dawn call-to-prayer, and Umm Kulthum with 'When Love.' Everything else is just a pile of straw mixed with dust!"

Ahmad Akif was anxious not to leave the subject of modern music without injecting a bit of philosophizing. "People who admire modern singing and European music," he said, "fall into the category of the ruled being influenced by their rulers, as Ibn Khaldun pointed out."

Ahmad Rashid still remained silent in spite of the way Ahmad Akif had attacked his position. That brought an end to the conversation about singing. Without any particular connection, talk now shifted to the topic of Sulayman Ata Bey. Kamal Khalil observed that he had stayed in his village longer than usual.

"So God has given us two merciful weeks of respite from his shameless behavior!" commented Sayyid Arif.

"It won't be long," said Abbas Shifa disapprovingly, "before he gets married again."

"But what a bride!" Sayyid Arif continued regretfully. "I tell you, by God, I've never seen a woman more beautiful than Yusuf Bahla's daughter!"

"Isn't your friend aware," Ahmad Akif asked, "that no one would want him for a husband if it weren't for his money?"

"No doubt about it," said Abbas Shifa. "Youth, beauty, morals, they're all missing!"

Needless to say, that particular description was not to Ahmad Akif's liking at all. In more than one aspect, he felt, it described him as well: youth, beauty, and morals, all lacking, to which he could add in his own case, no money either. For a moment he fell back into the fit of utter depression that the conversation had thus far managed to dispel. Worried that the mood might take over again, he plunged into the argument once again.

"What is it," he asked, "that makes Ata Bey give in to these hankerings?"

Now Ahmad Rashid looked directly at him. "What's so surprising about that?" he asked with uncharacteristic modesty. "Along with youth and beauty isn't money one of the primary motivations that endear a man to a woman? In fact, money may be the one that endures longer than the others!"

But he soon put his sarcasm to one side and adopted a more serious tone. "Look," he said, "An old man of Ata Bey's age isn't interested in the kind of love that gets young people so worked up. Whenever he manages to acquire a precious bride, he is actually gratifying both his dwindling

libido and, far more important, his more dominant posses-
sive instinct."

"Youth gets transferred by contact," commented Abbas
Shifa. "From his new bride our old friend expects to regain
some of the sparkle of youth. With things the way they are,
it's not out of the question that our friend the Bey will
change fairly soon from an ape to a donkey!"

"So, are we to understand," Boss Zifta asked, "that he's
descended from apes?"

Naturally enough Boss Nunu was not entirely happy
about the way they were poking fun at old people. "What
counts when you're old," he commented, "is how healthy
you are, not how old. My father got married when he was
sixty, and had children. Just look at Sayyid Arif for example (and here he let out a guffaw), what's his youth done
to him?"

Everyone laughed, including Akif.

"Don't be so quick to laugh, Boss Nunu!" Sayyid Arif
was forced to respond. "Pretty soon things are going to
change. I've heard about some brand new pills. You'll see!"

That was as far as Ahmad could go in keeping up with
their chatter. He felt like a swimmer whose strength is flag-
ging and whose resistance is growing weaker by the minute. He had no idea how he managed to change the subject
to war news nor how it came about that Sayyid Arif started
counting off the German victories in Russia, proudly rattling off the way Vyazma, Bryansk, Orel, Odessa, and
Kharkov had all fallen and the Crimea had been overrun.
At that point Boss Nunu stood up to leave and perform the
Friday prayer. Ahmad got up too, excused himself, and left
to go home.

When he got there, he stood in the hallway for a while wondering whether Rushdi was still in his room. He walked along the hallway and stood by the door of his brother's room. He could smell cigarette smoke wafting its way through the gaps in the door, so he turned round and went back to his own room. For the first time ever, Rushdi was spending his weekly day off (or rather their weekly day off) at home! More likely than not, he would not be going out either, and she too would be staying close by the window. God knows how many times they had already exchanged waves and smiled at each other, and how many hopes had arisen.

Taking off his suit, he put on a gallabiya and skullcap, then sat down on the settee next to the bookshelf. He was feeling utterly miserable, and yet there was no jealousy, or, at least, nothing that showed. He managed to convince himself that whatever went on in the other part of the apartment was simply child's play and of no interest to him. Was this just a temporary feeling on his part? How could he know? Even so, he felt badly done by. How could it all have happened so quickly, he asked himself. Was the emotion that he had convinced himself was real love truly this superficial?

He let his feelings calm down a bit, then went to the bookshelf and took down Imam al-Ghazali's book, *Goals of the Philosophers*. Now, here was something far more deserving of his attention, one of those treasures about which Ahmad Rashid knew absolutely nothing. He opened the book up to the chapter on theology and tried reading the preface to the division of the sciences. Before long he realized that he was devoting so much energy to concentrating on what he was doing that it was impossible to enjoy the actual process of reading. He closed the book and put it back on the shelf. He decided that his mind had used up a good deal of energy that day on the process of forgetting—no matter what kind of effort was involved—so he could afford to give it a day's rest.

It had all been a silly piece of emotionalism. How could that girl have possibly made him happy when he was so intelligent and learned while she was totally naive and uncultured? Truth to tell, his younger brother had just saved him from making a mistake that might have been the end of him. From now on, he needed to keep his eyes wide open and abandon forever any thought of getting married. How absurd to even think that he could ever find a suitable woman! Even so, she had betrayed him in a way that was both mean and reprehensible. Hadn't she flirted with him? Hadn't she been happy enough to have him as an admirer? How could she have changed her mind so unbelievably quickly? He asked himself whether God had ever created a more repulsive sight than a two-faced girl. Telling himself to "get over it and move on" was all very well, but what a paltry world it was where feelings could be turned upside down at the drop of a hat!

"God damn the world!" The loud voice interrupted his feverish ruminations, and he realized that Boss Nunu had just come back to his store from the Friday prayers. He was delighted to be distracted from all his woes in this abrupt fashion. Moving over to the window on the side that was still new to him, he looked out over the neighborhood that he had come to know and already found tedious. If only the family had never left al-Sakakini! Not only that, but he also found himself secretly wishing that his younger brother had never come back to Cairo from Asyut. If he hadn't come back, his peace of mind would not have been shattered so completely. But no sooner did the thought cross his mind than he felt a deep sense of pain. He dearly loved his brother; there was no doubting that. It would be impossible to fake the real affection he felt for his brother who was almost his son and foster child. What was really odd and wrong was that he loved him and hated him at the same time. Had Rushdi not come back to Cairo, Ahmad would now be engaged.

Before realizing it, his whole inner self started gushing sentimental about married life, completely ignoring all previous misgivings. The number two was sanctified, he decided. Pythagoras may have said that the number one was sanctified, but he was wrong—it was two. Humanity can lose itself in groups, but drowns in misery when left alone. A life companion can provide succor. Mutual revelation, profound love, shared companionship, delight of one heart in another, and infinite serenity, all of them are the deep delights that only happen between two people. Ahmad was utterly fed up with his own misery, exasperated by his loneliness, and resentful of the void in his life. Now his inner self was contradicting him, by expressing a great longing for love, sympathy, company, and affection. Where are those lips to give him a smile of affection? Where is the heart to share its beats with another? Where is the bosom from which to nurse some droplets of repose and to which to entrust his innermost thoughts?

His exasperation reached its peak. He went back and sat on the bed, shaking his head in anger. It was almost as if he were trying to block out these sad feelings so that he could recover his anger and severity, not to mention his insane belief in the virtues of loneliness, arrogance, and contempt for human emotions. His jealous feelings might cool in the long run, and his emotions might flag as well, but, when it came to his sense of his own importance, it was an entirely different story. That was an ulcer that could not be lanced. How on earth could that be? Whenever it repaired itself, his blind conceit would remove the scab.

"That girl has got to realize," he said between grinding teeth, "that from now on I have decided to give her up without so much as a second thought!"

26

On Saturday morning he woke up exhausted. He had not slept at all well, and he was now paying the price for the joyful interlude of love, however short it may have been. What was past was past. True enough, but, as long as the possibility of forgetting it all still lurked behind all his sorrowful memories, then consolation in some form or other was still something to be devoutly desired. Where was that lovely Jewish girl from al-Sakakini now with her ideal kind of love? By now time had done its work, drawing a veil of forgetfulness over the past and swallowing up all such memories. Still he clearly understood that from now on he needed to remain unaffected, or at least to make a show of doing so. He had to show Nawal that he was barely even aware of the fact that he had been jilted by a young girl.

When he went to the bathroom, he noticed that his brother's door was ajar. He could see him getting dressed, which was amazing in itself because his brother always got up later than he himself did. He also noticed his brother looking up at the window opposite. That gave him a jolt, as though someone had stuck a needle into him. He let the cold water flow over his head for some time as a way of calming his shattered nerves. Back in his room he put on his suit, then went to the table to drink his cup of morning coffee, smoke a cigarette, and eat something light. He had decided to greet his younger brother in a perfectly normal way, not least because he was anxious to keep his real feelings hidden. Rushdi came in wearing a suit and fez, and gave him his usual smile.

"Good morning!" he said.

"Good morning to you too!"

Ahmad was surprised to see his brother wearing a fez, since he would usually appear for breakfast bareheaded. "Why the hurry to put on the fez?" he asked.

"I'm going to eat breakfast elsewhere," his brother replied, still smiling. "I've some urgent business to attend to."

"What can be that urgent?"

"I have to finish some things for work."

Rushdi bade him farewell, as he did to his mother who was making breakfast, then, with his graceful appearance and his radiant smile, he left. Not for a single second did Ahmad believe this story about "urgent business." He was pretty sure that Rushdi had got up so unusually early and rushed out of the house because he was going to meet Nawal somewhere on her way to school. That at least is what his gloomy heart told him was going to happen. Had the two of them really made such an arrangement? He recalled angrily how, for the duration of their relationship—such as it was—he had procrastinated and had been unable to make up his mind what to do. However, where his brash younger brother was concerned, it was just the blink of an eye between by his boldness as he was by the way he had managed to strut his youthful appearance and slender figure in front of him just a couple of minutes earlier. However, mixed in with the admiration he felt was a strong dose of self-contempt and defiance, with a bit of malice and anger thrown in as well. It was as though he were swimming in the eternity of the Creator but all the while lamenting the ephemerality of the created world itself.

After a while he put on his own fez and left the apartment. He decided to walk along al-Azhar Street as a way of calming his nerves. He kept to the sidewalk on the left-hand side and walked fast.

"Just forget about the root causes of this profound sorrow you're feeling," he muttered to himself sagely. "There's no need to keep it all stored in your consciousness. Simply heave it into the bottomless abyss of oblivion. If reading has not as yet guided you to wisdom, then learn a lesson from someone like Boss Nunu who's happy."

At which point Ahmad visualized Boss Nunu, with all his good health and merriment. Why, he asked himself with a deep sigh, was he trying to bear the burden of so much misery, like the bull that, as legend has it, carried the globe on its horn? How could he possibly be so abjectly incapable of finding any kind of happiness in life? Why didn't he go looking for people who are always laughing and consult them about the best ways to laugh and be happy? There was no point in going through life feeling this miserable and woebegone. Somehow he had to find a way to bring a little bit of joy into his broken heart.

He kept repeating these thoughts to himself until he reached Queen Farida Square. He got on a trolley that was packed, so he had to stand squashed between all the other standing passengers. He was naturally averse to crowds, so once again his anger mounted; it had only had the briefest of respites in any case. A strange and terrifying idea occurred to him: how would it be if the world could be devoid of human beings. He was not sure whether the idea came to him because he was on a packed trolley or whether there might be other reasons. It was not the first time, or so he imagined, that he had thought to himself how nice it might be if Cairo could be emptied as the result of a bombing raid. But then he felt ashamed to be contemplating such apocalyptic thoughts of terrible destruction, all because he had been adversely affected by a truly lovely young girl. Even so, he repeated to himself in disgust, "Isn't betrayal as vile as destruction?"

27

Rushdi Akif left the apartment unusually early without eating any breakfast; but, in any case, he was quite used to changing his habits and eating breakfast late. When he reached the New Road, he spotted the girl just in front of him; she was walking toward al-Darrasa on the way to the desert road leading to Abbasiya. He slowed down a bit so that there was a greater distance between them, then followed her. She was already aware that he would be following her—he had signaled as much to her via the window. That seemed to please her, although she managed for the most part to conceal most of her emotions behind a veil of coquetry and bashfulness. At times, however, her real feelings emerged in the form of a smile or attempts at suppressing a smile; and that was enough for him. In fact, Rushdi had very little time at his disposal, but, where he was concerned, time was like gold and diamonds. Ever since their first encounter on the roof—in fact, ever since he had first set eyes on her—he had been watching her closely, then following and flirting with her. This pursuit had involved a use of all his natural gifts—his youth, handsome appearance, sense of fun, and patience; so much so that she had come to regard him as a fixed part of the window.

From the outset he had had no doubts concerning his eventual triumph, nor for that matter had she. If that were not the case, then why did she keep appearing at the window as though on cue, submitting to his eager looks and responding so willingly to his smiles and gestures? If he had any lingering doubts on the matter, then the last smile she had given him had removed them completely and put an end to such concerns. However, she was not prepared simply to surrender without some pause for thought; she was a bit scared about the direction her heart was leading her. The image of the elder brother—Ahmad—kept coming back to her, and that made her feel rather ashamed and awkward. But then the fresh new face that had come into her life had made her all too aware of the faults in the elder brother. Why did Ahmad always look so scared, she wondered. Why did he behave like a mouse, scurrying back to its hole as soon as it hears the slightest noise? Why was he always so stiff and formal, never moving or doing anything? Actually, she was just as shy as he was, and that was why she needed someone brash and forward to appear on the scene and tackle her shyness straight on. He would never have been able to answer her needs, or perhaps she had only come to realize that when someone else had appeared who could really respond to them. And then there was the palpable difference between a young man full of vigor and someone already middle-aged and gradually wilting; handsome on the one hand, and tense and inscrutable on the other, the difference between a joyful happiness and a lonely misery. The truth is that she had fallen for Ahmad because he was a man and he was around, but it was Rushdi who had managed to find a place in her heart and stir her emotions. For that reason she had rewarded his patience with a radiant smile, a gesture that was to mark the beginning of a whole new story.

They both went up the road toward al-Darrasa, then turned off on the desert road. She was in front and he followed behind. It was a crisp, damp morning, a little chilly. A gentle breeze was blowing, bringing with it intimations of November, which mourns for the flower blossoms of lovers. The sky was full of bright clouds. Sometimes they were clustered together, but then they would break up and turn into frozen lakes that refracted the early morning rays of the sun from the horizon. The way their fringes sparkled in the sunlight was eye-catching. It was a scene to soothe the human heart, and yet there were two hearts that were completely lost in each other.

After the turn-off he quickened his pace and caught up with her. The girl could hear the sound of his footsteps as he drew closer, but did not look round. Even so, his steady approach did have its effect: she started blushing and, without even realizing it, her lovely, clear eyes formed themselves into a smile. Finally he was walking alongside her and almost touching her.

"Good morning," he said gently.

She tilted her head in his direction and glanced hesitantly at him. "Good morning," she replied in a soft voice.

As usual she was carrying her school bag under her arm.

"Would you let me carry that bag for you?" he asked with a smile.

"Oh no," she replied. "There's no need for that. It looks big, but it's not heavy. It's no problem for me to carry it myself."

"But, for two lovely delicate hands like yours," he said, "it must be a bit heavy!"

"No, it's not," she replied. "I can handle it quite well. Please don't spoil me!"

That made him laugh. "But surely it's wrong for me to have my hands empty while you're carrying that big bag."

She began to feel a bit flustered, but she decided to humor him. "What's wrong about it?" she asked. "I carry it myself every morning and evening."

"You're obviously scared I'm going to steal it."

"Oh, if only you really could! It contains all my nasty homework. Arithmetic is not even the worst."

That made him laugh again. "God curse the knowledge that gives you grief!"

She gave him an encouraging smile. "Are you really cursing knowledge just for my sake," she asked, "or does the hatred go back a while?"

"No, it's entirely for your sake," he replied, "although I have to admit that there's a certain amount of enmity from the past as well. What are your favorite subjects?"

"History and languages."

He was the complete opposite: his favorites were sciences and math. Even so he pretended to be delighted. "So we think the same way!" he exclaimed.

She was amazed at how happy he seemed. "Why should you be so overjoyed?" she asked.

"How can you possibly not know the answer to that question, my dear?" he replied with his habitual smoothness. "The fact that we share the same intellectual preferences can surely serve as a firm basis for a more spiritual agreement of the kind we're experiencing now!"

She blushed and turned away, something she usually did when her shyness got the better of her. She didn't respond.

"Don't you agree with me?" he asked her.

She remained silent, or, more accurately, silence retained its hold on her.

"So, am I to read into your silence the answer I'm hoping to hear?" he asked gently.

He looked at her and thought he saw the glimpse of a smile. Now his enthusiasm took over. "I knew the answer from your very first glance," he commented softly.

"The very first glance?" she could not avoid asking, with a clear sparkle in her eyes.

"Yes indeed!"

"Unbelievable!"

"Don't you believe in love at first sight?"

"Aren't you exaggerating? Are the things people say about love at first sight really true?"

His lovely honey-colored eyes sparkled as he replied, "No doubt about it!"

Now she changed her tone. "But we don't even know each other yet!" she said.

He realized that she was trying to find a way to escape from the gold collar he had put around her neck, but he was not about to let her get away.

"Don't change the subject. We're bound to know each other better before long; either that, or else it'll all come to an end, and my name will become a mere memory! But the one thing I want to tell you is that, if it's not love at first sight," (and he deliberately used the word "love" as though it was something spontaneous), "then it's not love at all."

Once again she remained silent.

"I don't mean," he went on, still smiling at her, "that love has to occur at first sight. What I'm saying is that the very first glance is enough to reveal that there are people with whom we share spiritual ties that may turn into real love. Don't they say that souls can talk to each other without invoking the senses at all? Through a single glance the soul can transcend all expectations. As for love, that is engendered by time and fostered by intimacy, it has to be regarded, more often than not, as a product of either habit, benefit, or other values that involve careful deliberation. What do you think?"

She hesitated for a moment, looking somewhat puzzled. "Are you saying," she asked, "that there can't be...," (she didn't mention the word "love") "unless it's at first sight?"

That made him realize that he had been prattling on for too long. He was afraid of what might happen if he had to explain what he meant. "No, no," he replied anxiously, "that's not it. What I meant was that the first glance may well be a good indicator of the goal toward which one's emotions may lead."

She gave a gentle laugh. "Your philosophy is tricky," she said. "It doesn't involve either history or languages!"

With that he dissolved into laughter. He was utterly delighted by her response and dearly wished that he could kiss that tiny mouth with its delectable nectar.

"Actually it's much simpler than either history or languages, because it's based on innate instincts. The clearest proof is that the two of us have met under its inspiration. God willing, we will never be parted."

By now they had gone about half way, and the City of the Dead was looming ahead to their left, shrouded in its eternal gloom and all-pervasive silence. She stared at the tombs with her honey-colored eyes.

"It's my lot," she said to hide the awkwardness she felt listening to his sweet talk, "to have to look at those tombs every morning. What a gloomy scene!"

The young man wondered why it was that she had to take such a long route in order to get to Abbasiya and then back again in the afternoon. Why didn't she take the trolley along Khalig Street? Then the truth hit him; he realized that she justified the exhaustion involved—or rather her father justified it for her—as a means of cutting down on expenses. Kamal Khalil Effendi was considered to be a minor civil servant, one of those people who strive with genuine determination—and in difficult circumstances—to lift their families up to a higher social level. Rushdi recalled that his own family had had to go through similarly hard times, especially his beloved brother who had steadfastly and patiently kept misfortune at bay. His whole heart blossomed with affection, love, and admiration.

"You won't have to look at the tombs after today," he said.

"How can that be?" she asked with a frown. "Am I supposed to walk blindfolded or something?"

"No. Our conversation will be enough to distract your attention!"

She gave a gentle laugh as a way of showing that she understood.

"It's a long walk," she said. "You won't be able to stand it for long, particularly since winter's on the way."

"We'll see about that."

They carried on walking, with only desert on the right and tombs on the left. They proceeded through the tombs toward the west. Rushdi pointed out a wooden tomb with a small courtyard, lying to the right, the third one in.

"That's our family tomb," he said.

The girl looked to where he was pointing and noticed the small tomb. "Then let's recite the Fatiha," she said.

They did so together.

"Here's where my ancestors lie," he said. "The most recent are my grandmother and grandfather on my father's side and my youngest brother."

"When did your brother die?" she asked.

"A while ago when we were still young."

With that they left the tombs and talk about them behind and returned to happier topics without even thinking about the glaring contrast between talk of love and tombs. For example, they did not spoil the mood by asking themselves how much remained of their lives on this earth or what would transpire in their lives before they too would be laid to rest in this tomb or another like it. None of that concerned them.

At this point she plucked up a bit of courage. "We don't even know each other yet," she said.

"Aren't we neighbors?"

"Yes, but I don't even know your name."

"Heaven forbid. It's Rushdi. Rushdi Akif."

"But you don't know my name either!"

"Oh yes I do!"

"Did you know that from the very first glance as well?"

Rushdi laughed and gave a nod.

"So what's my name?" she asked.

"Ihsan."

She laughed out loud. "Is that how you make up names?" she asked.

"No. That's your name!"

"No, sir, you're wrong. Maybe you were after someone else. So feel free to go back!"

"But I can distinctly remember my mother talking about yours on one occasion. She called her Umm Ihsan."

"So you thought Ihsan was me?"

"Yes...."

She laughed again, loud enough to make her face turn red. "That's my elder sister's name. She got married two years ago!"

Rushdi gave an awkward smile. "Forgive me," he said. "So what's your name?"

"Nawal."

"Long live beautiful names!"

She hesitated for a moment, then gave him a crafty look. "Are you at school?" she asked.

"Yes," he replied, "I'm a student at the Abbasiya School for Girls!"

"So you're a civil servant then?"

"With Bank Misr."

"And I'm an employee of the Ministry of Education!" she replied in turn.

They had a good laugh. They were now approaching Abbasiya, and Rushdi realized that his first encounter with his new love was about to come to an end.

"Okay," she said, "this is far enough. We must separate here."

They stopped walking. He took her hand and held it tenderly. "Good-bye until tomorrow morning," he said.

"Good-bye," she replied with a nod of her head.

She hurried away, while he stood where he was, watching her with unalloyed delight. "At first she was obviously shy," he told himself, "but then she opened up and became friendlier than a fragrant breeze. She is so pure and delicate; may God protect her from all evil demons, myself among them!"

Up until now his routine had involved flirting with a girl, then getting to know her, and finally loving her. But on this particular morning he found himself making his way back, listening as his heartbeats beat out the prelude to a love song on the silence of the road.

Meanwhile, Nawal kept walking down the street to her school, telling herself how kind, handsome, and sweet he was. If only dreams could come true, she told herself.

28

Ahmad had kept his eyes wide open and immediately noticed the change in his younger brother's demeanor. That Saturday afternoon Rushdi seemed drunk with happiness, so much so that he looked as though he were in a daze. Ahmad noticed that he changed his normal habit of taking a nap between noon and sunset—the time when he took off for al-Sakakini; instead he rested for just one hour, then woke up—eyelids drooping—combed his hair, put on some cologne, then made his way to his beloved window. His middle-aged brother, meanwhile, read in his room, or rather tried to read until the time came for him to go to the café—that being the new routine in his life. He was pinning all his hopes on the process of forgetting, waiting for it to happen just as a despairing patient anticipates the end. His heart was still being battered by feelings of love and failure, of disdain and jealousy. He loved his brother and hated him at the same time. His feelings fluctuated between the two without settling on either one, and the whole thing was almost making his head burst.

Toward evening Rushdi burst into his room. There was nothing unusual about that, and Ahmad smiled up at him, making a big effort not to look sad or melancholy. His young brother gave him a sweet smile and offered him a cigarette.

"Sorry to disturb you," he said apologetically but with obvious happiness. "But I've some really great news for you!"

"I hope it's good!" replied Ahmad, his heart pounding.

"A friend in the government service has told me that they're thinking of instituting some kind of restitution for overlooked workers."

"That's terrific news!" Ahmad responded with a relief that his brother was incapable of appreciating.

"It's a terrible miscarriage of justice for someone like you to spend twenty years in the eighth administrative grade."

Ahmad shrugged his shoulders. "You know full well that I'm not bothered about grades or government posts in general."

They chatted for a while, then Rushdi went out so as not to waste his brother's valuable time. After Rushdi had left, Ahmad started thinking about his feelings toward his brother, and the whole thing exasperated him. He felt utterly miserable. Was it possible to forget that he had loved his little brother from the cradle onward? Was it possible to deny that Rushdi loved him even more than he loved his own parents?

Just before sunset he hurried over to the Zahra Café, relieved to be out of the house. He spent a couple of hours with his friends there, using the conversation as a way of escaping his misery and his disturbing thoughts, then went back home. Rushdi, of course, was still out, spending his evening at the casino. This girl of his seemed to have purloined the time of day—from noon until sunset—when he would normally have been asleep, with the result that his entire day had turned into one continuous unit of wakefulness and exhaustion. Ahmad looked angrily at the window—which he had vowed never to open while he was at home. Would she have noticed that he wasn't by the window any more? he wondered as he changed his clothes. Would that bother her as much as it should? How he longed for her to be aware of the contempt he felt for the way she had deceived him! His sense of pride was still bleeding and a fiery anger was still blazing in his heart.

He went to bed earlier than usual in order to avoid reading. He was woken up by the air-raid siren. He got up quickly, put on his coat, left his room, and bumped into his parents in the lounge. His mother was in a panic because Rushdi had not returned from his night out; she kept wondering where he was and beseeching God to keep him safe. The weather outside was cold and damp.

"Things are always worse during winter," his father said.

They went to the shelter and took up their usual positions. His father looked at his watch and discovered that it was 2 a.m.

"It would be an act of mercy," he said in a sarcastic tone, "if Rushdi stayed outside. Then he wouldn't have to bother about coming home at this time of night!"

Ahmad decided he'd keep an eye out, but just then he spotted Rushdi hurrying down the shelter stairs and looking around for them. Once he found them, he came over with a smile; his lingering inebriation clearly fortified him enough to face up to their questions—especially those of his father. He greeted them all.

"We were in al-Gamaliya when the siren went off," he told Ahmad, "so I ran like the very devil in the dark."

His father rounded on him. "You're the devil incarnate, no doubt about it!" he said. "Can't you manage somehow to curb your rowdy behavior in such tense times as these?"

Ahmad could not bring himself to glance at his brother's face. Rushdi was not prepared to sit and listen to such talk, so he got up and started pacing around the shelter. Ahmad allowed his gaze to wander as well, and he looked over at the far corner where the family of Kamal Khalil was sitting. He spotted her sitting next to her mother and looking down at the floor; only the right side of her face was visible. He wondered whether she had noticed him. Did she still imagine he did not know about what she had done? Wasn't she suffering just a few pangs of anxiety and misery? Or was he the only person who was fated to suffer those feelings? At that precise moment, he remembered the apocalyptic desire that had occurred to him previously, the one about the air raid that would destroy everything. He shuddered at the thought and raised his eyes to the ceiling. "O God, be merciful, Most Merciful of all!"

Just then he spotted Kamal Khalil and Sayyid Arif standing close to the former's family chatting to his brother. Ahmad was utterly astonished. How on earth had his brother managed to make their acquaintance? When had that happened? Did Rushdi have a specific goal in mind? He was certainly self-confident and brash, traits that he, Ahmad, could not even conceive of imitating. At that moment his feelings toward Rushdi were a mixture of admiration and hatred, but he did not have the chance to reflect further on the matter because there was a huge explosion that deafened everyone. Soon afterward the sound of rapid anti-aircraft fire could be heard. Like a ravenous kite swooping down on a clutch of terrified chickens, a horrible feeling of panic hovered over their pounding hearts. There was only one explosion, but the anti-aircraft fire went on for some time. Then silence returned and everyone recovered their breath. A quarter of an hour later, the all-clear siren went off.

When Ahmad looked for his brother, he could not find him. People were leaving the shelter in groups. He had a feeling of déjà vu; searching for Kamal Khalil's family, he spotted them close by waiting for the crowd by the shelter door to thin out. But he didn't see Nawal with them. It all reminded him of that night when she had gestured to him to catch up with her but he had hesitated and been a coward. Rushdi however would never behave that way!

29

Life resumed its normal course. Even though Rushdi and Kamal Khalil had only known each other for a short while and they were so far apart in age, their friendship was soon on a firm footing, not least because Rushdi was so elegant and astute. Kamal invited Rushdi to the Zahra Café, and he came and sat down with his brother's friends—and his brother as well. His mild manner and bright expression both insured that he soon earned their admiration.

He liked this group of friends and decided to spend some time there once in a while. Soon afterward, Kamal Khalil invited him to visit his home. Rushdi was, of course, delighted to do so, and bonds of friendship soon developed. The elder man trusted Rushdi to such a degree that he even introduced him to his wife and daughter, thus lifting the veil separating Rushdi from Kamal's family life. For Rushdi the invitation came out of the blue. He had never expected anything like it from a family in the al-Husayn quarter, which was very conservative in its values. Actually, his own family was considered extremely conservative even though there were no daughters. Neither he, nor his brother—let alone their father—would even consider introducing a strange man to their mother. Even so, Rushdi was delighted by Kamal's gesture; it thrilled him to find himself trusted to such an extent. He now managed to portray himself as a serious thinker and put on a display of stolid conservatism. As a result, he found himself taking over Professor Ahmad Rashid's position as tutor to Nawal and Muhammad.

When Rushdi's brother heard about this turn of events, he was thunderstruck; he did not know how this had come to pass. It was as though Rushdi had become a member of their neighbor's family. In a single day he had somehow managed to train himself to achieve this kind of responsible position, one that Ahmad had not managed to achieve in twenty years! Once again Ahmad found himself staring at his brother with a blend of amazement and envy, but he managed to put on a show of complete ignorance about what was going on. He had already closed the window on his miseries, so now he would have to turn a blind eye to all this as well. He surrendered himself to patient endurance, with which he had long become inured.

From the outset their mother was fully aware of exactly what was going on. Rushdi was not one to hide secrets. Whenever he was at home, he would be by the window; when time came for tutorials, he would rush over to their neighbor's home. A passion had grabbed him by the heart; signs of it were visible in the way he paid unusual attention to his appearance, in the nostalgic tone in his singing, and in the fact that he went out so early in the morning—the real reason for which was no longer a secret from anyone.

In fact, the neighbor's family seemed to be just as aware of something to which he had long since become inured; they all seemed to have high hopes for a happy outcome. Sitt Dawlat, the boys' mother, was well aware of all of this. She questioned herself about it, but could not come up with any strong objections to the idea.

"How long, O Lord," she would sometimes mutter to herself sorrowfully, "How long must I wait until I can be like every other mother and celebrate my own sons being happily married?"

But did Nawal really deserve her son? Why not? She was pretty and educated, from a good family; her father was a civil servant. Everything seemed right. But one thing troubled her: could Rushdi get married before his elder brother? But what was she supposed to do? She would have to wait and see what transpired in the days ahead, all in accordance with the all-prudent will of God Almighty.

This time Rushdi had fallen victim to his own love game. What had started as a usual case of flirting had now turned into true love. He was feeling a genuine affection for Nawal. After all, she was his beloved neighbor at the window; companion on the morning road to the hills garlanded with fluffy clouds; infatuated student with whom he could exchange loving looks over the table while they did arithmetic, algebra, and geometry; and cinema companion every Friday morning. Love hovered over these two joyful hearts and joined them together in a craving for affection and felicity.

By now Rushdi's life had turned into a never-ending string of activities, one that preyed on his body and nerves. He was either focusing on his job at the bank, floating in a haze of passion, or carousing at the Ghamra Casino. He could only snatch a bit of sleep early in the morning. This new love of his had not managed to break his habits when it came to chronic gambling, indulgence in heavy drinking, or indeed in illicit sex. He told himself he was quite capable of handling such pleasures without any problems, and the plain fact that they had become habitual led him to forget entirely that they were actually major flaws in his character. Not for a single moment was he willing to forego his indulgence in all of them, nor did it occur to him that somehow his life might need to change. Money, booze, and love, those were the things he worshipped, although he may have had the occasional qualm over the amount of money and trouble this lifestyle managed to cause him.

"When I get married," he used to say by way of consolation, "I'll put a stop to it all!"

If he had been really honest with himself, he would have decided to forget about all this inappropriate frivolity in his life and to focus on marriage. However, what allowed him to make light of it all was that one day he managed to deposit the sum of fifty pounds in the bank—his profits from gambling. He told himself that if he could save enough of his salary for a whole year and add it to that amount, he would certainly have enough for his marriage expenses. But when would that year need to start?

It was this plan that he kept postponing, surrendering himself instead to the tyrannical demands of his own desires. He had yet to learn how to control his passions, impose limits on his desires, or curb his will. Eventually, however, he did begin to pause to contemplate his dilemma, with one eye on the debauched life he had been leading and another on the girl he desired.

3o

November went by, and the weather got a lot colder, the kind of cold rarely experienced in Cairo. Rushdi Akif got influenza, something he probably caught walking back to Khan al-Khalili very late at night. Ignoring all the symptoms, he just took a few aspirins whenever his headache was really bad. He kept up his normal activities, but the next day his condition worsened while he was working at the bank. First he shivered; then, teeth chattering, he started shuddering all over. He felt so weak that he had to close his eyes. Leaving the bank, he took a taxi home and stretched out on his bed feeling utterly exhausted.

The bank's doctor gave him a week off, but his condition worsened even more. His health collapsed incredibly quickly, and he lost a lot of weight; he looked like someone who had been ill for an entire month. Ahmad now realized that his younger brother no longer had the necessary resistance to disease that had allowed him to resist these attacks before.

"You're living in a dream world," he told his brother, unable to resist the desire to preach. "Your body can't cope any more with the strains you're putting on it."

Rushdi was used to listening to these kinds of comments from his elder brother. "It's just a cold," he replied with a wan smile. "I'll get over it."

"If you didn't abuse your health so much," Ahmad said angrily, "it wouldn't have been able to make you so ill!"

But nothing could deflect Rushdi from his usual behavior. "Haven't you noticed that I don't spend the entire evening on my own? All my friends are as fit and healthy as mules! It's just a cold. God willing, it'll go away!"

Ahmad was well aware that his brother would stubbornly defend his lifestyle, so he stopped making pointed comments. He was no stranger when it came to offering Rushdi advice and encouragement, but now the exasperation and displeasure he was feeling made him go even further. It was as though he were using an excessive display of affection and concern to conceal his own feelings of sorrow and shame.

"I still love him as much as ever," he kept telling himself, "and he deserves nothing else. Had he known how I felt about the girl, he would never have done what he did. He's entirely innocent. He loves me, and I do him."

But how could he ignore the anger and defiance boiling inside him? How could he forget the way he'd wished that his younger brother had never come back to Cairo? Indeed, how could he forget that for a single instant he'd actually wished that the world would be emptied of people, his brother among them of course? These thoughts and others like them made him feel miserable and plagued him with malicious ideas.

One night, when Rushdi's fever was particularly viru-
lent, Ahmad had a strange dream. He had only managed
to fall asleep after a good deal of agonized thought. In his
dream he saw himself sitting on his bed. He was looking
hopefully out of the window at Nawal's balcony, but,
before he knew it, there was Rushdi sitting on a chair
between him and the window, smiling a sweet smile. That
annoyed him, and he turned away from the window to
stare at his brother. Rushdi tried to distract his attention
by pretending that he had no idea what the problem was,
but he did not succeed. Then he watched as Rushdi gradually turned into a huge balloon; the shock he felt made him
forget completely about how angry he was. Such was his
surprise at what he was witnessing that he was unable to
suppress a loud cry. He watched his brother—shaped like
a huge balloon—slowly floating upward as though he were
about to head out of the window and high up into the sky.
However, the window blocked his ascent; he stayed there
stuck between the two sides of the window and blocking
out all the light. At first Ahmad was merely shocked, but
then he began to be afraid as well. His brother started
laughing sarcastically at him; that got on his nerves, and
he became very angry. It seemed to him that his brother
was playing deceitful games and scoffing at him. He
remonstrated with him, but his brother paid him absolutely no heed and kept on laughing. Ahmad went over to
his desk, brought back his pen, and stabbed it into his
brother's stomach until it snapped. A cloud of smoke now
appeared, filling the entire room with dust. His brother's
body started deflating slowly until it was back to its normal
size, at which point he collapsed at Ahmad's feet. Twisting

in sheer agony, he started chewing the chair legs, screaming and coughing until his eyes bulged and blood came
streaming out of his eyeballs. Ahmad started to panic and
was overwhelmed by a fearsome terror, at which point he
woke up and realized that he had been dreaming. Good
heavens, a pox on all dreams!

No sooner had he recovered from the dream-induced
terror than he heard a groan from beyond the closed door
of his room. He listened and realized that it was his brother
making the noise; he was groaning and grunting. He leapt
out of bed, put on his slippers and went quickly to his
brother's room. He found Rushdi in bed moaning and his
mother beside him rubbing his back, while his father sat
close to the bed.

"What's the matter?" Ahmad asked.

"Don't worry, son," his mother said. "It's just the pain
of the fever breaking."

Rushdi realized that Ahmad had come in.

"I'm so sorry," he said stifling his groans for a moment.
"I've kept you all awake."

They all gave him encouragement and prayed for him.
Ahmad sat down beside his mother, took his brother's
hand, and started stroking it tenderly, as though he felt the
need to compensate for the angry feelings he had expressed
during his dream. An hour of agony went by, with the
family feeling as much pain as the sick young man. They
all stayed by his bed until dawn.

31

Rushdi recovered and left his bed. It had not been easy for him to stay there for a whole week, particularly since he was the kind of person whose only delight in life involved games, nightlife, and pleasures. For that reason he balked when his brother suggested that he should stay at home and get some rest so he could recoup his energy.

"It's bad enough that I've wasted a week already," he chuckled apologetically.

Ahmad who had devoted most of his adult life to his brother got angry. "I think it's a very bad idea to plunge straight back into the kind of life you've been leading. You keep squandering your youth away as though it's an inexhaustible resource. You never get enough rest. What kind of insanity is this?"

Rushdi detected in his brother's tone of voice a note of jealousy because he, Rushdi, was always so healthy.

"You're a wonderful big brother!" he said with a beatific smile on his face. "May God grant me always to have the benefit of your large heart."

"It's all for your own good!"

"Do you think I have the slightest doubt about that?" the loving, grateful younger brother asked.

Even though Rushdi did indeed have no doubts about his brother's affections, he still ignored his advice. Next morning, Ahmad watched as Rushdi resumed his early morning departure. He was astonished.

"What on earth are you doing?" he asked.

"Going to the bank," Rushdi replied somewhat nonplussed.

"What's the rush?"

Rushdi decided to be brutally honest with his brother. "My dear brother," he said, "this house makes me sick!"

Ahmad was well aware of what was actually making him play fast and loose with his health. He was very distressed to hear what his brother had said, but hid his feelings by staring at his cup of coffee. Rushdi left. Their mother was sitting at the table as well, and she did her best to soften the blow caused by Rushdi's unwillingness to follow his brother's advice.

"Your brother's cure is in the outside world, Ahmad," she said as a way of apologizing for Rushdi's behavior, "not inside the house. Don't blame him too much."

When Ahmad did not say anything, she assumed that he was still angry. "Isn't he his mother's son?" she asked with a smile. "Anyone like his mother can't do too much that's wrong. Don't you notice how restless I get if I have to stick around the house and don't get the chance to visit my friends? Both of us hate staying inside."

She chuckled with laughter, while he mustered a wan smile. It was obvious that nothing on earth was going to dissuade Rushdi from resuming the lifestyle he loved so much, so now once again he was about to throw himself into the quagmire of love-making, gambling, drinking, smoking, and women. He had recovered much of his usual energy, but his health had not recovered along with it. He was still very skinny, and his complexion was turning paler and paler, almost as though his illness had never actually left him.

Ahmad spent a good deal of time offering his younger brother advice, but the latter had his mind on other things. One afternoon Rushdi came into his brother's room—just before he was to go out to meet his friends at the Zahra Café. Rushdi gave his brother a sweet smile.

"Can I talk to you for a bit?" he asked.

Ahmad looked up. "Of course, Rushdi. Go ahead."

As Ahmad looked at his brother's handsome, pale face, he could see that he looked unusually serious. That surprised him somewhat. He wondered what had made the perennial playboy turn so serious. He recalled that the only times he had seen his brother look this way were on those few tense occasions when he had heard that he had failed in some of his school exams. Ahmad was a bit worried and raised his eyebrows inquisitively.

Rushdi sat down on the chair. "I need to talk to you seriously," he said. "Life is not all fun and games."

If the entire topic were not one that touched a raw nerve for Ahmad, he would have burst out laughing. Instead he tensed, guessing with a degree of panic what topic his brother was about to broach.

"You're absolutely right," he said quietly, "life is not all fun and games."

"When I need advice," Rushdi said, "you're the one I turn to. I've come to see if you agree to the idea of my getting married."

His heart leapt as though what he had just heard was a complete surprise, something that had not even occurred to him. Even so, he was unwilling to show any sign of distress and put on a show of innocent surprise, indeed of happiness at the idea. "So at last you've come to talk about marriage," he replied. "I'm utterly thrilled!"

"That's right, brother," Rushdi told him excitedly. "Does that make you happy?"

"Of course it does. This may be the very first time we're both happy about something!"

There now followed a moment of silence. Ahmad realized that the natural thing was to ask about the bride-to-be, but he was hoping that his brother would open the subject without him having to ask the question. Rushdi said nothing, however, so Ahmad saw no alternative but to swallow hard and ask. "So have you chosen a nice girl?"

Rushdi sat up straight. "Oh yes, Ahmad!" he replied. "She's the daughter of our dear neighbor, Kamal Khalil Effendi, your friend and mine."

All the advance planning he had done in order to ward off the impact of this announcement only helped a little. The mere hope of avoiding the penalty was of no use when the actual sentence was pronounced. But he fell back on his self-esteem and proceeded calmly.

"May God grant you success in pursuing your happiness."

"Thank you so much, dear brother!"

"Even so I need to ask you a question, just as a precaution.

Have you learned everything you need to know about the family of which you're proposing to become a part?"

"I've gotten to know the family from close up. Not only that, but I know the girl personally."

That admission reopened his own wound, so he doubled his efforts at keeping calm and collected. "I'd simply remind you," he said, "that, if word of this gets out, then any decision to back out will turn into a real scandal."

"My fickle days are over. I've made up my mind."

"Have you spoken to anyone else about this?"

"No, except the girl herself, of course."

Again his heart leapt, and his imagination started forming a picture of the two of them alone together, talking about this wonderful, yet risky move. But he immediately squelched the image. "With God's blessings then...," he said in as happy a tone as he could muster.

"Can I ask you to raise the topic with our father? Once that's done, we can take the next steps."

Ahmad paused for a moment. "Yes, I'll let our father know," he said. "As far as next steps are concerned,..."

"I'll do anything necessary."

"We won't set things rolling until you have fully recovered your health and at least regained the weight you lost when you were ill."

"That's easy to do!" responded Rushdi with a laugh. "We won't have long to wait." He stood up to leave. "Thank you for everything, and I wish you likewise."

Rushdi changed his tone of voice, as though he had just remembered something. "By the way," he went on, "why don't you think of getting married too? Isn't it proper for me to congratulate you before you congratulate me?"

Should he now explain to his brother the decision he had come to about marriage? Ahmad wondered. Rushdi had no idea what he was saying; for that reason he was blissfully unaware of the fact that he was aiming poisoned darts at his elder brother. The mere question aggravated him; the long tongue of fate, it seemed, was mocking his misery even though he thought he had finally rid himself of it.

"Oh," Ahmad said derisively, "the time for me to marry is long past."

"Past?"

"Forget about it, Rushdi. You know how busy I always am. God only gives a man one heart."

Rushdi left the room, shaking his head sadly. Ahmad looked at the floor, his expression a reflection of profound sadness and resignation to fate and despair. Now it was his task to arrange Rushdi's marriage; in a sense he would be weaving his own shroud. The process would inevitably be painful, but at the same time there would be certain elements of pleasure and consolation. At least he would be able to feel that obscure pleasure that pain can bring, like a moth flitting around a lamp. There would be the additional pleasure of surrendering to the dictates of all-powerful fate and reflecting on those hidden feelings that kept disturbing him. Last but not least, there would be the pleasure of indulging his wounded self-esteem.

32

Ahmad got dressed and made his way to the Zahra Café; he had managed to rid himself of the regret he normally felt when he abandoned his lonely ways. He started participating in the conversation more than he had before—if only with Ahmad Rashid—and allowed himself to laugh more than he ever had. It suddenly occurred to him that he could join their other evening session, the one he had heard about before but never actually attended. The idea attracted him, and he really wanted to do it. However, he was his usual diffident self and had no idea how to broach the subject. It was still on his mind when everyone stood up to leave.

Boss Nunu usually went home first, then caught up with his friends at their other meeting place, so Ahmad left the café in his company. While they were walking, he managed to pluck up the necessary courage.

"Boss," he asked shyly, "would you allow me to join you with the rest of the group?"

"Of course! May God continue to guide you well!"

"But I have to tell you," Ahmad went on, "that on this particular subject I am dumber than the proverbial donkey."

"Allow me to be your guide," Boss Nunu responded boastfully. "In any case, it's a lot easier than all those books of yours and produces much better results."

They continued to walk along narrow winding alleyways enveloped in total darkness. Entering a building, they climbed the stairs to the third floor. Boss Nunu pressed the button for the bell.

"If you're on your own and want to get in," he said, "you need to press the bell five times in a row. Then remember the password that I'm going to say now."

They heard Abbas Shifa's voice asking who it was.

"God damn the world!"

The door opened, and Ahmad went in feeling not a little bashful, followed by Boss Nunu. They crossed the hallway to a large room where a large group of people were seated. A soft blue light, like the delicate hues of dawn, enveloped the room, coming from a lamp covered with a blue cloth. All eyes were focused on the new arrivals, especially the newcomer. Ahmad felt so embarrassed that he almost tripped. They were all seated on cushions strewn in the form of a circle. In the middle was all the necessary equipment: the brazier, water pipe, and tobacco.

The two of them greeted everyone else and then sat down next to each other. Ahmad was now able to take a good look around him and noticed that all his friends from the Zahra Café—except for Ahmad Rashid—were there. His attention was drawn to the center of the assembly where a striking woman was seated on a huge cushion of her own. She was striking indeed. Even when seated she was as tall as someone else standing up. She was broad-shouldered and long-necked, with a full, round face and clear features. Her complexion was somewhere between Egyptian and Ethiopian. Her hair was curly and chestnut-colored, tied up in a short, thick ponytail. The most amazing thing about her appearance was her huge eyes: prominent without making her look ugly, they had a gleam to them and could stare through anyone. Her size and strength were enough to inspire awe, while the animal magnetism in her gestures and the allure of her sensuality were clearly sufficient to arouse desires. She was wearing a striped shawl over her shoulders.

She started staring hard at Ahmad with her flashing eyes, and he realized at once that she must be Aliyat al-Faiza whom they all called "husband lover." Her husband, Abbas Shifa, was sitting on her right and Boss Zifta, the café owner, was on her left. Boss Nunu introduced Ahmad to her, and she held out her henna-decorated hand and greeted him kindly. Boss Zifta gave him a look of reproof.

"So," he scoffed, "at long last you've come to realize that God exists! How many years have you spent buried away in that room of yours? Why have you tortured yourself that way? You're not married, but you're not an old man yet either. How can anyone do that to himself?"

Boss Nunu was anxious to give his friend a break and make excuses for Ahmad's behavior. "My friends," he said, "my instincts never fail me, and my ever-watchful eye is always on the lookout. From the very first moment I saw him, I realized that our good friend, Ahmad Akif Effendi, was a child of chance, but that, for a while at least, circumstances had decreed that he would go off track, and I would have to be the one to guide him back to the true way, God willing."

Kamal Khalil was also worried that these jokes would annoy Ahmad, since a combination of new factors had contrived to make Ahmad someone important to him. "Dear friends," he said, "our learned friend, Ahmad Akif, likes to read a lot, but there's nothing wrong with him trying to get a bit of pleasure out of life. After all, it can't be all hardship and nothing else!"

Boss Zifta waved his hand in exasperation. "Why on earth do we voluntarily subject ourselves to hardship, whether it's ongoing or not?" he asked. "Ahmad's a ranking civil servant. If you'll excuse me for saying so, why on earth does he have to keep studying as though he were still a schoolboy? So, Ahmad, promise us that, after tonight, you will never miss this gathering of ours!"

Ahmad gave a tentative smile, and his diffidence only increased when Aliyat al-Faiza responded to Boss Zifta.

"Take it easy, Boss!" she said, looking straight at Ahmad. "How can he possibly make such a pledge when he may not find our little gathering to his liking?"

Ahmad blushed. "Forgive me, Hanem," he said as quickly as he could.

The others all usually referred to her as "Sitt" so, when Ahmad used "Hanem" with her, it sounded strange.

"You're always welcome here!" she replied.

Abbas Shifa was busy preparing the wads of tobacco, arranging the coals, putting them on the water pipe, and then offering it to his wife. Ahmad kept eying the water pipe nervously. He leaned over to Boss Nunu.

"Shouldn't I be a bit worried about taking the water pipe?" he whispered in his ear.

"If someone like you is scared of it," the Boss chided him in a low voice, "what are our children supposed to do?"

Abbas Shifa was sitting in the middle of the circle and started handing the water pipe round from one person to the next. It came ever closer and reached Boss Nunu. Putting the pipe to his mouth, he inhaled deeply, causing the bubbles to make a loud noise and exhaling dark smoke from his nostrils. Finally, Ahmad saw the pipe reach his own lips, with everyone's eyes on him. He wrapped his lips around it and took a short puff as though he were really scared.

"Inhale harder...harder," Boss Nunu shouted at him. "Swallow the smoke."

So he swallowed the smoke, then blew it out quickly, feeling as if a hand was stopping his breathing. He started coughing so hard that it wracked his entire body and made his eyes tear. Boss Nunu was watching him anxiously.

"How are you feeling?" he asked.

"I should only take small puffs to start with," he said with a sigh. "You're a really tough teacher, Boss!"

"Just as you wish," Boss Nunu replied with a laugh. "It's best to take things slowly."

Abbas Shifa sent the water pipe round five times in a row; the smoke rose everywhere and formed into clouds. Ahmad smelled a strange scent, one that took him back to olden times, a scent very similar to this one—in fact, it was the very same scent. Where and when had he smelled it, he wondered. He did not have to wrack his brains for long. It had been the first night in Khan al-Khalili. This strange smell had wafted up to his room and worried him so much that he could not get back to sleep. It had been nothing other than the smell of this incredible, frightening narcotic. Maybe it had come to ease his transition to the new room and to the remarkable quarter to which he had moved, one where it was quite likely that every breath inhaled was like the one he had just taken. He was utterly delighted to have remembered that earlier moment, not least because by now the drug had started to work its magic on his nerves and calm them down. He even managed a smile.

Abbas Shifa went back to his seat to rest a little, while Boss Zifta started loading up the tobacco in preparation for the second round.

All of a sudden Aliyat al-Faiza spoke up. "Have you all congratulated Sayyid Arif Effendi?" she asked.

Everyone looked at her.

"I hope it's good news," Boss Nunu said.

"A really clever doctor's told him about some new pills," she said with a smile. "He said they're bound to work."

Everyone there—the friends from the café and the others—had a good laugh.

Boss Nunu turned to Sayyid Arif. "With all my heart," he said, "I hope that one day I'll see you acting just like us."

"That shows just how bad your intentions are!" Sayyid Arif replied somewhat exasperated.

They all asked him about the new pills, but he refused to say anything about them in case of complications.

"Actions always reveal intentions," Boss Nunu said.

Whatever the occasion, he was always inserting aphorisms, proverbs, and Prophetic sayings into his conversations, whether relevant or not, without being the slightest bit aware of the total inappropriateness of what he was saying to the matter at hand. Even so, only a few of those present ever noticed this trait of his.

Sulayman Bey Ata could not stand the noise, and his ugly face assumed an expression of sheer misery.

"Quiet, quiet!" he yelled angrily as was his wont when he disliked something. "This special gathering of ours has its own protocols, you know!"

"So what are they?"

"This amount of noise," the monkey replied angrily, "is the kind of thing you encounter in a bar where people are blowing their minds on drink. A hashish circle like ours is the exact opposite; it should be peaceful and quiet. Hashish is a sultan that demands humility and silence from his subjects. It is that silence and peace that allows the drug to best achieve its effects. Your entire disposition is purified and your imagination becomes crowded with a host of dreams. Humanity can thus overcome all its daily problems and difficulties. As you can ponder them without hindrance, they are all solved one after the other."

"But we all come here to get away from problems and difficulties, not to ponder them!"

"Bad idea! Running away from problems doesn't make them go away. All that happens is that you forget how bad they are. When they return, they're worse than before. The wisdom provided by hashish gives us a confidence that can confront all those difficulties with a will strong enough to treat them as mere trivialities. That way, they are swilled down memory's drain and erased from existence."

"This isn't a hashish session we're involved in," commented Sayyid Arif with a laugh, "it's a confession!"

Boss Zifta agreed. "True enough," he said, "this is priestly hashish talk! Whoever said, 'Goha, count your sheep!' spoke the truth."

Boss Nunu was not happy with the way the conversation was going. He looked over at Sulayman Bey. "How can anyone with no worries stay silent?" he asked.

"How can anyone have no worries, unless they're an animal?"

"How can you be sure they don't?!"

At this point, Sayyid Arif chimed in with, "Maybe he's a heron!"

Abbas Shifa, his hair all bedraggled and looking like the devil himself, stood up and started the water pipe on its second round. The sound of the bubbles drowned out the conversation. This time Ahmad took deeper puffs, relying on a devil-may-care attitude he had never felt before and a deep-seated desire to forget his troubles. Even though he hated Sulayman Bey Ata, in this particular case he admired his philosophy. He dearly wanted to be rid of his own profound sorrow; that was what had brought him to this stifling assembly—the hope of finding release. Now the drugs were taking control; his eyelids drooped, his eyes turned bloodshot, and his neck slumped a little. Just then he had a terrible thought and leaned over to Boss Nunu.

"Shouldn't we be worried about the police?" he asked. "What happens if one of them comes to the door and yells, 'God damn the world'?"

Boss Nunu laughed. "We reply, 'And God damn your own father!'"

Once the second round was over, Abbas Shifa sat down beside his stunning wife. Tongues started wagging again.

Boss Zifta the café owner kept at it. "I've good news for you all," he said. "Once Hitler has managed to conquer Egypt, God willing, he's going to annul the ban on hashish. Instead he'll ban drinking English whisky!"

"Hitler's a wise man," said Boss Nunu. "I've not the slightest doubt that hashish is the reason why his strategy is so clever to begin with!"

"How can we put him in touch with Abbas Shifa?" asked Kamal Khalil Effendi.

"He has no need of Abbas von Shifa," Boss Nunu replied in a serious tone. "Bunker 13 is chock full of the purest hashish."

The Boss shook his head sadly. "Haven't you all heard," he asked, "that the Japanese are distributing drugs to the peoples they conquer?"

Boss Zifta reacted in the same tone. "If only the English were hashish addicts!"

"Fifty years of British occupation wasted!"

At this point Sayyid Arif stood up suddenly, signs of extreme worry written all over his face. He put on his fez as though making ready to leave. Everyone was astonished.

"Where are you off to, brother?" Aliyat inquired.

He hurried around the edge of the group and sped toward the door. "The pills have worked," he said as he made his exit.

In a flash he was gone. Everyone burst out laughing.

"Can that be true?" Kamal Khalil asked through a hacking cough.

"False propaganda," Sulayman Ata interjected sarcastically, "just like that of his German friends."

"We'll know the answer in nine months!" said Boss Nunu.

"All in good time!" Aliyat chimed in.

They kept up their banter until Abbas Shifa stood up yet again, holding the water pipe. This was the cue for everyone to stop talking. This time round, Ahmad was in a drugged stupor. He said not a word, feeling unwilling or even unable to talk. He had the feeling that he had lost all control of his limbs. He tried to move his arms to convince himself that he was still in control, but a strange, yet powerful feeling persuaded him not to bother and suggested strongly that there really was nothing in the world that warranted any effort or movement. Slumber, submission, and contentment, they were the best things life had to offer. Through the clouds of smoke he could make out the other people; they all looked like specters from some strange world or inhabitants of another planet. He had no idea where this strange sensation was coming from, but he decided to laugh—a long, elongated chortle whose opening measures sounded like a sigh, while the coda resembled the bubbling of a water pipe. The others could not help laughing too. Even though he was completely stoned, he was aware that they were laughing and sat up in his seat so he could claim to be still awake—to the extent possible.

Now something remarkable happened. Aliyat stood up, and her incredible, sleek body extended itself upward and outward, offering an eyeful to all those present. Her dress was extremely tight fitting and clearly revealed her gorgeous figure. Her magnificent procession now moved off, with her holding on to the edge of her shawl and thus revealing her arm shrouded in gold bracelets. As she passed by in front of Ahmad, he was shaken awake and saw a robe that parted at the hips to envelop a pair of buttocks the like of which he had never seen before: plump, fleshy, and quivering, placed atop thighs that were as finely crafted as the very best woodwork. He could hardly believe his eyes. Boss Nunu noticed how amazed he was.

"Watch out!" he said. "She's letting you in on a secret that has been the downfall of the quarter's husbands. That's not just a pair of buttocks. That's a treasure!"

"It's almost inconceivable!" Ahmad commented almost inaudibly.

"And, as if that were not enough, they manage to combine two entirely separate qualities: from one point of view, they're as firm as an inflated ball; from another, they're so soft that your fingers can glide over them!"

"That's one of life's great mysteries!"

"We ask God to keep us safe!"

"Amen," replied Ahmad without even thinking.

Abbas Shifa was looking at them. "So what are you two talking about?" he asked Boss Nunu, faking annoyance.

"We've plans for the most expensive furniture in the house!" replied the Boss with his usual raucous laugh.

They stopped talking so they could listen to Boss Zifta who was chatting on the other side of the circle and apparently offering advice to some of the newcomers.

"There are three things you should do your best to acquire in quantity: gold, copper, and Persian rugs. They retain their value, so you can sell them when things get rough and make full use of them when it comes to preparing for your daughters' weddings...."

A man in a turban named Boss Shimbaki reacted negatively. "Oh, a curse on all daughters, wives, and mothers!"

Abbas Shifa pointed at the speaker. "Are you all aware," he asked, "that Boss Shimbaki's wife left him in a huff?"

Everyone voiced their regrets. At this point Aliyat came back, just in time to hear the last comment.

"Why did that happen, Boss?" she asked. "I do hope it wasn't my fault...."

"Oh no," Shimbaki replied. "It's my son Sinqur's marriage that's the trouble. I wanted a quiet, modest affair to be in line with the times, but she's insisting on singing girls and the whole routine. 'How come,' she asked me insolently, 'your money's forbidden for me and my children here but is permitted to you over there?'"

"And 'over there' means my place!" Aliyat commented with a guffaw.

Shimbaki went on in an angry, yet regretful tone. "Here's what she said to me as she left, clutching her bag of clothes: 'I'm going to remember you as a man who's never given me a single day's happiness!' Listen, for heaven's sake. Is that anything for a companion of thirty years to utter?"

"Curse her!" said Aliyat in a bitter, censorious tone. "Too bad you wasted the best days of your life on her. Listen to me, Boss. Show her the way things really are by marrying someone else!"

The man gave a nod, as something resembling a smile crossed his lips. "Is there enough of life left?" he muttered.

"Heaven forbid, Boss," she replied immediately. "You're still in the prime of life!"

Now Boss Nunu was warming to the idea. "People who claim that nothing trains a woman better than having her husband marry another wife have it right! Our Lord instructed us to marry four of them."

"God forbid! God never ordained any such thing. What He did do was to make it legal as long as all four are treated equally."

"Any other constraints to share with us?"

"Bless the Prophet! I'm an old man. Nothing's to be gained from this kind of talk."

"You should get married, using those new pills Sayyid Arif is taking as a blessing!"

At this point Boss Zifta resumed the conversation he had been having before Boss Shimbaki interrupted with his family problems.

"You should try buying Persian rugs in particular. Gold can go down in price, and so can copper. But the value of Persian rugs always increases over time. An old woman isn't worth a solitary penny, but a rug...."

Aliyat slapped him on the chest.

"Oh God," he yelled, "the only molar I have left just fell out...."

"Listen, you crazy pot-head," she told him, "we're talking about marriage. What are you going on about rugs for?"

"Don't get mad. Patience is the gateway to solutions. As long as you're determined to get Boss Shimbaki married off again, I'm going to tell him a joke that'll make him want to do it."

With that he turned toward Shimbaki.

"A shaykh came home after a long evening out," he went on, "and saw his wife asleep on the bed. She'd been bragging to him about how beautiful she still was, to such an extent that he felt harassed. Passing by her on his way to bed, he muttered, 'The siren's asleep!' when suddenly, she grabbed the edge of her nightgown, saying. 'And God curse whoever woke her up!' "

Ahmad felt as though he were suffocating. He could not stand the atmosphere in the room any longer. His patience had worn thin, so he staggered to his feet. Everyone stared at him.

"Where are you going?" Boss Nunu asked.

"I've had enough," he replied almost inaudibly.

"This is just the end of the beginning! We still have time ahead of us for punning, singing, and real intoxication."

But Ahmad insisted on taking his leave, and he did so with slow and heavy steps.

"Have the pills worked for you as well?" Boss Zifta joked as he left.

He left the apartment, clasped the banister, and went slowly, very slowly, down the stairs until he saw the steps leading to the street. Once on the street, he staggered his way home to his room. It was the riskiest journey he had ever taken in his entire life, the time being almost two o'clock in the morning. He undressed wearily, turned out the light, and fell onto his bed. He did not fall asleep as quickly as he expected. He realized that, while his eyes might be closed, he was still wide awake in a peculiar and alarming way and his heart was thumping fast, almost as though to lift the covers off the bed and throw them down.

Images kept crowding his imagination, then dissolving and vanishing. Only one image lingered, that incredible woman. Did he want to have sex with her just as much as did all the others? But slowly now...what would he do with her? If she embraced him, he would feel small and puny, like a flea in an elephant's armpit. No, she was no real woman, but rather a symbol of the world of steaming passions, on which shore his feet had sunk and on whose horizon his eyes had gazed. His heartbeat doubled and his throat felt dry, and he imagined himself falling from a great height into a bottomless abyss. Terrified, he sat up in bed. Fear and despair gripped him and for what remained of the night until daybreak he endured incredible pain, both physical and psychological.

33

Ahmad made up his mind not to repeat this adventure. Boss Nunu did his best to reassure him and convince him his reactions that night were due to the fact that he hadn't eaten something sweet directly after smoking hashish. Ahmad refused to accept these explanations, tempting though they were.

"It's very clear," he told himself in his normal tone of self-pity, "that the intellectual mind is simply not equipped to enjoy these types of pleasure."

Even so, he told himself that he would not need these drugs in order to forget his miseries. If his younger brother married to the girl fairly soon, he would be free to forget. However, the problem was that Rushdi continued his reckless ways and refused to put an end to his irresponsible behavior. He had not even fully recovered his health; in fact, it had deteriorated. No one could ignore any more how thin he looked, added to which was the fact that his paleness had now turned a sickly yellow color. He began to cough violently and lost his appetite. Ahmad was horrified by his condition.

"It sounds to me," he told his brother in a tone that brooked no argument, "as though the way you're neglecting your health has put a monkey wrench into your hopes and plans. Why don't you straighten out so you can get your health back? That's why you haven't recovered from your first illness, and now you've got this violent cough. From now on, you should give up going out regularly at night and drinking. What on earth are you doing to yourself?"

For a change Rushdi did not object since the coughing fits were already weighing him down. "Okay," he said, "I agree."

"You'll need to get well, Rushdi," said his brother who was used to self-torture, "before you can fulfill your promise to Nawal's family."

The sick young man now started to display some genuine resolve. He stopped going to the Ghamra Casino and only left the house in the afternoon in order to give his private lessons to his two pupils, that being an obligation that was dear to his heart and a source of much pleasure. For the first time since he had left his childhood behind, he made a point of going to bed at ten o'clock, something that aroused in Ahmad a sense of total amazement at the magical workings of love. However, Rushdi refused to give up his morning walk out to the hills even though it exposed him to bone-chilling cold; after all, it, too, was something dear to his heart and nourishment for his fondest dreams. For several days he endured this utterly respectable way of life, but there were no signs of any improvement in his state of health; in fact, the cough went down into his larynx, and his voice turned hoarse. As a result he could no longer sing his favorite songs.

The celebration of the Eid al-Adha was about to happen, and, as usual, the family was busy making preparations. The sacrificial sheep was brought in, and, since there was nowhere else to put it, they tied it to the kitchen window by the neck. Sitt Dawlat, the mother of the family, busied herself making the bread loaves. As usual Ahmad had complained about the rise in the cost of a sheep and suggested that they might well not be able to afford one next year, a thought that appalled his mother.

"I spit on the very notion!" she laughed. "Don't even mention such dire thoughts."

The feast arrived during the very first days of January 1942. The family, indeed the whole neighborhood, gave the occasion a joyful welcome. The table was piled high with meats of various types and sizes. What was amazing was that Rushdi stuck to his new regime even for the feast; truth to tell, he would not have had the strength to match his desires even if he had wished to do so. Ahmad spent most of the holiday at the Zahra Café, but he did not succumb to the temptations that Boss Nunu put in his way, namely cajoling him bit by bit into paying a return visit to Aliyat al-Faiza's house. How could he ever forget the way that hellish night had ended?

The fourth morning of the feast came, and something happened that Ahmad would never forget. He had woken up at eight-thirty and made his way to the bathroom as usual. There he found Rushdi bent over the sink, coughing so violently that his entire skinny body was shaking. Ahmad moved forward and stood beside him. As he stretched out his hand to clasp his brother's shoulder, he happened to look down into the sink. There was a red smudge! His hand froze where it was, and his heart leapt violently.

"O my God!" he exclaimed, his voice quavering.

He stared at his brother in a panic. Rushdi had stopped coughing, but he still seemed in a daze; his chest was moving up and down, he had trouble breathing, and his eyes were red.

Ahmad waited until his brother had recovered his breath somewhat.

"What's that, Rushdi?" he asked, pointing at the red smudge in the sink.

Rushdi gave him a desolate look. "It's blood," he replied in his hoarse voice.

"O my God!"

Rushdi looked utterly depressed. Totally losing control, he burst into tears. "I'm ill," he said in a barely audible voice, "and now it's all over!"

"Don't say such a thing!" replied Ahmad pleadingly.

"That's the bitter truth, brother," Rushdi said despondently.

Ahmad turned on the faucet to wash away the blood, grabbed his brother by the arm, and took him back to his—that is, Rushdi's—room. He went over to the window and shut it. Rushdi sat down on the bed, and his brother brought over a chair and sat directly facing him.

"What can you tell me, Rushdi?" he asked, swallowing hard. "Tell me the absolute truth!"

"Finally I went to see the doctor," he replied softly. "He told me that I have incipient tuberculosis in my left lung!"

34

The truth of the matter was that, even since the middle of December, Rushdi had been feeling a pain that boded ill. One day at the bank he had had a terrible fit of coughing. He had taken out his handkerchief in order to spit into it, and had been terrified to see that it was bloody. The whole thing had sent him into a panic, and he had hurriedly put the handkerchief into his pocket in case anyone else found out. Leaving the bank, he had gone to a specialist on chest diseases. He had sat in the waiting room, absolutely terrified, staring at all the wan faces with their thin bodies hacking away. Had he fallen victim to that dire disease, the very mention of which made anyone shiver in fear? He had heard a friend of his once say that tuberculosis was a disease with no cure, and his heart pounded as he recalled the occasion. He had never had any serious illness before, and it worried him that this fatal disease might be the first really bad experience he would have. His panic only intensified as he sat there waiting to go into the consulting room, but he was patient until his turn came.

As he went in, he was making a mighty effort to control his terror. He took a quick look around at all the equipment and machinery and lastly at the doctor himself, who was leaning over a small sink washing his hands. He stood there waiting, while the doctor dried his hands and then turned toward him. He was short and thin, and fine featured; his head, however, was large and bald. His eyes bulged, and he had a sharp stare. Rushdi greeted him by raising his hand to his head.

"Welcome," said the doctor in a loud voice, "please be seated."

Rushdi sat down on a large chair. The doctor walked round to his neat desk and sat down behind it. He took out a large notebook, opened it, and started asking questions: Rushdi's name, profession, and age. Rushdi responded to all of them and then gave the doctor a traditional, inquiring look.

"I need you to check my chest," he said.

No sooner had he said this than he had a violent coughing fit. The doctor waited until he had stopped and could breathe properly again.

"Have you had a cold?" he asked. "When?"

"I had influenza over two weeks ago. It was a bad case. I obviously went back to work before I'd fully recovered. I'm still feeling tired. Then I started coughing violently like this, and my health's gone downhill ever since."

Rushdi described how much the coughing hurt and how much weight he had lost.

The doctor interrupted him. "When did your voice go hoarse?"

"At least a week ago."

The doctor told him to strip to the waist. The young

man stood up, took off his tie, then his jacket, shirt, and undershirt. He looked lean and emaciated. The doctor put his stethoscope to his ears and started placing it at the spots on Rushdi's chest and back where he was tapping with his finger. Rushdi noticed that he went back several times to one particular spot at the top of his chest on the left. The doctor now told him to get dressed again.

"Have you been spitting blood?" he asked.

Rushdi's heart leapt, and he paused for a moment. "Yes," he replied in a lowered voice, "I've noticed it two or three times."

The doctor brought over a blue vial and told him to cough heavily and spit into it. A short time went by as Rushdi stood there breathing heavily, like a defendant awaiting the verdict to be delivered.

"I suspect that there is something wrong with your left lung," the doctor said. "There's no point in stating anything definite at this stage. But you need to go and see Dr. So-and-so immediately so he can take some X-rays and you can bring me back the results."

The doctor warned him not to do anything that required effort. Rushdi stood where he was with a frown on his face. He was feeling utterly miserable.

"I may be wrong," the doctor went on. "But, even if I'm right, it's not serious."

He went to the other doctor to have X-rays taken, then waited in agony for days, worried out of his mind in addition to all the pains of the coughing. Normally he was not by nature someone to give in to fears and anxieties, but now he suddenly found himself at the mercy of a deadly illness. The very word "illness" had a very bad effect on him.

Taking the X-rays he went back to visit the first doctor. The latter looked at them carefully and then turned to his patient. "Just as I thought," he said. "You can call it a slight lesion or a surface infection, if you like."

His hopes began to fade, and his honey-colored eyes had a desperate look about them. He stared blankly at the X-rays, not understanding what it was he was looking at— "a slight lesion or a surface infection"! Was his entire life now going to be hostage to such apparent trifles?

"So let's call it what you want," he told the doctor. "My question to you is: does this mean that it is a case of incurable tuberculosis?"

The doctor gave him a disapproving look. "Don't let the word 'tuberculosis' alarm you," he said. "Forget about all those kinds of fear. They have no basis in truth or science. You'll certainly recover if you follow the instructions I'm about to give you."

The doctor paused for a moment of reflection.

"People say," Rushdi said anxiously, "that there's no cure for tuberculosis."

The doctor shrugged his shoulders in contempt. "I reject such ideas," he said. "You should know that I had the disease at one point. Even so, you must only eat the very best food, take a complete rest, and live in clean, dry air. All those things you can find at the sanitorium. Get to Helwan as soon as you can."

"How long will the cure take, do you think?"

"I'd say, six months at the most."

Rushdi's heart sank. He was sure that a period as long as that would mean that he would lose his job. If this piece of news got out tomorrow and reached "the neighbors," he would lose his girl as well. For both these reasons the idea of the sanitorium did not appeal to him at all.

"What if these conditions were also available at home?" he asked.

"Where do you live?"

"In Khan al-Khalili."

"As far as I know, that's a very damp area. The sanitorium is by far the best place for you to be. And don't forget that you'll need the very best care as well."

He began to warm to the idea of a home-cure system; that way, no one would find out his secret. He would be able to keep his job and his girl.

"What if I can't go to the sanitorium?" he asked.

The doctor shrugged his shoulders again. "In that case you'd have to take extra special care in the house, particularly where rest and food are concerned. You'd have to stay in bed, of course. I'll describe the medical process to you...."

While the doctor was busy writing out the medical protocol for him, Rushdi suddenly thought of a crucially important question. "I've just thought of another issue," he said after a brief pause. "Can I...I mean, when can I get married if I have this kind of disease?"

For the first time the doctor smiled. "I would hope that, with the necessary care, you'll be cured in about six months," he said. "You'll have to stay under observation for a full year after that. Then it would be a good idea to wait another six months...."

Once again, he advised Rushdi to go to the sanitorium if it was at all feasible and then recommended that, if he could not do so, he should certainly come to see him from time to time. Rushdi went home bearing with him the entire weight of his misery. To him, everything now seemed like a terrible dream; his ears, in fact his entire world, were filled with that dreadful word—tuberculosis. Should he believe what everyone said about it, or believe what the doctor had told him? Had the doctor decided to tell him the truth, or was he trying to allay his fears? He had told him quite frankly that he had suffered from the disease himself, so Rushdi saw no reason to disbelieve him. Yes indeed, six months was a long time, but he would have to put his trust in God and endure it patiently. Had he been free to do what he wanted, he would certainly have preferred going to the sanitorium, but two things stood in the way: his job and his beloved. What was he supposed to do?

His health, which he had never even bothered about until now, was in imminent danger. Before today he had never had occasion to look back with nostalgic regret on his health. It had never occurred to him that health might be something that could vanish or change drastically. But what was the point of being healthy if he lost his job? What purpose did it serve if it placed a roadblock between him and the girl with whom he was so in love? The best thing would be to stay at home, get accustomed to looking after himself, and take his medicine without anyone finding out about his secret. That way, he could get better without having to give away his secret or lose both his job and his beloved.

That is the way his thought processes developed. What made it much easier for him to convince himself was that he still had his basic functions in place and was able to move around. While keeping his condition a secret, he had in fact begun the prescribed routine, until quite by chance his brother had come into the bathroom; after that his secret had been no more. The truth is that he was not sorry, not only because his elder brother was so much a part of himself, but also because the process of keeping it hidden away was preying on his mind, so he felt a sense of relief when his brother found out. He unloaded all his sorrows on to Ahmad, except the part involving the sanitorium, about which he still felt a need to be a bit cautious....

35

Ahmad listened silently to his younger brother talking, his heart full of the most profound sadness. He completely forgot about the mixed feelings he had felt toward his brother, wavering between love and aversion. All he could feel now was just one irrepressible, instinctual emotion—a genuine love in which was combined extreme worry and overwhelming sadness. Memories from the recent past still impinged, but he squelched them immediately, feeling not a little ashamed. He was even annoyed with the girl who was the root cause of them.

When Rushdi finished the account of his visit to the doctor, the two brothers stared at each other, sadness and worry written all over their faces.

"This is God's will," said Ahmad, "but we'll never despair of His mercy. We have to believe what the doctor says. It's not like doctors to offer false hope to their patients. The lesion is a small one, he says. From now on, we'll have to devote as much care and attention as we can to treating it. I must say that I'm shocked that you didn't tell me as soon as you knew about it!"

"I only found out just before the feast," Rushdi replied quickly, even though he knew it was not the truth. "I didn't want to bother anyone. I was waiting for the right moment to tell you, and only you, about it."

"It's God's will," said Ahmad sadly. "So let's endure His judgment until such time as He bestows a cure, He being far more merciful to us than we are to ourselves. Now, tell me what you've decided to do."

The question made Rushdi panic, and he looked warily at his brother. "Needless to say, I'm going to follow the doctor's instruction," he said. "He's told me to take things easy, eat good food, and have some injections."

Ahmad's expression made it clear that he was not entirely convinced by what he had just heard. "But people with this disease normally go to the sanitorium," he said.

Once again Rushdi lied to his brother. "The doctor doesn't think it's necessary."

Ahmad now looked more hopeful. "Well, Rushdi," he said, "maybe it's a minor attack after all!"

"For sure! That's what the doctor told me."

"Maybe you won't need to take a lot of time off."

Once again Rushdi felt awkward. "I'm not going to ask for time off," he told his brother in a low voice.

That shocked Ahmad. "How on earth can you recover then?" he asked in disbelief. "You may have been told it's a minor case, but don't treat this illness lightly, Rushdi. We've had enough of that kind of behavior already!"

"Heaven forbid, Ahmad, that I should play fast and loose with my own life! From now on, you'll see that, apart from going to work, I'm going to take things very easily. I'll compensate for the effort I put into going to work by eating carefully and taking fortifying medicines. If I request sick leave, it'll put my job and future at risk."

"Aren't you exaggerating?"

"No, Ahmad, certainly not! If the bank's doctor finds out about my illness, I won't be allowed back until I'm completely cured. That may require a long time, and I've no guarantee that I won't be dismissed. Actually, it's virtually certain in such cases, in view of the fact that I've taken sick leaves both here and in Asyut before."

Ahmad frowned and looked even more anxious. "Good God," he protested, "health's far more important than a job. How can you possibly get better when you're still working hard?"

"The doctor told me I can do it," Rushdi replied optimistically. "He knows best. God willing, I can be cured without sacrificing my future or raising any kind of scandal."

Now Ahmad was really annoyed. "Scandal?" he said in disbelief. "There's no scandal involved. God is testing you. Everyone is liable to get sick unless God ordains that they be protected and saved. What I'm afraid of is that...."

"Don't be scared," Rushdi interrupted. "Pray to your God for me. You're going to be happy with the way I handle things."

Ahmad felt overwhelmed and said nothing more. Rushdi sighed in relief and started telling his brother about the precautionary measures he was proposing to take. He would get some carbolic acid so he could sanitize the bath and sink every morning and would buy special cutlery and crockery for when he ate and drank. He would tell his parents that they were a present from a dear friend of his. His brother listened carefully. For the first time he started to worry about himself, thinking about the possibility of infection. He was a bit of a hypochondriac in any case.

At this point Rushdi made ready to broach another sensitive topic no less tricky than the first one, if not even more so. "There's something else, Ahmad," he said, "something that's of extreme importance to me. I'd like to ask you to stick to it as carefully as I'm going to. I want this entire conversation we've had to remain between us only."

Ahmad was utterly astonished. Then he remembered the way Rushdi had just talked about the crockery and cutlery being a present. "But what about our parents?" he asked.

"They don't need to know anything about it," Rushdi replied firmly. "There's no point in getting them all worried. If my mother gets scared, that'll be enough to publicize the whole thing."

Ahmad felt distinctly uneasy, realizing that all this implied a peculiar and unhappy family life. "Have it your way, Rushdi," he sighed. "If you start getting better, then maybe we can keep things a secret, but if not, then...."

"Don't worry! From now on recklessness is no longer an option."

Ahmad realized full well what Rushdi's motivations were in wanting to keep it all a secret from his parents. Rushdi was worried that the news would soon spread to the girl's family; for that reason he was making light of the whole thing. This realization had a profound effect on Ahmad, and he was deeply saddened by it. Rushdi may have been staying at work because he was anxious for the girl and her family to think he was still fit and well, but in fact his longing for the girl was causing him real harm. At this point he plucked up his courage and turned to Rushdi again.

"Rushdi," he whispered, "if you wanted to request a leave without revealing your secret, then I'm sure we could come up with some kind of pretext other than your illness to justify such a request."

Rushdi shook his head angrily. "Oh Ahmad," he replied wearily, "it's all settled. Don't go back to it again!"

Ahmad said no more. After a while he stood up. "Be strong then," he told his brother, "and act like the kind of man I've always known you to be. You know that whether you get better or not is entirely in your own hands. May God protect you and care for you!"

Ahmad went back to his own room feeling sad and depressed. News of this dangerous illness had managed to arouse all his latent anxieties, and he felt a genuine sympathy for his beloved brother. At this moment he entirely forgot that his brother had been the instrument that fate had used to demolish his own hopes or that Rushdi had been the one to hurt his self-esteem and crush his pride. Now he could see Rushdi as he really was, a beloved younger brother, someone who had grown up in his embrace and given him a sense of fatherhood for twenty years.

He looked over at the closed window that he had once named Nawal's, then looked away in anger. His heart was still unwilling to remember the girl; the mere act of doing so involved committing an unforgivable crime against his sick brother. This new disaster now required that all such memories be expunged.

"It's all over and done with," he told himself. "Any pangs of regret I may feel are a stinging blow to the deep love I have for my own brother."

Just then he became aware of quite how furious he was as he talked to himself. In truth, the fury was self-directed. He could not forget the way he had wanted to see the whole of Cairo obliterated and the fearsome dream he had experienced when he had woken up to the sounds of his brother's fever-induced moans. Good God, he asked himself, what kind of atrocious devil was residing inside him to spew forth such ideas?

36

Rushdi set about confronting his dangerous illness with zeal. He regularly took the medicine and injections that the doctor had ordered for him and, in addition to the usual food he ate at home, he started eating other things that were especially nutritious: yogurt, eggs, honey, liver, and pigeon, all of which cost him quite a bit of money. He kept his brother fully informed about the steps he was taking so as to allay his fears.

January went by with its freezing cold wind, and everything seemed to be going well. Rushdi made do with one single hour of pleasure each day, the one he spent with his two pupils. No later than ten o'clock each night he would go to bed and fall fast asleep. The hoarseness in his voice disappeared, and his cough improved too, almost to the point of stopping completely. That thrilled him since it seemed to confirm that he was on the road to recovery. But he was still skinny, and his color did not come back. Every ten days he went to see the doctor who continued to give him advice and suggested that he maintain or even increase his self-care.

The early days of the illness were black indeed. He fell victim to all sorts of worries and delusions and felt such despair that it actually scared him. Life seemed almost at an end, and yet his *joie de vivre* was certainly no less than that of other people. Whenever he recalled that he was staying in Cairo, when the best thing for him was to stay at the sanitorium outside the city in Helwan, and that he was carrying on working when he should really have taken a leave. All of which made him feel even more afraid and anxious. However, emotional types like him never know how to pause for thought when it comes to pursuing their desires; their thought processes are just like those of a criminal who has a clever lawyer working for him. Thus, even when these worries were at their peak, he still managed to convince himself that he was on the right track. When his voice lost its hoarseness and his coughing stopped—or almost—he was delighted. His self-confidence, sense of security, and hope all came back. This new feeling of calmness afforded him a degree of tranquility and respite.

However, this situation did not last very long. His old brashness and ribald tendencies came back, bringing with them a deep-felt longing to indulge in life's pleasures once again. His illness and the dangers it posed no longer bothered him much. He was full of admiration for his patience and willpower, as he recalled the month of January when he had trained himself to do exactly what he had promised his brother to do. It shocked and amazed him at the same time; it was almost as though he believed himself incapable of changing direction and living an upright existence for

an entire month. Now, with hope smiling at him, he could
hear life's pleasures—his own life's pleasures—summoning
him with magic whispers, like the songs of the nightingale
in the early morning.

In his current lonely state he remembered his friends,
the Ghamra Casino, and the nights of revelry. Their happy,
smiling faces appeared before him, and his ears rang with
echoes of their pealing laughter; the way they called him
"the Lionheart," the nickname he loved, relished, and was
afraid to forget. What wonderful friends they were! Life
could be nothing without them—so much fun and such
good company! How could he ever forget the way they had
pestered him with phone calls at the bank when he had
stayed away.

"Where are you, brother Rushdi? Why this long absence?
When you were in Asyut, it seems, you were closer to us
than you are now in Cairo! Is the Lionheart's chair to
remain empty? And we're missing your cash too!"

How hard he had laughed with them, parried their pro-
tests, and then offered important business as his excuse for
his prolonged absence. He longed to see his friends, to have
a bit of fun. The life of pleasure kept beckoning him.

He started to wonder whether one night would be all
that harmful. Could it really be fatal? Truth to tell, his relish for life had not diminished because of his illness; if
anything, it had become that more acute and vigorous.
Eventually, the temptation proved too much and he threw
caution to the winds. The very thought of being released
from the tortures of despair thrilled him, and he started
humming to himself the tune, "I Can't Forget You." He
hadn't sung anything for a month and a half.

When evening came, he put on his coat, slung a scarf around his neck, and went to al-Sakakini. No sooner did he spot the garden of the Ghamra Casino than he yelled out from the very depths of his soul, "Hello, hello, how wonderful to see you!" His friends were overjoyed to see him again, and he simply surrendered himself to their unstoppable energy. They chatted in their usual crazy way, then went inside to smoke, drink, and gamble. He was afraid of not indulging himself in case they started getting suspicious. At the same time he was anxious to forget—such was his hope at the time—that his left lung was infected with that disease whose very name made people shudder in fright. He smoked and drank two glasses of cognac that warmed up his cold body. He gambled as well, although he hesitated a bit because the costs of the drugs he was taking were playing havoc with his budget. But fate smiled on him, and he won almost two pounds.

He left the casino feeling happy, although he could feel a certain hotness burning his tissues. It was very hard for him to walk in the freezing cold. When he reached home, he was utterly exhausted. No sooner had he closed the door than Ahmad's door opened, and he came out. He invited Rushdi into his room. The younger brother followed him, feeling not a little ashamed and nervous.

"What on earth have you been doing?" Ahmad yelled. "Have you gone mad? Is this the agreement we made?"

Rushdi remained silent, although the semblance of a smile showed on his face, a mixture of contentment and worry.

"This is unbelievable," Ahmad went on. "I only found out because your bed was empty. I was feeling anxious, so

I was only sleeping lightly. Then I heard the front door. Is this what we agreed to?"

"As you know full well, brother," Rushdi finally said in a low voice, "I've kept to the agreement for a whole month. Now my inner self urged me to break it, just a bit...."

"Only someone who's either completely ignorant or pretending to be could possibly say something so stupid. Don't you realize that the kind of behavior you've shown tonight can negate a whole month's precautions?"

"But I'm feeling a whole lot better!"

"You're kidding yourself!" said Ahmad angrily. "Your crass stupidity is doing you harm. Allowing you so much freedom is obviously a huge mistake. If the doctor knew the kind of tomfoolery you've been up to tonight, he would immediately demand that you go to the sanitorium for a check-up."

Rushdi looked defeated. The whole effort of coming home and facing this had completely worn him out.

"Don't be unkind to me, Ahmad," he chided his brother. "You don't usually behave this way...."

"Now you don't seem to be able to tell the difference between caring and unkindness," Ahmad responded. "You call me unkind, when I've stayed up in a complete panic wondering where you were. It's yourself and me you're being unkind to!"

Rushdi now felt even more tired and worn-out. Tears welled up in his eyes. That made Ahmad cool his temper and feel both sorry and unhappy for his brother. He put his hand on Rushdi's shoulder.

"Enough of your exhaustion and my pain. You've never cried, so don't start now. I won't bother you any more.

God alone can tell you what the right thing to do is. My heart is afraid for you and is begging you to do what's right. Go to bed and trust in God to make you well again."

As Ahmad went back to bed, he started wondering whether his brother would revert to his old ways despite his serious illness.

37

Early February was greeted by a world that was as concerned as usual about its strong winds and freezing storms. The sky was covered with a thick layer of dark clouds. The ground was like a chicken sitting on its eggs, waiting for the advent of spring that would crack open the dark cloud cover and reveal the clear sunlight and the scent of flowers.

Rushdi still looked very skinny. Deep inside him there lurked a flame consisting of emotions and feelings that would not be quenched. He wanted to throw off the chains that his illness imposed on him. The doctor had given him another check-up and told him that his chest condition had not improved. All his hopes were dashed, and the joy he had felt when his voice and cough had improved simply vanished. He had been patient for so long, abandoning the life that he loved. He kept on hoping and hoping, but when was he going to get better? What was even worse was that the doctor had insisted that he must find a way to get to the sanitorium in Helwan. Had he given up on the idea that Rushdi could be cured while staying in Cairo? So what then was the point of enduring all this patience and agony? Apart from all that, his brother made it clear to him that he was not happy about how thin and pale he looked. As a result Rushdi was permanently disgruntled and resentful.

One evening he was giving his two pupils their lesson. Nawal asked her brother to go and get a cup of water. When the two of them were alone, she asked Rushdi why he wasn't meeting her every morning any longer. Couldn't he do it just once? His heart leapt for sheer joy.

"How about tomorrow morning?" he immediately replied, totally oblivious to the consequences of what he was saying.

It was then that he thought of his brother who was now serving as his jailer. He told himself that, if Ahmad acknowledged that he had to go out at nine o'clock in the morning, then how could he object if he went out three-quarters of an hour earlier?

The next day Rushdi got up early, had his nutritious breakfast, waited until Ahmad went into the bathroom, then hurriedly left the apartment. He spotted his beloved girl a few steps ahead of him, wearing her usual gray coat and with her school bag under her arm. He was so overjoyed that he forgot all about his own miseries. As he followed her up the road to al-Darrasa, he fondly recalled the times when he had felt fit and well as he did this routine. The entire idea made him sigh in regret.

"How precious health is," he told himself.

He looked up at the Muqattam Hills shrouded in cloud.

The sky always put him in mind of his Lord, and he now begged Him to take him in hand.

After the turn off in the road he caught up with her and clasped her right hand in his. She turned toward him with a smile.

"So," she teased him in a tone that was not without a touch of reproach, "you have decided that this little jaunt isn't worth your time, you fickle boy?"

He shook his head remorsefully. "It's this awful cold," he muttered.

"You're supposed to have gotten over your cold a while ago," she said. "So why so slow?"

"You're right. It's hanging on, but it's nothing really. The truth is that it's my negligence that's to blame."

Obviously she was aware that he had stopped their morning excursions because of his cold. Since the cold had now gone, she encouraged him to resume their walk together since she was keen for them to be alone together.

She sneaked a quick glance in his direction. "Do you know what my grandmother says about you?" she asked.

His heart gave a leap, fearing that he might be about to hear something relevant to the question of an engagement. "What does she say?"

"She asked me with a laugh, 'How come your professor is as thin as a rake? Do you want me to suggest some recipes to put some weight on him?'"

Nawal gave a gentle laugh, and he laughed with her so as to cover up the intense feeling of sorrow that came over him. He started to feel alarmed, but could see no way out of his predicament other than to put a bright face on things.

"I don't need to get fat. Being thin is all the rage now. Thank your grandmother for me and tell her that I'd actually like to get even thinner!"

Just then she frowned as though she were remembering something. "By the way, you naughty boy," she chided him, "sometimes when we're gathered around the table for our lessons, you play footsie with me. You seem to forget that you're wearing shoes but I'm barefoot!"

Rushdi blushed. "My heart and soul would sacrifice itself for your lovely little feet!" he laughed.

They were passing by the café called The Desert Club. She pointed at the waiter who was eating his breakfast. "Do you realize," she said, "that cunning waiter over there has cottoned onto our rendezvous every morning? As soon as he spotted me walking on my own these last few days, he started clapping his hands whenever I walked by.

"'Where's your mate, little bird?' he'd say as though talking to himself. 'All lovers work in pairs!'

"Good heavens! How embarrassed I felt; it almost made me pass out!"

Once again they burst into laughter. They had almost reached the turn in the road where the Akif family's wooden tomb lay on both sides. Nawal looked over at it.

"You owe me at least a hundred prayers," she said. "Every single day I recite the Fatiha by your family tomb."

"My dear Nawal," Rushdi replied with a smile, "you're a mercy for my grandfather who's buried there and a gigantic tease to his grandson!"

He too looked over at the tomb. Suddenly a scary thought crossed his mind, like some demon emerging out of a graveyard. Would fate soon decree that this girl of his would be walking past this tomb and reciting the Fatiha over his departed spirit? His heart froze, and he looked wonderingly at her lovely face. She was his everything in life, he realized; if there was one single thing that could scoff at death, it was surely the deep love shared by two hearts. He now had a very powerful motive for his relationship with her, for holding her close to his heart, indeed inside his heart if possible. She looked back at him and noticed his dreamy-eyed gaze.

"Why are you staring at me like that?" she asked.

"Because I love you, Nawal," he replied with a break in his voice. "Looking at those graves by the light of your lovely eyes, I've come to realize the true meaning of the saying that life is love. The graves have told me that every hour we allow ourselves to be apart from each other is in fact a crime whose penalty is the darkness of the tomb. I heard a voice yelling at me: 'What a fool you are! All you bother about is trivialities. You're gambling away the real pleasure of life.' "

She blushed, and her eyes sparkled with emotion. Neither of them felt the cold wind that was blowing in from the desert. He clasped her hand, and they walked on together. He started asking himself how he could possibly avoid bringing up the topic of an engagement after everything he had just said. For her part she was expecting him to raise the much beloved topic with every step she was taking. But he said nothing more until they were at the end of the road. They said farewell and parted. He slowed down and watched her walk on, his gaze full of all the love, emotion, and sadness he was nursing in his heart. She turned off toward Abbasiya, and he headed for the trolley stop. It was only then that he began to feel totally exhausted. He felt short of breath and so dizzy that he almost threw up.

Rushdi now made a point of talking to his brother about the possibility of an engagement and the bad impression her family would get if he did not raise the subject. His brother was already annoyed because Rushdi had gone out so early in the morning and so told him that he was not prepared to broach the topic with Kamal Khalil Effendi until he was completely cured.

"You can make whatever excuses you like," he told his brother. "You certainly know how to do that. But it's not right to make anything official until you're completely well again, God willing. The engagement announcement can be a reward for getting better. We'll see how strong your resolve really is!"

Ahmad found that he could not dissuade his brother from going out early and exposing himself to the cold. He gave up and entrusted his brother's welfare to God, begging Him to show mercy and kindness. Ahmad was one of those types who take the sufferings of their nearest and dearest on themselves. In such weak hearts, deeply buried fears and worries can find fertile ground for all sorts of sorts of sorrows and delusions. From the very first his brother's illness had become his overriding concern, a poisonous thorn in the side of his own sense of security.

His anxieties extended to other spheres as well, so much so that he ended up having to deal with the most delicate of ethical issues, one that had not even occurred to him before. He was well aware that his brother was meeting the girl every morning; he may even have spent time alone with her in the evening when he was tutoring her. If passion got the better of him—as happens when people are in love—and he stole a kiss, might not the girl be exposed to some serious kind of harm. Did Rushdi not realize the risks he was taking? Was his conscience not serving as a kind of restraint? But then, how could someone who was treating his own life with such levity give any value to those of other people? Ahmad thought about this for a while. He was both exasperated and worried, but he had no idea how to rescue this innocent girl from disaster. His indecisiveness was based entirely on the purest of ethical motives; he was convinced of that and also of the profound moral obligations on which it was based. Even so, he did not seem to realize his natural propensity to indulge in self-examination, or that all too often the eye only sees what it wants to see, so he was both exasperated and worried, both of which only complicated his thinking even more. He could not tell Kamal Khalil the truth since such a betrayal of his beloved brother would be an appalling crime, nor could he reveal his fears to his brother, since that would strike his sensitive soul in its most vulnerable spot. The reluctance, fear, and worry that Ahmad was feeling were all torture for him, but now as always he had neither resolve nor will to act. Disconsolate and confused, he gave up. His worries continued to plague him and prick his conscience, so much so that the entire process wore him out and made him desperate.

"Perhaps the kind of stupor that Boss Zifta enjoys is better than the kind of life I'm living!" he thought to himself in despair.

38

Rushdi's health went from bad to worse, and he became even thinner and paler. Even so, he refused to change his behavior, as though the whole thing had nothing to do with him. From this point on, he was no longer content merely to take his early morning walks. Whenever he felt like seeing his friends at the Ghamra Casino, he would rush over there and spend a riotous evening with them.

"Are you trying to commit suicide?" Ahmad would rail at him.

The truth is that he was on a downhill slide toward suicide without even intending it. He was utterly incapable of resisting his natural inclination to indulge in life's pleasures and surrendered to a frightening new instinct created by the disease itself, while his propensity for risk-taking and optimism shielded him from the dire outcome involved. He never gave up hope, or rather only occasionally; and remained the daredevil he had always been, contemptuous and always smiling.

Then suddenly his cough came back; in fact, it came back much worse than it had ever been before. Now it was almost continuous, and once again his sputum had blood in it. His fellow workers in the bank noticed how badly he was coughing and began to get suspicious. Work now became pointless, and his parents began to be aware of how dangerous the condition that threatened their son actually was. They advised him to stop working until he had recovered, and yet he still crazily insisted on pretending he was well. Ahmad could take it no longer; one day he called him into his room.

"Are you ignoring how dangerous things are?"

"What are you implying?" his brother asked him in a resigned tone he had not been expecting.

"You can't keep working any more. Let alone going out at night and carousing!"

"So the scandal is out, is it?"

"This illness isn't a scandal!" Ahmad responded emphatically. "Necessity has it own rules."

Rushdi looked at the floor. He had lost all will to resist. "It's all in God's hands!" he said with a sigh.

The way Rushdi had given way so suddenly was a sign of exhaustion, not of conviction. No sooner did the bank's doctor establish the real cause of his illness and give him sick leave than his strength completely collapsed. He retired to his bed, feeling utterly weak and wracked by coughing fits. Ahmad still kept the true facts from his parents, but Rushdi's condition deteriorated with frightening speed. His mother noticed the blood in his sputum, and his father heard about it. Both of them were terrified. Rushdi's condition demanded a consultation with the doctor. Ahmad suggested inviting him to the house, but Rushdi decided they should both go to his clinic. He got dressed, helped by his mother who was now deeply concerned about her younger son. They took a taxi to the doctor's clinic, and Ahmad went with his brother into the consulting room. The doctor had not seen Rushdi for a couple of weeks.

"What on earth have you done to yourself?" he asked in his usual loud voice as soon as he set eyes on Rushdi.

"I'm coughing a lot and feel very weak," Rushdi responded with a wan smile.

The doctor examined him. There was a long pause. "Just one word to you," he said. "The sanitorium now!"

Rushdi's sallow face showed a frown. "Is it worse?" he asked softly.

"Undoubtedly," the doctor replied with raised eyebrows. "You clearly haven't been taking my advice. But if you get to Helwan as soon as possible, there's no need to worry. Get there today if you can. You'll find me there right beside you."

"Will he need to stay in Helwan for long?" Ahmad asked.

"Only God knows the answer to that," the doctor replied. "I'm not a pessimist, but it has to be done now."

The two of them returned home to find their parents waiting impatiently.

"What's the matter with him?" the father asked Ahmad.

Ahmad realized there was no point in lying any more.

"He needs to go to the sanitorium," he replied with deliberate terseness.

There was silence. Sitt Dawlat's eyes turned red, a sign that she was about to burst into tears.

"God be kind to us!" their father muttered.

"There's no need for alarm," said Ahmad trying to reassure them. "But he must go to the sanitorium."

Rushdi still did not want to go there, but he did not dare refuse now that his condition was so bad. He called his brother over. "Okay then, so be it: the sanitorium," he said in his mother's hearing. Then pointing to the window he went on, "but please don't tell them the truth!"

Ahmad was overwhelmed and felt utterly depressed. "Don't worry," he said. "I can easily say that you've some fluid in your lungs and you need to go to the sanitorium."

"Will that be enough, do you think?" Rushdi asked sadly.

"Getting rid of fluid in your lungs takes a long time," Ahmad replied. "Whatever the case may be, it's more important now to look after your own health than anything else."

39

Without wasting any time Ahmad followed the instructions of the doctor who had been treating his brother and immediately started making arrangements to have Rushdi admitted to the sanitorium. A bed had become available at the beginning of March because the patient involved had completed his treatment. It was therefore decided to take Rushdi to the sanitorium on that date. Only a short wait was involved, but during that period the family suffered all manner of emotions, a mixture of worry and hope.

Rushdi's coughing was causing him a great deal of pain and making it difficult for him to sleep. His parents sank into a deep depression, the serenity of their life totally destroyed; the expressions on their faces were a mixture of hope and anxiety.

Now Ahmad fell victim to all his pent-up anxieties, feeling gloomy and worried all the time. Kamal Khalil Effendi came to visit and assured Rushdi that fluid in the lungs was nothing to worry about. Sitt Tawhida and her daughter,

Nawal, also called in when Ahmad was not at home. The mother told him that his insistence on staying so thin was what had made him so ill; with a laugh she assured him that, once he got better, she would make sure that he got fatter. With Rushdi's parents listening, Nawal did not know what to say; even he could not risk looking at her all the time. Even so, they managed to exchange fleeting glances that communicated messages of love, thanks, and silent sorrow.

Rushdi was very happy that they had paid him a visit, the kind of happiness he had not felt since he had taken to his bed. When mother and daughter had both left, he shared with his mother his fears that the true nature of his illness might become public knowledge, but the poor woman managed to reassure her son that it would remain a secret known only to the people who loved him the most.

On the first of March a taxi took the two brothers to Bab al-Luq Station. The last thing Rushdi heard inside his parents' home were his father's prayers; the last thing he saw were his mother's tears.

"If the cure takes a long time," Rushdi told his brother on the way, "I'll be fired for sure."

"Even if that happens, heaven forbid," Ahmad replied confidently, "it'll be easy to get your job back. The only thing you should be worried about is getting better."

They got on the train, which soon left for Helwan. They sat side by side. Ahmad remained silent, his thin face a mirror of deep anxiety. Rushdi coughed from time to time. Ahmad was struck by the string of bad luck that had afflicted his family. They had already lost one child, and now here was Rushdi afflicted with a very serious illness. He himself had been set up by fate for a series of failures and missteps. If only fate had made do with him alone, that would have been tolerable to him, but unfortunately it had not. Glancing at his younger brother, he was shocked to see how thin he was, how scrawny his neck looked, and how bleary his eyes were. Where was that bright, mocking gleam that had once been there?

"O Lord," he prayed silently to himself, "will this tragedy ever end? Will I ever be able to open my eyes and not be confronted by specters of memories long past?"

Staring out of the window, he watched as a long line of buildings and villas went flashing by. The train then took them through lush, green fields and captivating rural scenery, before finally approaching the beginning of the endless, barren desert, fringed on the horizon by lofty hills. The progression of buildings, fields, and desert made him feel sad, and he found himself once again sliding into a deep depression.

The train reached Helwan, and the two of them left the train station. The journey had exhausted Rushdi, so they took a taxi to the sanitorium. It went down a deserted road, until the sanitorium loomed in front of them at the foot of the mountains, like some forbidding castle. Both brothers stared at it, their hearts beating fast.

"Let us pray," said Ahmad, "that our Lord will take you by the hand, bestow a cure on you, and let you leave this place fully restored to health."

When they got to the sanitorium, they took the elevator to the third floor, where the nurse showed them to the room they were looking for. It consisted of two beds, on one of which a young man of Rushdi's age was lying down; he looked just as thin and pale as Rushdi. They all exchanged greetings, and Rushdi sat down to recover his breath. With his brother's help he changed his clothes and lay down on the bed. Ahmad sat down on a comfortable chair, then pointed to the other young man in the room.

"I'm sure he'll be a good companion for you," he said. "You'll be able to help each other kill time and avoid feeling lonely until you both get out of here, hale and hearty, God willing!"

Ahmad spent some time chatting with his brother and the other young man. He discovered that his name was Anis Bishara; he was a final year student in the School of Engineering. However, it was obvious that the journey had exhausted Rushdi—he simply lay there on the bed in a kind of stupor—so Ahmad chatted with them both for a bit longer until he was sure that Rushdi was settled in, then he stood up to leave. As he clasped his brother's hand to say farewell, he could feel tears welling up inside him and had to grit his teeth to stop them emerging from his eyes. Once he had left the room, it occurred to him that Rushdi had also been on the verge of tears when bidding him leave. He was on the point of going back, but rejected the idea and continued on his way out of the building. Walking down long corridors with patient rooms on either side, he shuddered as he noticed ghost-like human beings all wearing billowing white garments. On his way back to the station he kept looking back at the imposing sanitorium building and muttered yet another prayer.

The Akif family spent a miserable evening together. The father looked totally distracted, and the mother wept so much that her eyes were red. Ahmad tried to make things easier for them by talking in hopeful terms, but the fact of the matter was that he too needed someone to lighten his own burden of misery.

40

The family had to wait impatiently until Friday, which was visiting day at the sanitorium. Kamal Khalil decided that he and his family would go with them. Both families made preparations for the visit. Ahmad bought his brother a box of chocolate biscuits, while Sitt Tawhida, Nawal's mother, prepared a pastry dish for which she was renowned. At noon they all went together—the three men, two wives, and Nawal—to Bab al-Luq Station and sat opposite each other, the men on one side and the women on the other. That is how Ahmad found himself directly opposite Nawal. From the very first moment he avoided looking at her. He had not seen her since that fateful day when he had discovered what had been going on between her and Rushdi, but the fact that she was sitting so close to him now brought back old memories and triggered some painful feelings. He was afraid of succumbing to his emotions, so he decided to avoid the possibility by engaging Kamal Khalil in conversation for a while and then reading the *al-Ahram* newspaper. However, even though he managed to avoid looking at her, the flood of emotions he was feeling got the better of him. How was he supposed to forget his thwarted hopes or the bitter anger he had once felt toward his own brother? How could he overlook the terrible disease that had converted his anger into an unstaunchable wound in his own conscience? How could he forget that at one point he had even been worried in case the girl herself got infected? He had even considered accusing his brother of exposing her to all kinds of risk. All these worries had turned his entire life into a firetrap. He was quite ready to believe what he had once told himself, "Rushdi may have a lung disease, but my disease is in the mind!"

He started wondering what kind of feelings Nawal was having now that she was sitting directly opposite him in the train. Sorrow? Shame? Wasn't it reasonable for her to feel sad that the illness had afflicted her beloved and to pay no attention to his middle-aged brother? There was absolutely nothing unfair or unreasonable about that. But he still had to ask himself: what was the point of his own life, and how was he supposed to make use of the fact that he was healthy? He immediately began to feel the familiar sensation of being persecuted, one that was both painful and enjoyable. There was something else as well that he had to admit: he was happy to know she was there in the train compartment with him, even though he was avoiding looking at her. Why was that? he wondered. Was he testing his ability to forget and feel dismay? Or was it rather that he wanted to slake his old urge to show her how easily he could ignore her and rise above his feelings?

He came to himself for a moment and decided that it

was wrong to be entertaining such thoughts when he was on his way to visit his dear brother at the sanitorium. Such was the pain he felt inside him that he found himself wishing that there were some kind of operation that could suture the wounds in the human soul as was possible with the limbs of the body.

The journey came to an end, and everyone walked along the road, their eyes glued to the sanitorium looming in front of them. Even though Rushdi had only been there for three days, the fact that he was now forced to relax and take things easy led Ahmad to hope that his brother would already be feeling better. He walked ahead of the rest of them, went into the room and looked at Rushdi's bed. His brother was lying down. Even though he was aware of their arrival, he did not move. He received their greetings with a wan smile on his pale lips, and then they all gathered around his bed. Ahmad's hopes rapidly faded. His brother's appearance shocked him, and he immediately realized that his condition had actually worsened since the day he had brought him there. That confounded him, and his heart sank. Rushdi's visitors sat down, and Ahmad put the chocolate biscuits and pastry down on a small table near the bed.

"I'm hardly eating anything," Rushdi said weakly as he spotted them. "I don't feel hungry at all."

His mother kept staring at him, trying desperately not to show how absolutely devastated she was. "Don't you like the sanitorium food, Rushdi?" she asked.

"The food's fine, but I've lost my appetite."

"Don't worry," Sitt Tawhida said. "This always happens when the disease is in its early stages. Tomorrow this pure, dry air will make you feel hungry again."

Rushdi gave her a smile and then Nawal too, since she was sitting beside her mother.

"The last three nights have been dreadful," he told Ahmad. "I keep waking up and can't get back to sleep. The pain is much worse, and the...."

He didn't finish the sentence. Ahmad realized at once that he was avoiding the word "coughing." It was at this moment that he realized that the decision to bring Kamal Khalil's family with them had been a huge mistake. Even so, he was anxious to give his brother as much encouragement as possible.

"You heard what the lady said," he told him. "This is typical of the first phase in the illness. With God's help you'll be past it in no time and then you can get well again."

"Wouldn't it be better for me to come home?" Rushdi pleaded.

Ahmad noticed that his mother was on the verge of agreeing to the idea. "God forgive you!" he said hurriedly. "Absolutely not. You're not going to leave this room until you've completely recovered. Then you'll be able to walk back to Cairo! Fortunately, you're already looking a lot better."

Kamal Khalil wanted to put an equally positive face on things. "That's right, Rushdi Effendi," he lied, "you're definitely looking better."

The boy's mother took a closer look to see if what they were saying was believable.

"You need to be patient, Rushdi," said his father, his calm voice cracking a little. "Be patient. May God care for you and take you by the hand."

Rushdi said nothing, although not willingly. Ahmad was

well aware of that, knowing that Rushdi was only ever convinced by his own opinions and used them alone as a basis for his actions. Ahmad was sure that if Rushdi disliked the sanitorium enough, he would not be patient nor would his stay there produce any beneficial results. That thought depressed him even more.

Just then he noticed a movement in the other bed and watched as his brother's roommate sat up in bed. Ahmad was embarrassed because the overwhelming sadness he was feeling had made him forget to say hello to Rushdi's roommate.

"I'm terribly sorry, Anis Effendi," he said raising his hand in greeting. "How are you?"

"No problem!" the young man replied with a laugh. "Rushdi's obviously eager to get out of here and leave us!"

"I've kept you awake a lot," said Rushdi apologetically.

"There's no need to apologize," the young man replied. "I don't mind being awake at night."

"You seem to be a night owl," Ahmad said with a laugh, "just like Rushdi!"

"Absolutely right! And now here comes fate to tell us we have to abandon the things we used to love."

They all wished the two young men a speedy recovery. Ahmad's mother went over to the table and brought over the box of chocolate biscuits. She put one down beside Rushdi where he could reach it. "Won't you try one, Rushdi?" she begged.

He shook his head. "Not now," he said firmly. "Later...."

That made her sad, but she managed to put on a good front as she put the box back. Even now, she could not forget the necessary etiquette, so she went over to Anis's bed and offered him some too.

Ahmad kept staring disconsolately at his brother, but when Rushdi turned toward him, he managed to fake a smile. He was utterly stunned to see how weak and pale his brother looked. He seemed exhausted and listless; he just lay there, a prisoner, with no interest in the outside world. He looked scared as well, and the expression in his eyes betrayed both pain and resignation to fate. Ahmad got the impression that Rushdi wanted to tell him something; so strong was this feeling that he thought that he should spend some time alone with Rushdi after his visitors had left. But then the thought occurred to him that Rushdi was going to beg to be brought home, and that made him change his mind. He clenched his fist for his brother in a show of solidarity, pretending to make light of the whole thing.

Time came to leave, and everyone said fond farewells. They all left the room, with prayers for a speedy recovery on their lips. Rushdi's mother was the last to leave, kissing her younger son on his cheeks and forehead. On the way back she broke down, and tears welled up in her eyes. Nawal too was tearful and had no idea how to hide it. For his part, Ahmad kept his grief to himself until he got home and went to his own room. He remained optimistic and told himself that next time he would find Rushdi much improved. God, when would he ever recover that bloom, energy, and *joie de vivre* that he had possessed before? Would he ever again hear his brother's touching songs, that gentle teasing and ringing laugh?

The Akif family slept that night feeling the same sorrow

and grief they had felt on the night they'd parted with Rushdi. Early next morning they were all jolted awake when the doorbell started ringing. Ahmad sat up in bed. The bell kept on ringing as though no one was taking any notice. A horrendous thought suddenly occurred to him; he leapt out of bed and rushed out of his room. There he found his parents almost running toward the apartment door. No one mouthed a word, as they surrendered to whatever the fates had ordained. Swallowing hard, Ahmad made for the door, turned on the outside light, and opened it. Looking outside, he found nobody there. But the bell kept on ringing.

"There's no one there!" he told his parents flabbergasted.

He went over to check on the bell's battery, took off the cover, and separated the wires. Immediately the bell stopped ringing. As he closed the door, he felt tears welling up in his eyes. They all looked at each other, completely devastated.

"God protect us from Satan the accursed!" was his father's reaction.

"Wouldn't it be better to bring Rushdi home, if that's what he wants?" his mother said with a sigh that came from the depths of her heart.

"My revered mother," said Ahmad, "you must put your faith in God Almighty!"

41

On Sunday afternoon Ahmad was sitting with his parents, sipping coffee. A letter arrived, and Ahmad immediately recognized the handwriting.

"That's strange," he said. "It's Rushdi's handwriting."

His parents both sat up and watched as Ahmad slit the envelope open. The letter was written in pencil and in a sloppy hand totally unlike Rushdi's normal script:

8/3/1942

My Dear Brother,

Greetings to you and my parents! I'm writing this at 2 a.m., but don't be surprised at that; I've been robbed of the pleasure of sleep forever, and no sleeping pills have any effect. Just imagine, yesterday I took a dose of a well-known sleeping medicine; when it had absolutely no effect whatsoever, the doctor gave me a powerful drug and told me I'd sleep like a lamb. I'm still wide awake.

This torture just goes on and on, and I'm actually sitting up—or rather resting my back against the pillows—because lying down aggravates my cough, which is now much worse. That means that I have to sit up in bed; the only way I can get any rest is to fold the pillow, put it in my lap, and then lean my head on it.

Dear Brother, I hate to cause you any sorrow or pain, but there's a bitter truth, one from which there is no escape, that I have to share with you. After all, you are my first and last resort. Well, dear brother, I now know the results of the X-rays that were taken the day after I arrived here. I have a new spot on my right lung, and the old one on my left lung has created a cavity the size of a quarter. My general health is grave. Here's the report of the resident physician: "Absolutely no tolerance for food, no sleep at all, clear cough, breathing continuously impaired." I'm going to die, there's no doubt about that, none whatsoever. As I write these words to you, tears are pouring down my face, and I can't even see the words I'm writing to say good-bye to you. Every time I think of you all, I burst into tears.

So that's the way things are. The only thing I beg you to do now is to bring me home so I can spend my final days at home with all of you until I die. This time please don't raise any objections. Once again, I'm sorry to cause you so much grief, but what am I supposed to do? Don't tell our parents about this. God's blessings and peace upon you.

Your ever-loyal brother,
Rushdi

Ahmad read the letter in a kind of stupor, then reread parts of it over and over again. When he had finished, he felt almost dizzy, unwilling to accept what his brother was telling him. Even so, by the time he looked up he had managed to recover some of his self-control and could face his mother calmly enough to tell her an outright lie. His consideration for his mother's feelings and the fact that she was sitting so close to him allowed him to forget about himself for a while and keep a firm grip on his nerves. He looked at his parents and saw that they were both anxiously waiting for him to say something, like a person waiting to be shot by a firing squad with no blind over their eyes.

"Rushdi's insisting on coming home," Ahmad said, feigning exasperation. "What's the matter with him?"

"But he's doing fine!" his mother said.

"All's well and good," Ahmad went on, "but he loathes the sanitorium."

"Bring him home to me, Ahmad. There's no point in keeping him at the sanitorium against his will."

Ahmad stood up. "I'll go to Helwan tomorrow and bring him back," he said.

With that he gave his father the letter and went to his own room, with his mother behind him.

Next day he went back to Helwan without delay or hesitation. All the way there he felt conflicted and agitated. For the first time in ages he was contemplating the prospect of death as an imminent reality, considering its direst aspects and feeling the pain, despair, and fear that came with it. He could envisage the family tomb far away, the one that had swallowed up his baby brother and that would now pile up its earth again to create a hole to envelop his dear brother, Rushdi, someone without whom he had no idea how to live his own life. As he drew ever closer to the sanitorium, he became more and more depressed. Terror now had its heavy foot planted firmly on his chest. Good God, he wondered, how would he find Rushdi today, when he hadn't been getting any sleep at all?

The sun was slowly setting as he walked out of the train station. Taking a taxi to the sanitorium, he went up to the third floor without paying attention to anything else. As he approached the door to Rushdi's room, his heart was pounding. He went in and looked straight at the bed. There was Rushdi, exactly as he had described himself in his letter, sitting up, with his head leaning on a cushion folded in his lap.

"Rushdi!" he exclaimed, swallowing hard.

His brother looked up quickly. Ahmad noticed how very pale his face was and how hard he was finding it to breathe. A glimmer of happiness showed in Rushdi's eyes.

"You've come," he said in a quavering voce. "Take me out of here, please...."

"That's why I've come, Rushdi," Ahmad said to calm himself down a bit.

He turned to Anis Bishara, and they exchanged greetings.

"Poor Rushdi!" Anis said in a tone of voice that clearly showed how worried he was. "He never gets any sleep. Last night was terrible. It'll really be better for him to spend this next week at home. But he should come back here later!"

Ahmad nodded his head in agreement. "Do you know what the procedures are for requesting to take him home?"

"Go and ask the doctor immediately," he replied in the same serious tone of voice.

Ahmad encountered no difficulties in getting permission; in fact, he was not a little scared by the alacrity with which the doctor agreed to the request.

He went back to his brother's room and collected his things. Rushdi could not take his pajamas off and put on outdoor clothes, so he made do with a dressing gown. They brought a wheelchair to take him to the elevator. Anis Bishara accompanied him to the outer door of the sanitorium to say farewell and shook his hand warmly as he uttered a prayer for his recovery. Ahmad watched as his brother submitted meekly to the arms of the people carrying him; his eyes rolled and he looked so incredibly thin. Ahmad could not help remembering how fresh and handsome his younger brother had always looked, and how elegant, witty, and energetic he had been. Ahmad was so devastated that he could not avoid biting his lip, sensing as he did so a huge sob rising from the very depth of his soul.

42

When they got home, they found his parents and Kamal Khalil's family all waiting for them. Sitt Tawhida and Nawal had come to pay a visit to the sick young man's mother. When they heard that his elder brother had gone to the sanitorium to bring him home, they both stayed on until he arrived. When Rushdi finally appeared, everyone was completely shocked, and no one made any effort to hide their feelings. The young man seemed to have no idea of what was going on nor did he seem to realize that anyone else was there. They sat him down on his bed; his chest was heaving up and down and his eyes were closed. Everyone stared at him, unable to say a single word. Sitt Dawlat, his mother, turned pale and started trembling. She rushed over to his bed and sat behind him so he could lean back on her much-troubled breast. After a while Rushdi opened his eyes and looked round the room at the people gathered there. There was now a glint of awareness and recognition, and a hint of a smile appeared.

"Thank God!" he said in a husky voice that seemed to

come from the depths of his chest, "thank God, I'm back in my own room!"

Everyone repeated a prayer of thanks, and Sitt Tawhida reiterated it.

"God willing, I'll get better here," he said with a smile. "Please don't leave, dear lady!"

She kissed him on the shoulder. "I won't, dear Rushdi, God willing!" she replied. "My heart can't deceive me."

His eyes met Nawal's several times, and on each occasion he was greeted by a sweet smile that managed to combine in one all her prayers, hopes, and fears. Ahmad moved off to one side, never taking his eyes off his brother. Every time Rushdi's eyes glazed over, Ahmad shuddered. "God Almighty," he thought to himself, "show us your mercy!"

"It would be best," said Rushdi's father wisely, "for us to leave him so he can get his breath back and rest."

Everyone went out except for his mother. The two visitors went home. For a while Ahmad stayed in his own room, but he could not stand it for long and went back to his brother's. There he found Rushdi still pleased to be back and talking to his mother.

"I'm so happy to be home," he was telling her in a soft, quavering voice. "The sanitorium was so awful; I didn't eat anything and I didn't get any sleep. I saw one patient bleed so much that he basically drowned in his own blood. They went past our room carrying another patient to the isolation wing where they put people who are close to death. It was a shame that my poor health had a negative effect on Anis Bishara, my roommate. I got the impression that my condition scared him, so he started crying. Now I feel much more relaxed...."

He looked up at Ahmad. For a moment he said nothing,

his chest still going up and down. "I'm so sorry, Ahmad," he went on. "I've worn you out. Don't hold my disobedience against me. From now on, I'm going to take care of myself, I promise. I'm not going to go against any advice you want to give me. If God grants me a cure, I'll never play fast and loose with my life again."

Ahmad had to grit his teeth to stop himself from bursting into tears.

"There's no need to blame yourself, Rushdi," he said with a smile. "Everything happens in accordance with God's command. God willing, you'll start getting better tomorrow. You'll remember this entire ordeal the same way people remember nightmares after they've woken up!"

The young man was delighted with his brother's words and gave him a smile. He asked him to bring over the table so it was close to his bed and to put his bottles of medicine on it. Ahmad did so, placing it within his brother's reach and arranging the medicines: a box of calcium, a bottle of sleeping pills, and caromin.

Rushdi thanked him. "I'm going to need a nurse," he said, "to give me a calcium injection every day."

"I'll get the pharmacist to send one," Ahmad said, "and make the necessary arrangements with her. You should stop talking now so you don't overexert yourself. May God take care of you and keep you safe!"

Rushdi took some sleeping medicine, and with that he managed to relax. He had been kept awake for so many nights that he actually managed to fall asleep, although he had several coughing fits that cruelly interrupted his slumber.

43

Now came the really dreadful days. Rushdi was wracked with pain. His poor broken-hearted mother did her best to prop him up. He almost never got any sleep. Even though he took sleeping medicine, he could only doze off for a short while just before dawn. All too often morning would arrive, and he would still be sitting up in bed, his entire frame wracked by coughing fits. He stopped eating, and, whenever he forced himself to try a few bites, he would vomit them up in a horrendous fit of coughing. By now the coughing was continuous and wracked his entire body. No sooner had one bout come to an end than the veins in his neck would bulge out and prepare to launch another one, leaving his eyes red and streaming. He would seem to be going rapidly downhill, so that any thought of a cure was out of the question, but then he would appear to cross that hurdle. It was not so much that he got better, but simply that, as time went by, he kept on resisting and putting up a brave front.

Then the violent coughing began to subside, and he started getting some regular sleep. He even managed to eat some food and was finally able to lie on his side. This seemed to augur well for his recovery, and yet March went by with him still incredibly weak and exhausted. He could not get out of bed and got thinner and thinner, so much so that he was reduced to mere skin and bone. His visitors were shocked when they saw his legs, his emaciated face, his drawn cheeks, and sunken eyes. He had a sallow look about him, and his head seemed larger than usual, so much so that his neck seemed on the point of snapping because of its heavy load. The expression in his eyes was grim, a reflection of his determination to keep going, but also of pain and resignation. The very sight of it made Ahmad ache with pain, and it wore him out. Every time he looked in on Rushdi, he could see that same unforgettable expression on his face; it all compelled Ahmad's already overburdened heart to take on all the pain and suffering his brother was going through, leaving bleeding wounds deep inside him. Those looks in Rushdi's eyes plunged him into new depths of pain, disease, and despair. Good God, how many times was his heart destined to be torn apart and his tear-ducts to pour forth?

On one occasion Ahmad went into Rushdi's room and discovered that he had sat up in bed and put his legs down on the floor. His mother was not there, and Ahmad was scared that this maneuver might indicate that Rushdi was going to do something that could harm him.

"Wouldn't it be better to stay in bed?" he asked.

Rushdi looked very hurt, but then his expression changed to one of frustration. "Listen, brother," he said somewhat exasperated, "can't you see that time keeps going by, and I'm stuck here in bed, not moving at all. I stay in bed all day and half the night until that soporific we call sleep takes over. Good God! How restricted my life has become! I'm bored sick of staying in bed."

Ahmad had no idea what to say. Rushdi's obvious exasperation made him feel particularly miserable. "Be patient, Rushdi," he said gently. "That's the only way you're going to get better."

They all had to live with it; that was all there was to it. Rushdi dealt with the oppressive march of time by reading newspapers and magazines. He used to talk to his mother as well—she would hardly ever leave his room—and to his father and brother too. In spite of all the pain and tedium he still managed to avoid the kind of despair that had led him to write the letter that he had sent his brother from the sanitorium. He was still hoping to live his life and be cured of this dreadful illness. However, the pain that had etched such a profoundly melancholy expression onto his countenance had by now made him fully aware of the reality that lies behind the suffering subsumed within the essence of this worldly existence. He did indeed feel pangs of agony as the cold breaths of death hovered over him. Life's span would probably prefer that everyone become familiar with those chilling sensations, and yet it only manages to reveal their reality to the aged and to pour them into the mouths of those who are to die young.

What was amazing was that, in spite of all the pain and frustration, Rushdi did not forget about matters of the heart. The disease could not erase thoughts of love. It may not have pulsed through his veins in the way it had once done, and yet it could still make his heart race. So many happy memories were associated with his love, memories that shone a bright light into his heart, which created its own pulsating rhythm in his ear. His heart was stimulated like a flower inspired by the breath of spring—gleaming smiles, the desert road, honey-colored eyes, they all flashed before his eyes, while his ears could hear the sounds of pacts and pledges of love. But what would happen now? What was the unknowable future hiding? Would he ever recover his former youth, energy, hope, and love? Would he ever again be able to strut about with a supercilious elegance, the way he had before? To laugh out loud without provoking a violent coughing fit? To have tunes and melodies running through his head? To have his friends spot him and yell, "Here comes the Lionheart!" To take Nawal's arm in his and walk with her up the mountain road, the two of them shrouded from view by the clouds? Was there any hope left of buying the engagement ring and getting married?

Nawal would come to visit him with her mother, and the two of them would exchange fleeting glances full of a passion whose ardor only they could feel. O God, why could they not be left alone, if only for a moment? How he longed to hear a loving word from her, one to dampen the burning heat of his feverish heart!

March came and went, and with April came a change. Nawal no longer came to visit him, and a whole week went by without a visit from her. By the middle of the month she still had not come; only her father came. April came to an end with neither of them seeing the other. He was visited by his friends from the Zahra Café and their families, his

friends from al-Sakakini, and many relatives and former
neighbors. The house was always full of visitors, but never
Nawal. She had suddenly vanished from his life, as though
she had never been a tangible reality and a devout hope in
his life. He was quite sure that his parents and brother
shared his pain and disappointment, but they did not say
anything about it so as not to upset him even more. His
self-respect made it impossible for him to ask his parents
why Nawal had stopped coming to visit him.

Was it that they had found out what his illness really
was and assumed that the situation was hopeless? Was it a
fear of contagion that made them keep her away? Had he
now become an evil to be avoided after being a beloved
suitor for so long? Had love gone back on its word? He
started mulling over his grief in silence until he could stand
it no longer. One day, when Ahmad was the only one in his
room, he broached the subject.

"Do you see how she's stopped coming?" he said.

Ahmad realized full well to whom he was referring and
feigned indifference. "Don't think about such things," he
replied. "You're fighting for your health, so don't deliberately weaken your own resistance."

"The worst thing in life," Rushdi went on as though he
had not even heard what his brother had said, "is for a
friend to shun you for no good reason, or for the only reason to be that bad health has kept him away."

"Don't bother about it and don't give in to such dark
thoughts!"

"I won't be bothering about it any more," Rushdi muttered sadly, "but such perfidy is evil!"

Ahmad shuddered to himself as he recalled that he

himself had used exactly the same phrase earlier on. "Just remember," he said, concealing his own emotions, "our hearts are with you. We still love you and will never treat you badly."

Rushdi smiled. "I can't remember when I learned these lines of poetry:

Why is it I see people shunning me,
Only stealing glances in my direction?
People never pay attention to the sufferer;
They are only interested in the healthy."

Ahmad frowned. "Are you trying to kill me with grief?" he asked.

"Good heavens, no!" Rushdi replied. "I love you even more than the idea of getting better!"

Ahmad went back to his own room. "Dear God," he asked sadly, "how can she have cut him off when he is her victim?"

44

What had actually happened is that Kamal Khalil had been concerned about the exact nature of Rushdi's illness. He soon shared his doubts with his wife. In order to put an end to any lingering doubts, he went to visit a friend of his in Bank Misr and inquired about Rushdi's illness. The man told him the truth, which made Kamal Khalil very sad because he sincerely liked Rushdi and regarded him as the best possible husband for his daughter. The news hit Sitt Tawhida with all the force of a lightning bolt, and all her hopes for Nawal's happiness vanished into thin air. Husband and wife sat down together.

"What do you think?" he asked with a frown.

His wife preferred to say nothing rather than reveal the painful truth.

"I don't think Rushdi is going to recover from this terrible disease," he said.

"God be kind to him!" she replied, clearly upset.

"And even if he does survive, he certainly won't be fit for married life."

"So what do you think?"

"I think that we have to protect my daughter's health. She's still young. Going into his room the way she has now done several times is exposing her to severe risks. She has to be told the truth so she won't continue to live on fantasies or be exposed to contagion from a disease that few people ever recover from."

"The whole thing is in God's hands," she replied, her tone one of sorrow and resignation.

They called Nawal in. She arrived, completely unaware of what they were about to tell her. She was looking downcast, a sign of how miserable she was feeling. Her father asked her to sit down on a chair opposite him.

"Nawal," he said in a grave tone, "I called you here to tell you a very important secret. I've always known you to be an intelligent girl, and I expect you always to behave properly. You have to know that our neighbor, Rushdi, is much, much sicker than people are saying...."

The girl's face went very pale. Her father's serious tone had gone straight to her heart, and she was suddenly terrified.

"What illness is it, Daddy?" she asked.

"I'm sorry to have to tell you that Rushdi is stricken with tuberculosis. As you know, it's a dreadful disease. God's mercy is wide; however, everyone has an obligation to take care of themselves and not to do anything rash, whatever the reason may be. Let's all pray that our friend recovers and remember the words of God Almighty in the Qur'an: 'Do *not cast yourself into perdition by your own hands.*'"

Tuberculosis! God in heaven! What was her father telling

her? Had her beloved Rushdi now turned into something she had to shun? Had this dreaded disease really lodged itself in his warm heart? Were all their hopes dashed and their dreams shattered? She looked back and forth between her two parents, utterly bereft. Her mother realized the agonies her daughter was going through, but had to keep the knowledge to herself in the presence of her husband.

"God knows well how sad and sorry we all are," her mother said, "and He alone can heal our wounds. But your father's right, Nawal. You're still very young, and that means that you're an easy target for this disease. So let's do what is right for both you and us, and pray to God that Rushdi may recover. God hears and answers...."

Nawal's father observed her expression from beneath his bushy eyebrows, trying to read what he could see and what she was hiding. "Now you surely understand, Nawal," he said, "why we had to call you in to talk about this. I'm sure you respect my views on the matter. I'm your father, and I'm more concerned about you than you yourself are. That's why I'm telling you that from today you cannot visit our dear sick neighbor any more. There's no reason to feel guilty about that; no intelligent, fair person can possibly hold it against you. Whatever the case may be, I don't care what other people say or whether or not they choose to blame me for something, as long as it makes sense to me. So what do you have to say?"

Nawal did not have the courage to say what was really going through her mind. The respect she had for her father was such that she could not argue with his point of view. She said nothing, and he had to prod her into saying something.

"I'll do as you say, Daddy," she replied softly.

That was all he wanted to hear. He was afraid that if they kept on talking she might reveal her true feelings, so with a sense of relief he stood up. "That's exactly what I expected of you," he said and then left the room.

No sooner had he gone than Nawal looked straight at her mother.

"How can this be, Mother?" she asked.

"It's unavoidable, Nawal," her mother replied sadly.

"How can I not visit him?" she sobbed. "How can I stay away? When someone is afraid for herself, is that a good enough reason to desert friends in their time of trial? What's the point of having friendship or decency in this world of ours?"

She could not go on, but burst into tears. Her mother almost did the same, but she realized that, if she weakened now, she was putting her daughter at risk.

"There's no point in anyone catching a fatal disease for the sake of a friend who won't be any use to you if you get sick yourself. Your father wants to make sure that you stay young and healthy, and in that he's absolutely right."

"Okay, Mother. I'm willing to let myself be deluded by such horrible talk, but it'll never do me any good. This illness is not the only evil thing in this world. Faithlessness is much worse. What will Rushdi think of me? Not only that, but how am I going to defend myself in front of him and everyone else?"

"You'll tell them that your father strictly forbade you to visit him. Your father can deal with the problems, and you have to do what he says. No one can argue with a father's right to control his daughter's behavior."

"You're so unkind, Mother! I feel as if I'm going to die of grief!"

"It would be a thousand times better for people to curse me than for me to condemn my own child to perdition."

Hot tears were still running down Nawal's face, and her voice broke. "He's going to hate me," she said in a different tone. "He'll despise me. Then, if he gets better...."

She burst into tears once again.

"That's your fate," her mother said with a sigh. "What are we supposed to do? But remember, you're still young, and there are a host of opportunities in front of you. God will heal your wounded heart. Let's pray to God that He gives Rushdi back his youth and compensates you for what you have lost."

"How can you be so unkind?" her daughter sobbed. "You're cruel and unkind!"

She ran off to her own room. By now it was evening. Teary-eyed she went over to the window and looked toward the much-beloved window opposite. It was closed, and there was a faint light visible through the cracks. She could imagine Rushdi lying on his side in bed, with that gloomy look on his face, then coughing violently.

"How sorry I feel that you have to lie there helpless, Rushdi," she said to herself, "your eyes betraying the pain you are feeling. Where have our young dreams and ideals gone, our conversations, our hopes, where have they all disappeared? O God, what wretched luck I've had, and what a gloomy world I live in!"

She threw herself down on the settee, sobbing uncontrollably. She kept trying to stop crying, but it was hopeless; the whole thing had totally sapped her energy. Her thoughts ranged far and wide with no focus to them. In a single instant her life with Rushdi flashed before her eyes, providing whatever confirmation she might need that fate had dealt her a cruel blow. She had noticed how sad and despondent both her parents had been as they spoke to her. Suddenly she became really scared. The only thing she knew about death was the word itself, but now here it was looming in front of her like a wild beast just waiting to pounce on her heart. O God! And now her parents were telling her not to visit Rushdi and placing themselves between the two of them with a merciless determination. Her teary face showed a frown, and she felt a cold shudder go through her entire body. Placing her hand on her chest, she felt deep down that she was as scared of this disease for herself as she was for her dear beloved Rushdi: bed rest, coughing, emaciation, and agony. Misery, despair, sadness, and fear—all these emotions hit her at the same time. Between her worries about her beloved Rushdi and her concerns for her own health and happiness she found herself being ripped to shreds. O God, hadn't she been living a devout, secure, and hopeful life up until now? What required her to go through all this hardship and misery?

The following afternoon she returned from school to discover that her parents had changed her room; she was now in another one far removed from the window overlooking Rushdi's. Her contact with that ray of light in her life was now forever severed.

45

Rushdi no longer mentioned Nawal's name, which came as a surprise to Ahmad. He wondered whether his younger brother was suffering his agonies in silence or rather was trying to forget by rising above things. Ahmad devoutly wished that his brother would manage to put it all behind him and find a little peace. From looking at Rushdi he could not tell what was going on inside his head. His expression was frozen, and the look in his eyes was almost permanently grim and depressed. Ahmad continued to commiserate with his brother, feeling hopelessly confused, as did his parents. It wasn't the emotional aspect of the affair that concerned them, but rather its effect on Rushdi's health, since he was fighting for his life. What made things worse was that as time went by their initial despair turned into a glimmer of hope. If anyone were to have asked why that was, the only answer would have been that time kept passing and things remained essentially unchanged. Rushdi could still not get out of bed, and his thinness still caused a good deal of alarm and worry. His complexion had a yellowish hue to it with a bit of blue mixed in, and his cough only gave him occasional respite.

In the first half of May, Rushdi was visited by the bank's doctor for another examination and extension of his sick leave as he saw fit. He gave Rushdi a cursory examination.

"As I believe you're aware," he said, "your official leave ends on May 30, 1942."

Yes indeed, he was well aware of that, and yet it was as though he were hearing it for the very first time.

"Really?" he said softly. "Yes, I do know that...."

"The amount of sick leave you still have is clearly not enough for a full recovery; that's going to take a long time. For that reason, you'll have to be fired by the bank as of May 31."

The doctor's voice sounded strange to Rushdi's ears. "Is there no hope of my being cured," he asked in an even weaker voice, "before the remainder of my sick leave comes to an end?"

The doctor was completely nonplussed by the question. "Do you really think you can get better, recover your strength and normal weight, and resume your job at the bank with just twenty days to go?" he asked. "That's out of the question. You've at least a year ahead of you before you'll be well again."

Rushdi stared at him distractedly and then looked at the floor. The doctor handed him a form stating that his sick leave would come to an end on May 30, 1942, and that he would be considered dismissed from his job as of May 31, 1942, if he had not returned to work before that time.

"Please sign this form indicating...," the doctor said in a tone that made it quite clear that he wanted to leave as soon as possible.

He thought of his brother, Ahmad, as though summoning his aid in this crucial moment. Rushdi looked first at the doctor, then at the piece of paper, clearly sensing that the man was running out of patience. He was not a little flustered, but managed to take his pen and sign the form with a trembling hand. The doctor left the room, and his mother came in to check on him, her expression showing clearly how much it was all taking out of her.

"Mother," he told her, his voice cracking, "I've just signed the form officially dismissing me from my job at the bank!"

His mother's heart gave a jolt, but she managed to control herself by not giving way to her true feelings. "Is that all that's making you sound so sad?" she asked, making light of it all. "My dear son, God has blessed us by saving you from a dangerous illness, so we should mention His name with all due gratitude. Everything else is trivial. Don't worry about it. You may lose your job today, but, God willing, you'll get it back."

"It's all over!" he said in the same tone, as though he had not heard a single thing she had said, "I've lost my job. Now past and future are forever gone!"

"Rushdi," she went on, gritting her teeth to stop herself from bursting into tears, "don't give up and don't be so sad. Through God's command and mercy, this misfortune will be removed, and you'll get your job back or find an even better one. You may be glum now, but, by God, you're going to end up smiling. May my heart prove me right!"

But he did not hear what she was saying. His eyes had wandered off to unknown horizons, and his mother had disappeared from view.

"How vile it is to be so sick!" he said as though talking to himself. "The direst pain and agony! It turns strength to weakness, youth into old age, and hope into despair. It brings down those who stand upright, idles those who work, and disfigures the loved one. My future is lost forever, my light has been extinguished, my bones have been weakened, and my hand has been crippled. O God Almighty, protect us all from the evil of disease, protect us all from the evil of disease."

With that his mother lost all control and burst into tears. "Have some pity on me, Rushdi," she sobbed.

"God doesn't want to show us any pity!" was his angry reply.

That afternoon, when his father had come home from the al-Husayn Mosque and Ahmad had come back from the ministry, the two men had a long chat with Rushdi in which they both tried to make light of what had happened and expressed the hope that he would get something better. Eventually Rushdi actually seemed to listen to them and even find some consolation in what they were saying. Ahmad realized that the cost of the medicines was going to become—in fact, had already become—more than Rushdi's salary could pay for; it was now fully one quarter of his monthly earnings, and that would be stopped after a while. And Ahmad's already overburdened salary was not going to be able to compensate for this loss.

"Rushdi," he told his brother, "you're already better than you were just a short while ago. I think you could stand spending some more time at the sanitorium. Don't you think it would be a good idea to go back there so you could have the fresh air and nursing care that you can't get here?"

The very mention of the word "sanitorium" made Rushdi shudder. "At this point," he replied, "there's no way I can even make it to the second floor, let alone transfer to the third."

"But don't the rooms on the third floor have better air and treatment than you can get in your room here?"

Rushdi shook his head, which still looked huge on his thin, elongated neck. "Life out there is foul," he said. "The sick people there frighten me. O God Almighty, protect us all from the evil of disease."

Ahmad did not continue the conversation. That evening, Rushdi and his mother were passing the time as usual chatting and listening to the radio, the sound of which floated up from the neighboring cafés. The announcer introduced Rushdi's doctor, who announced to the listeners that he was going to give his first talk about tuberculosis. The mother shuddered at the very mention of the word that kept her awake at night, but Rushdi perked up and started listening carefully. Nor were they the only two people listening; the father who was reading the Qur'an in his room also lifted his head toward the window in order to listen. Ahmad was sitting with his friends in the Zahra Café, but he stopped listening to their chatter in order to concentrate, heart pounding, on the radio broadcast. The doctor talked about the way the microbe responsible for the illness had been discovered and the various phases of the disease, describing each one in detail. He went on to discuss the problem of marriage for people who recover from the disease and how many years people with the disease could expect to spend in each phase. He finished by suggesting that the government should establish a special village for people who survived the third phase, somewhere in the desert by Helwan, a kind of isolation facility where people could spend a good part or even all of their life.

The members of the family all listened to the radio from their various places. The mother made an effort to hide the tears in her eyes, while the father went back to his reading. Ahmad's heart was weeping, although he made an effort to seem happy at what Boss Nunu was telling him. Rushdi said nothing, as he thought over what he had just heard. All of a sudden memories of his life came flooding back: his happy childhood, his love of fun and games, and his magical love—fleeting images of faces, groups, and places, all crammed together. His heart was full of regret as he plunged from the acme of hope to the very depths of despair. He forgot that his mother was there with him.

"Dear God," he yelled in despair, "if You have determined to put an end to my time on earth, then I beg you to make it quick."

His mother was stunned. "Rushdi!" she chided him.

He gave her a sad smile. "It looks as though you'll never get to see me married as you would have wished," he told her in a mocking tone of voice.

When he saw her burst into tears, he felt badly and said no more. "I'm so sorry, Mother," he apologized. "I've robbed you of food and sleep, and darkened your days. And now here I am torturing you with my drivel. Dear God, forgive me!"

46

Next day he woke up feeling more relaxed and at ease with himself. When Ahmad came into his room to say good morning, Rushdi asked if he could borrow the Qur'an. Ahmad went to get it, and Rushdi received it gladly.

"Isn't it wrong for me to touch it," he asked Ahmad, "when I haven't bathed for a month?"

"God will accept your excuse!" was Ahmad's reply.

He started reading the sacred text; if he wasn't afraid of coughing, he would have recited it in his sweet voice. He found the process calming and pleasurable; the very mention of God soothed his troubled heart and helped him forget about his longing for happier days in the past, his regret at what he had missed, and his remorse over the excesses he had committed. In fact, it even helped him forget the permanent pain which was now part of his life, the despair of any cure that was the result of the doctor's visit the day before, and the fear of imminent death that now loomed before him. At last he could escape all the pain and fear he had experienced, relying instead on a spirit of resignation, patience, and trust in God Almighty. By submitting to God's will and judgment he found a certain peace. He realized that the all-powerful nature of that very will contained within its folds both his past and future. That allowed him to submit quietly to its care just as he did to his mother's arms when he had a coughing fit.

The days went by with Rushdi peaceful, calm, and patient; there were no outbursts, no anger, and no complaints. No longer did he raise objections to anything or make sarcastic remarks. On the rare occasions when the air-raid siren went off, no one in the family left the apartment; instead, everyone felt their way to Rushdi's room in the dark and sat around his bed, hearts pounding and nerves on edge.

Time went quietly by, but then something important happened. It was late afternoon in mid-May. The father had gone to the al-Husayn Mosque to pray the evening prayer, and Ahmad was sitting in Rushdi's room chatting to him along with his mother. All of a sudden the doorbell rang and the door opened. The patter of feet could be heard as two women entered the room: Sitt Tawhida and Nawal! Utter amazement showed on everyone's face, and both brothers could feel their hearts pounding. Why had Nawal come now after so long? By doing so, she was running the risk of opening up again the wound that had at last begun to heal itself. Ahmad stood up and moved to one side, close to the window. Rushdi looked up, his eyes encircled by two bluish halos, his expression one of disbelief and even denial. But the shock soon left him, to be replaced by an intense anger that roiled his newly found calm.

Sitt Tawhida was very cheerful. She told him he looked much better. For her part, Nawal just stared at him, horrified by how thin and weak he was. She was completely overcome and could not think of anything to say. All that came out, and in the quietest of tones, was "How are you?" He did not feel like responding, but simply lifted his chin and spread his hands out, as though to say, "Just as you can see!" It was obvious to everyone that Rushdi had changed. He looked agitated and annoyed; deep inside he was feeling intense pain. With her usual aplomb Sitt Tawhida made every effort to lighten the atmosphere. She chatted away and kept laughing, doing her desperate best to get the others to laugh with her.

"I've some good news for you, Rushdi Effendi," she said. "In a dream I saw you carrying heavy loads and crossing a long bridge. You reached the other side safe and sound. That means that, God willing, you'll get better very soon!"

Rushdi's response was not a little gruff. "The doctor's already given a different interpretation of that dream," he said. "He's assured me that it'll be at least a year before I can get out of bed."

"Heaven forbid, Rushdi Effendi!" the women chided him. "You're always so pessimistic." She pointed at her daughter. "Here's Nawal," she went on. "She's come to see you. She wouldn't have stayed away if she weren't so busy with her studies, and if she hadn't gotten ill recently. She will be taking her exams at the end of this month...."

"Exactly the same date that I'm due to lose my job," Rushdi fired back.

Nawal turned pale as she realized how angry Rushdi was and why.

"That's shocking," Sitt Tawhida said, "absolutely shock-ing! Every calamity has to come to an end...."

"Except this one," said Rushdi clasping his chest. "The only end will be when my own life is ended."

"My dear Rushdi," she said, "your illness is not that severe. God willing, you'll get better."

He shrugged his shoulders."What illness are you talking about?" Rushdi shot back, his hands still across his chest. "This one is called tuberculosis. Haven't you heard of it? It's tuberculosis; it's eating away at my chest; it's turning my saliva into blood. It is a very severe, dreadful disease. And it's very contagious, so take care!"

The whole thing was too much for him and he was over-come. His mother begged him to stop talking, then begged her two guests to go into the lounge with her. She apolo-gized for the fact that Rushdi's illness was making him so intolerant. The two brothers were now left alone.

"It would have been better," said Ahmad sadly, "if you hadn't lost your temper."

"My dear brother," Rushdi replied emotionally, "she doesn't deserve the slightest sympathy! Her lack of loyalty was disgusting. As you well know, that girl is to blame for the calamity that has brought me down. If it weren't for her, I would have realized how dangerous this illness was and rid my life of it for ever. It was my fondness for her that forced me to keep it all hidden. Now you can see for yourself what it has done to me."

He sat up in bed. "What on earth possessed Nawal's mother to bring her over here?" he asked, still upset. "The crafty old woman's thinking long-term. What's more likely, a cure or death? She's holding the options close to her chest. But, I can tell you, Ahmad, from now on I'm never going to even think of getting married. Should God will that I get better, I hereby pledge to do whatever's necessary for my shattered body. Even if things work out for the best, all that lies ahead of me is genuine old age under medical supervision. Dear brother, I've a sum of money on deposit in the bank that I was saving up for marriage. I'm going to take it out and then go back to the sanitorium in Helwan. Once I'm there, I'm going to put myself at the mercy of the fates until God decides to execute His ordained decision. Take the money out tomorrow, and buy me some clothes and necessities. I'll be at the sanitorium before the month is out. And let God's will be done...."

47

At noon the following day (a Friday), Ahmad did what his brother had asked. He took his money out of the bank, bought him some pajamas, household clothes, and a few other necessities, and then returned home. He was delighted that his brother had decided to go back to the sanitorium in Helwan.

When he got back to the apartment, he found his brother smoking a cigarette. He was utterly shocked. Rushdi had stopped smoking as soon as the disease had made its first appearance. He looked sheepish as his brother came in and gave him a bashful smile.

"Who on earth gave you that cigarette?" he shouted, forgetting all about the things he had just purchased. "What on earth are you trying to do to yourself?"

He gave his mother an inquisitorial look.

"Rushdi insisted," she said by way of self-defense, "and I couldn't resist. He wouldn't keep quiet until he got what he wanted."

"Don't be hard on me, Ahmad," Rushdi said without putting the cigarette away. "I had this sudden irresistible urge to smoke a cigarette."

"This is absolute insanity!" Ahmad replied angrily.

"One cigarette's not going to hurt," Rushdi said by way of excuse. "It's so good! Let me take a few puffs in peace." He finished smoking his cigarette with obvious relish. "Don't get angry, Ahmad," he said. "That's my last cigarette. Now, what new clothes did you buy?"

Immediately after lunch he suddenly felt very weak, but did not feel like lying down. He sat on his bed, stretched his legs out, and rested his back against a folded pillow. His legs looked like two sticks, and his complexion was a pale yellow with a tinge of blue. There were dark circles around his eyes, and his eyes had an unfamiliar look to them, different from the normal sadness, as though gazing at some distant point invisible to the eye.

Late in the afternoon Ahmad came to chat with his brother before taking off for the Zahra Café.

"Are you going to the Zahra Café?" Rushdi asked him. "Say hello to all my friends there. How I wish I could spend the evening with my friends in al-Sakakini!"

Ahmad was much affected by his brother's words. "God willing," he replied, "you'll get better, then you can go back to your friends and their Sakakini nights!"

"Am I ever going to get better?" Rushdi asked despondently. "Just look at my legs. Will they ever look like human legs again?"

"Do you think God cannot make that happen if He so wishes?"

Rushdi shook his head, spoke to his brother in a way he

had never done before, as a kind of sage counselor. "Always keep a close watch on your health, Ahmad," he said. "Never treat it lightly."

For a second he stared at the floor. "Illness is like a woman," he went on in a different tone of voice, "it sucks the youth out of you and destroys all hopes."

Ahmad wondered to himself why Rushdi was talking like this and stared at him despondently.

"Microbes work unseen," Rushdi went on. "Once they have grabbed their victim, they finish him off."

"Rushdi, what are you saying?"

"I'm sharing a truth before parting. You may not see me any more after today."

"What do you mean, Rushdi," Ahmad asked in a panic, "I may not see you after today?"

Rushdi paused for a moment's thought. "Isn't it likely that you'll lose patience?" he asked as though in his normal sarcastic tone. "You'll either get fed up with the illness or else your studies will keep you preoccupied, so you'll forget all about me in Helwan!"

"Heaven forbid, Rushdi, heaven forbid!"

Rushdi gave him a very odd look. "Why don't they simply burn sick people?" he asked. "That would put them out of their misery and stop making them a burden on others!"

"Rushdi," Ahmad protested, "why on earth are you talking this way?"

Again Rushdi paused for a moment. "God curse all illness," he went on. "May God protect you from the evil of disease!"

Ahmad was totally stunned. His mother came back

with a cup of coffee that he sipped in silence. He was worried in case Rushdi started talking the same way with his mother there, but he said nothing. Ahmad relaxed a bit and assumed that he was back to his normal behavior. He stole a glance in Rushdi's direction and was struck by how weak and pale he looked and how skinny his legs were. "Can this really be you, Rushdi?" he asked himself sadly. "A pox on this disease!"

It was late when he got to the café. He always found that his time there helped calm his shattered nerves and grieving heart. He stayed there until nine-thirty, then came back to the apartment. As he walked past his brother's room, he noticed that Rushdi had taken a sleeping pill to help him sleep but was not asleep as yet.

"Good evening!" Rushdi greeted his brother. "You're back!"

"Yes," Ahmad replied looking at his brother carefully. "How are you feeling?"

"Praise be to God. How was the tea at the Zahra Café?"

"As usual."

"Drink it in good health then," Rushdi said in a barely audible voice.

Ahmad left him to get some sleep, went to his own room, and got undressed. He was feeling tense, and his nerves were on edge. He could smell something foul, and that made him even more tense and nervous. Could the anxieties that populate the deepest recesses of the human soul actually smell bad? For an hour he tried to take his mind off things by reading, then he got up to go to bed. He spent a long hour, lying there prey to dreadful thoughts and misgivings.

Next morning he woke up early to the sound of movement inside the house. His senses were immediately on the alert. Looking at his watch, he saw that it was five o'clock. He wondered what could have woken anyone up at such an early hour. He got out of bed and rushed out of his room in a panic. Before he had gone even a couple of steps toward Rushdi's room, the door was opened suddenly. Their mother emerged, holding her hands above her head as though begging for help. Then she lowered them and started slapping her cheeks violently, crazily....

48

It was a truly awful day, one long procession of pain, grief, and agony. The very memory of it grieved Ahmad, digging a pit inside his heart as deep for him as it was for his poor parents.

It began with him going into Rushdi's room, quaking in fear at the very idea of what was awaiting him there. Looking toward the bed, he saw Rushdi lying there. His mother had covered his body with a blanket, and his father was standing close by, weeping, his head downcast. Ahmad went over to the bed and pulled back the blanket. There was Rushdi, lying there as though he were sleeping, his appearance and pallor unchanged. Had the disease left anything for death to change? Leaning over, Ahmad kissed his cold forehead, then pulled the blanket back over him. Now he surrendered to the flood of tears that, fueled by so much grief, had been gathering inside him day after day until they clustered together in the chill of death and flowed in profusion.

Then his stop at the store in al-Ghuriya. As Ahmad purchased a shroud, he remembered that only yesterday he had bought his brother some clothes for this world. He had chosen the brightest colors because he knew how much Rushdi liked to look well-dressed. In a complete daze he watched the salesman's hands as he measured out the cloth and then folded it up.

Next he had to go to get a burial certificate.

"Name of the deceased?" asked the official casually.

Ahmad dearly wished that he could not hear his own voice. "Rushdi Akif," he replied.

"Rushdi Akif has died," he told himself. "How horrible can this reality be?"

"How old?" asked the official in the same cold tone.

"Twenty-six," he replied.

"What illness?"

As he told the official, he felt increasingly angry. How could he ever forget what it had done to his ill-starred brother? The way his legs and neck had looked, the color of his skin, the hacking cough? He now received a copy of the document that was required before Rushdi could disappear into the bowels of the earth forever. He expressed his thanks to the official and left. The way this official and the bank's doctor had acted in such an unfeeling fashion had aroused his anger against all human relationships in general. How could anyone be so casual about death when it was the direst thing that ever happened in life? Did a day ever go by without the sight of a coffin being carried on people's shoulders? How could they be so casual about the whole thing, as though it didn't bother them at all? Shouldn't everyone envision themselves being carried in such a coffin?

Then the profiteers of death. They came in succession, carrying washing equipment and the coffin itself. Eyes glinting, arms flexing, they all invoked false expressions of sympathy in order to hide the glee they felt as merchants about to make a good profit. For them Rushdi's beloved body was merely a commodity.

Then the casket proceeded on its way, carried on the shoulders of men decked in the white garb of youth. Ahmad let his gaze follow it as it went on its usual downward path, passed from hand to hand and shoulder to shoulder. A fez was placed on top, reminding everyone that its owner had always tilted it to the right until it almost touched his eyebrow, a sign of someone with a rakish streak who was well aware of how attractive he was. My God, all his friends were there in force, crying their eyes out. Kamal Khalil was crying too, while Ahmad Rashid looked stone-faced. Ahmad was far from delighted to see the latter among the mourners. He also avoided looking at Boss Nunu, who was flippant by nature; unlike Ahmad, he would always make light of misery and smiled his way through misfortunes.

Rushdi's father walked directly behind the coffin, his intense sorrow seeking solace in faith and piety. When the funereal procession reached the mountain road, Ahmad's emotions got the better of him—this very road had been a witness as morning after morning Rushdi had played the role of the young lover in pursuit of his love, heedless of his deadly illness. The love in his heart had been bought at the expense of his health, but then he had lost both of them. Dear God, could this road really bear witness, as the saying goes, to a friend's deceit? Could it lead him to conclude that the girl who had watched as Rushdi committed suicide for love of her had started to worry about catching the illness herself and cast him off into the wilderness?

The family tomb loomed ahead of them newly cleaned. The ground was covered with sand, and chairs had been set up in rows in front of the entrance. Water carriers moved among them. The tomb's entrance looked like a mouth yawning in irritation as it watched life's tragedy being repeated. The coffin was placed on the ground, and the covering was removed. Rushdi, wrapped in the shroud that Ahmad himself had chosen, was lifted up and clasped by hands, which then placed him into the ground. A moment later they re-emerged and started relentlessly piling earth on top of him. In just a few minutes he had completely disappeared, and the ground was level again. They then poured some water over the grave, as though somehow the crops had not been sufficiently watered yet.

Thus did a beloved person vanish forever and a life come to an end. In the blink of an eye a much-loved person simply disappears, and neither tears nor sorrows are of the slightest use. Now everyone went back, their emotions shattered. The wisdom that only yesterday had decreed that Rushdi should be a much-loved person now willed that he be forgotten. The apartment was gloomy, and the two parents were beside themselves. Rushdi's room was cleaned, then the door was locked.

Around midnight, Ahmad went to his room, his mind full of reflections. Just then he smelled something in the air. Good heavens, that foul smell was still there, the terrifying stench of death! Next morning it was still hovering in the atmosphere. He worked out that it was coming from the street leading into the old part of Khan al-Khalili. He opened the window and looked down. On the sidewalk he could see a dead dog, its stomach bloated and its flesh all puckered; it looked just like a waterskin and was covered in flies. For a while he stared at it, then looked away, his eyes welling with tears.

The days that followed were truly grim. Their father began to salve his bleeding wound with faith, but not even belief could find a way to assuage their mother's abject grief. In fact, such was her agony that she actually started blaming God, "What harm would it have done to Your world if You had left me my son?"

She then turned to her husband. "This is an unlucky quarter," she said angrily. "I agreed to come here against my will, and I've never liked it. It's here that my son became ill and died. Let's get out of here and with no regrets!"

Now she turned to Ahmad. "If you want to do something kind for your mother," she said, "find us somewhere else to live."

She hated the quarter and everyone who lived there. Ahmad had come to dislike it as well, but how was he supposed to find somewhere else when Cairo was going through such difficult times? Even so he spared no effort to respond to his mother's wishes, commissioning all his friends to look for a place anywhere in the Cairo area; not only that, but he himself decided that one way of dealing with his own intense sense of loss was to wander far and wide around the city's streets on the pretext of searching for a vacant place to live. Boss Nunu noticed how miserable Ahmad looked and did his best to cheer him up and draw him into their conversations. On one occasion he even invited Ahmad to visit Sitt Aliyat's house again, but Ahmad declined.

49

In the days that followed there were a number of significant developments in the war. The Eighth Army withdrew from Jisr al-Fursan, and in the second half of June Tobruk fell into German hands. People kept talking about the danger of invasion. The friends gathered at the Zahra Café discussed the events in their usual way.

"This time," Sayyid Arif commented gleefully, "Rommel's march can't be stopped!"

"All you German-lovers," Ahmad Rashid commented sarcastically, "do you really imagine that if the Germans invade Egypt they're going to come in peace? Isn't it more likely that there'll be a bloody war that will demolish everything standing?"

"What do we own in this country to worry about?" was Boss Zifta's flippant comment. "Rich folk who don't realize that the whole world is transient can worry all they want."

"All I have," Boss Nunu said, "is my own soul and those

of my children. They're all in God's hands, and Rommel will not have them unless God so decrees. That goes back millions of years, before Rommel was even created."

He let out one of his guffaws. "I've made a pact with God," he went on. "If Rommel enters Egypt and I'm still alive, I'm going to invite him to spend an evening at Sitt Aliyat's house. Then he'll see that Egyptian guns are much more effective than German ones."

Ahmad shared with his parents the opinions that he kept hearing, telling them about the dangers of invasion and people's fears that the air raids would now become more frequent and severe. It was almost as though he were trying to take their minds off their misery by making them scared instead.

One evening, Ahmad came home some four weeks after Rushdi's death. He found his mother waiting for him.

"Nawal came to visit me this afternoon!" she said.

The name made his heart leap, and he grabbed hold of his tie.

"Why did she come?" he asked in amazement.

"She was very upset," his mother went on. "We had barely greeted each other before she burst into tears. Her voice kept breaking as she spoke to me. 'I know you're angry with me,' she said, 'I know that you're all angry. I'm sorry, but God knows, it wasn't my fault, dear lady. They said I couldn't visit him; they stopped me coming and kept a close eye on me. They refused to listen to me when I begged to see him and totally ignored my tears. I would never have behaved that way if I had had my way. In spite of everything, I never gave up until I forced my mother to bring me over when my father was out. That's how we came to visit you on that awful day that I can't forget, that I'll never forget as long as I live. Oh, dear lady, Rushdi gave me such a look, full of contempt and hatred. It tore my wounded, innocent heart to shreds. I realized, of course, that he was getting his revenge and how much he hated me. How I suffered because of that, and I'm still suffering now. But one day he'll find out the truth; he'll know that I didn't do him wrong and I was never unfaithful to him.' "

Ahmad's heart was pounding as he listened to his mother. "Do you think she's telling the truth?" he asked.

His mother thought for a moment. "What I heard was her speaking from the heart," she replied deliberately. "I can't see why she'd take the trouble to tell lies now that it's all over. I believe she was telling the truth, although I have to say that it only increases my hatred for her parents."

Ahmad was deep in thought as he changed his clothes. Like his mother, he was inclined to believe the girl, and that made him happy. How sad that Rushdi had died, despairing of love just as he despaired of a cure. How unlucky they both were, the one who had died and the other who was still alive. Memories came flooding back to stir up his misery yet again.

"I beg Your forgiveness, O God!" he muttered to himself. "Couldn't you have chosen me instead and left my brother alone? My life has been a failure and doesn't deserve to continue, whereas Rushdi's was rich and fulfilling and should have gone on forever. Again I beg Your forgiveness, O God!"

Just at that moment he felt a sudden urge to visit his brother's locked room; he had wanted to do so several times, but had decided not to. This time, however, he could

not resist the temptation, moved as he was by feelings of
both love and sorrow. As he left his own room, it was completely quiet; his father was asleep. Approaching the door,
he was beset by a wave of depression. He turned the key in
the lock, went inside, and turned the light on. He let his
gaze wander distractedly around the empty room. A musty
smell filled his nostrils; furniture had been piled up, and
the desk was covered in a layer of dust that he wiped off.
Everything suggested farewell. God, why had he ventured
into this room when his tears had yet to dry? As he looked
around, his eyes were drawn to the drawer in the middle of
the desk and he remembered that Rushdi had kept his
diary and photograph album in it. His heart told him to
take them both back to his own room since the furniture
was going to be sold either today or tomorrow. Opening
the drawer, he took out the diary and album and blew the
dust off them. Casting one final look around the room, he
went out, convincing himself that he had gone there specifically to get the diary and album. He put them down on
his own desk and stared at them long and hard. Opening
the album at its first page, he discovered a large photograph showing Rushdi standing with his hands in his
pockets. How handsome and full of life he looked! Just
then he remembered the dead dog that had fouled his
life for two whole days, and that made him even more
morose.

He was anxious for the album to preserve its secrets, so
he did not look any further. He picked up the diary without feeling any need to pry into its secrets, but even so he
could not resist the urge to thumb through the final pages.
He skimmed some of the headings: "new love," he read,

"mountain road," "talk of love," "our hopes," and then, "the kiss that kills." That made his heart thump. What could that mean? Hadn't Rushdi used the same expression sometimes when he was feeling particularly miserable? The heading was dated the 12th of January 1942, in other words when he had first found out that he had tuberculosis. Ahmad could not stop himself reading that section, his entire being throbbing with emotion:

Monday, January 12, 1942

O my God! From today and as long as God so wills, I'm a dangerous person. Inside me is something that is harmful to other people. I am someone whose very breaths threaten God's servants; a tower about to be demolished by fatal microbes. I've played a dangerous game so as not to lose Nawal. It's no problem for us to meet each other, but I must be careful: Nawal is denied you; you certainly can't touch her. Kissing her, something that would cure the soul, is totally out of the question. She keeps on chiding me and wondering why I'm behaving this way. Maybe she's asking herself why I don't still make good use of the fact that we're alone on the road and kiss her as I used to do. Does she think that I've had enough of her lips? Is my love fading away? No, no, my love, my heart has not tired of kissing your lips nor has my love faded away. But I'm scared for you; I have to protect your lovely mouth from certain destruction. It's not my fault. My heart still feels the same way toward you, but inside my chest lurks an evil foe. I'm afraid for you and have to protect you from it.

Ahmad closed the diary and started pacing around the room, staggering as though he had just received a bang on the head. Throwing himself down on the bed, he started banging his forehead.

"O God," he yelled, "how I wronged him! How often I accused him of being thoughtless!"

It felt like a saw cutting into his heart, and he let out a groan of pain.

50

The rest of June went by, ushering in the incredible heat of July. The family was still in mourning, and a general atmosphere of gloom pervaded the house. Out of pity for his parents Ahmad was still diligently searching for somewhere else to live; in fact, he was tired of Khan al-Khalili as well. The shock of Rushdi's death had badly affected his sensitive nerves, and his old insomnia returned. This nervous sensitivity brought with it other symptoms: he could become emotional very quickly and often fell prey to worries that drove him into depression. Sorrows over both past and present clustered together inside his churning heart, and he was permanently fearful about what griefs, worries, and sorrows the future might be holding in store.

"Whatever happiness we may feel toward our loved ones today," he told himself with his parents in mind, "is merely a pawn for the tears that we'll be shedding when we say farewell to them on the morrow."

He recited a line of poetry by Abu al-Ala' al-Ma'arri: "If

calamity does not strike at night, then fortune's decision will find you on the morrow!"

His nerves were useless when it came to enduring fate's vicissitudes or life's troubles, and he was on the point of falling prey to his old illness. All of which helps explain why he was so keen to leave the quarter, added to which was the fact that sirens kept going off day and night (although the city was not actually bombed as had happened the previous September).

The general situation became much more tense when Axis forces kept on advancing, crossed the Egyptian border, and penetrated deep into the country. They moved on past Marsa Matruh which was generally reckoned to be the most significant defense point for Egypt, then overran Fuka and Dab'a. When the invasion got as far as al-Alamein, general panic reached its height. The city of Alexandria was now in the invaders' sights, and people started saying that the necessities of war were such that they threatened to turn Egypt into a crumbling ruin watched over by hooting owls and a mosquito-breeding swamp.

On the day German forces reached al-Alamein, the friends gathered at the Zahra Café as usual. They were all delighted to see each other, and there was much laughter. None of them had thought about leaving the quarter or stocking up on food. Not a single one of them had bothered to assess the potential impact of an invasion on the city; or, if they had, they were treating the whole thing as something to joke about, as though it really did not concern them at all.

"The whole thing's in God's hands," was the word of the hour, "so whatever happens to everyone else can happen to us as well!"

Ahmad Akif did not disagree with what they were saying. On that day in particular, he found being in their company especially enjoyable; it was as if their tiny gathering were serving as a kind of retreat whereby he could escape from the general alarm that everyone seemed to be feeling. He was afraid and happy at the same time. Thinking about what might happen, he started to worry. Before his eyes there loomed a situation in which everything would be turned upside down, all sense of responsibility would disappear, and values would collapse. Deep down he felt a nervous thrill. The anticipated invasion would do away with all his worries and sorrows. Along with everything else, all traces of the past, including his own, would be swept away.

"Just listen to the latest news," said Sayyid Arif using the tone of someone in the know. "Rommel has divided his forces in two: one pointing toward Alexandria, the other toward the Fayyum oasis."

"I've heard that Alexandria's being bombarded by air and land," said Ahmad Rashid. "People are leaving the city and going to Damanhur."

"Are the English really done for?"

"They're burning their papers and evacuating their women."

"When will the Germans reach Cairo?"

"Tomorrow or the day after...."

"Unless they move their victorious army toward Suez...."

"I've heard for sure that parachute troops have been landing in the fields."

"And what would any of you do," asked Boss Nunu, "if

one of those parachutists landed near you and asked you for directions to the war zone?"

"I'd take him straight to Sulayman Bey Ata's house," Sayyid Arif responded immediately, "and tell him 'Look, here's the British ambassador!'"

"You'd be much better off offering him some of those pills you take for your illness!" Sulayman Ata replied angrily.

"I'll tell you what I'd do," said Boss Zifta. "I'd take him to Abbas Shifa's apartment and show him the biggest pair of you-know-whats in Egypt!"

"How long are we going to joke around like this?" asked Ahmad Akif in amazement. "Don't you all realize that there's a real threat of our having to leave our homes? We may well be sent out to some filthy villages."

"Oh, for the wonderful life in the village!" yelled Boss Nunu in reply.

"Aren't you afraid of death?" Ahmad Rashid asked.

"Let me live long enough," said Boss Zifta, "and throw me at Rommel."

"True enough," said Boss Nunu, faking a serious tone, "the Germans are monsters. When they invade a country, they spread out all over the place and disguise themselves in a whole variety of ways. By tomorrow you may come across Germans wearing turbans or women's clothes. By God, I'm worried in case I turn on the water faucet to perform my ablutions before I pray and a German diver comes out...."

At that very moment, as if on cue, the air-raid sirens went off.

It was seven o'clock in the evening. They all leapt to their feet, and the smiles rapidly vanished from their faces. They all rushed for the bomb shelter, many of them afraid that this would be a really fierce and destructive raid, as usually happens before an invasion. They had only to remember Alexandria, Suez, and Port Said, not to mention Warsaw and Rotterdam. It took only a few minutes for the shelter to be bulging with people. Ahmad sat with his parents. Everyone was very scared. It was all too much for his mother, and he could see tears in her eyes. Twenty minutes passed in an agony of waiting, then the all-clear siren sounded. Everyone was astonished and looked relieved and happy.

"It was just a reconnaissance mission!" someone yelled, while others suggested that the plane had come close to Cairo but then turned round and changed direction.

Everyone made their way toward the exit, and Ahmad joined the crowd. Close by the exit he spotted Nawal holding the arm of her little brother, Muhammad. The two of them were laughing as they hurried back to their apartment. His heart gave a thump, something that usually happened whenever he saw or remembered her. He watched as she moved toward the exit and then disappeared around the corner. Suddenly he felt angry and miserable. The way she had been laughing infuriated him, as though he had caught her committing some foul crime. He was so upset that he decided not to go back to the Zahra Café until he had taken a walk to calm himself down.

As he strolled down al-Azhar Street, he started to feel calmer. Actually, his mood returned to normal much more quickly than he had expected and he asked himself why he had been so angry. What had upset him? Was it her laugh? Did he really expect her to spend her entire life weeping?

Didn't he laugh sometimes at work or in the café? Didn't even his mother smile once in a while? Why shouldn't Nawal laugh, and why should it annoy him if she did? No, the process of forgetting was the real culprit—that bitter pill that comes when mourning is finished and sorrow takes over; mourning for our pain, sorrow for ourselves. We tell ourselves that, thank God, we have forgotten; that is one of life's laws.

He gave a deep sigh, but then a thought occurred to him, one that was by no means new but at the same time one he had been avoiding. He was afraid to confront it, but this time he told himself that it was useless to run away and pretend it wasn't there. He had to confront reality. Did he still love Nawal? Why was his heart still pounding every time he saw her or thought of her?

He pondered all this as he continued his stroll, his pale face flushing in embarrassment as though his secret were now known to everyone. "Love," he told himself, "was something buried under layers of anger, sorrow, and terrible memories. To be loyal to such a love, I would now have to trample underfoot both my sense of honor and my brother's memory. That, of course, is out of the question. So, my brother and my pride stand between me and my love, and it is not worth my life to show such contempt for two things that are so very dear to me!"

But it was all true: he was still in love with Nawal; in fact, he had never stopped loving her even though his various sufferings might have kept the fact hidden from him. Even so, what would be the point of acknowledging such a love, even if it was the strongest force of all? How long could he tolerate being so close to the flame that was burning him up?!

51

At the end of August Ahmad Akif found an empty apartment in the al-Zaytun neighborhood. It was in a place owned by a civil servant in the Accounting Department at the Ministry of Works. He had heard that Ahmad was looking for somewhere to move, and by chance the civil servant who had been living there had to break his lease because he was being transferred abroad. The owner invited Ahmad to visit him, discussed the possibility, and rapidly reached an agreement, namely that the family would move in at the beginning of September as soon as the other tenant moved out.

Everyone in the family was delighted that they would soon be leaving Khan al-Khalili with all its gruesome memories. Even now they were having to leave with a broken wing. The father was suffering from high blood pressure that interfered with his retirement, while the mother continued to grieve, which made her lose a lot of weight. Her innate jollity was quashed under the burden of it all, and she began to look very old. Ahmad was just as sad, and yet he could see stars twinkling on the horizon. People started talking about fair treatment for workers who had been overlooked for a long time, and it seemed as though a promotion to the seventh grade was within the realms of possibility. He had always despised ranks and civil servants who held them, but deep inside he was happy about the anticipated promotion. He would be in charge of four employees in addition to the incoming mail and genuinely aspired to turn the position into a new initiative in government administration, one that would serve as a model for his boss, "the all-knowing." Who knows what the future might hold? He could still look forward to some twenty years in government service, so maybe he would be promoted even further. At long last, the government would be getting things right!

Nor was that all. He had taken his mother with him to look at the new apartment. The owner of the house had invited them both to his own apartment. While Ahmad had drunk coffee with him in the lounge, his mother had been invited into the women's quarters. On their way back to Khan al-Khalili his mother had been full of praise for the owner's wife and his sister as well. Concerning the latter, his mother had told him that she was a cultured and attractive widow of fifty-three. That set his imagination working: the sister a fifty-three-year-old widow, cultured and attractive, and himself a bachelor of forty and colleague of her brother, both of them living in the same house. As far as he was concerned, the age difference was not significant; she was not that old, nor was he any spring chicken either. So life was not without its hopeful prospects, and only God could know what lay in the future.

Even so, such thoughts could not coincide with wearing a black tie. Good God, how could these dreams of his be floating around so openly? At that moment it occurred to him that from now on Nawal might well be casting her glance somewhere else, at Ahmad Rashid, for example. That's the way life proceeded on its course, oblivious to everything; it was almost as if it had not been just the day before that it had bid farewell to someone who had played such a prominent role. Life was dumb and cruel, like the dirt of the earth, and yet it could nurture hope just as easily as the earth did fresh flowers. Ahmad was still sad, but hope was there as well.

Thus the family started preparing to move. Carpets were folded up, cupboards and beds were taken apart, and utensils, books, and pieces of furniture were put in boxes. The move was to be the next day.

That afternoon the women of the apartment building all arrived to say farewell to the family. Ahmad was still in his room. Sitt Tawhida and Nawal were among the women who came to visit for the last time. They all sat in the central lounge since that was the only place in the apartment where anyone could sit. After the other women had left, Sitt Tawhida and Nawal stayed behind. By that time Ahmad was due to go out to the Zahra Café to say farewell to his friends there. There was no way he could avoid walking past the two visitors. When he came out of his room, Sitt Tawhida stood up.

"How are you, Ahmad Effendi?" she asked, offering him her hand.

"I'm well, thank God," Ahmad replied softly in his usual flustered manner. "Thank you."

Nawal had stood up as well. He turned to her and offered his hand. Their hands touched for the first time ever, and his body shuddered. He did not say a word or even look up at her.

"I'm still apologizing to your mother for the way we behaved," Sitt Tawhida said. "I hope you can find it in you to forgive us as well, Ahmad Effendi. As God knows full well, your late lamented brother was very dear to us...."

Ahmad was not a little bewildered. "We can all forgive you," he replied. "Necessity has its own imperatives, dear lady."

Sitt Tawhida deftly steered her way around the subject. She thanked Ahmad for his politeness and understanding. He then excused himself, said farewell to Sitt Tawhida, and held out his hand to Nawal. This time, as their hands were touching, he snatched a quick look into her eyes, but then headed straight for the door. It was the first time their eyes had met up close; he had barely looked at her since those early days when, bolstered by his initial hopes, he had flirted with her between his window and the balcony. In her eyes he could still detect the same purity, kindness, and curiosity he had seen before. As he quickened his pace, his heart kept pounding and his eyes twitched nervously. Maybe the problem was that they were saying good-bye. Farewells tend to arouse feelings even in people who normally do not get emotionally involved, so it was this farewell psychology that he invoked as an excuse for the fact that he was now feeling so emotional and upset. It was all intensified by the memory of Rushdi; his beloved image appeared before Ahmad's eyes with a chiding smile on his face. Ahmad found himself addressing his brother's image:

"I'm sorry, Rushdi," he said, "I was just saying good-bye. You know about that better than anyone. It was painful too, and you know about that too. You won't need to chide me any more, I promise."

Ahmad reached the Zahra Café; God alone knew when he would have the chance to go out to a café again. His friends greeted him warmly, as was only appropriate for a farewell occasion. They all stopped talking in order to concentrate on saying good-bye to their dear neighbor.

"Do you think you'll forget us?" Boss Nunu asked.

"Heaven forbid, Boss!" Ahmad replied, entirely unclear as to whether or not he was telling the truth.

"Al-Zaytun's a long way away," Boss Zifta said. "You can only get there by train."

"Train rides shouldn't keep friends apart!" Ahmad replied with a smile.

Abbas Shifa raised his eyebrows as though he were recalling something significant. "I know al-Zaytun just as well as I know Khan al-Khalili," he said. "A while back I used to go there at least once a week. I'd come back with the very best hashish!"

Ahmad grinned. "So can I expect to be seeing a lot of you?" he asked.

"Oh, those days are long gone!" Abbas Shifa said sadly. "They threw the seller into prison, and that's where he died."

Everyone said how sorry they were that he was leaving. They complimented him on his fine family and gave their condolences for the loss of his brother. Even Sulayman Ata had nice things to say. At this final moment Ahmad's heart was bursting with affection for all of them, the ones he

liked such as Boss Nunu and the others he did not like such
as Ahmad Rashid. He was surprised to realize that, when
it came time to say farewell, his heart was always sorry to
leave anything, however tedious and burdensome it might
have been.

At this point everyone started talking as usual about the
war situation. They mentioned that the German advance
had been halted at al-Alamein. It was Ahmad Rashid's
opinion that the Germans had now lost the battle for
Egypt. Sayyid Arif had another take on it. According to
him, Hitler had ordered Rommel to halt so as to avoid
attacking Egypt—the throbbing heart of Islam—and all
the suffering that an invasion would cause. If it weren't
for the Fuhrer's merciful judgment, the Germans would
already have been in Cairo a month ago. Ahmad stayed
with them, listening to their conversation and banter, but
when it was nine-thirty, he stood up to say farewell for the
last time. Shaking their hands one by one, he received their
best wishes with thanks. With that he headed back to the
apartment.

Once in his room, he opened the window and looked
out on the quarter. It was the middle of the month of Shaaban, and the moon was gleaming brightly in the clear
August sky. All around it stars were twinkling coyly as
though to express their regret that the moon had again
appeared in its youthful guise, something that they had
always known would not last. The moonlight bathed the
entire quarter in a shimmering silver glow that banished
the lonely darkness of night and imbued street corners and
alleyways with a particular magic.

It was the night of mid-Shaaban, and the prayers for

that holy night could be heard through the neighboring windows. You could hear a boy shouting in his high-pitched voice: "O God, the one and only Bestower, Possessor of Majesty and Honor," and the family repeated it after him. And he was the only silent one among them. What kind of prayer could he offer to his Lord, he wondered? He thought for a while, then lifted his hands toward the shining moon.

"O God," he said humbly, "Creator of the universe, Ordainer of everything, envelop him in the broad expanse of Your mercy and let him dwell in Your spacious heavens. Grant to his grieving parents solace and perseverance, and to my own heart bring peace and tranquility. In the days ahead grant that I may find consolation for what is past" (and at this point Ahmad put his hand over his heart). "This heart of mine has endured a great deal of pain and swallowed failure and frustration."

Was he remembering the day he had arrived in this old quarter, with the same quest for change in mind? Well, change had certainly taken place, but all it had brought were tears and despair. Ramadan would soon be here again. What memories! Could he still remember the last Ramadan, with him poised by the window waiting for the sunset prayer, then looking upward and seeing her there?

Now here was history itself, passing in front of his eyes just as it had been recorded by the onward march of days and nights, written with the ink of hope, love, pain, and sorrow. So this was the final night. Tomorrow he would be living in a new home, in a different quarter, turning his back on the past...a past with all its hopes and dashed aspirations.

Farewell then, Khan al-Khalili!

Translator's Afterword

At my first meeting with Naguib Mahfouz (d. 2006) in 1969, the discussion began with the topic of translation, but not of his own work. At the time I was revising my doctoral dissertation on the renowned narrative of the Egyptian writer Muhammad al-Muwaylihi (d. 1930), *Hadith 'Isa ibn Hisham* (which was originally published in 1907; my translation and study of it eventually appeared in book form as *A Period of Time* in 1992). Mahfouz was delighted to hear of my interest in that work, since he acknowledged to me that it had long been a favorite of his family and had had a great influence on him as a teenager as, it would appear, it did on another great Egyptian storyteller, Mahmud Taymur (d. 1973). Inevitably, however, the conversation gradually shifted to his own works, and I told him that I had read and greatly admired many of the short stories in his recently published collection, *Khammarat al-qitt al-aswad* (Black Cat Tavern, 1967). When I asked him if he would allow me to translate some of them, he readily agreed and asked me to make a list of the ones I particularly liked. Once I had recorded the names of five or six stories, he asked if I was interested in any of the novels. Because its political context is set during and after the 1952 revolution, I had recently purchased *al-Summan wa-l-kharif* (1962; *Autumn Quail*, 1985), and thus that title was added to the list. Mahfouz signed his name to the paper (which I still cherish in my files), and my career as a translator of Mahfouz began.

In fact, it began, somewhat unusually perhaps, not with his novels, but rather with a collection of short stories— the ones on the list that I had chosen myself, and others that I proceeded to translate with an Egyptian colleague, Akef Abadir. The collection, *God's World*, containing a selection of short stories culled from all his collections up until the year 1970, was published in 1973 and was mentioned in the Nobel Committee's citation in October 1988 (although most critics in the Arab world incorrectly assumed that it was a reference to the Arabic collection *Dunya Allah* (1962), from which we had selected its title story for inclusion in our own collection).

Over the ensuing decades that short story collection was to be followed by my translations of *Autumn Quail* (1985), *Mirrors* (1977, 1999, based on *al-Maraya*, 1972), some individual short stories, and finally *Karnak Café* (2007) (a translation of the highly controversial novel, *al-Karnak*, 1974). This translation into English of *Khan al-Khalili* (1945), certainly one of the earliest, if not *the* earliest, of his "novels of the 1940s," thus takes me back to a much earlier period in his novelistic output. It is to the impressions that such a return to beginnings has brought about for a translator that I would now like to turn.

The novel, *Khan al-Khalili*, is named for one of the most famous quarters of the old city of Cairo, the one founded in the tenth century following the invasion of Egypt by Shi'ite Fatimid forces. The new city was constructed in the area immediately below the Muqattam Hills. At its center was the mosque of al-Azhar, originally established in 972 CE as a center for Shi'ite learning but one that over the centuries has become a primary source of both education and doctrinal discussion within the Sunni community. However, the most prominent Islamic monument in the Khan al-Khalili quarter itself is the mosque–shrine of al-Husayn, the grandson of the Prophet Muhammad, who was slain during the tragic schism that, within decades of Muhammad's death in 632, had split the early Islamic community in two. The mosque itself contains some of the relics of al-Husayn and is thus a shrine frequently visited by devout Muslims, among whom we may list both the father of the Akif family in the present novel and the mother of the 'Abd al-Gawwad family in Mahfouz's renowned trilogy of novels; during her visit to the al-Husayn shrine, she is knocked down, with tragic consequences for herself and her family, as recounted in *Bayn al-qasrayn* (1956; *Palace Walk*, 1990).

The Akif family moves to Khan al-Khalili from the suburb of al-Sakakini, a change that is in the opposite direction to that of the one Mahfouz himself made as a child. Having been born and grown up in al-Gamaliya, equally close to the al-Husayn shrine, his father moved the family to the more rural (at that time, at least) suburb of Abbasiya. However, as any number of articles and television programs have pointed out, Mahfouz never lost his deep and abiding affection for the quarter in which he grew up, and evidence of that is abundant in the descriptions to be found on the pages of *Khan al-Khalili*, as well as other novels penned during the 1940s and into the '50s, culminating in the trilogy, *Bayn al-qasrayn*, *Qasr al-shawq* (1957; *Palace of Desire*, 1991), and *al-Sukkariya* (1957; *Sugar Street*, 1992). Many too are the photographs that show Mahfouz, by now the well-known Egyptian novelist, sitting in the Fishawi Café in Khan al-Khalili that, like its analogue, the Zahra Café in the novel *Khan al-Khalili*, lies in the shadow of the al-Husayn shrine. Is it any wonder then that this novel and the others in this "series," with their utterly authentic portraits of every aspect of life in these ancient quarters, continue to hold such a central place in the hearts of Egyptian readers?

In this novel, place plays a crucially important role, as it does in all the other "quarter novels," but so does time. Following Mikhail Mikhailovich Bakhtin's notion of the chronotope, we can note that the two are almost inevitably linked to each other. The Akif family's move to the Khan al-Khalili quarter is not a voluntary one, but is rather the result of panic caused by a bombing raid. The novel's time period is that of the middle of the Second World War, and *Khan al-Khalili* records in vivid detail the often-neglected direct effects of the Africa Campaign on the Egyptian capital city. The social effects of the war and the continuing British occupation of Egypt (that started following the 'Urabi Revolt of 1882) are very much to the fore in the long-famous novel, *Zuqaq al-Midaqq* (1947; *Midaq Alley* [sic], 1977), in which the climactic scene sees the young Egyptian, Abbas, battered to death by British soldiers as he confronts Hamida, the quarter's beauty, who has become a call girl. In *Khan al-Khalili* however, the impact of the war is, if anything, even more direct and vividly described. The tenants of the neighborhood into which the Akif family moves regularly find themselves being woken up in the middle of the night by the dreadful sound of air-raid sirens. The bomb shelter to which they all descend may be a haven from the potential destruction above, but the descriptions of these panic-stricken hours spent underground are used by Mahfouz as an effective means of portraying the clashing emotions Egyptians feel as they confront the consequences of other people's wars. The conversations among the group that gathers every night at the Zahra Café are another device whereby the novelist is able to illustrate the wildly contrasting attitudes of the various social strata of Egyptian society as they react to the war going on around them.

Many commentators on Mahfouz's career have suggested that it was precisely the dire impact of the war on contemporary Egyptian society during the early 1940s that led Mahfouz to abandon his plan, as usual carefully elaborated, to write a whole series of novels set in ancient Egypt. He had, in fact, already published three of them (along with some short stories): *'Abath al-aqdar* (1939; *Khufu's Wisdom*, 2003); *Radubis* (1943; *Rhadopis of Nubia*, 2003); and *Kifah Tiba* (1944; *Thebes at War*, 2003), but his plans for a whole series of others, based no doubt on his long-standing interest in ancient Egypt, were put aside in favor of a concentration on the current travails of his fellow Egyptians. In this context it needs to be added that, at various stages in his very long career, he was to return to the ancient Egyptian theme, of which *Amam al-'arsh* (*Before the Throne*, 1983) and *al-'A'ish fi-l-haqiqa* (1985; *Akhena-ton, Dweller in Truth*, 1998) are merely two examples.

Mahfouz's inspiration to write these "pharaonic" novels may well have come from both his youthful enthusiasm for ancient Egypt and its impact on Egyptian nationalist ideals and from his readings of the perennially popular historical novels of Jurji Zaydan (d. 1914), which had taken episodes from Arab and Islamic history as their chronological frame of reference. However, the turn to the contemporary period and to the process of writing novels about the Egyptian society of his own day was clearly the consequence of a concentrated course of study that he had initiated during the 1930s under the inspiration of his mentor and (then) publisher, the renowned Coptic Fabian intellectual, Sal-ama Musa (d. 1958). It was this figure who encouraged the young graduate student in philosophy to consider a career as a writer and suggested that he investigate the tradition of fiction writing in the West. One work that we are told Mahfouz consulted was *The Outline of Literature* (1923) by John Drinkwater, with its "handy list" of novel titles as an appendix. Mahfouz, it would appear, made his way methodically and steadily through the works on the list, which included the most famous novels from the various European traditions, comprising examples of historical romances, bildungsroman, family sagas, and the like. This ongoing process of reading European fiction (mostly through the medium of English), coupled with his own wide knowledge of and devotion to the pre-modern heri-tage of Arabic literature, was to provide the inspirational framework for the lengthy and variegated career in fiction writing that was to follow.

Within the earlier phases of this developmental framework, *Khan al-Khalili* emerges as a remarkably successful
contribution to the family saga, a sub-genre of the novel
that was to be seen again at the end of the 1940s in his
Bidaya wa nihaya (1949; *The Beginning and the End*,
1985) and, almost immediately afterward, in the three volumes of his trilogy—in which the narrative of the life of
the 'Abd al-Gawwad family is heavily focused on the story
of Kamal's upbringing (a character, the features of whose
life and times have long been associated with those of
Mahfouz himself). In the case of *Khan al-Khalili*, we are
dealing with the Akif family, although, as the narrative
progresses, the narrative focuses in the main on the two
sons and, even more specifically on the elder of the two,
Ahmad; descriptions of his movements both start and conclude the narrative. Ahmad clearly regards himself as the
ill-starred victim of his family's circumstances: the indo-
lence of his father that leads to his compulsory early retirement and the resulting need for Ahmad to assume the
burden of supporting the family as a whole and, in particular, his younger brother, Rushdi, as he goes through
school and university. However, the novel's narrator also
provides the reader with a portrait of Ahmad as a rather
pathetic middle-aged man whose lack of initiative, intellectual arrogance, escapism, and chronic shyness have all
led inexorably to a situation in which life has essentially
passed him by. The move from the suburbs to Khan
al-Khalili provides a jolt to his complacent existence, but,
in spite of the new acquaintances that he makes—most
notably at the Zahra Café—his attitude toward life and
people remains essentially unaltered. It is his fleeting

encounter with the neighbor's teenaged daughter, Nawal, which rocks the static monotony of his existence. An agonizingly hopeless and unfulfilled "relationship" ensues, involving traditional exchanges of glances across the alleyway and brief encounters in the air-raid shelter during bombing raids.

Into this painfully slow scenario bursts the figure of the younger son, Rushdi, returning from a period working in the southern city of Asyut. The two brothers, who dearly love each other, could hardly be more different. Rushdi is young, handsome, dashing, and reckless, devoted to a nightlife of carousing, drinking, sex, and gambling. Having spotted the beautiful Nawal, he chases her, walks her to school, and wins her heart. However, just as a genuine love is blooming (and gradually being acknowledged and even accepted by both families), Rushdi becomes ill. Tragedy has struck the Akif family once again. It is tuberculosis, and Rushdi needs to go to the sanitorium. In spite of Ahmad's pleas and eventual anger, Rushdi refuses to acknowledge the extent of his illness and carries on with his reckless behavior. Eventually he cannot avoid accepting the inevitable and goes to the sanitorium. By this time, however, it is much too late, and Ahmad brings his brother back to Khan al-Khalili where he dies in the arms of his devastated mother.

The family now decides that it must move again. As the novel ends, they have found a new apartment. Ahmad's mother even intimates that their new landlord has a sister in her fifties who might be a suitable partner for him. Although Ahmad bids a nostalgic farewell to his friends at the Zahra Café, there are a few glimmers of hope for the

Akif family as it prepares to move against the backdrop of the allied victory at al-Alamein.

Khan al-Khalili shows clearly that Mahfouz is already the master of novel construction, albeit within a series of modes that, from a twenty-first–century perspective, can be described as "traditional" (and certainly based on European models). The novel opens with detailed descriptions of time and place, as Ahmad travels along an unfamiliar route to his family's new abode. Khan al-Khalili and its denizens are lovingly described, and Ahmad and his career are placed within this changing framework as the family sets itself to adjust to new surroundings. The first glimpse of Nawal in the stairway leads to a series of chapters in which Ahmad contemplates his career and his future. The return of Rushdi (chapter 16) changes everything, and the center of the novel is concerned about his developing love affair with Nawal and Ahmad's silent agony as he watches it develop. It is on the day of the Eid al-Adha (chapter 33) that the dreadful news of Rushdi's illness is first revealed, and the developing tragedy leading to his death and burial follows its inexorable course. At the end of the novel the family's second move in such a short period is placed once again within the broader framework of Egyptian society as it tries to cope with the consequences of a global conflict on its soil.

Many commentators have remarked about the accuracy of Mahfouz's description of place in this series of "quarter novels," but we need also to point to the poetic quality of some of his descriptions, a feature that is to emerge in starker relief in his later novels, especially those of the 1960s. Here, for example is his description of the sky as Rushdi is walking Nawal to her school in Abbasiya:

It was a crisp, damp morning, a little chilly. A gentle breeze was blowing, bringing with it intimations of November, which mourns for the flower blossoms of lovers. The sky was full of bright clouds. Sometimes they were clustered together, but then they would break up and turn into frozen lakes that refracted the early morning rays of the sun from the horizon. The way their fringes sparkled in the sunlight was eye-catching.

Or this depiction from the very last scene in the novel as Ahmad looks out of his window for one last time:

It was the middle of the month of Shaaban, and the moon was gleaming brightly in the clear August sky. All around it stars were twinkling coyly as though to express their regret that the moon had again appeared in its youthful guise, something that they had always known would not last. The moonlight bathed the entire quarter in a shimmering silver glow that banished the lonely darkness of night and imbued street corners and alleyways with a particular magic.

Another feature of novel writing where Mahfouz's developing technique appears in this novel is that of dialogue. While, in accordance with his views on language (that are certainly not shared by all writers of Arabic fiction), he writes his conversations in the standard written language *(fusha)*, he is still successful in conveying both the context and mood of the occasion involved. This applies particularly to the conversations at the Zahra Café, of course, but it is equally in evidence in an entirely different situation, the love-chatter between Rushdi and Nawal (chapter 27).

Mahfouz's narrator is, to use one of Bakhtin's terms again, "monologic." This more traditional aspect of the narrative craft comes to the fore frequently in *Khan al-Khalili* when the inner thoughts of characters need to be revealed: the often furious and agonized musings of Ahmad throughout the work, and Nawal's bemused comparison of the two brothers (chapter 27). The same narrator is also not above providing the reader with some more generalized thoughts and opinions on the evils of gambling (chapter 18), the value of singing and singers (chapter 25)—a favorite topic of Mahfouz—and death (chapter 43). Here, above all, is one feature of narrative technique that Mahfouz was to develop and refine further, particularly in the novels of the 1960s.

It goes without saying that the ways in which Mahfouz makes use of all of these various narrative features have had an impact on, and are reflected in, the process of translating this novel into English. The "more traditional" aspects of *Khan al-Khalili*—the carefully organized and chronologically linear approach to time and the lovingly detailed descriptions of place (the apartment's bomb shelter being merely one, more obvious, example)—are characteristic of phases in novelistic development that are, to quote E. M. Forster—a similarly "traditional" critical source—reflections of a narrative strategy that relies on "telling" rather than "showing." Beyond that, the philosophical and ethical musings of Ahmad in the face of his own failures, his tortured affection toward Nawal, and above all the complex sentiments that result from his own deep and abiding love for his brother, Rushdi, these reflections and emotions are couched in often lengthy and aphoristic passages that clearly reflect an earlier phase in the development of the novel genre in general and of its Arabic context in particular. In noting that I have made no attempt either to eradicate or gloss over these features of *Khan al-Khalili* in this translation, I would suggest that there is great value in observing Naguib Mahfouz, generally acknowledged as being the foundation-layer of modern Arabic fiction, in the process of honing his fictional craft in this novel. In such a context, two points of comparison might be made: the first is with the justly renowned *Trilogy* (published in 1956 and 1957) with which the series of "quarter novels" from the mid-1940s and early '50s may be seen to culminate, and where there is a clearly visible development in the process of balancing the various elements of "showing" and "telling," including descriptions of time and place, dialogue between characters, and the various modes of reflection; the second point of comparison is with the novels that Mahfouz published in the 1960s— *al-Liss wa-l-kilab (The Thief and the Dogs)*, for example, *Tharthara fawq al-Nil (Adrift on the Nile)*, or *Miramar*— where descriptions of time and place are much more terse and allusive, and the techniques of dialogue and interior monologue are invoked in order to reveal ("show") to the reader the innermost feelings of the characters. By the 1970s, the above-mentioned and more traditional features of *Khan al-Khalili*, characteristic of a much earlier stage in his development as a novelist, have all but disappeared. I might add here that, as the English translator of his *al-Karnak* (1974; *Karnak Café*, 2006), I have almost automatically been made abundantly aware of quite how far Naguib Mahfouz traveled in his career as a novelist in quest of new narrative techniques and appropriate levels of discourse and, in that process, quite how much he contributed to the genre's development throughout the Arabic-speaking world.

This novel then provides us with an excellent example of a master novelist giving his readers a vivid and detailed portrait of his native Egypt and one of its capital city's most ancient and august quarters during a crucial stage of the Second World War. Beyond the importance of that historical context, however, it is also an example of the careful research and planning, not to mention the artistry and craft, which were to remain features of his fiction for the next fifty years or more.

Glossary

Abd al-Hayy, Salih (d. 1962): an exponent of the classical style of singing, he became well known during the 1920s, particularly for his performances of the popular poetic genre of *mawwal*. He also sang with Munira al-Mahdiya (see below).

Abd al-Wahhab, Muhammad (d. 1991): Egypt's most famous male singer in the twentieth century, renowned for incorporating western instrumentation and melody into his songs.

al-Alamein: on the Mediterranean coast of Egypt, the site of a turning-point battle in 1942 during which Allied forces led by Field Marshal Bernard Montgomery stopped the advance of Axis powers under General Erwin Rommel.

Ali ibn Abi Talib: the Prophet Muhammad's cousin and son-in-law who became the fourth Caliph of Islam and the founding figure of the Shi'a subdivision of the Muslim community (Shi'a being an abbreviation of Shi'at Ali—Ali's party).

Almaza: a district of Cairo to the northeast of the center, between Heliopolis and the suburb of Madinat Nasr.

al-Azhar: the world-renowned mosque–university in Cairo, founded in the late tenth century.

Bayt al-Qadi: literally "the judge's house," a section (and square) of the old city of Cairo between the al-Husayn Mosque and the northern gate, Bab al-Futuh.

Bulaq: a district of Cairo adjacent to the River Nile. It gave its name to the first printing press in Cairo during the reign of Muhammad Ali.

City of the Dead: formerly this name was applied only to Cairo's southern cemetery, but for some time the name has been used to refer to both the southern and northern ones (the latter being formerly known also as "the tombs of the caliphs"). It is this latter cemetery that is referred to in this novel.

The Complete Work (al-Kamil) by al-Mubarrad, *The Scribe's Manual (Adab al-katib)* by Ibn Qutayba, *The Book of Eloquence and Clear Expression (Kitab al-bayan wa-l-tabyin)* by al-Jahiz, and *The Book of Anecdotes (Kitab al-nawadir)* by Abu Ali al-Qali from Baghdad: all these are titles of major works that form part of the library of compendia on secretarial writing within the tradition of Arabic prose.

Dab'a: a town on the Egyptian Mediterranean coast, the scene of fighting during the 1942 campaigns.

al-Darrasa: an area that was formerly right on the eastern edge of the city of Cairo, but is now an inhabited suburb close to the City of the Dead (see above) and the Muqattam Hills.

"Do not cast yourself into perdition by your own hands": Qur'an, Sura 2, verse 195.

Eid al-Fitr and Eid al-Adha: the two great festivals in the Islamic calendar; the first celebrates the end of the fasting month of Ramadan; the second occurs on the the tenth day of the pilgrimage month, Dhu al-Hijja.

farsi, naskh, ruq'a, thuluth: the names of the scripts utilized in Arabic texts.

Fayyum: a depression and oasis to the southwest of Cairo.

Fuka: a small town on the main railway line between Marsa Matruh and Dab'a on the north Egyptian coast.

ful mudammis: a dish made of beans, probably the most characteristic breakfast dish in Egypt.

gallabiya: the floor-length loose garment worn by Egyptian men.

al-Gamaliya: the district of old Cairo immediately to the north of the al-Husayn Mosque. The name is used to designate the entire area between the al-Azhar Mosque and the northern walls of the old city of Cairo.

al-Ghazali (d. 1111): One of the most prominent Muslim theologians, best known for his work, *Ihya' 'ulum al-din* (*Revival of the Religious Sciences*).

Hafiz, Ibrahim (d. 1932): the Egyptian neoclassical and nationalist poet, known as "the poet of the Nile."

Hanbali: one of the four schools of Islamic law, founded by Ahmad ibn Hanbal.

Hanem: a Turkish word for a woman, but in Egyptian terms a woman of breeding and stature, an honorific title. The use of "Madame" in English parlance conveys something of the same effect.

al-Husayn Mosque: the mosque–shrine in the Khan al-Khalili quarter, dedicated to al-Husayn, grandson of the Prophet Muhammad who was martyred at the Battle of Karbala in 680.

Ibn Khaldun (d. 1406): the theoretician of history whose *Muqaddima* (*Introduction*) is regarded as a foundational work in social science. His career took him from North Africa, to Spain, and finally to Egypt. His latter years are the topic of a recent novel, *al-'Allama*, by the Moroccan writer Bensalem Himmich, available in English as *The Polymath* (The American University in Cairo Press, 2004).

Ibn Maymun (Maimonides) (d. 1204): the renowned Jewish philosopher and physician, born in Cordoba, who spent the latter part of his life in Cairo.

Ibn al-Mu'tazz (d. 908): the one-day Abbasid caliph, but more renowned in his role as both poet and critic.

Ibn Qutayba (d. 889): a scholar of wide-ranging interests, he composed works on philology, history, theology, and literary criticism. The breadth of his learning is indicated by the scope of his most seminal work, a compendium entitled *'Uyun al-akhbar* (*Springs of Information*).

al-Jahiz (d. 869): one of Arabic's greatest polymaths and the acknowledged master of classical Arabic prose style.

jubba (gibba): a broad-sleeved outer garment.

kunafa: a sweet Egyptian dish served especially during Ramadan. It uses shredded wheat as a base, to which is added honey and a variety of other toppings.

al-Ma'arri, Abu al-Ala' (d. 1057): one of Arabic's most renowned poets, known for his pessimistic outlook on life expressed in poetry of great complexity.

al-Mahdiya, Munira (d. 1965): an Egyptian actress and singer, particularly during the 1920s when she was a rival to Umm Kulthum (see below).

mahmal: the ornate camel litter sent to Mecca each year for the season of the Hajj ("Pilgrimage").

al-Manfaluti (d. 1924): an Egyptian essayist who made his reputation by publishing a large number of sentimental and moralistic articles in newspapers that were later collected into two volumes, *al-Nazarat* (*Views*), and *al-'Abarat* (*Tears*).

al-Manyalawi, Shaykh Yusuf (d. 1911): a singer in the classical

style and model for many modern singers. His record-
ings date to the era before the First World War.

Marsa Matruh: on the Mediterranean coast of Egypt to the
west of Alexandria. Now a seaside resort, it was the
scene of fighting during the campaigns of 1942.

al-Mubarrad (d. 898): the grammarian of Basra who spent
the latter part of his life in Baghdad. His most famous
work is *al-Kamil* (*The Complete*).

Muhammad Ali Street: a key artery in Cairo that connects
Khalig Street (so called because it was formerly a canal,
now called Port Said Street) with the square beneath
the Citadel.

al-Mu'izz (d. 975): a ruler of the Fatimid dynasty, during
whose reign Egypt was conquered and the old city of
Cairo constructed.

Mutran, Khalil (d. 1949): known as "the poet of the two
regions," he was born in Lebanon but spent much of his
life in Egypt. His poetry combines neoclassicism with
hints of an emerging romantic tendency.

al-Muwaylihi, Muhammad (d. 1930): an Egyptian writer and
journalist, best known for his pioneering narrative,
Hadith 'Isa ibn Hisham (1907), available in English as
A Period of Time (Reading: Ithaca Press, 1992).

New Road (al-Sikka al-Gadida): the road that connected the
newly built nineteenth-century part of Cairo, named
al-Ismailiya after the Khedive Ismail during whose reign
it was constructed, with the old city, the al-Azhar
Mosque, and the eastern edge of the city.

Night of Power (Laylat al-Qadr): falling between the twenty-
seventh and twenty-eighth day of the month of Ramadan, the night during which the Prophet Muhammad
received the first revelation of the Qur'anic text (an
event recorded in Sura 97 of the text).

al-Qali (d. 967): a famous philologist who moved from Baghdad to Cordoba in Spain. His best known work is *al-Amali* (*Dictations*).

Rud al-Farag: an area of Cairo to the north of Bulaq, renowned for its fruit and vegetable market.

al-Sakakini: one of Cairo's middle-class suburbs (like al-Abbasiyya where Mahfouz spent the latter part of his childhood) that sprung up outside the bounds of the old city during the latter part of the nineteenth century. It lies immediately to the south of al-Abbasiyya.

Shaaban: the eighth month of the year in the Islamic calendar.

shahada: the Islamic statement of faith, "I bear witness that there is no god but God and that Muhammad is His Prophet."

Shawqi, Ahmad (d. 1932): the Egyptian neoclassical poet, renowned for the musicality of his verse, who was given the title "Prince of Poets."

shisha: the local name for the water pipe, narghileh, "hubble-bubble."

Sitt: by contrast with "Hanem" (see above), "Sitt" is the commonly used word for the female head of a household. It means "woman" but implies something close to the English "Mrs."

taamiya: a characteristic Egyptian dish, made with fried beans and garlic.

Umm Kulthum (d. 1975): "the Star of the East," the Arab world's most famous singer of the twentieth century and a personal favorite of Mahfouz himself.

Zaghlul, Saad (d. 1927): Egyptian nationalist leader who was a personal hero of Mahfouz. References to him appear in many of the novelist's works.

zar: an exorcism ceremony conducted by and for women.

al-Zaytun: a district in the central northern part of Cairo, between Shubra and Heliopolis.